Hashim & Family

Shahnaz Ahsan

JOHN MURRAY

First published in Great Britain in 2020 by John Murray (Publishers)
An Hachette UK company

I

Copyright © Shahnaz Ahsan 2020

A CIP catalogue record for this title is available from the British Library

Hardback ISBN 9781473665224
Trade Paperback ISBN 9781473665231
eBook ISBN 9781473665248

Typeset in Bembo Std by Palimpsest Book Production Limited, Falkirk, Stirlingshire
Printed and bound in Great Britain by Clays Ltd, Elcograf S.p.A.

John Murray policy is to use papers that are natural, renewable and recyclable products and made from wood grown in sustainable forests. The logging and manufacturing processes are expected to conform to the environmental regulations of the country of origin.

John Murray (Publishers)
Carmelite House
50 Victoria Embankment
London EC4Y 0DZ

www.johnmurraypress.co.uk

Hashim & Family

For my grandparents Fatima Nahar Begum,
Habib Ullah, Ramjan Nessa, and Ahmad Ullah,
who gave and braved so much

My home belongs in every home; I am tired of searching for it.
My country belongs in every country; I will struggle to find it.
Immigrant I am, wherever I go –
I feel I have a place there, though,
I have to find a way to enter it.
I wander from house to house to search for those I love.

Probashi, Rabindranath Tagore

Part I

1960–1964

I

HASHIM PULLED HIS jacket tightly around his chest and fastened the shiny buttons with numbed fingers. He couldn't tell whether it was the icy wind making him clumsy or the fact that the buttonholes were sewn up too tightly, but as he tried to force the last fastening into its hole, it fell away from the jacket into his hand. Hashim inwardly cursed the slick-tongued salesman who had persuaded him to spend the last of his savings on this ugly, overpriced three-piece suit.

'It will make you stand out the minute you step off that plane,' the tailor had purred. 'It's the latest cut, and the cloth is even better than the stuff that comes out of those English mills. Besides, it's a necessity. Nobody goes abroad without a suit.'

The last bit at least was true, he conceded. Everyone knew that one required a crisp suit and a starched collar if one was intending to head *bilath*. Abroad. England. A tie was donned for the pre-departure farewell, but soon loosened and pocketed once the journey was under way and the handshakes and *salams* with neighbours and friends, well-wishers and nay-sayers alike, who all flocked to the village station to wave the train off, were over. And so here he was, standing outside Manchester Central railway station waiting for Rofikul in the freezing cold with a blazer that was tight on his shoulders, slightly too short in the sleeve, and already falling to pieces in his hands. The plane had landed at Heathrow in the early hours of that morning, and Hashim had somehow managed to navigate his way to Manchester, a city he knew nothing about other than the fact that it was where his cousin lived.

Rofikul had been living and working there for the last few years. He had been one of the first to go abroad. But then, he'd always been the pioneer. Unlike Hashim, he had attended three years of college in the city before dropping out in order to pursue his chances abroad. He was the one who had got Hashim's paperwork in order, sent money for the flight, and made the whole process seem so straight-forward and so manageable that Hashim wondered why all the other young men in the village weren't setting off on the same adventure he was. It had been almost ten years since Hashim had seen his cousin and he worried whether it would still be the same as it had been when they were teenagers spending their summers together at their grandparents' home. In any case, Rofikul had a place where Hashim could live, and, more importantly, the promise of a job.

'There are three phrases you need to know to get by in England,' Rofikul had written in his last letter. 'These are "thank you" and "sorry", closely followed by "please", in order of importance. Make sure to use these liberally if you want to get on as smoothly as possible.'

Hashim's first task of purchasing a train ticket for his journey northwards had involved ample declarations of all three phrases to the surly man at the ticket booth who had printed out the little cards on a creaking old machine before handing them to Hashim.

'Platform 11, you've got twelve minutes. Don't be late, train won't wait.' The official gestured to the platform with a nod of his head. Hashim desperately wanted to ask him so many questions: was it true that it rained all the time in the city he was going to? Where could he get something to eat? Was it always this busy here? But his command of English existed largely in theory rather than in practice. And so Hashim nodded a *thank you* and hurriedly boarded the train that chugged along the length of the country, leading him to the city he had tied his fortunes to. He had no intention of staying in England more than five years. Enough time to make money, send it back home, have a house built there and live comfortably. That was the plan. Well. As his wife would tell him years later – plans change.

'*Zoldi, zoldi*, hurry up! We need to leave!' Rofikul strode through the narrow hallway of the rickety terraced house, his heavy tread shaking the floorboards. He rapped loudly on the flimsy chipboard door of the downstairs bedroom that was shared by three of his umpteen housemates.

'Atiq? Hey! Get *up* already, Hashim is going to be wondering where we are.'

Atiq emerged from the room, rubbing his eyes, his inky-black hair rumpled. He wore a blue checked *lungi* and his white vest was stained with ochre sweat marks beneath the armpits.

'All right, *all right* – no need to make such a racket, I'm coming. Just let me put a shirt on.'

'I swear to God, I'm about a heartbeat away from strangling you . . .' Rofikul swore in exasperation.

'Yeah, and then who would drive you around? Let's not forget that I'm the only one with wheels around here.' Atiq tossed his keys to Rofikul. 'Here, go and start the car. I'll be out in five minutes, and we'll arrive to meet your little friend in plenty of time.'

Rofikul caught the keys and walked out of the small brick terraced house towards the rusty Ford Popular that was parked outside. The street was full of houses packed tightly together, with washing lines draped across backyards. On weekend mornings when he didn't have to work, Rofikul was often woken by the chattering of the housewives as they pegged out their laundry, gossiping over their fences with a Woodbine dangling from the corners of their mouths, their limp English hair bound up tightly in rollers.

As Rofikul slid into the driver's seat, he allowed himself a momentary feeling of satisfaction, turning the key in the ignition and enjoying the purr of the engine beneath him. Atiq sometimes let him drive around the derelict car parks behind supermarkets, and occasionally at an airfield several miles out of the city, where they drove illicitly round in circles and parked to smoke cigarettes and talk. Atiq never let him drive on the road, though; irritating, as a car would have made Rofikul's social calendar a lot more manageable, not to mention more discreet. He thought about Helen and her soft auburn hair and her gentle brogue that he still sometimes struggled to fully understand and felt a warm flutter in his stomach. Yes, he definitely had to work on acquiring a licence and – somehow – enough money for a car.

'He's a *darkie*? But Helen!'

'Shush, Marie! Sweet Jesus, do you want the whole pub to hear you? Keep it *down*. And don't call him that, it's not nice.'

'All right, all right – but what do you want me to say? I mean, Helen! I know you're after a young man – aren't we all? But, Jesus, couldn't you have found someone . . . you know?'

'No, I don't know – like what?' Helen's voice turned cool. She pushed her gin and tonic across the table.

'Well, a bit more like . . . well, like *us*.'

'Like what, Marie? Like that Tommy you ran around with last year? Who could hardly stand up come half past eight on a Friday night and cried like a baby in the mornings? Or did you have someone more like my father in mind?'

Marie sighed and reached for Helen's arm. 'Look, now – I'm sorry for upsetting you, I didn't mean to be unkind. I'm sure he's a sweetheart. I just . . . well, you know how people talk. And sometimes they can be right. You know Colleen?' Marie glanced at Helen tentatively before continuing. 'She was with a chap from the West Indies for months, absolutely mad about him she was. Had a terrible row with her mam and dad when he got her into trouble, so she moved in with him, and by the time the baby was six months he'd taken up with another poor girl right under her nose, and she had nowhere else to go. And that dark— sorry . . . the baby's father, well, he has nothing to do with the child of course. So, you see . . .'

Helen shrugged off Marie's hand. 'No, I don't see. And besides, not that it matters, but Ray isn't even from the West Indies. He's Indian. Well, from near there anyway. So you mind your opinions if you please, Marie.' This was not how Helen had hoped the conversation would go. She had wanted Marie to be excited for her, full of questions and demands to meet her 'young man'. She had never introduced anyone to Marie before, but these last couple of months had just been so deliriously happy that she needed to share the news with somebody.

Marie nodded. 'All right, love, all right. Another round? On me. Come on, it's New Year's Eve, let's not get riled

7

about silly things.' Marie slid out of the booth where the two girls were sitting. The faded red velvet upholstery rubbed against her stockings and caused her flimsy dress to stick to the backs of her thighs as she stood up. She rearranged her skirt and sashayed over towards the dark wooden bar to place her order of two G&Ts, ice with lots of lemon, and idly flirt with the portly, married barman.

Helen watched her from the booth. *Silly things.* So that's what her friendship – relationship, whatever it was – with Ray was to Marie. Something silly and unreal. Well, it had felt real when they'd met in the café that first afternoon. She'd just ducked in for some shelter from the sudden rain shower. He'd been sitting at a corner table reading a large red book, his hand cupped around a mug of tea. She came to learn over the months that he took his with hot milk and three sugars, and sometimes he liked to break up little pieces of fragrant bark and put that in too. The first time he'd done that she'd been aghast.

'What on earth are you doing?' she'd asked as he added a curl of cinnamon to the small tin pan of steaming milk and tea.

'It makes it sweeter.' Ray had grinned at her. 'Try it.'

And she did. The woody aroma soon became synonymous with Ray in her mind, and for months thereafter she struggled to explain to Nanna why she'd started putting bits of tree bark in her tea.

Since the afternoon in the café, when she had shyly asked to share his table, they'd met up whenever they found the time. Nights at the pictures, walks in the park; sometimes they even caught the bus outside the city and spent long afternoons in the Peak District. He would marvel at the craggy rocks and the beautiful rough landscape and tell her stories about where he was from. *Sylhet.* He told her that's where tea grew; yes, the very tea that she had poured in his cup that morning.

She was too embarrassed to admit that she thought all tea came from China. Isn't that what folk said? *Not for all the tea in China,* her mam would say, when a neighbour asked her if she'd ever yearned for a son after her eight pregnancies yielded six healthy daughters and a couple of babies whose sexes remained unknown, lost in a pool of blood and heartbreak before their time. Helen knew that was a lie though. That was the reason her mam and dad's marriage was a miserable one. *Six expensive, useless, idle daughters,* her father would rant. And no lad to help shoulder the burden. Then he would leave the house for the pub where he'd knock back a pint or six – one for each daughter – and then when he came home to the mousey woman he had the misfortune of calling his wife, he'd smash his fist into her face, or, if he felt so inclined, he would set about the act of siring a male heir. Across the hall, in the room she shared with two of her sisters, Helen would pull the pillow over her ears trying to muffle the sound of her mother's sobs and her father's drunken slurs and the steady, oppressive banging of the bedframe into the cold, plastered wall.

And so, on the morning of her seventeenth birthday, before anyone else in the house had been roused from sleep, Helen had packed a few possessions into the only suitcase they had in the house, a beaten-up leather bag, and slipped quietly off to the station to catch a train that would take her away from the docklands of Liverpool. She decided on Manchester as her final destination. Her mother's great-aunt, who they called Nanna when they were children, had been a former Brunswick mill girl, and lived in the inner city in an area Helen vaguely remembered was called Ancoats, where a few old mills were still creaking along. She was sure she could

9

seek refuge there. Helen tried not to imagine the thundering rage of her father and its manifestation on the body of her mother, the scarlet welts screaming of Helen's betrayal. It was not her soothing presence, but her vital earning power that would be missed. By denying her family its dues from her weekly pay packet, Helen's crime was not simply absconding: it was theft.

Over the three years she had since been living in Manchester, Helen had sent money back home and letters inviting her sisters to join her, describing her life – careful not to brag about her newfound freedoms, but hinting that their fortunes would be richer here than by the docks. But she had yet to receive a single note back from her mother or sisters; an injunction no doubt laid down by her father, though she was disappointed that they had not cared enough about her to risk flouting it. Still, she continued to write – light, breezy letters, shielding the reader from the guilt that she felt as her ink crisscrossed the page. The envelopes stuffed with notes were never returned, which gave her some comfort: if the money was helping, then at least some good had come of her estrangement.

'Helen!' Marie stood over her, wielding two full tumblers topped with ice and lemon. 'Come on, drink up! I can't wait till midnight, I'm ready for a new year!'

Helen smiled and took the glass from Marie's wobbling hand.

'To a new year!' They clinked rims, and each took a sip.

Helen thought about Ray, how his unexpected tumble into her life had made the preceding year the best one yet, and she made a silent prayer to Mary, mother of Jesus, that the next one would be just as special.

*

'Hey! Hey, it's him – there he is, I told you he'd be waiting outside! Idiot, why didn't he just stay in the waiting room?' Rofikul banged on the window of the car as Atiq swung it into the pick-up area outside the station.

'*Ar-eh*, are you trying to smash the glass? Leave my car alone, would you, and go and get your cousin before someone else does. He's asking to get jumped standing around like that.'

Rofikul did not hear Atiq's admonishment; he'd bounded out of the passenger door before the car had drawn to a standstill and was running over to where a very cold-looking Hashim was standing on the cobbled crescent of road outside the station. His suit was creased, and the leather suitcase that lay at his feet had seen better days. Rofikul noted that Hashim's side parting was perfectly neat, though, and he spied the comb in the breast-pocket of that awful cheap suit. He grinned – another dapper young man to take around town with him. The two of them would be hits.

'Hey! Cold, isn't it?'

'Bhaiya!'

Rofikul pulled Hashim into a tight hug and thumped him heavily on the back.

'It's so good to see you! You survived the flight, I see. Isn't the food awful? Well, let me tell you, that bit doesn't get better now you're here. But those air hostesses . . . eh? Eh? With their shiny legs? Almost makes the journey worthwhile!'

Hashim laughed and shook his head. 'I see you haven't changed a bit then, Bhai – all jokes, and no time-keeping?'

Rofikul feigned contrition by slapping himself on the head and sticking out his tongue. '*Aha-re!* You can lodge a complaint with Atiq about that, I *told* him we would be late, but you can never get that man out of bed unless you bribe him with a cup of tea and a *porotha*, and I haven't got time to spoil him like that. Anyway, he's waiting for us with the car over there – come on, let me take that bag. And here, you take this.'

Hashim found a heavy woollen coat thrust into his hands.

'I knew there was no way you could have brought something thick enough. You'll need that tonight. I borrowed it from one of the boys at home. Anyway, wear it for now, and we'll take you shopping to get a proper winter coat soon.'

Hashim gratefully donned the dark grey overcoat, the padded shoulders swamping his narrow frame, and plunged his hands into the deep pockets.

'They weren't joking about this weather, were they?'

Rofikul grinned. 'It's dark when you leave the house, it's dark when you come back; and sometimes in the mornings you wake up to little threads of ice dangling on the inside of the windows. You don't ever get used to it, but you will learn to start dressing better for it.' Winding a scarf tightly around his neck, Rofikul led Hashim over to where Atiq was waiting with the engine running and sprang open the tiny boot of the car. He tossed the suitcase in between a tow-rope and a canister of petrol, and cheerfully banged the lid shut.

'Do you mind not destroying my vehicle, you brute?' called Atiq from the driver's seat. He nodded towards the newcomer in acknowledgement. 'I'm Atiq. Welcome.'

Hashim tentatively stood by while Rofikul walked around to the front and flung open the passenger door.

'The front seat for our new arrival! Come on, Hashim, this way you get the proper view . . . of the roads . . . and the cars . . . and the roads . . . and the cars . . .' After shoving Hashim into the front, Rofikul slid into the back seat and slung his arms over the seat backs in front of him. 'Atiq Bhai, take us home.'

With a lurch, Atiq slid the car into gear and pulled away

from the kerb. Hashim peered over the grey dashboard, into the shadowy night flecked with yellow lights. As the car picked up speed along the smooth roads, Hashim settled back into his seat and closed his eyes to the sound of Rofikul's voice, interrupted occasionally by Atiq's monosyllabic retorts. *Home*, he thought. *Yes, take me home.*

2

AFTER FOUR MONTHS Hashim had grown fond of the red brick of the city, the flashes of colour providing welcome respite from the relentless grey of the clouds overhead, the grey fumes of the factories, and the grey of the roads beneath him. And everything seemed greyer still because of the constant rain that never seemed to fall with any conviction, but instead feebly pattered down from the sky. He could get used to the cold, he had decided. But it was the dreariness that weighed him down, the absence of any hint of greenery. Still, though, there were certain elements of daily life that he had warmed to, and the clattering of the milk-cart over the cobbles before sunrise became a familiar background noise as he washed for dawn prayer, splashing icy water into his face. As he spread out his threadbare prayer rug on to the nondescript carpet of the shared bedroom, Hashim felt a sense of comfort enfold him as he murmured the holy words his father had taught him. Some of the other men he lived with also prayed regularly, though most were a little lax, missing a few prayers in the middle of the day by necessity – factory hours were not built around the ever-changing prayer times – but they did not seek to make them up once they were home. Hashim privately tried to compensate for his missed prayers, doubling up the foregone noon and afternoon prayers with the one at sunset. He wasn't sure if this was a legitimate practice, but he hoped that Allah would be understanding of his predicament.

His new housemates were, for the most part, jovial and welcoming, although he had concluded that Atiq's apparent surliness was not reserved just for Hashim, but was simply the way Atiq preferred to communicate. Aside from Rofikul and Atiq, there were about eight others, many of whose names and faces all seemed to blur into one generic pool. These housemates worked further out of the city, usually on night shifts, so his path rarely crossed theirs. But among the dozen or so grown men there was a distinct sense of homeliness, for which Hashim was grateful. There was a system, not codified by rules, but one in which everyone seemed to know his part. There were the shoppers who took care of the groceries, and the cooks who ensured there was always a steaming pan of something delicious and filling left on the stove, even for the night workers when they arrived back in the early morning after the milkman had been and gone. The cleanliness left a little to be desired, not due to any lack of individual effort, but simply the result of having almost a dozen adult men living in a space meant for half that number. But still, there was always company and warmth, and despite the shabby decor and the peeling linoleum, Hashim felt settled into his new home.

Work was a different matter. On his first day Hashim had tried to introduce himself to the foreman, a dour-faced man of about fifty whose skin looked as though someone had hewn over it with a rake.

'Good morning, sir. My name is Hashim.' He said it exactly as he had rehearsed in front of the cracked mirror in the pantry that morning, razor in hand, with Mamun or Ilyas or one of the other housemates banging on the door yelling for him to get a move on. The foreman had glared at him.

'And . . .?'

Hashim faltered. 'Today is my first day . . .'

'So what, you want a special announcement, do you? 'Ere – Ray!' He bellowed at Rofikul and motioned for him to come over. 'This that cousin of yours you was chewing my ear off about?'

Rofikul nodded. 'Yessir, this is my cousin, Harry – you can call him Harry.'

Hashim shifted his glance from the foreman towards Rofikul and raised an eyebrow. Ray? Harry? What was this, did he now have to change his name too?

'Right, well, show 'im where 'is overalls are and set to work – you know where he's meant to be. Jones can give him t'walkaround and then put 'im on the bagging line, would you?'

'Yessir.' Rofikul – or Ray as he was now apparently known – nodded and dragged Hashim over to the hooks and benches where other workers were already changing into their overalls.

'Harry? So I'm Harry now?'

'You think they can manage Hashim? It's just easier for them to remember; they won't say much to you anyway, it's just in case they need to get your attention for something.'

Hashim said nothing, but his turned back as he changed into the dark work clothes radiated annoyance.

Rofikul watched as Hashim struggled to get the hair net over his slightly large head. 'Here, let me help you.'

'How can you let them call you what they want? Why an English name?'

'Look, Hashim, there are a hundred other things you'll need to worry about living here. I'm telling you, what people

16

call you is the least of your worries. At least Harry is actually a name. Better than "darkie" or "ey you" or worse. So just shut your mouth and get on with it. *Harry*.'

And so Harry learned to get on with it. He was paid at the end of the week, not handsomely, but it was enough to cover his rent and contribution to the food and the electricity, as well as wiring some back to his family in Sylhet. After several months of this continuing pattern, Rofikul began to notice that Hashim was sending the entire remainder of his wages back home. One night, as they sat at the small kitchen table playing cards over a cup of hot, sweet tea, Rofikul decided to broach the subject.

'So, Hashim, what are your savings looking like?'

Hashim looked blankly at Rofikul, his hand still raised holding a run of four spades, two aces and an annoying, superfluous jack of hearts he was trying to get rid of.

'What savings?'

'Ah, that's what I suspected,' Rofikul said, slapping down his hand of cards. 'Rummy.' He lit a cigarette, inhaled, and then expertly puffed the smoke upwards. 'Look, Hashim. You're doing all right. You have enough to cover the house expenses. You're sending enough back home. Don't you think you should start, you know, keeping some here?'

'Why would I need that? Sending it all back is the reason I came over in the first place.' Hashim looked confusedly at his cousin, wondering whether this conversation was more about Rofikul and whatever thoughts were brewing in his mind, rather than much to do with him.

'Hashim, listen. You need to start thinking about your future. You don't want to spend the next ten years like this. Don't you want to save for things? Some better clothes, even. A car maybe, one day. I don't know, but you at least need to have enough for an emergency. What if something happens

17

and you need to fly back straight away?' Rofikul stubbed out his cigarette on the corner of the table and sighed. 'Anyway, forget about all that. What about *bhabi*?'

'What about her?' Hashim's voice rose slightly.

Rofikul reached out and placed a hand on his cousin's arm. 'You should be together, Hashim. If you're not careful . . .' He paused, choosing his words. 'Just trust me, Hashim. You shouldn't be apart from your wife for so long.'

'Have you gone completely mad? Why exactly would she want to come here? What would there be here for her?' Hashim realised his hands were shaking.

'You. That's exactly what I'm saying, Hashim. You should be together, you've not even been married a year, and half of that time you've been here. You should bring her over. Show her what life is like here. Think about it.' Rofikul pushed his chair back and walked over to open the kitchen window to let out the curls of smoke.

Think about it. Did Rofikul think Hashim was an idiot? He'd done nothing except think about it, for months. Every time he awoke to the damp cold mornings and came downstairs to one of the housemates clad in a *lungi* and jumper stirring a pan of milk on the stove, he imagined what it would be like to walk into the kitchen and see Munira there. When he got home after work to a steel pan of congealed lamb curry and lukewarm rice set on the stove, he thought about how much more civilised it would be if his wife was there ladling it out into small serving bowls, and how she had always declined to eat with him, despite his invitations to do so. In the few weeks that they had actually spent as newlyweds they hadn't once dined together. It wasn't the done thing for a wife to eat with her husband in the communal home. There was a distinct order: all the children would be cajoled, caressed and beaten into eating first. Then the men

18

– Hashim, his brothers, any uncles who might have been visiting – would eat at great leisure, being served all the choicest cuts of fish, the freshest rice, and then finally Munira and her sisters-in-law would sit down to eat whatever remained, but not before Hashim's mother had authorised their turn and had been served herself.

Hashim reached for the box of Woodbines on the table and slipped one of the slim rolls of tobacco between his lips. As he held the lit match close to the tip he drew in a breath, deeply, and watched the end glow a satisfying burning orange. Shaking out the flame, he exhaled and sighed.

'How am I supposed to bring her? I don't even know if she'd want to come.'

Rofikul smiled. 'Have you asked her? Not many do bring their wives over, but it can be done. We can find someone to talk through the paperwork.'

Hashim thought about the conversations he'd had with Munira in the weeks they had spent together. He hadn't even seen her until their wedding day; their union was based upon the knowledge that he had a visa to go and work in England and the fact that her father was a respected *alim* from his mother's home village. Unusually, Munira had completed high school, which was far more education than he himself had achieved. He flushed at the thought of being too stupid, too dull, for the quietly intelligent, beautiful woman he called his wife. After the wedding ceremony, they were left alone together for the first time in one of the smallest rooms of the house, which had been temporarily vacated for the new couple. Completely at a loss what to say or how to act, Hashim's first question had been to enquire what her name was. After a mortifying silence, during which Hashim's face had turned every shade of crimson, while his wife's remained covered by her bridal shawl as she lowered her head, there finally came the name that he hadn't been able to get out of his head for weeks – *Munira*. He cleared his throat awkwardly and asked a few more questions, ones he also already knew the answers to: how many siblings she had, what class she had studied until. Politely, if a little aloof, she had answered his questions. They were supposed to sleep together that night, on a bed adorned with flowers arranged by Hashim's female relatives, as distant to one another as they had been before the ceremony; before the white garlands had been wrapped around their necks, before Munira's face had been daubed with *kumkum*, before he had placed a gold band on her finger.

They had become slightly less awkward with each other over the following weeks. Although they spent most of the day in different quarters – Munira with the women or sequestered in her room, still exempt from the usual daily chores, and Hashim with his friends, or visiting neighbours – they found time in the evenings to talk and gradually begin to know one another. Through these lamp-lit conversations, he learned about the books she enjoyed reading, that she had been teaching herself English with the help of her older brother, ever since she discovered that her future husband would be working in England, that she was her father's favourite and that, thankfully, she interested Hashim. And it seemed as though he interested her. He remembered with pride the day he first managed to amuse her, recounting a story from his school days and how it had made him feel six feet tall to see the twin crescents deepen in her cheeks as she laughed. But she had been so formal the day of their parting, betraying such little emotion that he wondered if she was relieved that he would be gone soon, and that she would not have to deal with the tiresome demands of a husband. Since his arrival in Manchester though, her letters suggested otherwise: there was a veneer of propriety to them, but he felt that he could delve between her lines, and eke out some emotion beneath the surface of her words.

Hashim slipped his hand into his pocket and pulled out his wallet. He removed the black and white print of a young woman with thick brows, a small nose and dark eyes. Perhaps Rofikul was right. Perhaps he could look into what it would mean to bring his wife – he was still so unused to the word – over to join him. He wondered if it was something she would want, whether the prospect of leaving her country and her people, for him – a man she hardly even knew, despite the gold band she wore – could possibly be appealing. There was nothing to do but to ask her, he decided. Whatever her response, he would accept it. As he lay in bed that night, turning the idea over in his mind, he realised how much he hoped she would say yes.

3

M UNIRA PUT DOWN her pen and let out a sigh as she began to braid her thick, raven hair. It was dark outside and the only light in the room came from a dimly lit hurricane lamp. In the corner of the room a quivering mound covered by an embroidered blanket rose and fell intermittently, occasionally releasing a guttural wheeze. She glanced over and saw the rhythmic inflating and deflating of Khala Moni, Hashim's spinster aunt, and concluded that Khala Moni was indeed still alive despite her constant proclamations of imminent death. Satisfied in the knowledge, Munira began to re-read the page she had just written.

Assalamu alaikum,
I pray that Allah is keeping you safe, and that you are in the best of health. From your letters it seems as though you are working long hours, and I worry your mother worries that you may be tired. I try to remind her though that you sound happy in your letters. Everything must still be so new and exciting, and although your descriptions are so colourful I struggle to imagine it as you must be seeing it. I know you said the rain was cold, but I still can't imagine what that feels like – the warmth of our rain is all that makes the wet bearable.
Things are very well here, by the grace of Allah, so have

no concern for us. The farm is doing well, the planting has been done for the year. I write to my parents every week too, and they ask after you and Rofikul Bhai.

The photograph that you sent us of you in the studio is kept in the almari. *Your mother shows it to guests when they come to visit, and everyone says how smart you look.*

Be well,

Munira

Something felt a little cold about the letter. She picked up the pen and added a final line:

Sometimes I take the photograph and look at it when your mother is asleep.

Satisfied, she folded the page into quarters and slipped it into a thin envelope with red and blue striped edges. It was probably somewhat forward to admit that she was stealing glances at her husband's picture, but the envelope was sealed now, and she didn't have a spare one she could use, so that was that. He'd have to make of it what he pleased. Even though they had been married for over a year, Munira was still unsure as to how her husband really saw her. She had tried to temper her instinctive boldness since adolescence, at the behest of countless aunts and even her own mother, who ruefully implored Munira to act with more propriety. It was an unbecoming trait for a young woman to favour her brothers' school books over her domestic chores, or to prefer to sit in on the conversations of her father and uncles about religion and politics, rather than listen to the complaints of the womenfolk about their ailments, their pains, their children and their husbands. Munira's mother declared that her only daughter's unbending will was the fault of an indulgent father and that no other man would permit such behaviour. When the proposal had

23

come from Hashim's family, Munira's mother had simply refused to believe it.

'They must have got her confused with a different girl,' she declared to her sisters-in-law as they sat in a semicircle in the courtyard, crouched on low wooden *khats* sorting the grit from lentils, and peeling the stringy threads from bean pods.

'What other girl exactly could she be confused with?' asked Munira's eldest aunt, whose own brood of dutiful, insipid daughters somewhat bored her, though she could never publicly admit so. 'There's no other *alim* in the village so they specifically meant your husband's daughter – and you have no other girls, so who else apart from Munira could they have meant?'

'But, it's just . . . well, they don't even know her. Or us, really, so I can't see why they'd—'

'Since when has that made a difference? Did your in-laws know you before you got married? Has anyone ever truly known the families they marry their children into? If they did, maybe they'd be less disappointed when it turns out they pretty much detest one another, but the point is, they said Munira. You've done your homework, haven't you? The boy, he looks decent, doesn't he? No paunch, all his hair? And he's going *bilath*, isn't he? So if he is a brute, she's safe while he's in England. And if he's a nice boy, then she'll have time to find out, won't she?'

Munira overheard the conversation from inside the small barn on the edge of the courtyard where she had been tending the chickens. She had been more taken aback than anyone by the proposal but couldn't help feeling a little stung by the force of her mother's incredulity. After all, she knew she was attractive – everyone told her so, though the compliment was always veiled in a put-down. *Oh Munira, your hair is so thick, it must be impossible to style in any way other than a braid. Oh yes, that Munira, a lovely smile but it does make her look a little . . . you know . . . careless.* And she came from a good enough family; her father was a learned and respected religious man. Her brothers were bound for college or were already there. They weren't a wealthy family, but they were well regarded – why on earth shouldn't she be considered the catch that she was? To her mother's mortal horror, Munira saw no reason why she ought not to share her opinion with her aunts in the courtyard, and yes, her watching, doe-eyed, open-mouthed cousins too, for that matter.

That evening, Munira heard her mother rapidly recounting the event to her father in a pitch higher than usual. She could not discern her father's response, but she imagined she was due a reprimand once the conversation was over. When her mother flounced into the room where Munira was reading and announced that her father wished to see her before bed, Munira sighed and marked her page with a piece of folded card. Padding into the room that her father used as living room and study, she prepared for the admonition.

'Baba, is what your mother told me true?'

'Yes, Abbu.'

'So you want to get married, is that it?'

'No! Yes – well, no, I just meant . . .'

'Well, it sounds as though you took your mother's reservations about it quite to heart.'

'I didn't mean it like that, I just – well, they were all making it sound as though anyone would be crazy to want to marry me.'

'I see. Well, luckily for us, I suppose someone – or at least his family – is crazy enough. I've spoken to your mother.

It sounds as though you aren't against this. I've done some research on their family and I'm satisfied. There's no reason this can't happen before the winter.'

Munira had gone to bed that night feeling blank. She was not unhappy with the prospect, but she did not know how to be excited about the idea of marriage when it seemed so distant to her. Even when the saris were being laid out in front of her in a quest to find the perfect bridal shade, or when the wet, brown *mendhi* paste was applied in floral patterns to her hands by her aunts, or when her face was being daubed in smears of yellow turmeric in the pre-wedding ceremony, the thought that this was preparation for *marriage* did not seem to penetrate. She knew that this was all necessary preparation for a *wedding*, but what lay after it – the relationship she would have to form and navigate, the entire new person she would have to learn to live with – remained a mystery. It was not until the day of her actual wedding that she realised that everything she knew would soon be gone, and all that lay ahead was uncertainty. She hoped her husband was kind.

It had surprised her, once the ceremony was over and she and her new husband were left alone in the room together for the first time, that he had seemed more nervous than she was. She noticed his shaking hands as he sat beside her, his voice barely registering above a murmur. When he had asked her name, it had taken every inch of self-control not to stare at him incredulously. A part of her was annoyed – *she* was the bride, the one who was separated now from her family. As the sheltered only daughter of loving parents, it was her prerogative to be nervous, falteringly shy, to weep, should she so wish, all the way through the night. She had wept when she had parted from her parents. It was the first time she had seen her father's tears and suddenly the world and her future felt hollow without the thought of him being in it every day. So she had answered Hashim's banal questions out of politeness. She recognised that he meant well and that his nerves were not because he was displeased with the marriage, but simply because, like her, he had no idea how to act in this situation. Their whole lives, elders had instructed them on everything: the correct way to address relatives; how to enter and leave a room; the etiquette on speaking first or speaking too much in a social gathering – but nobody had thought to instruct the newlywed couple how to behave on their first evening together as husband and wife. When she had finished answering Hashim's questions and had run out of her own to ask, Munira was so tired that she fell asleep where she had been sitting, on the bridal bed, still fully clad in her heavy silk sari. She awoke at dawn the next morning to find a soft embroidered blanket draped over her, and saw her new husband sleeping in the armchair in the corner of the room, one foot tucked beneath him. He had not even tried to join her on the bed. He was a good man, she decided. Shy. But kind. Quietly, she went to the jug and basin in the corner of the room where she washed her face and hands, preparing herself for the morning prayer. She had much to give thanks for.

Their first morning together as husband and wife had been as awkward as the night preceding it. After Munira had quietly prayed and reapplied her *kajal* and straightened out her bridal sari, she sat on the bed and waited for her husband to stir from the armchair before her. She did not have to wait long; there was the briefest of ceremonial taps on the door before it was flung open by Munira's eldest new sister-in-law, armed with a green silk sari, a hairbrush and a smile that was more curious than kind. Hashim woke with a start and jumped up from his armchair.

'*As . . . assalamualaikum bhabi,*' he greeted his older brother's wife, his eyes on the ground, not meeting hers for fear of the smirk on her face. He knew she had taken in the scene, the fact that he had been asleep in the chair, and that Munira was sitting perfectly poised on the middle of the bed, still in her full bridal attire. His neck grew hot as he imagined the gossip and speculation that would be flying through the kitchen in moments. His sister-in-law ignored his greeting, instead addressing Munira with a steady stream of questions and exclamations.

'Oh, look, there you are still perfect, look, aren't you perfect? *Shundori*, even your jewellery is still all exactly in place. You look as though you slept right there sitting up; doesn't she look like she slept sitting up?' she asked no one in particular. 'Right, we need to get you ready for the other guests now, you'll have a lot of visitors today. Choto Bhai, you need to get out of here now, we need to get your wife ready. Yes, no need to look so shocked – she is your wife, you know, or hadn't you noticed? Did no one tell you? *Ahare*, see what happens when you don't pay attention. Come, come, go straight to the kitchen, one of your *bhabis* will make you *porotha*; not you, Munira dear, sorry, you have to look beautiful first and *then* we'll let you eat.'

The sister-in-law grinned in what she fancied was a playful fashion, revealing her red tobacco-stained teeth and slightly receding gums. Hashim had bolted right out of the room, but not before flashing a thin smile at Munira whose expression had set into the stoic serenity of a martyr. Munira was left to the mercy of her new *bhabi*, who puffed and primped, prodded and praised, forcing Munira to turn her head this way and that while her hair was fixed, the *urna* pinned firmly

28

into her hair. It felt as though the pins were being drilled through her skull by *bhabi*'s fat fingers.

At first Munira had endured the endless attention, the coiffuring and beauty advice from her sisters-in-law, recognising that, for the most part, it was well intended and came from genuine pride and affection for their newest sister. But since Hashim had gone to England, it was as though Munira herself had ceased to exist. Now the only woman without a husband present, Munira was often overlooked, and treated like one of the older female children of the family, rather than as a new bride. She had even been forced to be roommates with the ancient Khala Moni, the strange spinster aunt whose actual lineage and attachment to the family were by all accounts uncertain, but who had been around for so long that no one thought to question it any more. Munira did not include any of this in her letters to her husband – after all, there was nothing really to complain about, she was hardly being maltreated. But she did not care for the gossip of her sisters-in-law and as a result had inadvertently gained the reputation of being a little aloof. She had no one to talk to, no father to indulge her in her theories, no brothers to discuss her ideas with, no mother to listen to her stories, and now, as she sealed her letter to Hashim, she realised that she missed her husband.

4

WHEN THE COUNTRY had been declared 'open for business' a decade earlier, no one could have predicted that those three thousand economic migrants who arrived each year would eventually swell to an eye-watering one hundred thousand immigrants, and counting – one of whom, hoped Hashim, would be his wife.

Hashim was sitting in a greasy spoon café in Ardwick quizzing Rofikul about the papers he was clutching in his right hand. The acrid smell of frying bacon hung in the air and the net-curtained windows were foggy with condensation. Two steaming mugs of tea stood on the table before them.

'You're sure? You're absolutely sure these are the right ones?' Hashim shook the facsimiled documents at his cousin excitedly.

Rofikul nodded, a grin spreading across his face. 'They're her papers.'

Hashim shook his head in disbelief and drummed his fingers on the once-white surface of the Formica table top, now stained with years of mug rings. He was holding his wife's immigration papers, the documents to say that she was welcome in this country – to come to Britain – on a spousal visa. Munira could be with them almost as soon as he booked her flight.

'But they said it would take months!' He looked at Rofikul, half expecting his cousin to laugh and declare the whole thing an elaborate joke.

Rofikul returned Hashim's gaze. 'Well . . . it did.'

'But . . . I thought it would be more months.' Hashim was now fiddling with the glass condiment bottles on the table in front of him, picking off the tangy crusts of brown sauce from the white screw top. He looked almost pleadingly at Rofikul, as though willing him to say something reassuring.

Rofikul softened, a little surprised by Hashim's range of responses to what Rofikul had imagined would be unequivocally positive news. 'Hashim,' he asked gently, 'do you want it to be more months?'

Hashim looked down at the table and shook his head slowly. 'No, of course not. This is wonderful news, I – thank you – no, really, thank you, this wouldn't be happening if it wasn't for you, finding that lawyer, getting the vouchers and papers sorted and everything . . .' He trailed off. It was true; the idea had been Rofikul's in the first place, and had it been left to Hashim, none of this would have happened. It was Rofikul who had found, on several people's recommendations, an immigration specialist who was affordable, spoke Sylheti, and seemed to know what he was doing. Rofikul had set up the first meeting for Hashim, had instructed him how to dress for the meeting, had suggested he might need a copy of Munira's passport and their marriage certificate for proof, and had even organised the process for Munira back home, instructing her via Hashim to arrange a visit to the British Embassy in Dhaka and advising what she would need to take with her.

Rofikul inclined his head slightly in acceptance of Hashim's thanks, added another sugar cube to his mug of tea and stirred, waiting for Hashim to find his words again.

'It's just that I thought I had more time. You know, to get it ready, to make it nice for her.' Hashim paused again. 'How can I bring her to that house? It isn't ready. *I'm* not ready.' He laid the papers down on the table and gestured towards them helplessly. 'What will I be bringing her over to?'

Rofikul offered Hashim a Woodbine and they lit up. The anxiety and uncertainty of a new challenge billowed from the ends of their cigarettes in puffs of white smoke that merged with the aroma of bitter coffee and forbidden animal fat and fried eggs. After a couple of minutes of silent inhaling and exhaling, Rofikul stubbed out his cigarette in the thin metal ashtray on the table and spoke firmly.

'Hashim. There is nothing wrong with the house – you've told her about the living arrangements, haven't you? She understands about the sharing, so it will be fine. And of course, we'll rejig the other rooms so that you and *bhabi* can have your own bedroom, that's no problem.' He stopped, realising that his cousin's anxieties were not limited to concerns about housemates and sleeping arrangements. He took on a jovial tone to mask the seriousness of addressing what he sensed were Hashim's real concerns.

'As for the rest of it . . . look, nobody knows how this will turn out. None of the rest of us have brought any wives over, you're our pioneer! So, yes, it might take a bit of getting used to, but think how wonderful it will be to have her here. A real woman's touch around the house. You don't know how much you'll miss it, trust me. Think how nice it will be to come home to her after work, how much fun it will be showing her new things, enjoying life together. She'll be happy to be with you and you'll be happy having her here. Really. It will be all right.' He grinned at Hashim. 'And if she's a real witch, we'll just get immigration control to send her back.'

Hashim laughed despite himself, Rofikul joined in, and, before long, their guffaws had filled the little café and the other customers were turning to stare at the two young brown men in their overcoats who were laughing so hard their shoulders were shaking amid plumes of tobacco smoke.

5

HELEN SLIPPED HER stockinged foot into the red leather shoe and bent down to fasten the buckle around her slim ankle.

'Marie! Get a move on, would you? We're going to be late!'

Marie sauntered into the room, clad in a towelling bathrobe, her hair arranged in a crown of setting rollers.

'Stop mithering, it's not even seven o'clock yet. And we can be late, they'll wait for us.' She sat down in front of the small dressing table and began to take out her rollers, gently unfurling each section of hair and giving it a light misting of hairspray before moving on to the next.

Helen watched as Marie unwound the silky brown strands from the hollow plastic cylinders and thought how ridiculous it was that women had to go through such time-consuming preparations before daring to venture out in public. Still, that was the way it was. Holding up a hand mirror to the light, Helen shaded in her brows with a pencil and added a final coat of lipstick to her mouth – nothing too flashy, just a peachy coral to make her look a little less washed out. The summer was not kind on her pale Irish skin, which had a tendency to go straight from milky to puce without so much as stopping for breath, so she tended to avoid the sun. Marie, on the other hand, was blessed with skin that tanned a light umber, a gift from her Italian grandmother. As she pointed out, though, she had also inherited that side of the family's tendency towards hirsutism and Catholic guilt, a thought that somewhat consoled Helen. Marie had finished back-combing her hair and was now clasping a metal device on to her eyelashes to make them curl.

'Marie, no one will even notice your lashes – what they will notice is that you're wearing a bathrobe. Hurry *up!*'

'Eyelashes are exactly what blokes will notice, and they don't even know it. Here, pass me that brush, will you?' Marie dipped the tiny brush that Helen handed her into a small pot of black and swept a winged line along her upper lashes. Turning her head to check for symmetry, she nodded at her reflection in approval and winked at Helen. 'Calm down, love, look – I'm ready!'

She slipped off her robe, revealing a pretty shift dress that hung elegantly from her tiny frame and fell just above her knees. She grabbed the bottle of White Shoulders that stood on the dresser and dabbed a little on her wrists and neck before proffering the bottle to Helen who copied the ritual. Marie put her arm around Helen's waist and drew her close, so they could both see themselves in the full-length mirror that leaned against the chipboard wall in the corner.

'See? Not even late, and even if we were, we'd be worth it.'

Helen smiled at the girls in the glass, who both beamed back. Marie's dark waves were thick and glossy, and her matte red-stained lips added an air of silver-screen glamour that Helen could only dream of. Helen was taller, slimmer, and paler than her friend. Her grey-green eyes were honest where Marie's were playful, and while Marie's quick and easy laugh made her popular wherever they went, people often mistook Helen's quietness for hostility. Still, though, tonight they were going

35

out with Ray and his cousin Harry, and some friends from work said they'd be around too. It was Saturday night and the long summer evening held all the promise in the world.

'What do you mean they both look the same?' Rofikul exclaimed, waving the shirts maniacally in Hashim's face.

'Well – they're both blue . . .' Hashim's voice trailed off as he realised that this was not the response that Rofikul was waiting for.

'*This* is royal blue,' bellowed Rofikul, raising the hanger in his right hand, 'and *this* is baby blue.' The hanger in his left hand danced so close to Hashim's face that he could smell the detergent from Poppy's Launderette down the road where the household took all their washing.

'There is a very clear difference between these two blues. All I am asking is for you to express a preference for which blue. It isn't that hard. Choose.'

'All right! All right, I'll wear the royal one – it sounds better than "baby" at least,' Hashim retorted, snatching the shirt from Rofikul.

'Excellent choice!' Rofikul beamed and tossed the rejected shirt on to the pile of clothes in the middle of his bed. 'Now don't forget to pair it with a black belt – oh, you don't have a brown one anyway, do you? Just as well, navy and brown make you look like a sailor.'

Hashim buttoned up the shirt and considered responding before deciding against it; Rofikul was mad at the best of times, but tonight he seemed especially excitable. He had been pestering Hashim to go out with his 'friends' for months and Hashim had resisted for as long as humanly possible in the face of the persistent tornado that was his cousin. Finally he had relented, and agreed to accompany Rofikul on a night at the pictures and then 'out', whatever that meant.

Tucking his shirt into his best trousers, Hashim called out to Rofikul, who was fiddling around with the wireless in the corner. 'Hey, so these friends of yours then, these . . . girls . . .?'

Rofikul twiddled the dial into a patch of static trying to find a radio station to no avail. Irked, he flipped the switch off.

'Damn it, we need to get a record player. Yes, they're girls – what about them?'

Hashim paused to fasten his cufflinks and consider how to phrase his question. 'Well, what are they like? How do you even know them? Are they . . .' Again he trailed off, unsure as to whether he was offending Rofikul, who was peering into the small built-in mirror of the heavy wardrobe that loomed in the corner of their room. Rofikul was unsurprised by the question; frankly he had wondered why it had taken Hashim so long to even ask – it was a perfectly understandable query. Using the edge of his comb to draw a crisp line along the side of his head, Rofikul parted his hair and smoothed down the stray wisps with his fingertips.

'They're nice girls. It's not . . . it's not like that.' He paused. There was a reason he hadn't introduced Helen to any of his other friends. They'd get the wrong idea, writing her off as a passing infatuation at best, or, at worst, a cheap, worthless distraction who would simply be cast aside once Rofikul returned back home. How could he even begin to explain what was happening? That ever since that first day in the café when she had come stumbling in through the door without an umbrella, utterly drenched and dripping water all over the floor, he had been unable to think of anything or anyone else. She had been so polite when she asked to join him at the only free seat at a table, and had been so enjoyably curious, asking about the book he was reading, and where he came from.

He soon learned that Helen was not from Manchester either — her accent gave that much away — and it became apparent that she had made few friends in her three years in the city. She was the only person since he arrived, several years previously, who had ever shown a real interest in him as a whole person, not just a more experienced *probashi* who could help navigate the uncertainties of life in Britain. She asked him questions about his life back home, about how he found living in England, and soon enough he found himself confiding in her. As the daughter of Irish immigrants, she understood a little of what it felt like to be perpetually on the margins of the society that he had tried so hard to melt into, and which had resisted him continuously. He had been suspicious at first, wondering why a young white girl would show such an interest in him, but her demeanour was always so matter-of-fact and unselfconscious that he relaxed into their friendship. Their conversations were punctuated with long, comfortable silences, when simply being around each other was enough to feel warm and rooted and, for the first time in many years for both of them, secure.

And she had been so patient with him, even though he knew that his reluctance to acknowledge her existence to his friends must have hurt dreadfully. Helen had introduced 'Ray' to her best friend, Marie, within the first few months of their knowing each other. Marie had behaved coolly towards Rofikul at first, giving one-word answers to his polite questions and doing nothing to fill the cavernous silences that opened up across the small tea-room booth. Helen had sat beside him anxiously, a reassuring hand on his knee underneath the table, while she looked imploringly at Marie, willing her to thaw a little and give poor Ray a chance. But Rofikul had respected Marie's demeanour, correctly reading her hostility as fierce protection of her friend. That loyalty showed that she cared as deeply for Helen as Rofikul did, and he appreciated that. In time, Rofikul and Helen had progressed from meeting at the café on weekend mornings, to long walks across the nearby moors, to the occasional evening out together – always with a chaperone, usually Marie. But then Hashim had come back into his life, and Rofikul felt, for the first time, that he had a real friend other than Helen, and realised that he wanted Hashim's approval.

'I'm sorry . . . I didn't mean anything. I mean, I wasn't saying . . .' Hashim looked over to where Rofikul was still facing the mirror. He realised that this was probably not the first time that his cousin had attempted to discuss whatever was bothering him. There were other occasions when it seemed as though Rofikul was about to say something important, and then changed his mind, and made a throwaway comment instead.

'No, I understand. It's hard to explain, that's all.' Rofikul smiled wanly and shrugged.

'You don't have to.' Hashim nodded towards the door. 'Come on, let's go. We don't want to keep them waiting.'

The two men slung their light jackets over their arms and stepped out into the soft July warmth. The sound of the television set next door floated out into the street, and somewhere in the distance children were kicking around a tin can and shrieking. With money tantalisingly warm in their pockets and the long-held promise of a night out, Hashim felt as though he and Rofikul had never had it so good.

The Regal Cinema stood proudly in the middle of Stockport Road; it was an imposing building that boasted two screens, a mezzanine lounge where patrons could enjoy warm fizzy pop and over-chilled ice cream that still had slivers of ice embedded in the cardboard tubs, and a broad sweeping staircase that dominated the art deco foyer. Outside, the white backlit board proclaimed the new releases in oddly spaced letters:

T HE GU NS OF NA VARO NE | T HE YO UNG ON ES

The number 44 trundled to a halt and Helen and Marie hopped off the bus. The hazy sky behind the cinema was streaked with blush. The queues snaked out of the foyer and back towards the edge of the pavement, with couples standing arm-in-arm, groups of confident-seeming office girls with shoes as shiny as their hair, and even the occasional family, noticeable by the weary mothers and distracted fathers and their earnest attempts at making the most of the long summer evenings. The girls threaded their way through the crowds towards the doors. Standing with their backs to the entrance were Rofikul and Hashim, neatly turned out in smart jackets – Rofikul in grey, Hashim in blue – their hair slicked back and crisply parted. Helen's heart leaped to her throat as she walked over to them and lightly touched Ray's arm.

'Hello, Ray.'

Rofikul swung round, a smile already across his face. 'Helen!' Grabbing his cousin eagerly by the elbow, he beamed. 'Helen, Marie – I'd like you to meet my cousin, Harry!'

Hashim thought Helen was a very pretty girl; a little pale for his liking, but she had a kind face and a voice that soothed him when she spoke. Her friend – Marie, was it? – was smiling at him, all red lips and masses of lacquered hair, and he had no idea where to look. Tongue-tied, it was all Hashim could do to nod politely, his face flushing.

Marie whispered to Helen. 'He's a doll, isn't he?'

Rofikul had already bought the tickets – they'd opted for *The Young Ones* over *The Guns of Navarone*. Helen didn't really have a preference, but Marie had been strongly in favour of the new Cliff Richard musical; she'd already heard and memorised all the songs and was simply dying to see it on the big screen. Hashim had never been to a cinema in England before and wasn't even sure if he'd be able to follow what was going on but at least music was universal, Rofikul told him, and he'd enjoy that sure enough. The foursome made their way to Screen Two where the adverts were already playing. An anthropomorphised hotdog was dancing with a paper cup and straw on the screen. People in this country are quite mad, thought Hashim. Rofikul ushered them towards the middle of the theatre. He tried in vain to convince Hashim to sit next to Marie, explaining that this was only proper, but his cousin was resolutely defiant. In the end, Marie, Helen, Rofikul and Hashim seated themselves in that order to appease both cousins: Rofikul who was adamant that he wanted to sit next to Helen, and Hashim who was adamant that he would only sit beside Rofikul. Marie seemed unfazed.

'He doesn't talk much anyway does he, really?' she murmured to Helen. 'Shame, he's got lovely eyes.'

They settled into their seats as the opening credits started to roll to a burst of orchestral music. A tiny prickling ran down the back of Hashim's neck. He had been to the cinema once before when visiting a friend in Dhaka – the atmosphere was charged with the huge screen and the music and everything silhouetted – he loved it. Out of the corner of his eye he saw Rofikul's hand clasped firmly around Helen's and he averted his gaze, embarrassed. Marie was fully absorbed in the film as Cliff Richard sashayed around crooning, surrounded by a group of earnest teenagers determined to save their youth club from the grasp of an evil millionaire. Hashim slurped his drink happily. This is what life in Britain was supposed to be like. He wondered if the cinema ever showed Hindi films, like the one he had seen that time in Dhaka. He wondered if Munira would like to see a film here some time with him and made a mental note to look into it.

As the closing credits rolled to the theme song, the lights came up in the cinema.

'Well, what did you think?' asked Rofikul, his hand still clasped with Helen's, Hashim noticed.

'It was magnificent!' Marie swooned. 'Let's see it again!'

'It was really very good.' Hashim pulled on his jacket. 'Let's see what else they have on another time?' They stood up and went out into the foyer where the bright lights made them squint after the darkness of the theatre.

'Well, all right, we can make it a regular thing – going to the pictures as a foursome, shall we?' Helen beamed around the group. It was so exciting to be out with friends and with Ray at the same time, feeling just like any other young couple.

'Absolutely, why not?' Rofikul draped his arm around Helen's shoulders and they all stepped out into the road outside the cinema. 'Now, where shall we go – drink? Or somewhere we can get a bite perhaps?' He stalled for a moment, his glance flickering over to the corner of the cinema where a group of young men were standing around smoking and staring intently at the foursome. Helen's eyes followed Rofikul's glance and she pulled her coat tighter around herself nervously.

'Let's . . . er, why don't we go straight back to our place, eh Marie? Maybe Ray and Harry can walk us back?' She felt a little silly for being scared, but you heard about things like this, groups of lads fighting coloureds and that, and it was always better to be on the safe side.

'But I wanted us to get a drink, it's only early yet!' Marie seemed oblivious to the stares they were getting.

Hashim sensed that something was going unsaid, but he wasn't sure what exactly the problem was.

'We can pick up some fish and chips on the way, how about that, Marie love? Nice quiet night in, the boys can come too of course.' Helen slipped her arm through Marie's and ushered Rofikul along with a look. 'Let's get going, we can jump on the bus, it should be here soon enough.'

The men in the corner seemed to notice that the friends were getting ready to leave. One of them stubbed out his cigarette and began walking towards them. The others followed slowly.

'Helen.' Rofikul's voice was low and steady. 'Take Marie and get back inside. Now.'

Marie had noticed the group now and had gripped Helen's arm. 'They don't look right friendly, do they?' she whispered.

Helen didn't want to leave the boys to the gang, but she knew that if she and Marie stayed, it would be even worse. Still gripping Marie's arm tightly, she edged them both away, keeping her eyes on the men before them as they backed through the side exit door and into the cinema. The door swung shut behind them.

Rofikul and Hashim were outnumbered by at least two to one. The lads were young but hard-looking. One of them stepped towards them, eyes narrowed, and spat squarely in Hashim's face. Hashim stepped back, startled.

'Oi,' Rofikul called out. 'There's no need for that.'

The leader of the gang cocked his head and turned to

the others. 'You heard that, lads? *There's no need for that.*' He laughed, and his friends joined in stupidly.

Like jackals, thought Hashim as he mopped the spit off his face with a handkerchief. He cast his gaze around to find Rofikul. He was standing squarely beside him.

'We aren't looking for any trouble, lads,' Rofikul began, one hand held up, palm flat to illustrate his point. 'We just want to get home.'

'Good idea. Go home. Back to where you lot come from.'

Hashim heard a crack and felt a blow that knocked his head sideways. Another grunt and a blow and he saw Rofikul being thrown on to his back on the pavement.

'And they're not your girls, you understand?' one of the men snarled into Hashim's face.

I know they're not my girls, Hashim screamed inwardly. *I don't want them to be my girls, I just want to get home.* He could hear the thuds descending on his body, and the grunts of the men, and occasionally Rofikul cry out, but he could feel nothing and soon enough blackness descended.

'Oh my God – oh God, are they – they're not moving.' Marie gripped Helen's arm as they ran towards Hashim and Rofikul. The gang had fled, leaving only evidence of their fists and feet behind.

'Wait here, miss, let me have a look.' The cinema manager strode over to the two motionless mounds of bloodstained clothing and black hair lying in the middle of the pavement. He gingerly prodded the figure with his foot and Rofikul moaned softly. Satisfied that the man wasn't dead, the manager called back cheerfully, 'He's fine!'

'Fine? You call that *fine*?' Helen screamed. She rushed to Ray's side, kneeling beside him and gently stroking the hair from his forehead. 'Did you telephone the police like I asked?

If you'd just rung them when I told you there were some troublemakers around, they'd be here by now.' Helen was seething. She'd asked at the ticket desk for someone to call for security but the woman behind the desk simply buzzed for her manager instead.

The moustachioed duty manager sniffed; he did not appreciate the girl's tone, and, besides, what business had she to be out with not one, but two of the coloureds who were taking over this city? Not that he condoned violence of course, but it wasn't right, that kind of carry-on. Not right at all.

'I see no need to get the police involved – looks like a small altercation, settled fair and square, and these lads just came off the worse. You should be glad they didn't get even more of a pasting.' The manager turned on his heel and strode away, shaking his head disapprovingly.

Helen and Marie were left alone in the empty street with poor Harry who looked as though he were in shock, and Ray who was barely conscious.

'What are we going to do, Helen?' Marie asked nervously.

'Nothing we can do,' Helen replied grimly, 'except take them home.'

'It isn't Ray.' Hashim winced as Helen daubed antiseptic on to his forehead. They were sitting at the kitchen table in Helen and Marie's tiny shared bedsit, while Rofikul lay passed out on the sofa.

'What?' Helen dipped a fresh cotton ball in the bowl of water and squeezed the drops.

'His name. It's not Ray. It's Rofikul.' Hashim blurted it out as though it had been searing him from inside. He didn't know why it bothered him so much but there was something about Rofikul's blasé approach to 'getting by' that rankled with him. Hashim had been made to answer to 'Harry' in order to make his white foreman's life supposedly easier. Rofikul's white lie had been taken to such lengths that he was seeing a girl who didn't even know what his real name was. Seeing the look of confusion on Helen's face, he felt guilty for adding a further complication to her already emotional evening.

'But he calls himself Ray . . .' Even as she was saying the words, Helen felt incredibly stupid. Did they even have names like that over there, where he was from? But it had never crossed her mind that he might be lying to her.

'Yes – but that's what people do here sometimes. My people. They – we – take names that make it easier for white people to say. To remember.' Hashim nervously shuffled in his seat. 'He wasn't lying, you know, he just . . .'

'I know.' Helen rose and picked up the bowl from the table and carried it to the sink. 'So . . . you're not Harry, are you?'

'I'm Hashim.'

'Hashim.' She repeated it. 'It's a nice name. Not hard to say. Not like Ro . . . Rof . . .'

'Rof-ik-ul.'

'Rofikul.'

Helen walked over to the sofa where Rofikul was sleeping. His cuts still needed cleaning; Helen had tended to Hashim first as he was conscious, but she needed to bandage up Rofikul now. Gently, she shook him awake.

'Rof— hey, Rofikul, love . . . it's me, wake up. Come on, love, wake up.' She laid her hand on his cheek and whispered his real name again.

Rofikul opened his eyes and recognition flickered across his face. He sat up and buried his face in Helen's chest as she put her arms around him.

Hashim quietly let himself out of the door and into the narrow, cobbled street. The half-moon hung desolately in the sky, and somewhere in the distance was the faint sound of a man shouting. As he walked home, his body aching, he thought about everything that had happened that evening. His first night out in Manchester had certainly been as memorable as Rofikul promised it would be.

6

M UNIRA'S MOTHER-IN-LAW WAS surprisingly pragmatic about the prospect of her youngest daughter-in-law leaving the familial home and travelling – alone, no less – across the world to a strange land. A place where, according to her son's letters, people ate cold food at lunchtime and it rained throughout the year. Imagine having no seasons! She hoped that her daughter-in-law would be able to look after Hashim while he was making sense of life in that barbarous land of cold weather and cold people. She was aware that Munira was afflicted with boredom in the communal home and realised that her other daughters-in-law were tiring of what they perceived to be Munira's snobbery. Her daughter-in-law was an intelligent young woman, no doubt about that, but she had been roundly spoiled by her father and brothers, who had indulged her desire for books and reading. Domestic life did not seem to suit Munira, but perhaps being with her husband again would reignite – if indeed, that flame had ever been lit – an interest in the charms of the home.

In some ways, Munira's mother-in-law envied her son and daughter-in-law the opportunities that lay before them. Since her marriage thirty years ago, she had never ventured beyond the confines of the family compound. Not that the outside world interested her that much – she had everything she needed right here within the home. She reared chickens, milked goats, tended to her kitchen garden and grew beans and gourds. Fish swam happily in the family pond where she and the rest of her family also bathed. Life in the *gram* was simple, although it was hard more than it was comfortable: this much was true. She and her fellow villagers had learned to exist in the shadow of disease and early death, those silent killers that reaped the lives of young and old alike with merciless abandon. Had she not lost several of her own children before their time? But all praise is to Allah, for He is the best of planners.

Munira's mother-in-law wiped her eyes with the edge of her sari and, in an unusual show of affection, threw her arms around Munira. They were standing in the open courtyard of the family home: Munira was about to get into the rickshaw that was parked by the gates and make her way to the train station, then the airport, with her brother by her side.

Despite the fake tears and the wailing from her sisters-in-law, Munira herself had eagerly anticipated this moment for months, ever since Hashim sent her the letter suggesting that she come over to live with him. *In England.* She had been lofty in her response, veiling her burning hopes behind what she fancied were dutiful proclamations that 'all things lay in God's hands and if He willed it, it would be done'. She wondered if her husband had seen through her pious nonchalance; she hoped so. It seemed so, anyway, given that he had pressed ahead in making arrangements with almost alarming urgency. He had written back many times instructing her what paperwork she needed to supply, that she would need to produce an official marriage certificate from somewhere, and finally – the last stage – had arranged for her appointment at the British Consulate in Dhaka. Her brother had accompanied her on that visit too, her first to the capital.

Munira knelt and placed both hands on her mother-in-law's feet and then on her own chest, three times, as a sign of respect. She then rose and climbed into the rickshaw, her heart pounding. She half feared that if she waited too long, someone might shout out that it was all a joke, and that she would have to turn back. As the rickshaw-*wallah* pedalled them away, Munira drew Hashim's most recent letter from the folds of her sari where she had tucked it into her petticoat – she didn't trust her sisters-in-law not to rifle through her drawers. Munira re-read her husband's slanted handwriting, drinking in the words again: the long-awaited confirmation that her passage to Britain was finally arranged, the address of the house they would live in: 45 Beresford Terrace, Ardwick, Manchester. She folded the letter and slipped it into the *Samsad Bengali–English Dictionary* that had lived on her bedside table ever since Hashim first suggested she should come and live with him, and that was now nestled in her handbag alongside a hairbrush, a handkerchief, and some wooden prayer beads that her sister-in-law had pressed into her hand as she left.

Munira had memorised five new words every evening, whispering them aloud, the foreign sounds feeling full and sprawling in her mouth. She was damned if she was going to arrive in England a timid mute. Unsatisfied by the dictionary alone, she had persuaded her elder brother to bring her some English magazines the next time he visited. Dutifully, he had arrived a few weeks later with a stack of glossy publications: most of them were women's household magazines with advertisements for cleaning products, modelled by various immaculate-looking white ladies with the longest and barest legs Munira had ever seen. But her favourites were the thicker, heavier magazines all about the English countryside. She had marvelled at the beautiful photographs and read about the different birds and flowers to look out for in the four seasons – for England only had four, compared to her motherland's six. Munira rapidly learned the names of the trees and how to identify them by their leaves; she was drawn to the star-shaped leaf of the chestnut, the reddy-purple of the copper beech, and the soft fronds of the drooping willow. She hoped that if she could recognise things that might seem familiar, then England would feel like home even sooner. With this in mind, Munira had learned the names of the rivers, as well as the flowers and the fish that populated the fields and streams of her soon-to-be home.

But now, all that seemed so far away. Munira still had almost two full days of travel ahead: a train from Sylhet to Dhaka, a flight to London, and then another journey from London to that unknown city: Manchester. Resignedly, she settled into the worn rickshaw seat, as the wheels rattled along the bumpy roads, inching her ever closer to her new life in a new land.

Thousands of miles across the ocean, Hashim lay awake in bed in the home that he was soon to share with his wife, as well as his already numerous housemates. Atiq and the others had been fairly neutral at first when he had proposed the idea of Munira coming to live with them, only really warming to the idea when Rofikul pointed out that with a woman in the house, the domestic standards would only get better for them all. Rofikul had moved out of the room he shared with Hashim to allow the married couple some privacy and was bunking in with Atiq and Ilyas in the room next door.

Now that the logistics were settled, and his wife would be arriving in his world in just a matter of weeks, Hashim could barely contain his nerves. He had no idea of how to be married – he'd only spent a few weeks in Munira's company, and even then his mother or a sister-in-law or some other family member was never far off, and so they were rarely left alone. But in this house, although the others would be around, it was different somehow. They would be a couple, a unit, in a sea of others, and while the idea thrilled him, he was alarmed at how it would all pan out. He wondered how Munira would adjust to life in England – dealing not just with an intemperate climate and Mancunian accents, but how she would react when she saw how her own people were living in this foreign land.

Hashim did not consider himself to be particularly traditional, but there were elements of the way his fellow countrymen conducted themselves in England that made him uncomfortable. Drinking. Girlfriends. Both he and they knew that such behaviour would not be tolerated back home. Hashim could see no justification for indulging in alcohol: it perturbed him when his housemates would casually pour themselves inches of brown whisky after a night shift and sit around the kitchen table talking and smoking. But taking up with girls, he understood to some degree. Rofikul and his other friends were young, and, for the most part, lonely. When these girls showed a kind-hearted interest in them – and for some unfathomable reason, they did – it was hardly surprising that the men reciprocated. And while Hashim might have frowned upon 'girlfriends' in theory, he was well aware that had he been single, there was a fair chance he might have found himself a girl to take the edge off the loneliness too. And knowing Helen softened his stance a little; her warmth and generosity touched him. He noticed how she looked out for Rofikul and the others: cleaning the house when she came around to visit, or by letting them know when such-and-such a place was hiring workers. Witnessing the tenderness between Helen and Rofikul had made Hashim more sympathetic towards these unorthodox couplings, but he wondered what his wife would think about it all.

Nobody was more on edge about Munira's opinion than Helen. It surprised her how much she wanted to be liked by a woman she had not even met. Rofikul had waved away Helen's concerns airily – why should she care what Munira thought? He loved Helen. If Munira had a problem with her, she would learn to live with it. But Rofikul's refusal to acknowledge Helen's concerns frustrated her. She tried to find the words to explain to him the source of her anxiety: that she felt like an imitation, an anaemic attempt at being the kind of woman that men like Rofikul actually wanted. Women who cooked the right food, spoke the right language, knew the right customs.

Helen decided to make use of her luxurious day off that week, and cook for Rofikul and the boys. She knew they liked curries, but the unknown powders and pastes involved intimidated her. She would make them something that she was confident in preparing: a stew. Resolved in her plan, Helen set about tackling the first hurdle: sourcing meat that the boys could eat. She knew they avoided pork, and that some of the men, Rofikul included, ended their dietary restrictions there. But Hashim and some of the others only ate meat that had been slaughtered according to the rules of their religion. Helen was fuzzy about the details, but she did know that it meant that all the meat for communal cooking had to come from one tiny butcher on Dickenson Road. When she had stepped into the dingy-looking shop she was assailed by the sweet smell of fresh blood. Chickens with their skin on and chunks of beef and mutton lay piled high on the counter in front of her. She pointed to a mound of mutton chops and smiled politely. *Two pounds of those, please.* A dour-looking man in a stained apron threw handfuls of the chops on to the metal scales. Helen placed the paper bag of meat and bones in her basket and went to the greengrocer on the corner to buy fat yellow onions, potatoes and carrots with their green fronds still attached. By the time she had finished her shopping it was close to two o'clock – Rofikul was finishing work at five. Hurriedly, Helen made her way to the house and let herself in through the back door with the key that the boys kept under the mat. Her heart was pounding; she felt as though she were somehow intruding, even though she'd been in the house countless times.

Helen set to work preparing the ingredients: trimming the fat off the mutton, peeling the potatoes, removing the papery skin from the onions and slicing them thinly. She found an abandoned casserole dish under the sink and arranged the chunks of browned meat at the bottom of it before pouring over the gravy she had made out of sticky sweet onions, flour, fat and salt and pepper. A few carrots and a layer of potatoes finished off the job, and by half past four the stew was in the oven. By five o'clock, the smell of cooking meat was wafting through the kitchen and the scuffed kitchen table was, for the first time in years, properly set with cutlery and as close to matching crockery as Helen could find in the cupboards. Helen smoothed her hair and reapplied her powder with only minutes to spare.

At twenty-five past five, Rofikul, Atiq, Hashim and Ilyas crashed in through the front door, mid-conversation. They were speaking in Sylheti, and, as always, it sounded to Helen as though they were having an argument. Rofikul had once explained to her that it was simply how they spoke when they got excited; emphatically raising their voices towards the end of their sentences, intonating to ensure that the listener had understood the point. But Helen never got used to the volume at which Rofikul conducted his conversations in Sylheti. Rofikul was gesturing to Atiq about something when he suddenly realised that Atiq, Hashim and Ilyas were staring beyond him. He turned around, seeing Helen sitting nervously at the head of the kitchen table. Her cheeks were flushed – either from excitement or embarrassment, or maybe even the heat of the stove, he realised, as his eyes took in the full scene. The laden table, knives and forks set out, the cooker emanating a heat that was dwarfed only by the warmth he felt spreading in his own chest as he looked at Helen. She was smiling now, rising from her seat. Rofikul thought she had never looked so beautiful.

'I thought I would cook for you all tonight. I hope you don't mind. I got the meat from the butcher, the one on Dickenson Road . . .' At this, she looked hopefully at Hashim, knowing that he was the most particular of the group when it came to maintaining his dietary laws, and hoped that this would reassure him enough at least to try her food.

'You went there today? Alone?' Hashim's concern at Helen visiting an unknown part of town was present in his voice but was drowned out by the sudden rolling of Rofikul's appreciative laugh.

'You did this? For us? She did all this for us, boys! Can you believe it?' Rofikul caught up Helen by the waist, swinging her around the tiny kitchen, laughing.

Hashim noticed the flicker that seemed to waken in Helen's eyes as she looked up at Rofikul, basking in his appreciation almost as a child would, and wondered if Munira would ever come to look at him that way. As the men washed their hands and faces in the kitchen sink, Helen took the stew out of the oven and set it on the table. She ladled out the brown meat and the crisp layer of potatoes, and poured over thick gravy on to each of the plates, explaining the provenance of the recipe: it had been passed down from her grandmother's mother, and yes, this was the type of food most people ate when she was growing up. Ilyas and Atiq inhaled their food in mute appreciation, but Hashim listened carefully to every detail of what Helen described, prompting her for more details. He asked how she had made the sauce so rich in colour and at what stage she added the vegetables, and nodded as Helen earnestly explained the use of gravy browning. As she spoke, Rofikul ate cheerfully, mopping up the gravy with pieces of the white bread Helen had cut. Hashim thought he saw a flicker of disappointment when Rofikul liberally added more salt to the stew on his plate and refrained from doing the same lest it hurt Helen's feelings.

After they had finished eating, Rofikul and Hashim insisted Helen stay seated while they cleared away the dishes, soaping them and stacking them on the metal rack by the sink. The scene was relaxed: the two cousins chattered happily as one washed and the other dried. Helen had removed her shoes and her stockinged feet rested on the edge of the hearth as she reclined in her seat and listened to them even though she could not understand their language. She wondered how Munira's arrival would change things, how having a stranger in their midst would disrupt their carefully balanced domestic peace. Helen feared being displaced, cast aside as a fake once the genuine article was safely delivered to the streets of Manchester. The woman who could participate in these conversations, who would not have to try as hard as Helen did. Again, Helen tried to push the idea out of her mind. There was no point fretting any more. Munira was coming next week. She would find out then.

7

MUNIRA HAD NOT been in England for long before she realised that her prior research on the country had been useless. The nature magazines she had pored over before her arrival might have taught her the names of trees, but offered no insight as to how one navigated bus routes across the city. There was no occasion to showcase her talent in discerning a brown trout from the silvery blush of a rainbow trout because there were no streams in the inner city of Manchester. Here, fish was either haddock or cod, dipped in batter and immersed in bubbling vats of what she later learned was beef fat. The difficulty in performing the simplest of tasks frustrated her: how one washed in the absence of a pond in which to bathe; how to launder clothes without adequate sunlight to dry them. She felt like a child, reliant on others for her survival.

During the first few days Hashim had hovered constantly, his nervousness making her even more on edge than she already felt. He fussed around her, pointing out the basic things she needed to know, showing her where the lavatory was outside and how to pull the chain to flush it. The sudden whoosh startled her, as did the tiny whirlpool in the huge porcelain bowl. He showed her the space he had cleared for her in the heavy oak wardrobe in their bedroom. *For your saris*, he had said, smiling tentatively, as though she might have thought it presumptuous that he would propose their belongings share any physical space. Now her colourful saris hung beside Hashim's muted work shirts, almost garish in comparison. They were a reminder to Munira that while Hashim could blend in here in England, she was still a stranger in a strange land.

At first, Munira had tried to keep her presence modestly contained in the bedroom, arranging her things neatly on one half of the dresser. Along the right-hand side of the mirror lay her hairbrush, hair clips, face cream and a small pot of kohl with a fine-tipped brush she used to apply it to her eyes. But over the course of the last few months, her existence had spilled out beyond the bedroom and into the rest of the house. Quilted, handmade blankets she had brought with her from home covered the sofas in the living room; small, low-relief pictures carved from bamboo adorned the walls. The scenes were of boats on rivers, buffalo tethered to a plough, a silhouette of a woman with a water urn balanced on one hip. They had been wedding gifts, and now they decorated her new home, the extended home she shared with her husband, his housemates their surrogate family. With the exception of Rofikul – and he hardly counted as one – she was without in-laws; an idea that seemed both unfathomable and delightful at the same time.

There were seemingly no expectations of her to prepare breakfast, or have dinner waiting: these men exercised an almost alarming level of independence. They reminded her of the dwarves in that fairy tale she had read, the seven little men who lived alone in a cottage in the woods until a mysterious princess wandered into their home, disrupting their way of life. In some ways, the boys did treat her with the kind of reverence she imagined was reserved for royalty. They always lowered their voices in her presence, stubbed out their cigarettes if she happened to enter the room. Munira knew that these were small signs of respect, afforded to her for being a woman as much as for being Hashim's wife, but it made her feel constantly on the margins. Other than Hashim and Rofikul, none of the other men really chatted to her; and while that was not exactly unusual in the shared compound back home where men and women had their own separate quarters, in a small house with no other female relatives, Munira was lonely.

Hashim was worried.

'She hates it here,' he said to Rofikul one day, as they were walking back from the factory. The weather was turning, and the men had turned up their coat collars against the autumn chill, burying their chins in the folds of wool.

'Says who?' Rofikul was swinging the lunch bag that had been filled with *rutis* and leftover *aloo bhaji* made by Munira the night before. 'She seems fine, she's just adjusting – it'll take time.'

'But she's lonely. We're out all day, she has no one to talk to, nowhere to go. All I can do is buy her magazines, but even she must get bored of reading them sometimes.'

'I wouldn't be so sure of that – your wife reads more than a professor could.' Rofikul peered at his cousin in mock disapproval. 'It's unwise to let a woman fill her brain so much, you know.' Seeing that Hashim was in no mood to joke, Rofikul adjusted his tone. 'If you like, I could see if Helen wanted to meet her. She's been asking about Munira. I'm sure she would love to take her out, show her around. What do you think?'

Hashim hesitated. For some reason, he had wanted to shield Munira from what he considered to be the more scandalous aspects of life in her new city: the drinking, the relationships with women. He felt guilty for thinking this way, knowing Helen as he did, and the depth of her kindness not only towards Rofikul, but to Hashim himself. She deserved more than being labelled as just another 'white woman'. She was a friend to them, and maybe she could even be a friend to Munira.

'It's not a bad idea. See what Helen says – maybe we could introduce them. I'll ask Munira whether she'd like that.' Hashim nodded slowly as he spoke, as though convincing himself of the wisdom of this arrangement. The look of gratitude on Rofikul's face touched Hashim. He understood that to his cousin, this introduction would go some way to recognising the validity of Rofikul and Helen's relationship.

And so Helen and Munira were introduced: two women whose only connection was the men they loved. Both had been nervous beforehand. Hashim had been surprised by Munira's anxiety; she usually seemed so self-assured.

'What if my English isn't good enough?' she had asked him. 'I've never spoken English to an English person before.'

'Well, Helen is actually Irish,' he had said stupidly, as though that would assuage his wife's concerns. 'But it doesn't matter,' he continued, 'you have the best English of us all! And she really wants to meet you, she's been asking about you a lot.'

Munira had refrained from asking too many questions about Helen and Rofikul and the nature of their relationship. Whether it was out of politeness or disapproval, Hashim could not tell, but when he had proposed that Munira meet Helen, his wife had positively leaped at the chance, so he supposed it was the former. Helen, meanwhile, had spent weeks grilling Rofikul as much as she could about the new woman in the house: what did she look like, how did she dress, was her cooking good? In the time since Munira had moved in, Helen had not been round to visit: partly because it was so much easier to see Rofikul in the relative privacy of the bedsit she shared with Marie, but partly because, until now, an invitation had never come.

Both women prepared for their first meeting almost as though it were a date, choosing their outfits carefully: Helen opted for a cream blouse tucked into a knee-length skirt of pale blue, while Munira wrapped herself in an apple-green sari with darker green stitching on the border. The plan was that Helen would call on Munira at three o'clock and they would have tea in the house, then Helen would take Munira to the park or perhaps to the market, depending on what she preferred. At two minutes past the hour, the doorbell rang. Munira slowly unlatched the door and smiled nervously in greeting at the woman who stood on the doorstep clutching her handbag so tightly that the skin was stretched over her already white knuckles, a bouquet of autumn blooms in her other arm.

Munira offered her hand. 'You must be Helen. Please, come in.'

Helen smiled back and followed Munira into the house that she already knew so well, but which was now the realm of another woman. She was startled by how beautiful Munira was, with her curtain of dark hair that hung down to her waist and plump, high cheekbones.

'Would you like some tea?' Munira motioned to the already laden table. There were teacups and saucers – Lord only knew where she had found them; Helen had never been able to find a matching set of anything in those cupboards – and a plate of biscuits. There was also a dish of a milky-looking pudding called *firni*, as Helen later learned, that would come to be a staple part of their tea afternoons.

'These are for you.' Helen handed the flowers to Munira.

'There should be a vase under the sink.' As soon as she said it, Helen worried that she had seemed over-familiar, territorial, even. But Munira didn't seem either to notice or to mind as she retrieved a glass vessel from the cupboard and began to fill it with water.

'These are beautiful. Dahlias . . . and what are these ones?' Munira pointed to the clusters of fluffy purple heads.

'I think they're asters.'

'I've never heard of them.'

'They have lots growing in Victoria Park.' Helen hesitated. 'If you like I can show you them this afternoon?'

Munira nodded emphatically. 'I would love that. I've barely left the house since I got here. My husband and brother-in-law are worried I'll get lost by myself but won't take me out themselves. I suppose that's why they asked you to babysit me . . .' She trailed off, worried that she had come across as petulant, but Helen's laugh reassured her.

'Not at all – I've wanted to meet you for ages. I've heard so much about you.' Helen stirred the bowl of pudding that Munira had ladled out for her. 'I know it sounds silly, but I've been so nervous about meeting you.'

'So was I – about you, I mean. They both spoke very highly of you.'

Helen smiled, almost gratefully. The kettle on the stove whistled and as she stood up to retrieve it, Munira thought that for the first time since she had arrived, the kitchen felt as though it had some life to it, simply just from the presence of another person during the long, empty days while the men were at work. She resolved to make sure Helen would visit again.

From that day on, Munira and Helen saw each other every week on Helen's day off, and usually at weekends too.

63

Sometimes they would meet in the park and take a walk before finding a bench to read their magazines and share a bar of Galaxy chocolate; at other times, they would wander through the outdoor market in Longsight, picking up fruit, vegetables and fresh fish. Munira was glad of the company and conversation, and Helen felt as though she were finally being welcomed into part of Rofikul's family life of which she had always been aware, but to which she had never been fully admitted.

Although Munira enjoyed her new friendship, her restlessness had not abated. She envied the others their sense of purpose: whether at the factory like the men, or in an office like Helen, at least they all had somewhere to be every day. Somewhere where they were needed. Munira realised that the same issue she had had while living with her mother-in-law had followed her across the ocean and into her new life in England: she had nothing to keep her mind *active*.

'You could join a library,' suggested Helen one afternoon as they ambled through the copper-coloured park.

Munira wrapped her scarf tighter around her shoulders, a few strands of hair having escaped from her plait.

'Is it far?' Although she didn't like to admit it, Hashim and Rofikul's caution had rubbed off on Munira.

'No more than fifteen minutes' walk, I should think. I'll show you.'

Later that evening, Munira showed Hashim her shiny library card with pride.

'Mrs Munira Begum,' Hashim read solemnly. 'Is that what you call yourself these days, hmm?'

'What should I be calling myself, then? "Wife"? "You"? Is that better?' Munira swatted her husband away and continued. 'Look what I got out today.' She pushed the pile of books over to her husband.

Hashim began to read out the titles. '*English Country Gardens*; *Birds and Hedgerows*; *Jane Eyre*; *Good Housekeeping Recipe Guide*; *Little Women* . . .' He looked up at his wife, astonished. 'And you're going to read *all* of these?'

'Well, that's the idea.'

'No wonder you've been bored until now.'

Munira shot her husband a slightly guilty glance. 'It's not that I've been bored. I just needed something to keep my brain busy.' She didn't want Hashim thinking she was bored with *him*. That wasn't the case at all. There was a safety, a solid reliability in being with Hashim that she had come to depend on, even love. She knew exactly what shopping he would bring home, what food he would be in the mood for, how he liked to spend his weekends. He didn't surprise her – and as someone who hated surprises, this suited Munira just so.

Munira spent the rest of her first long, cold season in England cocooned in books. The weather was too chilly now for walks in the park with Helen, so Helen would come around on her day off armed with needles and yarn, and they would knit scarves and sweaters, or read, or swap stories of their own lives before Manchester. When Helen left, Munira would bury herself in stories until Hashim and Rofikul came home, and then she would update Hashim as to where she had got to in the book as she served them all hot rice and chicken cooked with shredded cabbage.

'So she's run away now, from that house – the one with the old man.'

'And the crazy woman in the attic?'

'Well, yes, she's still there. But anyway, Jane's gone to stay with some cousins now.'

'But I thought her cousins were awful – didn't they beat her, or something?'

Munira beamed, pleased that Hashim clearly paid attention to her re-tellings of the great classics.

'Yes, but these are a different set of cousins – one's a clergyman. I think that means "church" man. Anyway, he wants her to go to India with him.'

Hashim had come to rather enjoy his wife's gentle education: through her he had learned names of famous authors and their books, and although he wasn't interested in reading them himself, he liked being able to share something that clearly made Munira so happy.

One morning in late December, Munira unlatched the back door to go out and collect the milk from the doorstep. She gasped as she took in the blanket of soft white snow that had silently enveloped the street overnight. It was beautiful and stretched as far as she could see: on the roofs of the terraced houses, on the tops of the stone walls, on Atiq's car, on the pavements. She had seen light snow earlier in the winter, had marvelled at the way the flakes danced down on to her outstretched hands: but, to her dismay, it had never settled for long on the ground. The milkman had clearly been unable to make his rounds, for there were no glass bottles neatly arranged like soldiers on Munira's doorstep. But – didn't those tracks in the snow look like those of a milk van? Munira looked closer and saw that the milk bottles *were* on her doorstep, camouflaged by the white. As she tried to tug them out, she realised, to her amazement, that they had frozen into the pile of snow that swamped them. There they would remain until the temperature warmed up a little and the ice thawed out. It could take days.

This country, she thought disbelievingly, was full of absurd surprises.

Dearest Baba,

I pray that you and Ma are in the best of health. How are my brothers? Please give them, and all the family, my salams and love.

It is winter here; the coldest I have ever felt. Everything you can see — houses, streets, the small patches of grass they call parks — is covered by a broad, sweeping white chador that has a different name here: snow. We keep warm by lighting fires in the house using coal. The lumps leave black marks on your hands and the fire that burns is a dirty, sooty flame, but it is warm and lasts a long time. We store the coal in sheds in the yard to the rear of the house. Houses here have two entrance doors usually, one at the front, and one at the rear — though nobody seems ever to use the front door. The houses all look the same too: red brick, square and squashed together like ants marching in a row. When I first got here, your son-in-law had to put a stick in the ground outside the house, so I would be able to tell which one was ours. The only thing that tells the houses apart are the front doors, but, as I say, everyone uses the rear, so it's of no use.

I have made a good friend here, Baba. Her name is Helen, and she's Irish — like Yeats, who you love so much, though she said she's never read him. She's been kind to me: showing me around, taking me out, accompanying me when we go shopping. Last week, I said that I wished I had a heavier sari for the winter time — but of course, no shops here sell saris. Helen had the brilliant idea of taking me to Lewis's, a big department store in town, where they sell fabric by the yard. We bought armfuls of thick material, each six yards long, and hemmed them, and turned them into saris. Necessity is, indeed, the mother of invention!

Your son-in-law sends his salams to you and Ma. And take a kiss from me for Ma and one for you. Please write to me soon with news from home.

Your ever loving,
Munira

8

NOBODY LIVED FOR the weekend the way the English seemed to, Munira observed. The way their faces lit up when they discussed their Friday night plans and their long lunches on Sunday seemed to be of almost religious significance. Helen and Marie were never without a fully-fledged programme of activities for the whole weekend, from going out, to shopping, calling on friends, and even properly scheduled lie-ins. Even Hashim and Rofikul had taken on this reverence for the weekend and its sanctity above all other days in the week. As the only one of their set who did not work, Munira felt a little left out from this excitement. To her, the days were all the same – an assortment of chores, reading, excursions to the market, and more reading – differentiated only by who else was around, which was nobody during the day from Monday to Friday, except on Helen's day off from the office which changed each week. But then the house filled up again at the weekends, and things seemed livelier and more colourful until even Munira could feel the magic of the two-day holiday.

At this very moment, Munira was in the kitchen preparing a Sunday late-morning brunch of omelette-topped *kitchuri*. She had washed the lentils with the rice, picking out bits of grit from the grains as she swirled away the milky water with each rinse. They were now steaming away in a pot on the stove with onion, garlic, ginger and woody sticks of cinnamon and bayleaf. She found the work therapeutic in its repetition although, unlike Helen, she would never quite describe herself as being at her most satisfied in the kitchen. A tap on the back door was followed immediately with a push, and Helen stepped into the light-strewn room.

'Hello, love.' Helen slipped her coat off her shoulders as she went over and greeted Munira warmly with a kiss on both cheeks.

'Perfect timing, Helen – everything's almost ready. I don't know where the men are. I heard one of them go out this morning.' Munira was beating tiny chopped onions and chillies into a bowlful of eggs and sprinkling in yellow turmeric and fat grains of salt. 'Rofikul, probably, gone to get the morning papers.'

'D'you want me to start on the tea?'

'Yes please – there's a pan on the side over there.'

Helen took the pan and heated some water and the milk, added a few teabags and let it simmer before stirring in the whole spices and sugar. This way of taking tea was a world away from the thin brews she had grown up with.

'What did you and Marie get up to Friday night, then?' Munira knew that however well you knew someone, you always asked how various aspects of their weekend had been.

'Just went to the pictures – Marie's fallen in love with the lead as usual, wants to see his next one when it comes out.' Helen glanced over at Munira who was now heating oil in a frying pan and pouring in the eggs. 'You should come with us next time, you know.'

'Mmm. Maybe.'

It wasn't the first time Helen had raised the idea, but Munira always seemed so hesitant about going out 'alone' as she called it – even though she wouldn't be alone, she would be with Helen and Marie – at night-time. It puzzled Helen; Munira always seemed happy enough to go to the market and parks and be out and about during the day, but this self-imposed evening curfew made little sense.

'You won't be alone, you know. Marie and I will be with you, it'll be fine. Like a girls' night out!'

'But what about Hashim?' Munira slid a yellow omelette flecked with chilli on to a plate and poured the next batch of eggs into the hot pan.

'What about him? He'll be home or maybe out with his friends too.' Helen removed the milk pan from the heat and blew on to it gently before starting to pour it out in the assembled china teacups. 'Doesn't he like you going out at night?'

Munira was quick to set Helen straight. 'It's nothing like that; if he were coming too, it would be fine. But it doesn't feel safe, just us women, out at night by ourselves. What if something were to happen to us?'

'What do you think might happen?'

'I don't know. You hear things . . .'

'What things?'

'I don't know, just – we never did it. Back home. We just didn't go out at night by ourselves. And I don't see the need to start now.'

Munira was using the voice that made it clear that the discussion was firmly closed. Helen relented, not wanting to upset her friend. The back door was flung open and in thudded Rofikul, a couple of newspapers under his arm and a glass bottle of juice in his hand.

'Beautiful day out.' He set down the things on the table and patted Helen's cheek affectionately. 'Where's Hashim?'

'Still upstairs.' Munira was ladling out the fluffy rice and lentils on to plates, topping each portion with half an omelette.

'I'll go and see what he's up to.' Rofikul slipped off his shoes and padded lightly up the stairs to the bedroom Munira and Hashim shared; the marital luxury he was not afforded. Even before he pushed open the door, he could hear the low melodic intonations: the rise and fall in pitch and the holding of long notes, as his cousin recited passages from the Qur'an that felt to him, Rofikul, at once familiar and alien. He hadn't heard those words for years, not in that style, the way their grandfather used to recite them. The way they had both learned during their shared summers at their grandparents' village, the one area of study where his cousin outshone him. Where Rofikul was impatient in learning to pronounce the words of a language he didn't even understand, Hashim was attentive to the nuances, mastering the art of holding vowels and subtle changes in the hard and soft consonants. Hashim's voice was gentle, coaxing the words from the page. Listening to the melodic rise and fall, Rofikul felt his throat tighten and, inexplicably, tears form in the corners of his eyes. The reciting stopped and there was a slight pause as Rofikul knew from behind the door that Hashim was wrapping up the holy book in its cloth and putting away the small wooden stand that was used to hold it while he read. Rofikul imagined Hashim slipping the white *tupi* from the top of his head and folding it the way their grandfather used to, before getting to his feet from his cross-legged position on the floor. Rofikul took a step back on to the landing just as the bedroom door swung open.

'Oh! Did Munira send you up to call me?' Hashim looked surprised to see Rofikul standing awkwardly outside the room. 'I'm coming now, I was just reading—'

'I heard.'

'All right.' Hashim paused. 'Was it disturbing you?'

'No! No. It wasn't, at all. It's just that it's been a long time since I heard it.' Rofikul pressed his hands together just to have something to do with them.

'Really?' Hashim seemed surprised.

'Well, yes. I don't make it to *jummah* often now, do I?'

'I suppose not – but plenty of people don't,' Hashim added hastily. It was true that while Hashim always tried to attend the Friday afternoon congregational prayers that were held in a makeshift masjid in someone's front room whenever he wasn't working, Rofikul had never seemed much inclined to make the effort.

'It wasn't just the recitation.' Rofikul paused. 'You sounded just like Nana Bhai. His voice, his style, it . . .' His voice flickered, barely enough to notice, but Hashim registered the pause in his cousin's voice. 'It just reminded me. I don't really spend much time thinking about *desh*, but hearing you made me feel as though I was right there.' He turned and started down the stairs. 'Let's go down – they'll be wondering where we've gone.'

Hashim nodded, following close behind. He didn't really understand how Rofikul could possibly avoid thinking of their homeland. Their *desh*. It was a delightful quirk of the Bengali language. The word literally meant 'country' but was also used to refer specifically to their homeland as though there were only one country in all the world, one that predated any borders or passports. The land had officially been granted many different internationally recognised legal names over the years, based on the whims of far-off governors. But those who hailed from there referred to it simply as *desh*. All other lands were collectively referred to as *bidesh*: abroad. In Hashim's mind, to avoid thinking about *desh* was impossible. It was the natural place his thoughts went to. And no matter how long they might stay, Britain would always be *bidesh*.

*

73

Brunch had been devoured appreciatively by everyone, including a steady stream of the other housemates as they passed through the kitchen, still groggy from their extended sleep. Helen stacked the dishes next to the sink as Munira rinsed the plates under the running tap. Privately, she couldn't imagine how Munira coped with living with so many people in a house that was hardly designed for as many as it now sheltered. She knew that Munira and Hashim talked occasionally about moving out to their own place, but it seemed a luxury. She also privately wondered when Rofikul would move out of the house and whether he would entertain the idea of moving in with her. Not that it would be an option without getting married, of course. It wasn't something they ever explicitly talked about and occasionally she worried that she was kidding herself over the whole thing – but he wouldn't have welcomed her so fully into his life, would he, unless he was thinking about them getting married? He'd been quiet over brunch; he joined in with the conversation and made a few jokes here and there, but he seemed distant somehow, as though his mind were elsewhere.

'Do you mind if I go and check on Rofikul? He seemed a bit quiet before.'

'Did he?' Munira continued her rinsing. 'Can't say that I noticed, but yes of course, go along – I'll get Hashim to help with the rest of these.'

'Thanks, Munira.' Helen made her way into the living room where Rofikul was sitting on one side of the sofa reading, his feet propped up on the coffee table. 'You all right?' she asked, leaning on the arm of the sofa. Rofikul put his book down beside him.

'Why wouldn't I be?'

'I don't know. You just seem a bit . . . quiet?'

'I'm fine.' He gestured for her to move from the arm and

come and sit beside him. She did, nestling her body close to his, relishing this snatched moment of intimacy before they could be disturbed by anyone else. 'I was thinking about home today.'

'Home?' It struck Helen that she had never heard Rofikul talk about where he came from in those terms before. He referred to it, of course, but not the way Munira freely spoke about her village, or Hashim about his family. In fact, she thought with an inexplicable sense of discomfort, Rofikul never really talked about anything to do with his – well, home. Helen had no idea about his family, how many brothers or sisters he had, or what his parents were like. Her only anchor to Rofikul's past was Hashim. 'Tell me about home.'

'Tell you?' Rofikul gazed over the top of her head, his hand stroking her auburn hair gently. 'I can't possibly tell you. There aren't the words.'

'Since when have you not had the right words for anything?'

Rofikul pulled her closer, feeling the jutting of her shoulder in his chest and relishing the slight discomfort her body caused him, making him even more aware of her proximity. 'Words don't always say what you wish they could.' He sounded sad.

'Do you miss it?'

'I don't know. Yes, I suppose I must, but I don't think about it often.'

'Why not?'

'I wouldn't know where to begin. Or where I should stop.'

'Why would you need to stop?'

'A person can't live in two places at the same time, Helen. Your mind, your soul even, it would be divided. Just half in each place, and never a whole, your thoughts always split. Never really functioning. I can't live like that.'

'No.' She squeezed his arm, tracing the tip of her finger along his brown skin. 'You shouldn't have to.'

'I won't. It's different for Hashim and Munira, they have each—' He stopped.

'What? They have what?' Helen loosened her grip on his arm. 'Each other? Is that what you were going to say?'

'Helen, no—' He tried to pull her back towards him but she shrugged him off.

'And what, having me – it's not enough?' She clenched her hands together, the skin stretching tightly over her joints. 'I don't, what – I don't count?'

'That's not what I meant at all . . . please, let me just—' Rofikul reached out for her again but Helen's hands remained tightly clasped in her lap.

'I ask you about it. You never want to say much. It's not my fault.'

'I know.'

'How can I be there for you? Understand how things are for you, if you don't tell me?'

'Helen, that's not fair, I do tell you things.'

'Not proper things. You talk about the weather and the seasons and how it changes so much more there than here; you talk about the fruit and how much better everything tastes. You don't tell me anything that matters. About you, what you did there. Even who you were there. I don't know anything.'

'What do you want to know?'

'Just something. Something real.'

Rofikul stood up. His head felt light; he had risen too quickly. Helen was looking at him, hurt – disappointed with him. He didn't know what to give her, what he could possibly tell her about himself that would satisfy her. 'I can't do this now.' He turned around and thudded heavily up the stairs.

Helen heard the door of the bedroom being pulled shut and decided against following him. Instead she sat very still on the sofa, replaying what had just happened. Had she been so very wrong to ask? Wasn't it natural that she should wonder, especially when he was ordinarily so open to talking about anything else? She wasn't prying, she just wanted to understand – to know something about him, something that counted, maybe even something that he had never told anyone else but her. Maybe then he would feel as though they had each other at least, the way Hashim and Munira had one another. She felt the tears forming in her eyes and knew that she didn't have the energy to explain anything to Munira right now. She got up and let herself out of the front door quietly, pulling the latch shut behind her.

For the first time in years, Rofikul dreamed about *desh* that night. He was with Hashim on the steps of the family pond in their grandfather's *bari*. It was summer, and the waterlilies floated demurely on their green pads. The boys were wearing white vests and had their *lungis* tucked up between their legs, and the sun beat down on their naked shoulders turning them a darker shade of brown.

When Rofikul returned to the town at the end of the summer his other grandmother would tut and scold and reprimand her daughter-in-law for allowing her son to run around like a hooligan just because they had spent the holidays in the village. *This is what happens when girls go back home to see their parents – they lose all sense of responsibility*, she would mutter, knowing full well that to deny her daughter-in-law the annual right of return to spend some time with her parents would be flouting a code of extended familial relations that pre-dated them all.

Rofikul loved going to his maternal grandparents' home

77

for the summer. His father sometimes accompanied them, but mostly was unable to leave his position as clerk at the district courthouse. Secretly Rofikul preferred it when his father was not there; his mother seemed more relaxed, lighter somehow, and less inclined to berate him for any number of minor misdemeanours.

It was different there. It wasn't just that he was allowed to get away with infractions that he would not have been able to at home. Everyone just seemed kinder to him. They were unquestioningly proud of his achievements in school when he told them about his class marks, rather than asking him why he thought that coming second was good enough. Their pleasure was more easily won and more generously given. Rofikul envied his cousin, Hashim, for living in this easy, more relaxed, atmosphere all the time. Rofikul's mother and Hashim's father were brother and sister, so while Rofikul's mother had moved to the town after her marriage to her urbanite husband, Hashim's father had stayed in the familial home, working on the farm and raising his children in the same life that he had known.

'Bhaiya! Look over there!' Hashim pointed excitedly to something flickering in the trees on the opposite bank of the large stretch of water. Rofikul strained his eyes to see but they were not as attuned to the fleeting movements of wildlife as his cousin's.

'What was it?'

'A peacock. We've seen it a few times but usually it comes down here when it's cooler, towards the end of the day. Listen, you can hear it.' The boys fell silent as they listened carefully for the plaintive mawing of the peacock, and then what sounded like an echo.

'Is there more than one?' Rofikul asked.

Hashim shook his head. Rofikul may have excelled in

mathematics and science and history, but when it came to understanding the immediate environment around them, Hashim left his older cousin far behind.

'No, it's just the echo, but it always makes it sound like there's more than one.'

'Maybe it's looking for a friend. It must be lonely.'

'Perhaps.'

'What do you mean perhaps; wouldn't you be lonely if you were the only peacock around?'

'You tell me – you *are* the only peacock here – I'm just a lowly crow.' Hashim grinned at his cousin. He cawed mournfully and they both laughed.

'Come, let's see if we can find it.' Rofikul was emboldened, even though the boys had always been told not to go beyond the nearest bank of the lake. *Don't walk under those trees*, their grandmother would warn them. *You don't know what spirits might be lurking there beside the water.* When they were younger they used to beg her to tell them stories of the beings who were said to haunt those banks: *spirits are attracted to stagnant water, you know – so don't spend time there and never go there alone.* She would tell them stories of long-dead ancestors who were said to sit near the water calling to their descendants, offering them promise of treasure if they would just dive down to the bottom of the murky depths. *Always tell them you don't want their offerings*, she warned, as though it could happen to them one day. *Say thank you, but you don't want it.*

Hashim had heard these warnings even more often than Rofikul but the sun was strong and the shade promised by the trees seemed appealing in this heat. He shrugged in agreement and they set off around the muddy banks of the small lake, Hashim barefoot and Rofikul shod in the rubber sandals his father insisted that he wear at all times. Twigs cracked underfoot and the rustling in the leaves high up in the trees betrayed the presence of monkeys. 'What are you going to do when we find it?'

'Kill it.'

Hashim looked shocked. 'You know it's bad luck to kill a peacock.'

'Have you ever tasted roasted peacock?' Rofikul pretended to fan himself. 'It's a delicacy in the towns.'

'You're lying.'

'Maybe I am, maybe I'm not. Maybe I want to use the feathers to decorate my new costume. I am designing one to look like the robes that the ancient Chinese emperors used to wear. Nanu will make it for me.'

Hashim looked at his cousin dubiously. 'Well, if you want feathers, you can just pick them up from the ground – they fall out naturally, you know. There's no need to kill it.'

'Relax, Hashim. Of course I wouldn't kill a creature as beautiful as that. Or any creature – you know as well as I do that I wouldn't know how.'

Hashim tried to conceal his relief. 'Obviously I knew you weren't going to. Have you really never killed anything though? Not even a fish? You've been fishing with us before!'

'A fish doesn't count, you don't really *kill* it, you just – well, pull it out of the water and let it die.'

'What about a chicken? You must have helped Nana slaughter chickens before?'

Rofikul shook his head, looking slightly embarrassed for the first time that Hashim had ever seen. 'Ma never lets me; and back home Baba just buys the meat from a shop.'

'Oh.' Hashim sounded surprised. 'I've killed a chicken before,' he said with a hint of pride. 'I mean, I helped Baba with it.'

'So, what's the difference between killing a chicken and a peacock – why is one bad luck and not the other?'

'You know it's not the same thing—' Hashim stopped. 'Bhaiya . . .'

Rofikul almost bumped into him at the abrupt stop. 'What? Why did you stop like that?'

Hashim held up a hand to motion Rofikul to be quiet and then stepped forward carefully, trying not to make a sound. Rofikul followed, peering ahead to try to catch a glimpse of what his cousin had seen. There in front of them the peacock lay dead, its plumage carefully spread out like a fan around it. A dark pool of blood gathered at the bird's throat.

Rofikul drew a breath. 'Foxes?'

'Now? It's broad daylight.' Hashim seemed perturbed. 'And we would have heard it. The scuffle, the cries – I didn't hear a thing, did you?'

Rofikul went over to take a closer look, and almost immediately recoiled.

'What, what is it?' Hashim asked anxiously, panicked at the sight of his unflappable cousin so visibly terrified.

Rofikul shook his head, unable to speak. He pointed to the crown of blue and green feathers that surrounded the dead peacock. Each one was placed an equal distance apart from the next and tipped slightly anticlockwise, as though someone had carefully plucked each one and deliberately laid it out in this pattern. Whatever creature had done this was not of this earth.

Rofikul woke in his bed with a start. He sat up, sweat dripping from his forehead and his breath coming in shallow, rapid gasps. It had all felt so real, the terror of that memory. Had it really happened? He tried to remember . . . he and Hashim had spent so many summers together, often daring each other to venture past a certain part in the forbidden stretch of land near those murky waters. But he couldn't recall that incident with the peacock. It must have been a dream rather than a memory, he told himself, but that thought was hardly of any comfort. What did it say of him that he was able to conjure up a dream like that? His breathing had slowed down a little but each time he closed his eyes all he could see were those carefully spaced out peacock feathers, the eyes staring right up at him.

He thought about hearing Hashim's recitation earlier that day, and from somewhere in the deepest corners of his memory he uncovered the short prayer his grandmother taught him when he was very young, the one to recite after a bad dream or after seeing something unpleasant. He whispered it once, hesitantly, the words seeming uncomfortable on his tongue. His words formed more easily the second time. And the third. He continued whispering his grandmother's protection against evil until that image in his mind faded and was eventually replaced by the gentle fog of sleep.

9

It had taken Rofikul over a week to win back Helen's favour and the task had not been easy. Hashim and Munira had kept themselves mostly out of it; Hashim from his own personal preference to stay out of confrontation, and Munira because she had been given no other choice: Helen had not confided in her, despite Munira's enquiries, and she had been left feeling a little hurt by her exclusion. *You'd better fix your falling out with Helen quickly*, she had told Rofikul crossly. *She isn't talking to me either and I'm not going to lose my only friend here just because you happen to be an idiot.*

He had tried apologising, begging, pleading, turning up at Helen's bedsit with gifts only to be met with Marie at the door as savage and as loyal as a protecting watchdog. *She doesn't want to see you, Ray* – Marie had never grown out of the habit of referring to him by the name he had used when she had first been introduced to him – before snatching the presents out of Rofikul's arms and banging the door in his face. In the end Rofikul had taken to waiting outside the office where Helen worked as a secretary, trying to catch her on her way out. The first couple of times she had walked straight past him. When she had seen him waiting in the rain on the third day she relented. *What do you want?* she asked. *We need to talk*, he had said. *So talk.* He had taken her arm. *Not here. Let's go somewhere else.* And he took her to the café where they had first met. *Interesting choice*, Helen had thought wryly. *Get me sentimental with all the memories and then try to get in my good books.* It had worked, though, as they both knew it would, but not as easily as Rofikul had perhaps anticipated. *We need to talk properly*, Helen had said. *An apology doesn't work if you don't know or understand what you're apologising for.* Rofikul had seemed contrite. *I was wrong to say what I did, and I didn't mean it the way it came out; all I meant was they can understand each other's experiences because they've both done it.* Helen hadn't given in so quickly. *But that's not what you said. You said 'they have each other' as though you didn't have me.* There was nothing Rofikul could say to that. *I was wrong, I never meant it that way. I'm so sorry, please forgive me.* In the end, his relentless apologising worked, and Helen agreed to see him for dinner that night. They had gone back to the tiny bedsit afterwards, Marie conveniently having chosen that evening to visit her family.

In the weeks that followed, things started to seem all right again in the world. Not just all right – full of actual possibility. Rofikul was going into business. Starting the garage had been Vincent's idea but Rofikul hardly needed much encouragement to jump on board. Working in a factory was fine until it wasn't, and it hadn't been fine for rather a long time. Clocking in, clocking out, keeping to someone else's time, gaffer always on at you counting your breaks, how often you needed to take a piss. And for what? The same old repetitive work, day in, day out, that needed no imagination, not even a shred of common sense, let alone creativity. 'Common sense' was a dirty phrase on the production line, where a man was supposed to do his designated task, and that task alone, and not concern himself with what came before or after in the process. Rofikul had been dreaming of a way out from the first week he had started working there.

He'd known Vincent for years; they'd both arrived in Manchester within a few months of each other and had met when they were lodgers in the same boarding house. 'Boarding house' was a generous term to describe their living arrangements: it was more like a rundown collection of rooms in a decrepit old Edwardian townhouse owned by an ancient couple who he learned were from somewhere in Eastern Europe. Still, theirs was one of the few establishments that did not have placards in the window advising who was and was not welcome, and so Vincent from Jamaica and Rofikul from East Pakistan found each other thousands of miles away from home. There were no joint houses in those early days, no system of people co-habiting with family friends or strangers of the same nationality. It had fallen to Rofikul to set up the first joint house for Bengalis; as one of the pioneers in the city, he had been the contact everyone back home recommended to their migrating relatives to look up once they made it to England. Rofikul Ahmed in Manchester. He was a good sort, he'd look out for them. But even when more of his countrymen had turned up in the great grey city, Rofikul had stayed in touch with Vincent, his first friend in this cold and sometimes pleasant land.

It had startled some of the new lads arriving from the motherland to discover that Rofikul counted a black man among his good friends. *How can you have anything in common with him?* they would ask. *Why would you spend time with an African?* At first, he had tried to explain to them that in this world, this land of the English, they made barely any distinction between black and brown and Irish and dogs, so why should he? *It makes no difference,* he used to say, *whether you're a Bengali or a black man; to the white man you're still the enemy, you're still worthless, and you're still not one of them.* But as the years wore on, Rofikul stopped bothering trying to justify his friendship with Vincent; it was a feature of his life, and the others could take it or leave it. He had been pleased that Hashim had not openly expressed any hesitation regarding this friendship; in fact, he had taken to it reasonably well, thought Rofikul, knowing that Hashim was conservative in many ways. But perhaps that was unfair towards his cousin; having traditional views did not mean that one had no taste in friends, after all.

Hashim had expressed concern about Rofikul leaving the relative security of a factory job with steady wages to strike out in setting up the garage, however. *You've got to think beyond just yourself,* Hashim had warned when Rofikul had joyfully announced his business partnership with Vincent, perhaps slightly heightened by the tumblers of whisky that had sealed their union. *You have responsibilities to uphold.* This had surprised Rofikul, because the very reason he was taking this step was precisely so that he could meet those responsibilities better, both here in Manchester with Helen and back home. He would never afford a car just on a factory wage, let alone be able to move out of the joint house and find a flat where Helen could join him. *I know what my responsibilities are, brother,* he had responded lightly, but pointedly enough to make his meaning understood. *Do you?* was all Hashim had said. Rofikul did not welcome the insinuation that he was somehow shirking his duties. It made him uncomfortable, this sense of judgement from his cousin. It was complicated, his situation with Helen and his duties to his family back home. But why should the one mean that he couldn't uphold the other? And anyway, what did Hashim possibly understand of all this, with his wife over here with him, fully participating in this life they now shared, and who knew all of him – both from home and abroad. Not everybody had that luxury; Hashim would do well to recognise that. In contrast, Vincent never gave Rofikul a hard time; another mark in favour of going into business together.

The garage started out in one of three ramshackle outbuildings on the outskirts of a nearby industrial park. At first, they relied on word of mouth, recommendations from friends to friends-of-friends, but soon word spread far enough for them to be getting custom from people with whom they had no personal connection. To Rofikul, that was the real marker of success: when patrons didn't come to you just because of some distant familial bond, but because they had heard of the service independently and chose you on a purely commercial basis. They served primarily the immigrant populations of central Manchester: Pakistanis, Bengalis, West Indians, even the occasional Eastern European or Russian. These were the circles in which their clients operated, and Rofikul and Vincent had the added benefit of attracting twice the usual loyal customer base thanks to their respective backgrounds.

They opened the garage with a little summer party down at the industrial park, just a few friends and a borrowed sound system and some tins – a bottle of something with bubbles to pop would have been nice, but perhaps a bit too extravagant so early on – some food, and a few folding chairs. It had been one of the happiest evenings of Rofikul's life. He remembered driving Helen home that night. They were the last ones at the garage; Rofikul had locked up after the others had left, Hashim and Munira home to bed, while Vincent had taken the rest back to his place for an after-party, fully intent on continuing the celebrations into the morning. Helen had been wearing a dress the colour of corn and her green-grey eyes had never seemed as deep as they did as she leaned back in the passenger seat and looked up at him. Gazing back at her, he held up his hand to her face and she kissed his thumb as he traced it lightly over her lips. He switched off the ignition and pushed back the front seat, holding out his arms for Helen to come over to him. She pressed herself against him, her body weighing almost nothing as he lowered the seat back and drew her closer to him, his hands lost in the thick mass of auburn hair as the moon rose in the inky sky outside.

There were times when Hashim found it difficult to believe that this was his life. He had a job in a factory, a steady income, a wife, and a roof over his head. It sometimes felt as though his gratitude would spill over, bubbling up within himself, before pouring out, sweeping up strangers and passers-by in his waves of contentment. Hashim thanked God often, fulfilling his obligation to perform the five daily ritual prayers. His mother had taught him that the surest way to peace was to be thankful for the things he had, and not to pursue dreams of things that were beyond his means. *Be grateful for your lot, Baba,* his mother had told him. *It is what is written for you.*

Hashim continued to send money back home each month. The letters he received in acknowledgement filled him with warm satisfaction. His father had been able to purchase two new cows, and they had hired hands to help with the harvest that year. But Munira had seemed less than enthusiastic when Hashim had read the letter to her. *That's good,* was all she said. She barely looked up from the book she was reading. *What's the matter?* Hashim had asked. Munira had shrugged. Hashim had got up from his armchair and gone to sit beside her on the sofa. *Isn't that good news, Munira?* Munira had nodded. *Yes, it is.* Hashim gently placed his hand on her book. *What is it?* Munira had sighed and looked up at him, weary-eyed. *Look at us. Where are we living?* Then she had turned back to her book and continued reading. Hashim had got up and left the room.

It had never occurred to him that Munira was unhappy with their living arrangements. The shared house was pleasant enough, if a little damp, and he and Munira had the luxury of their own room, being the only married couple. The other housemates were considerate, and never brought guests home – and since Rofikul spent so much time at Helen's there was a little more room in the house. *That was it*, Hashim realised slowly. Helen and Rofikul, not even married yet, were able to enjoy a little more privacy. But he and Munira were still there in that house, with no prospect of moving.

Hashim had started making enquiries the very next day. He circled adverts in the newspaper and secretly went to view possible flats, but each place was more rundown than the last. He wanted more than just a shabby bedsit for Munira. His mother's words rang in the back of his mind; it was true that he was contented enough with his lot, but he wanted to be able to give Munira what she deserved.

He had been standing in the local corner shop, rifling through the *Evening News* for the housing adverts, when he overheard the girl behind the counter talking to her friend. *Dunno how long I'll even have a job here*, she said miserably. *Old chap's looking for a new manager. Can't run it himself any more.* Her friend, seemingly uninterested, continued to flick through the magazine she was reading. *Says he'll shut it down if he can't find anyone*, the girl continued, *he's in a right state about it.* Hashim had shoved the paper back on the stack and made his way to the counter. *Excuse me, miss*, he had asked tentatively. *Did you say Mr Langley was looking for a manager?*

*

Hashim and Munira moved in a few weeks later. Mr Langley had seemed unconcerned about Hashim's inexperience in running a shop. *It'll come to you*, he had said. *It's in your folks' blood*. Hashim was to receive two weeks of training before Mr Langley packed up the flat above the shop and moved in with his son who lived in Leeds. Hashim had wondered why the son didn't come back to take over the family business but refrained from asking. The girl behind the counter had kicked off when she heard that Hashim was taking over as manager. *I'm not working for a darkie*, she had huffed to Mr Langley. *You'll want to see yourself getting a new job then*, was Langley's response. He had no time for that sort of carry-on; you were either an honest person, or you weren't. Besides, the neighbourhood was changing anyway – the shop might even get more custom with one of that lot as manager.

Munira was delighted with the flat. Two double bedrooms and a boxroom, with a living room, separate kitchen and an indoor bathroom. And the chance to work – she couldn't wait to start serving customers and strike up conversations with the regulars. *Are you sure this is what you want?* she asked Hashim as they stood in the new flat surrounded by all their belongings packed up in cardboard boxes. Hashim smiled. Factory work was work. This was a chance at a life of his own. He thought about what his mother would say, whether she would tell him to be satisfied with his lot. But this was it, he decided.

Some things about his new life – for he still considered it to be new even though he had already been in this country for several years – confused and, at times, intimidated Hashim. Since Munira had arrived, he had relaxed into the ways things were in England. He was relieved that Munira had adapted so well to this unorthodox way of living – more so than he had, in many ways – and it reassured him that she had adjusted well enough to be able to deal with some of the pressures their life invariably involved. Nevertheless, he fretted sometimes that the way they lived had drifted a little too far from the norms befitting a respectable wife. He was supposed to shield her from the indelicacies of the foreign land they were living in – and yet, somehow, he had brought her right into the heart of them. His wife's best friend was a white woman in a relationship with a man, albeit his own cousin, who she was not married to. His cousin's transgressions were hardly limited to that: Hashim was well aware that Rofikul, like some of the others, indulged in a drink from time to time, frequented snooker halls, and played cards for money. *Gambling, drinking, womanising.* Hashim knew the words and that the words described some of the worst kinds of sins, but somehow when Rofikul was the one committing them, they were hard to condemn as fervently as he knew he ought.

It was that time in the evening when the daylight had fully slipped into dusk. Hashim and Munira were reading together on the sofa in the dimly lit living room of the flat above the shop. Hashim loved these moments, which never came around as often as he wished they would. He wanted to sink into it completely, to cocoon himself in the warmth of Munira's body beside him and let the world outside continue to turn without them both. He found it unfathomable that anyone could possibly feel the strength of what he felt for Munira for anyone else. But he hoped that what Rofikul felt for Helen came close. She deserved that much.

'Do you think,' he began hesitantly before pausing, scrabbling around for the right words. 'Do you think it's possible to love someone very much and still do things that, well – aren't doing the right thing?'

Munira looked up from her paper in surprise. 'What are you talking about? Is this about leaving the milk out? I told you, it doesn't matter, darling, just next time put it in the—'

'It's not about the milk,' Hashim interrupted. 'It's not about, well, us.'

'Well, thank goodness for that.' Munira looked at her husband quizzically. 'You still look as though something's eating you from the inside though.'

'It's Rofikul.'

'Oh, is this about the garage?'

'It's not about the garage.' Hashim got up from the sofa and paced over to the fireplace agitatedly.

'Darling.' Munira put down her paper, concerned, and went over to where Hashim was standing. She took both his hands in hers and led him back to the sofa. 'What is it? You're starting to alarm me now.'

Hashim took a deep breath and lowered himself back into his seat. 'Do you think Helen wants to marry Rofikul?'

Munira looked startled. 'Well, I'd imagine so, don't you? I don't see why else they'd be spending so much time together if that wasn't something they wanted to do.'

'That's what I'm afraid of . . .' Hashim trailed off. 'Helen is a lovely girl, we all know that, and has been such a kind and generous friend to us . . . I just wonder whether Rofikul could do the right thing by her.'

Munira smiled. 'Are you wondering why your cousin is taking so long to ask her? I agree, he should get his act together soon. But I imagine he wants to get stable first.' She kissed Hashim's palm lightly before placing it gently back down on the arm of the sofa. 'It says so much about you, in the best of ways, that this concerns you. But they'll be fine, darling, in their own time.'

Hashim nodded gently at his wife and rested his hand on

her cheek. He wanted to share her optimism and good faith, but his concern continued to lurk at the back of his mind. He tried to suppress the uncomfortable truths he wished he wasn't privy to and returned to his book as the sun sank completely in the sky.

10

IT RAINED. SHE had not been to many, but it seemed to Helen as though it rained at every funeral she had ever attended. It made no difference whether it was summer or winter, or whether the deceased was saint or sinner: the heavens dutifully parted and rained tears down on the black-clad mourners. It was quite unnecessary really, given that the mourners would usually be sad enough without having the added trauma of raindrops trickling under collars and muddied wet feet. The priest recited sombrely in his funeral voice: *Earth to earth. Ashes to ashes. Dust to dust.* Mud to mud, thought Helen. She rested a little more of her bodyweight on the low, thin heels of her patent leather shoes, enjoying the slow feeling of sinking into the mud.

She had been in two minds about whether to ask Rofikul to come with her; she wasn't sure that her father's funeral was the right time to present her – what was he? Boyfriend? The word sounded so frivolous for their bond. But she couldn't call him her fiancé, not quite yet, given that he hadn't officially proposed and that when they'd all ask to see her ring, she'd have nothing to show. But there was a connection between the two of them that she alone in the whole world knew. She stroked her stomach gently and suppressed a smile. In the end the situation had righted itself: Rofikul had gripped her hands in his. *I'm so sorry, darling, but I don't think I'll be able to come with you – things are frantic at the garage and I just can't take time off. Do you mind terribly?* She had been at once relieved and a little hurt. True, he had spared her the awkwardness of trying to decide how she would present their relationship to her family. But rather than taking the step and accompanying Helen to support her as well as publicly affirm their partnership, he had simply made an excuse. Marie's reaction had put her out even further. *What do you mean he isn't coming with you to your father's funeral? What could possibly be more important?*

And Munira had looked genuinely shocked when Helen told her that she would be getting the train alone and had even offered to come with her. Helen had thanked her for the gesture but there was no need – in fact this was something she'd rather do alone. Munira was sceptical, disapproving even – in her culture women did not attend funerals at all, mourning instead from the confines and protection of their home – but if Helen must go, she shouldn't go alone. Helen brushed it off with a smile. *We do things differently here*, Helen said. *It's fine.* Munira seemed to accept the explanation – there was still plenty she didn't understand about the way the English did things – but she did badger Helen about all the aspects of the journey: which train she was taking, who would greet her at the station at the other end, would she be staying over? In the end Helen had had to write a full itinerary for Munira to be satisfied, including a contact name and address and details of her return journey. Finally mollified, Munira relented, but not before walking Helen to the bus stop herself to make sure she got the right number to the train station. Helen politely refrained from pointing out that she had travelled alone plenty of times. But it had never been for an occasion like this: the day she would have to bury her father.

On Helen's left stood her mother, sniffling and pink-nosed, the lower half of her face obscured by a white handkerchief into which she coughed pathetically between sobs. Helen was glad that Aileen flanked their mother on the other side, offering a solid arm for Mam to cling to. Their younger sisters clustered around their mother, unsure what level of sorrow they were expected to demonstrate, so opted for lowered eyes and bowed heads. Like Helen's, Aileen's eyes were dry, and they caught each other's gaze over the top of their mother's bowed head and exchanged something akin to a smile without moving their lips. The priest was saying something about committing the body to the ground, and then came the part about throwing earth on to the shiny lid of the coffin. A terrible waste really, thought Helen, to spend all that money on a box just to put it into the ground. And then her mother was scattering a handful of earth on the lid. It spattered across the mahogany and Helen wondered how many handfuls it would take to bury her father. It was her turn. Her hands closed around the damp, black earth and she cast it into the grave. *Dirt to dirt.*

The letter had lain askew on the doormat, obscuring the L in WELCOME, until Helen picked it up when she got home on a Thursday afternoon two weeks ago. The address on the letter was printed neatly in a rounded, girlish hand that seemed somehow familiar, and the postmark in the upper right-hand corner showed that the letter had been mailed from Liverpool, confirming her suspicions. Still standing in her coat, Helen had slipped her index finger under the loose flap of envelope and pulled it neatly along the edge to open it.

Dear Helen,

I hope you are keeping well. I'm sorry to write after so long with this news, but I don't have your telephone number, so I couldn't ring you. It's easier to write it down though, I suppose, than say it over the phone where I can't even see your face.

Pa collapsed at the dockyard yesterday. They called an ambulance, but by the time they got him to a hospital his heart had already stopped. (Frankly, I was just amazed that it actually worked in the first place.)

Mam is doing surprisingly well, actually. I expect she's probably relieved. (Don't even look at me that way, Helen – you know as well as I do it's the truth . . .) She said to tell you the funeral is on the 19th of this month and you can come if you wish but needn't worry if it's too much trouble. Who knows whether she actually means it or not, but I am passing on the message just the same.

In any case, it would be good to see you. Let me know if you'll be coming and I'll arrange to meet you at the station.

With love,

Aileen x

Helen had folded the letter up, slipped it back into the envelope, and leaned against the arm of the sofa. So her father was dead, and although everyone's collective lack of sorrow was obvious enough without it needing to be stated, that was Aileen's way. Certainly, no one could accuse her of those human foibles of sentiment or delicacy. If Aileen could miss the funeral, she probably would. But then again, if there was one thing Aileen understood, it was duty, and someone needed to stand beside Mam while she performed her final duties as downtrodden wife. Since Helen's departure, that role had fallen to Aileen who had borne it ungrudgingly, perhaps even enjoyed the sense of purpose it gave her. Well, she was welcome to it. However much Helen tried to have sympathy for her mother, she could not help the surging resentment she felt when she recalled all the instances her father had bullied and sworn and kicked and slapped and broken and roared at his daughters, and her mother had offered no resistance, simply waited for it to pass. True, she was no match for his brutish strength, true that once he had gone on the rampage there was very little anyone could do; true, too, that these rampages did always eventually pass. But it was unforgivable to Helen that her mother never even thought to tell her daughters that this was not an acceptable way to live, let alone try to defend them.

As the raindrops ran off the modest brim of her hat, it occurred to Helen that the reason she had not been back all these years was not the fear of her father spitting venom – that she could bear – but of having to be around Dáirine. As violent as their father was, Helen had a lingering suspicion that her mother was more interested in maintaining the status quo in the family for her own benefit, than disrupting it for the wellbeing of her daughters. She and Aileen knew that their mother was not above using her victimhood to elicit the sympathetic shaking of heads and muttered accolades of sainthood from neighbours. For Dáirine her domestic plight gave her some kind of status and a steady supply of attention.

The wake was a welcome relief from the rain and the pretence of grief. Surprisingly to Helen, it was also fairly well attended: aside from extended family members, there were also her father's workmates, neighbours and a few other people she did not recognise. But then again, this was Crosbie Street, and everyone knew that a good Irish wake meant free food and drink. The bar of the pub was laden with platters of triangular white bread sandwiches, sausage rolls, quartered glazed pork pies, potatoes baked in their jackets, slices of cake and tall jugs of sweet lemonade. A drab-looking barmaid pulled pints for a steady stream of thirsty mourners. All in all, the whole thing seemed almost like a party, with people standing around clutching foamy glasses and discussing the slowness of business. Even more surprisingly, Helen's mother seemed to be enjoying her centre-stage role of grieving wife. She accepted pressed hands and well-wishes, kisses on the cheek and declarations of sympathy, with a willingness that was almost desperate.

'She doesn't seem to be suffering too much, does she?' Aileen muttered to Helen. 'Mind you, what's there to miss really? Nice firm backhand from the love of her life? Besides, it's probably the most attention she's had in years.' Aileen sat down at a booth in the corner as far away from their mother as possible and buried her head in her hands. Helen sat down opposite her.

'Aileen?'

'Mmm?'

'Are you all right?'

Aileen lifted her head up and smiled wryly at Helen. 'I'm not crying under here if that's what you're wondering. I'm just . . .' She paused, as though the words she wanted to say were somehow too big. 'I'm so tired, Helen. You don't know what it's like . . .'

Helen shook her head guiltily. 'I'm sorry. You're right, I don't. I can guess though. Is she being very difficult?'

Aileen sighed. 'Like never before. You can't even imagine it. It seems I'm more useless than ever since Pa died, and she has suffered more than anyone has ever suffered before, and none of us can do anything right. Nothing makes her happy.'

Helen was startled at the bitterness in her sister's voice. Aileen had always been the mischievous one, the one who would devise games and pranks for the sisters to play on unsuspecting neighbours, even when it meant getting a flogging later on as punishment. To hear this defeated talk from her made Helen feel guilty for leaving the burden of her parents squarely on the shoulders of her favourite sister.

'Anyway, enough about the misery down here – I know that inside out. Tell me what's been going on with you over in Manchester?'

'Well,' Helen began, grateful for the turn in conversation. 'I'm still living with Marie – you must come and see our place sometime; it's small, but cosy, and we'd always make room for you. And let's see what else – I'm still secretary at the firm I was at before. Pay has gone up recently which is a help.' She paused. There wasn't much more she could add if she had to leave out everything else, everything about Rofikul and her friendship with Munira and Hashim by association.

'What? You're thinking something but not saying it. I can tell.' Aileen peered at her sister, carefully reading her face.

'Well, I – I'm seeing someone.' Helen blushed and fiddled with her coat buttons.

'Oh *really*? And you've kept it secret this whole time?' Aileen seemed to have perked up at this news.

Helen was glad if it meant they had something to talk about besides their parents. 'Well, not a secret – the occasion hasn't really come up to tell you until now.'

Aileen seemed to accept this grudgingly. 'Well, a letter wouldn't have hurt. Hang on – why isn't he here?'

'What was I going to do, say, "Hey, you haven't met my family yet, want to come to my estranged father's funeral?"'

'Well, it'd be better than having to come alone. And face a barrage of questions about what you're doing with your life. You could just point at your bloke and say "him".'

'Not sure if him being here would stop the questions or make it worse, to be honest.' Helen hesitated, wondering whether to confide in her sister. And how much to tell her.

'Why, what's wrong with him?' Aileen was always one to cut to the chase. 'He's not Protestant, is he?'

Helen shook her head. 'He's . . . he's foreign.'

'What, like a Frenchman? He speaks French to you, does he, all zissss and zaaaat?' Aileen flung her hands around theatrically.

'No, not French – he isn't white.' Helen stared ahead defiantly.

Aileen seemed amazed. 'He's never a darkie?'

'He's Indian. Well, actually he's from East Pakistan.'

'*Indian?*' Aileen's pale blue eyes couldn't get any wider. 'Does he wear a turban? Does he speak English even? Helen, how are you shacked up with an *Indian* fella?'

'Don't talk like that, Aileen,' Helen snapped.

'Sorry,' Aileen caught herself. 'I didn't mean it like that, I just . . . how did you even meet? Is it serious?'

Helen was tired. Tired of always having to defend her relationship, to convince people it wasn't just a frivolous encounter, that it meant something. She was tired of always having to be on her guard, to be second-guessing everything anyone said. It made her not trust her own relationship sometimes, made her believe that it was as fragile as everyone implied it was.

'Yes, it's serious.'

Aileen studied her sister's face. 'How serious?'

'We're expecting a baby.'

Aileen looked stunned. Helen felt a rush of relief and horror; she hadn't meant for it to come out this way. She hadn't even told Rofikul yet. But it had just happened, and for the first time ever Helen's little sister was lost for words.

'You are getting married, aren't you?'

'Well, of course we are,' Helen replied haughtily. 'It'll be soon. It's all very recent.'

Aileen let out a deep sigh. 'Helen – I . . . I'm happy for you. I really am. I just hope you know what you're doing. And that this chap, what's his name?'

Helen hesitated. 'Ray.'

'Right, Ray – that he – that he's good enough for you.' She took Helen's arm across the table. 'I just care, you know that.'

'Yes. And he is.' Helen tried to smile. 'He really is.'

The rest of the afternoon passed in a haze of pressing hands with increasingly inebriated mourners and Helen having to explain which of the sisters she was. It soon became apparent that *the one that went away* was the most straightforward form of identification. She spent time catching up with her younger sisters, too – all of them in some kind of education or gainful employment, she was pleased to hear, but they seemed awkward and shy in her presence and she didn't much enjoy feeling like an outsider. They had never really known her properly; Caitlyn, the youngest, must have been about ten years old at the time Helen left home. For the most part Helen tried to avoid getting embroiled in any conversation with her mother, and instead stuck to listening to distant relatives regale her with their aches and pains, and the trans-gressions of other family members. It suited her, needing only to express sympathy and understanding murmurs.

Such a tactic would only last so long, Helen knew. Sure enough, it wasn't far into a great-aunt's recounting of a slipped disc that Dáirine looked over at Helen and plain-tively held out her hand, gesturing for her to come over to her and join in the basking of condolences. Helen excused herself from the aunt, almost gratefully, and made her way across the room to where her mother and Aileen were standing in a horseshoe of guests. Dáirine's face was slightly flushed, the glass in her hand now containing only ruby-stained dregs, as she held forth on her now exhaustive experience of widowhood.

'It's the being alone that's the hardest.' Dáirine looked around plaintively at the semicircle of well-wishers who all peered back with softened eyes exuding the requisite sympathy. 'The nights—' Here she broke off and cast her eyes down as though the memory of matrimonial tenderness that had been untimely wrenched from her was too much to bear. Her self-conscious pause irritated Helen.

'Alone? Mam, I'd hardly say you were that.'

Dáirine looked up and surveyed Helen, her mouth settling into a slightly upturned line. 'Would you not, Helen?' she asked archly. 'You've always had your opinions, I'm sure.'

'There's Aileen, there's Cait, there're all the others . . . I mean, you've not been left to fend for yourself, they're always around. Aileen takes care of you . . .' Helen knew she was doing a poor job of keeping the impatience out of her voice, but she could not help it.

'Oh yes. She does – Aileen does. The girls do, yes.' Dáirine's voice carried the hard edge of her dead husband.

They do say couples become alike, thought Helen.

'But there's something different – about having a husband, the father of your children, being there, supporting the family. But I suppose you wouldn't understand.'

'Well, of *course* I don't understand – how would I understand? It was hardly as though Dad was there for us in any way that was good for us . . .'

'It's all very well to have ideas, isn't it? About what married life ought to be . . .' Dáirine took a step towards Helen, who could feel the horseshoe of bystanders fading at the edges around them as her mother drew closer.

'Mam,' Aileen tried to interject, but was swatted away by her mother's black lace-clad arm, fortified with grief and attention and drink.

'The thing is, Helen, my darling. How would you know?' Dáirine's eyes were glassy and her sweet-smelling breath felt hot on Helen's skin. 'You can't even get the fella who got you into trouble to marry you.'

So Dáirine knew. Helen sought out her sister's eyes anxiously, but Aileen's blanched face betrayed her. Around them bystanders shuffled with the pretence of embarrassment, but nobody looked away – the promise of a to-do was far too attractive.

'We . . . we are engaged. I'll be sure to send you a card with the date.' Helen tried to keep her voice steady, but she heard it giving and inwardly cursed herself.

Dáirine smiled sweetly. 'Yes, yes . . . please do, I should so love to come. Perhaps by then he will have seen fit at least to put an engagement ring on you?' All eyes swung to Helen's bare ring-finger, pale and vulnerable. 'And tell me – why isn't he here with you? Standing by your side at a time like this?'

Helen could feel her face growing hot but she steeled herself. 'He had to work. He sent his condolences, he—'

Dáirine spat out a shrill laugh. 'Oh, his *condolences*! Well, if they're as hard to come by as his engagement rings, I suppose we should all be so grateful!' She laughed again. 'Condolences! Let me give you a piece of motherly advice, my girl.' Helen's heart shrank. Her mother wasn't one who was above twisting the proverbial knife. 'Don't expect him to do the right thing. His sort never do.'

'And I suppose Pa did the right thing, did he? Beating

you up, turning up drunk every night?' To hell with not speaking ill of the dead, thought Helen. Her mother's eyes flashed with a kind of liveliness Helen hadn't seen before. She was enjoying this, Helen realised. This public humiliation of her own daughter. She'd always loved it.

'He knew his responsibilities,' Dáirine retorted. 'He stood by us. He wasn't perfect, but he was there for us. He never left.'

Low bar, thought Helen. 'More's the pity.' She turned and left the gathered crowd, feeling the heat of their eyes boring into her back.

'Send us an invite, won't you?' her mother called after her, before descending into another peal of laughter.

Helen gathered her coat from the corner booth where she had left it and made her way out of the rear entrance of the pub, stepping into the cool late afternoon air. Her sobs crept up into her throat until she could no longer hold them in. She wept noisily, hurt at how her family had managed to ruin something so beautiful before she had even had a chance to enjoy it. It felt sullied now, denied the initial rush of excitement and congratulation that every new promise of a life deserved to be met with.

'Helen.' Aileen, pale and red-eyed, had come out of the entrance behind her and stood nervously a few paces away. Her voice trembled. 'I'm sorry, I—'

'I don't want to hear it.' Helen started walking.

'I never meant—'

'I don't care, Aileen.' Helen stopped and turned to look over her shoulder at her sister. Aileen had been the lively one when they were younger, the adventurous one, the one who said whatever she liked, whenever she wanted, and to hell with the consequences. Now she looked tired, older than her age – and somehow as though everything around her disappointed her. She looked like Dáirine. 'I just can't believe you couldn't even wait a day to tell her. To let *me* tell her.' She shook her head. 'Did it make her happy? Did it make her like you more, or something? Did you feel better?'

'No, I – it wasn't like that. It's been hard . . .' Tears spilled down Aileen's face. 'I do everything, and she doesn't care and all she can say is—'

'Hard? You want to know what's hard, Aileen?' Helen wanted to scream. *Having to leave home in the dead of night because your arm's been broken by your own father. Being cut off from the rest of your family just because you dared to want something better. Never fitting in anywhere, not with your blood kin, not even with the man you love. Not even knowing if the man you love will love you enough back. That's what's hard.* But Aileen wouldn't understand, and she didn't want to miss the next train.

'Never mind, Aileen. I hope she loves you more now if that's what you wanted.' Helen took an envelope out of her bag and thrust it into Aileen's hands. 'That was to help with the costs for today. See to it that she gets it.' She turned away, ignoring Aileen's pleas, and set off down the road towards the station.

11

ROFIKUL HAD BEEN ecstatic when Helen told him she was pregnant. *You're sure? You're definitely sure?* Helen nodded. *I wouldn't have told you if I wasn't sure.* He had kissed her hard. *Do you think it's a boy?* he asked her. *What does it matter?* Helen laughed. Rofikul had smiled, delirious in his happiness. *It doesn't matter, really. Even if it's a girl. It's wonderful.*

And he was still happy, of course he was. But the constant nagging from everyone reminding him of his responsibilities was getting tiresome. It had been the first thing Munira had said to him when she had seen him after Helen told her the news. *You'd better get a move on and marry her, hadn't you?* No word of congratulation or good wishes. She could have been a little less barbed; he sometimes wondered how Hashim could stand it, but Munira never talked to Hashim that way. She seemed to reserve it all for Rofikul.

Hashim was even worse than he had been before the news, constantly badgering him about the garage and its profitability and asking about the long hours he was working. It was like some kind of role reversal, Rofikul thought wryly. The only person who treated him just the same as before was Vincent. 'That's great news, man!' Vincent had clapped him on the back cheerfully. 'Congratulations, my friend.' And that had been it: no lectures about responsibility, or how he needed to start looking for their own flat now, or questions about a date for a wedding. Unsurprisingly, Rofikul was starting to prefer spending most of his time at the garage. There was enough work to be getting on with, although he and Vincent also spent plenty of evenings playing cards and drinking whisky rather than balancing books or fixing engines.

But Rofikul was facing his new responsibilities squarely. He found a little flat not too far from the shared house and Helen had moved in soon after he had signed the lease, all her worldly things packed up in a brown leather trunk and a few boxes. It was wonderful coming home to her every night, seeing her presence in the space they now shared – her gown hung on the back of the bedroom door, her lotions and potions on the bathroom sink, her shoes lined up neatly in the hallway. Even when she wasn't home her presence was everywhere and he enjoyed the novelty of it all: it was like playing house. Everything was shifting into place and as long as everyone just left him to get on with it, it would all be fine.

Munira had insisted on accompanying Helen to her medical appointments when it became clear that Rofikul was unable to take time off from the garage. Helen was grateful for the company during the long stretches in the waiting room. At her first appointment, the doctor had made a point of staring significantly at her hand and then writing Miss Doherty at the top of his notes. Helen's face had remained impassive and she had answered his questions perfunctorily, but the air of judgement sank heavily around her. She cried to Munira later that afternoon once they were back at the house drinking tea. *I just hate that everyone is looking down on me.* Munira had stroked her arm, lips pursed. That evening Munira had rowed with Rofikul, without Helen's knowledge. *What's taking so long? Just make an appointment at the registry office, you've had weeks.* Hashim had stood awkwardly between them as though his presence would defuse the tension in the room. The next day, at dinner time, Rofikul slammed a piece of paper on the table in front of Munira. It was a date for an appointment for the application of a marriage licence. Her reply had been curt. *Good.* She was fed up with Rofikul and, by extension, Hashim too. *Why can't you talk to him about it?* she asked her husband as they were getting ready for bed. *He listens to you.* She had always known her husband had a deep aversion to confrontation, but his defence of his cousin – or rather, his refusal to condemn him – grated on her.

Hashim knew that his wife's irritation on the matter extended to him. He did what he could with Rofikul, dropping hints reminding him of his financial and practical responsibilities. But that was as far as he could wield any influence; he could not bring himself to add his voice to the calls for a swift marriage between Helen and Rofikul. He knew it needed to be done, for Helen's sake more than anything, and he understood why. But there were complicating factors that Helen and Munira were not privy to. Rofikul and he had never spoken of them openly, their aversion proof enough of their tacit understanding.

As for Helen, the reality that she was growing a life deep within her was becoming ever more apparent. Not just in the sickness that had riddled her body for the first few weeks, or the changing roundness of her shape, but in the changing sense of solidity she now felt. As though there were something that anchored her to this existence. Everything was now of more consequence than before. Since her father's funeral, and her first public acknowledgement of the pregnancy, she had felt guilty that this child she was growing within her was taking shape, losings its gills and growing fingers and toes, while all those around them were frantically discussing its 'legitimacy'. What a phrase to use, to deem an innocent child legitimate or illegitimate, as though a living being's mere existence could be wrong.

Helen had stubbornly refused all contact from Aileen. Letters sent to her old address, where Marie still lived, were thrown away immediately. Marie and Munira salvaged the letters when they saw them, carefully storing them away for a time when Helen might want to renew contact with her sister again. *She needs her family at a time like this*, Munira remarked to Marie more than once. On some level Marie agreed, but it wasn't as straightforward as Munira made it sound. Marie understood the situation that Helen had purposefully left behind, more so than Munira – an indulged, beloved only daughter – would ever be able to grasp. *We are her family*, Marie would reply. And to that, Munira couldn't help but agree.

Rofikul and Helen's application for a marriage licence took place on a Tuesday afternoon at the Registry Office. They had dressed as though it were an interview: a white shirt with dark blue tie and a suit jacket for Rofikul; a smart tan dress buttoned to the neck for Helen.

'You look very sensible,' remarked Rofikul to Helen with a smile, as they sat waiting on the grey plastic chairs in the foyer.

'I have to,' Helen replied. 'I'm a mother in training.' She offered Rofikul a mint.

'One who got into trouble before wedlock.' Rofikul frowned solemnly as he unwrapped the sweet. 'They'll never let you get married now.'

'Give over, you.' Helen swatted him with her handbag and they laughed.

A small bespectacled woman shuffled out of one of the rooms adjacent to the waiting area and called out thinly, 'Miss Doherty . . . and Mr . . .' She pushed her glasses up over her head and squinted at the paper. 'Ahmed.' She looked up and blinked as Helen and Rofikul stood up. 'Right you are, this way,' she said, ushering them into the interview room. She motioned for them to seat themselves at the large wooden desk and took her place on the other side. 'What can I do for you today? Birth, marriage or death? I would hazard a guess, but one can never be too sure.' She chuckled to herself, particularly pleased at this.

Rofikul wondered how many times a day she used the very same joke.

'We'd like to apply for a marriage licence please,' Helen said politely. 'We've brought our documents here with us like the letter said.' She took out a folder of carefully prepared papers, including her birth certificate and Rofikul's passport and immigration documents.

The woman took them from Helen and squinted at them carefully. 'We'll need to take copies of these,' she said. 'It shouldn't take too long.' She stood up and handed Rofikul and Helen each a form to complete. 'I just need you to fill these in and sign them, and then write a cheque for the licence fee.' She left the room, her arms laden with the documents for copying.

Helen glanced over at Rofikul. 'Here goes nothing!'

'Want to change your mind? It's not too late, I reckon she moves pretty slowly.'

'Not on your life, Mr Ahmed.'

The forms requested their fathers' names but not those of their mothers, Helen noticed. Not that she particularly would have enjoyed giving either. For her current address she wrote down the bedsit she and Rofikul now lived in. She glanced over at Rofikul's form, where he had written the same in his neat black print. 'Think they'll frown at that?' she asked Rofikul.

He grinned back. 'If they do, they've got a bigger shock to come . . .' He scanned through the options for the next section. Marital Status: *Never married. Divorced. Widowed.* His pen hovered above the boxes before inking a strong black X into the first box. He glanced over at Helen, who was signing and dating the bottom of the form. She saw him looking at her and smiled.

'Done.'

Rofikul signed and dated the piece of paper in front of him and smiled back. 'Done.'

Helen squeezed his hand under the table.

The registrar re-entered the room with copies of the documents and the originals which she returned to Helen and Rofikul. She looked over the completed forms and branded each one with a heavy black stamp, and then began filling in an official-looking piece of paper. She slipped it into an envelope and handed it to Rofikul.

'This is your licence,' she said slowly. 'It is valid for up to one year and you must hold your wedding ceremony in this jurisdiction. Do you have any questions?'

Helen and Rofikul shook their heads, beaming with excitement.

The registrar smiled back at them. 'Congratulations, Miss Doherty and Mr Ahmed. I look forward to hearing from you about confirming a date for your ceremony. You can book—'

Rofikul interjected, 'What's the earliest appointment you have available?'

Helen looked surprised but eager to hear the answer.

The registrar pulled out a heavy leather calendar and flipped the pages to the first blank page. 'The weekends are taken up much earlier in advance, I'm afraid. The soonest we can do is a Wednesday at three o'clock, six weeks from now.'

Rofikul looked at Helen for confirmation. *What do you think?*

She squeezed his arm tightly before turning back to the registrar. 'We'll take it,' she said steadily.

12

ROFIKUL AND HELEN were married on a Wednesday
afternoon in December just as the sky started to turn
the colour of slate. They were joined at the Registry Office
by Hashim and Munira as witnesses and Marie and Vincent
as guests. *You have to have a veil*, insisted Marie when Helen
maintained she only wanted a simple do. *You're only going to
do it once, you might as well.* In the end they had settled on
a short face veil, like the one Helen remembered seeing her
grandmother wear in her grandparents' wedding photograph.
It was one of the only photographs they had displayed in
the house growing up; one of the few that had been spared
destruction by her father. Whatever lack of tenderness he
had for his daughters and wife, was fully reversed when it
came to the memory of his beloved mother.

Rofikul wore a powder-blue suit and a navy tie. Hashim
had fervently shined his shoes for him the day before and
Munira had picked white chrysanthemums for both Rofikul
and Hashim to wear in their buttonholes. Helen and
Rofikul exchanged wedding bands; the only time Rofikul
would wear his. *Men shouldn't wear jewellery, Helen*, he
insisted. There were no readings – Helen couldn't think
of one she especially wanted, and Rofikul thought it absurd
to inflict readings on four guests. After the ceremony Vincent
made them all pose on the steps of the Registry Office

and he took as many photographs as he could against the fading daylight. Then they jumped into Vincent's car and drove to the little Italian restaurant in town where Marie knew the owner and had cajoled her way into getting a private room for the six of them. They stayed late into the evening, eating and drinking and smoking, and as Helen whispered to Rofikul that night when he carried her up the stairs to their flat, it was the most perfect wedding she could have imagined. Rofikul kissed her in reply. He was so fortunate that Helen seemed to be satisfied with what he was able to offer her. It was not enough, he knew that, and yet she never seemed to blame him. He wanted to be able to give her so much more; to offer his whole self in the way that he knew she craved. But it was not something he knew how to do; he had never really been able to place anyone above his own needs until now; he knew his failings, both now and in his previous life. He had no excuses for either; and it felt far beyond his control to change any of what had come before. That night as he lay awake hearing the gentle breathing of his new wife beside him, he resolved he would do everything within his power to make the best life possible for both Helen and their unborn child.

The bride was swathed in red, her bowed head covered with a heavily ornate scarf embroidered with gold threads. It was impossible to catch a glimpse of her face, but her hands and feet were dyed with patterns of *mendhi*. Gold bangles adorned her wrists and arms, and a delicate chain draped around her ankle. All around them, rhythmic clapping accompanied the traditional wedding songs being sung by their female relatives. The songs were of hope and love, of apprehension and sorrow. *How will the Princess leave her family?* they wailed mournfully. *What will the King and Queen do with this empty space in their hearts?*

She looked so small under the folds of sumptuous cloth, younger even than her fourteen years. Everyone said she was fair-skinned; not that he had had a chance to see her face yet. Wide-set eyes, his mother said. A perfectly formed mouth, confirmed his sisters. But it meant nothing to him – the descriptions, the promises – until he was able to see her for all that she was, his wife, a stranger. He could feel the heat from her body close beside him even though they were not touching. He stared resolutely ahead as he was obliged to; the first glimpse of his wife was to be done in private, with perhaps an aunt or sister-in-law there to witness the momentous occasion. Somebody pressed a sweetmeat into his hand and gestured for him to feed his bride. He tried to oblige but she kept her veiled face turned away in modesty. An aunt raised the veil slightly, telling her to open her mouth to receive the offering. Dutifully, eyes still lowered, the girl parted her lips, and his hand, directed by another aunt's firm grasp, placed the sweet into her mouth. Next it was her turn; her wrist was forcefully pushed towards her husband's mouth by an aunt. Her delicate patterned fingers placed the food into his mouth.

The singing started to die down and gave way to lamentations and sobs from the assembled women. Firm hands under his arms hauled him to his feet; beside him others were pulling his wife to stand. It was the time of the ceremony for the bride to be taken from her familial home and accompany her new husband to the unknown next chapter of her short life. His heart sank as she clung to her relatives weeping; it was expected of course, and no modest bride would dream of not crying at this moment. But her tears seemed so genuine that he felt brutal in taking the child away from the only place she had ever known. She fell to the feet of her mother whose loud sobs also filled the small room; the bride's father, tears streaming down his face, patted his daughter's cheek and mumbled comfort and blessings as he tried to pull her up again. They shuffled out of the room slowly, flanked by sobbing relatives and open-mouthed children bemused by the display of such raw and uncensored emotion. Somebody circulated a cloth-wrapped copy of the Holy Book over their heads as they inched out into the courtyard towards the waiting rickshaw that was to take them the twenty miles from the girl's village to the small town where her in-laws lived.

She had to be picked up and placed in the rickshaw by her uncles, her body wrapped in a thick shawl to protect her against the cold. Against me, he thought. As the rickshaw lurched away and on to the dirt-track road she had never gone beyond before, he felt her small frame pressed against him. He wanted to extend his arm around her, to hold her in so she wouldn't fall, to offer some kind of comfort. But she would not even look at him and he suspected that any physical touch from him would only add to her distress. Instead, grimly, he gripped the edge of the seat to hold himself steady from the jolting, so that his body would not be thrown against hers. The only sounds in the dark night were the cicadas and the dull croaking of frogs in the long grass, and the sound of the wheels spinning on the dirt track, away from her home and towards their future.

13

HELEN'S HEART DID not break. There was a swiftness associated with something 'breaking'; a discernible moment in time when something that was once whole is then destroyed. A vase slipping off a ledge and shattering into countless shards on the stone floor of a kitchen. There was something almost cathartic in the energy release of a breakage.

But Helen's heart was not fortunate enough to break. There was no neat snapping apart, with the hidden hope that the pieces might one day fall into place again. Instead, with every day that passed when Rofikul did not visit her or the baby, Helen's heart shut down, cell by sorry cell. Sure enough, it still beat as steadily as ever, but it did not sing, and it did not dream, and it soon became apparent to Helen, and all those around her, that perhaps it never would again.

While Helen shrank, her skin hanging from her shoulders like a pale oversized cloak, the baby grew fat and round. His soft edges and padded little feet cushioned his mother's bones as they lay together in bed, alternately sleeping and lying awake, often in tandem. He was what the midwives grudgingly admitted was 'a good baby'; he rarely cried and fed well. It was as though he knew that his presence needed to be as soothing as possible and to demand as little as possible, in order to help piece back together the woman who had given birth to him. For six weeks, the baby had no name. The hospital had simply listed him as Baby Doherty, awarding him his mother's last name by default when they saw there wasn't a father present. If Helen had had the energy she would have been furious at this assumption. There *was* a father, a father whose name she knew, and a name she wanted to attach to her child. The baby came from inside her; there was no doubting who his mother was. But the name would have been the only link her child had to his absent father, and now he was being denied even this. With no last name and no first name, her child spent his first weeks in apologetic anonymity. Eventually, Marie could tolerate no more and demanded that Helen bloody well give that baby a name.

'I don't care what it is, or how you pronounce it, but for the love of God he needs to be called *something*,' she had chided, while lovingly rubbing Johnson's baby lotion all over the baby's chubby thighs. 'It isn't Christian to have a nameless baby. And not that it matters, but I bet it isn't right, you know, in *his* religion either.'

Helen was sitting propped up in the bed, the once crisp sheets now as limp as her unwashed hair, clutching a stale mug of English tea. Marie had made it for her with a bag of PG Tips and a splash of silver top, fresh from the glass bottle. Marie had not known where the cinnamon quills lived in the cupboard above the sink and had not known that the milk needed to be heated on the stove to make a real cup of *cha*. Rofikul would have known all these things, given that these were Rofikul's rules. But Rofikul was gone – nobody knew where – and with him had gone Helen's ability and appetite to smell or taste or feel.

They had spoken once about names, the day when she finally asked Rofikul why he had introduced himself as Ray.

She hadn't even realised it wasn't his real name until she met Hashim for the first time that day at the pictures, that awful night when they were attacked outside the cinema. Helen remembered her shame on discovering that she did not even know the name of the man she professed to love. Later that evening, as she dabbed Dettol on Rofikul's broken skin, she had sounded out the letters. *Rof-ik-ul. Rofikul.* And then she had wept and Rofikul had looked on confusedly, not realising that her tears were not because he had kept part of himself from her, but because she had never made him feel comfortable enough to show her who he truly was. Later, they had talked about names they liked and disliked. He told her that people back home did not have surnames, and that women did not change their names when they married. Instead, people were known through familial asso-ciation. On giving birth, women would become 'mother of so and so' and although they had first names, boys were known as 'suchabody's son' until he became 'so and so's father'. The headmaster of the village school was simply known as 'Headmaster' and all teachers would be 'Master'. Families were identified and described by their location and profession, and not a collective name.

'But how do they keep records of anything?' Helen had asked, genuinely bewildered. Rofikul's guffaw in response made her blush, as though she ought to have known that the very idea of keeping records there was absurd. Rofikul had pulled out his passport and showed her his birthday: 1 January 1933. He then informed her that almost everyone from his village who needed official documentation shared the same birth day and month: 1/1 was easy to remember, and so 1 January became a standard date for all paperwork. Scandalised, Helen had asked when Rofikul's actual birthday was, and he had shrugged, and said in the spring sometime, according to his mother, and that the year was probably right. His nonchalance about not even knowing his own birthday was almost uncomfortable for Helen – as though he did not care to know when and where he had come from.

Then they had talked about names in common, and he had told her that some Christian names were the same as Muslim ones. Sort of. They were mainly names of the Prophets in the Bible. The Muslim versions were Arabic, and the Christian ones were – well, Greek or Hebrew, or something else, he wasn't sure what exactly, but they were similar enough. Rofikul told Helen that Moses was *Musa*, David was *Dawud*, Jesus was *Isa*, and that they even had a name for his cousin, John the Baptist, who was *Yahya*; and that they called Abraham *Ibrahim*, and Joseph was *Yusuf*. The only name that was exactly the same in both languages was Adam. The name of the first man for both their peoples, for all people. Adam, the first man and the first prophet.

Remembering this conversation years later, in the unmade bed of rumpled white linen, with Maric massaging the baby and while clutching a cold mug of colder tea, Helen named her firstborn child. *Adam*.

'Do you think she'll agree?'

'No, I don't, but I still think we should ask.'

Munira watched her husband unpack the crates, stacking the tall cardboard boxes of cornflakes on to the shelves. He was wearing a long-sleeved white work coat, like doctors wore on television, and had they not been in the middle of a serious conversation, she would have teased him for dressing like a surgeon. Hashim did not reply. His wife pressed him again.

'Do you see why I think we should at least offer?'

'Yes, I do. But, Munira, if she moves in here, you know how it will look. A single mother. And she's white. It's not good for her either—' Hashim stopped mid-sentence as he caught the furious gaze of his wife.

'And whose fault is it that she's suddenly single now? Answer me that.'

'Munira, I didn't mean it like that, you know I didn't.'

'Why don't you take this up with your cousin? Oh, wait – you can't, because he's absconded, and nobody knows where he is, and now his own baby is without a father and Helen has waited for him for six weeks now, in that tiny damp flat, and I think we all know that your cousin won't be coming back any time soon.' Munira spat the words out, the words that both of them knew were fair.

When they hadn't been able to track down Rofikul at first, they had thought that he must be busy tearing around the city searching for the perfect gift for the baby. He had known Helen was going into labour; Munira had telephoned him at the garage. He seemed to be living there, spending every waking moment working on cars with Vincent. Hashim and Munira had assumed he was working extra shifts to try to earn some extra cash in preparation for the baby's arrival. While they weren't wrong, neither of them could have predicted that as well as toiling over engines for money, Rofikul was trying to sweat out the guilt for what he was about to do, even though he didn't know it yet. He had sounded distracted on the phone when Munira gave him the name of the hospital and a list of things he needed to bring. But that was unsurprising, she had thought at the time – he was probably just in shock. It had been almost a month early, after all.

Helen had felt the first contractions while she was arm-in-arm with Munira walking through the park. Munira had flagged down a taxi, half a stale loaf of bread still in her hand – the ducks went hungry that day – and instructed the driver to get to St Mary's quick-time. The cabbie, not realising he had a heavily pregnant woman in the back of his car until it was too late, had no intention of paying a valet for any potential clean-up, and sped through three red lights on his way to the maternity unit. When Rofikul still hadn't arrived at the hospital two hours after Munira's phone call, she rang Hashim at the shop and instructed him to track down the father-to-be. Hashim called the flat to see if Rofikul was there. There was no answer, so Hashim tried the garage again and spoke to Vincent, who said that Rofikul had left hours ago. A further two hours later, when there was still no sign of Rofikul, Munira called Hashim again.

'Can you go to your cousin's flat?'

'Bhaiya's? I called but there was no answer – he must be on his way.'

'I hope he is. But maybe something happened. Please go around there and check. Make sure everything is all right.'

Hashim had hurriedly put up a 'back in half an hour' sign on the door of the shop and gone over to Rofikul and Helen's bedsit. When nobody answered Hashim's thumping at the door, he let himself in with the spare key he kept on his chain. Before he had even stepped beyond the front door, Hashim sensed that something was amiss. The cupboard doors were flung open, hangers strewn over the bed and on the floor. There was a clear, dust-free rectangle on top of the cupboard where Rofikul's leather suitcase used to be stored. Hashim imagined Rofikul shoving his clothes into the suitcase, bundling in shirts and socks and vests, pausing to consider whether or not he ought to take his smart blazer. Apprehensively, Hashim opened the top drawer of the dresser

123

and saw that Rofikul's diary and green leather passport were gone. His chest felt tight.

Munira's voice brought Hashim back to the present.

'We all know your cousin won't be coming back to bear his responsibilities. So. What do you say?'

Hashim placed the last of the boxes on to the metal shelves and looked at his wife. 'No, you're completely right. Ask her when you go around tomorrow, let her know she can have a job here at the shop too if she wants, although she doesn't have to work of course.'

Munira nodded and slipped her hand into the crook of her husband's arm.

'Thank you. It's the right thing to do, for all of us.'

By some unspoken bond of familial responsibility, both Munira and Hashim had taken on Rofikul's sin as though it were their own. Offering to take in Helen and her child was not only the right thing to do because they were friends, it was the only way any of them could seek redemption, so tainted were they by Rofikul's actions. Whether by blood, or by marriage, or by love, it seemed that somehow all their fortunes were now tied to each other.

When Munira went round to Helen's the next morning, armed with formula milk and a metal tiffin carrier of boiled rice with green bean and chicken *bhaji*, she was surprised to find her friend out of bed and fully dressed. Munira noticed that Helen had even tried to style her own hair; she'd missed teasing a few sections at the back of her head, but still, this was a heartening sign of the old Helen.

As Helen stirred the milk and the teabags and the warm, woody aroma of cinnamon filled the little kitchen, she looked over at Munira who was cuddling the baby, playfully biting each of his fat fingers in turn.

124

'I named him yesterday. He's called Adam. Adam Ahmed Doherty.'

Munira looked over and met Helen's steady gaze. I don't know how you do it, she thought. She nodded, not trusting herself to speak. She wanted to ask about the name; how Helen came up with it, whether it had been something she and Rofikul had discussed beforehand. But instead, she simply said, 'It's perfect.'

Munira was disappointed but unsurprised when Helen politely but resolutely turned down Munira's invitation to go and live with her and Hashim.

'I need to find a way of being our own family,' Helen said. Munira understood where Helen's pride came from, her aversion to being dependent on anyone else and the desire to feel stable on her own two feet. Instead, Helen and Adam would stay on in the flat with Marie moving into the tiny boxroom for company, to help with the bills, and – as Marie put it – 'to get away from that awful bedsit'.

Helen did, however, gratefully accept Hashim's offer of a job. There was no way she could manage going back to the office now, not with Adam being so young and nobody to take care of him all day. Instead, this way, Adam could be watched by whoever wasn't on the shop floor at the time, with Helen, Munira and Hashim sharing the job of looking after him. Helen took to shop work with the zeal of a first-time employee. She arrived fifteen minutes early every day and would not leave until she had ensured that all the shelves were neat and fully stacked, and that the purchase ledger was up to date with the orders for the next week. Before long Hashim was consulting with Helen on his ideas for expanding the shop, asking her opinion on price markdowns, special offers, and even how to dress the shop window and colours for the new sign. Her commitment touched

Hashim, and he recognised how deeply she cared for him and Munira and the success of their fledgling enterprise.

They continued comfortably with this arrangement for some time, until one day, shortly after Adam's second birthday, Hashim opened a letter that bore some unexpected news. It was typewritten on headed paper from Beale & Cromwell Solicitors, the executors of Mr Langley's will. It turned out that the old shop owner had died and left the business to his son. With no interest in returning to run the family business, the son had instructed his late father's lawyers to put the shop on the market at a price that would encourage a quick sale. The lawyers were writing to inform Hashim that the business he had managed, grown, and come to love over the last couple of years was about to be sold. Hashim pushed the letter across the breakfast table towards Munira, who was adding up the purchase ledger.

'What is it?' she asked, her eyes raking over the scratchy column of digits before her.

'Read it.'

Her husband's tone made Munira look up, surprised. She read the letter once. Then again. Finally, she put it down on the table, took off her spectacles, and fixed a firm gaze on Hashim.

'Well. There's nothing else for it. We have to buy the shop.'

It took them every scrap of their savings, selling the car, and taking out a loan, but, somehow, Hashim and Munira's bid was approved. By some trick of fate, they now owned their own business. It was more than either of them had ever hoped for. Even years after, Hashim still woke up in the middle of the night drenched in sweat, having dreamed that they were unable to keep up with their repayments and that the shop had to be closed down. He worked tirelessly to stave off the remotest chance of such a possibility. But while Hashim's focus was on making sure the books balanced each month, Munira was waging a one-woman battle to have the name of the shop changed.

'It's ridiculous,' she would declare, at every possible opportunity, either to Hashim, or to customers in the shop while Hashim was in earshot. 'It's absolutely ridiculous that the proprietor of this shop still has a sign above the front door with another man's name on it. Isn't that the most ridiculous thing you've ever heard?' Then she would sniff as she placed the customer's groceries into paper bags as though to indicate that she had nothing more to say on the matter – Hashim and Helen both knew otherwise – and then, when the customer left, the bell jangling as the door thudded shut, Munira would turn to her husband and ask, 'So what will it take for you to stop pretending that "Langley and Sons" still own this shop?'

He knew she meant well, but, wonderful as his wife was, Hashim realised that his fear of failing was something Munira simply did not recognise. He was perpetually worried by thoughts that the business might not succeed, that he would make some kind of mistake on the tax forms and they would be closed down or forced into bankruptcy. Such fears would be made all the more unbearable if the shop had his name above the door. It took months of running the business with a surprisingly healthy margin before Hashim was prepared to take the plunge. He broached the subject with Helen during a quiet lull one afternoon while she was balancing the credit book.

'But what shall I change it *to*?' Hashim looked at Helen pleadingly, almost apologetic for his lack of imagination. Rofikul would, they both knew, have come up with something bombastic, something catchy, something memorable.

And he could get away with it too, something almost lurid: *RAY'S ROYAL EMPORIUM* or *GREAT GREEN-GROCER*. 'Hashim's . . . Happy . . . Hut?' Hashim tentatively offered. Helen tried unsuccessfully not to laugh, and amid the peals of her mirth Hashim flushed. 'Well, I'm not very good with these things. That's why I'm asking you.'

Chastened, Helen tried to appease Hashim. 'Well look, how about you play on what we've got? *Langley and Sons.* Why not have it something simple, like *Hashim's*? Or *Hashim & Family*?'

Hashim repeated the words in his head. *Hashim & Family.* He did want to start a family soon. Being around Adam had brought out feelings from deep within him that he still hadn't entirely made sense of; it was somewhere between a constant state of anxiety and an overwhelming swelling in his heart that sometimes felt like it would take him over completely. He would often slip away from the shop and go upstairs to check on Adam, up to five or six times a day, even when he was being looked after by his mother or Munira. Hashim would claim that he had forgotten something: a pen, his watch, the list for next week's orders, but really these were just excuses to make sure that the child he was rapidly falling in love with was still breathing, still happy, still there. He had assumed this was a natural part of wanting to ensure the wellbeing of his own flesh and blood, but it wasn't until Helen had said the word 'family' that Hashim realised that was what he wanted.

Hashim and Helen kept the name-change a secret from Munira until the day the workmen came to fit the new lettering. Helen had helped Hashim choose a deep forest green for the lettering, with a chirpy yellow background.

'It's sunny,' she said. 'People will want to come and shop here if it looks like a happy place.'

Munira clapped her hands to her mouth in delight when she saw the new name hanging above the glass-paned wooden front door for the first time, and the joy in her face made something within Hashim bloom. Later that night in their bedroom, as Munira braided her hair before slipping into the sheets beside him, she had said to him, *And we are a family.* For a fraction of a moment, Hashim's breath stopped and he thought that Munira was declaring that something beautiful and coveted was growing deep within her body. Then his chest sank, realising that his wife had been referring to their unorthodox familial arrangement: his cousin's child, the mother of the child, Munira and Hashim himself. But as quickly as it arrived, his disappointment gave way to gratitude: Munira was right; they were a family. Together, the three of them watched Adam grow – sharing the delight in his hesitant early steps, the first time he uttered a word that may have been coherent, the long-awaited protrusion of a cream-coloured tooth – with such pride and love that it was as though they had all made him.

Years later, Munira would find herself for the hundredth time in her cold tiled bathroom willing her body, in vain, not to shed blood this month. And she would wonder bitterly whether Hashim had tempted the Fates by proudly and prematurely dedicating his shop to a family that did not exist and, by the look of things, probably never would.

Part II

1969–1972

14

LONDON IN THE springtime signified hope in the subtlest of ways. The edges of daylight started pushing further into both dawn and dusk, making the days longer and ever more full of possibility. Flowers across the city burst into bloom, finally releasing the colour they had contained in their bulbs all winter, hidden in the depths of the frozen earth. Nesting birds gathered twigs to build homes in empty chimney pots, oblivious to the smog and soot around them. This city had been Rofikul's newest iteration of home for almost five years and it was at this time of year, in spring, that it seemed most to hold out hope for the future.

It had been summer when Rofikul arrived in the city for the first time, all those years ago. The coach had pulled into Victoria station and creaked to a halt with almost a sigh. Rofikul sat rooted in his seat as he watched the other passengers clamouring to get off the bus and escape the oppressive stench of sweat, stale food and the mustiness of the vehicle interior. Normally he would have been the first one bounding off, merrily chatting and helping the driver unload the suitcases and swapping anecdotes, but not that day. On that day, Rofikul had just abandoned his wife and newborn child. In an unthinking haze he had thrown a few belongings and his passport into his suitcase, drawn out some money and boarded a coach to the city that had long intrigued him. He had determinedly tried not to think of either of them since then.

He had never visited London before. All the stories he had heard were, for the most part, unappealing: the noise, the overcrowded houses, the dirt. But there were tales of success too, from within the burgeoning community of Bengalis in east London that was rapidly cementing its position in the annals of migrant history. Rofikul had heard stories of the east London community through friends and relatives who had either lived there or knew of those who did: exotic-sounding place names such as Whitechapel and Stepney, Limehouse and Shadwell captured his imagination. He was familiar with the neighbourhoods of Manchester: Fallowfield and Longsight, Levenshulme and Ardwick, but London was new. London was a clean slate, with no obligations, no ties. In London he could be anonymous.

Rofikul was taken aback by the sense of freedom he gained from roaming the streets cloaked in his long-sought anonymity. Sometimes he would wander along the northern part of Brick Lane, where the Jewish bakeries sold plaited loaves and chewy rings of bread. If he turned west towards the City, he would happen upon Petticoat Lane and Spitalfields and their rowdy markets and hawkers. He loved listening to the cries of traders, many of whom had inherited their stall spaces through previous generations. Rofikul rarely bought anything – he was surprisingly frugal since moving to London – but as he made his way through the clusters of housewives collecting their week's groceries, or the young men boasting about the freshness of their produce, he allowed himself to melt namelessly into the comforting bustle. On days where he was willing to walk further, Rofikul would continue west towards St Paul's, where he would stop and rest on the benches in the garden that sat within the shadow of the magnificent domed building. It reminded him somewhat of the grand Ottoman mosques he had seen in books. He enjoyed watching the tourists clicking their cameras and ignoring the earnest guides. Sometimes Rofikul would tag along on these tours, which is how he came to learn about its creator, Sir Christopher Wren, the man who effectively rebuilt London after the Great Fire in 1666. It was amazing that the building had survived this long, thanks to the devotion of Londoners in guarding it fiercely against threat. Rofikul marvelled at the accounts of the volunteers who tried to protect the dome during the war, reflecting lights off it to try to dazzle the bombers. Such patriots.

When the weather was rainy – and it so often was – Rofikul sought refuge in the British Museum. He loved wandering among the countless treasures: sarcophagi of pharaohs; the Rosetta Stone – that mysterious key to unlocking so much of the language and knowledge that people still benefited from; mute and imposing statues from Easter Island; terrapins made of jade from the Mughal courts. The British really were masters of collecting and curating. Or, depending on how you looked at it, pillaging and displaying remnants from ancient civilisations – Babylonian, Persian, Egyptian, Greek, Mughal and so many others – now housed within the stone walls of this building, thousands of miles away from where the artefacts originated. The display cases in which the objects lay reminded Rofikul of glass caskets. Out of context, even the most impressive stone carvings and intricate jewelled breastplates looked anaemic – dead, even – compared to how he imagined they might have been when they were in use: living, breathing objects, pulsating with energy from the hands that held, wore, wielded them.

On days when he didn't feel like roaming the endless

marble corridors, Rofikul would settle himself in a corner of the museum teashop and read. There was something perversely pleasing about doing something so personal in a public place. He would dive into stories of forgotten tribes in South America through the *National Geographic*, find himself racing through the streets of Lahore with Kipling's *Kim*, engage in long ideological debates with the Enlightenment philosophers. Sometimes he would happen upon an abandoned copy of the *Sunday Times*, crossword always completed, and he would greedily devour it from start to finish.

When Rofikul had had enough of this anonymous freedom, he would retreat back to the place he had made his latest home. The heart of Whitechapel teemed with a vibrancy that he had never experienced anywhere else before. Jews, Irish and Bengalis all bustled along cheek by jowl, each with their own claim on the streets they shared. In the couple of square miles that made up the neighbourhood, factories stood alongside leather shops and bakeries, greasy spoon cafés and curry houses. It was a place of firsts: the first synagogue in England established under the auspices of the British United Synagogue was only a few streets away from the first mosque ever to be established in London. Surrounded by churches and chapels of varying sizes, and dotted with public houses on each corner, there was nothing that one could not find in Whitechapel.

One of Rofikul's most gratifying discoveries of life in this place had been that of a well-established community of like-minded *deshi* folk who met regularly for tea and *adda* – that unique style of light-hearted intellectual debate, and the sharing of food and advice – who had taken him in as one of their own. He had arrived in London with virtually nothing, just a suitcase and the address of a relative of an old college friend. The friend, Rofikul recalled, had been less than impressed by Rofikul's decision to move to England. *What do you want to go there for? Just to be treated like a labourer, with no status, no recognition. When they're done with you, they'll just cut you off with nothing. Don't expect anything better, my friend.* That was Tonmoy, always going against the grain. The whole world was making plans for going to Britain to work, at least for a few years, and yet here was Tonmoy trying to talk Rofikul out of it. When it became apparent that Rofikul would not be taking heed of his friend's advice, Tonmoy had relented, saying that it was Rofikul's mistake to make but if he must go to the imperial heartland then he ought at least to look up Tonmoy's uncle. Uncle Deepu was the renegade son of the family, an adventurer who lived and trained in Germany, Switzerland and other places besides, before finally settling in London and opening a homeopathic clinic. For almost eight years, Rofikul had failed to take up the invitation. But by the time he showed up unannounced on that midsummer evening, he was running low on options.

Rofikul had almost wept when Uncle Deepu greeted his unexpected visitor with such warmth. He had recognised the name after some prompting and had ushered Rofikul into the tiny flat. Rofikul had respectfully removed his shoes and left them neatly by the front door. The place smelled of *dhup kathi*, the incense used to perform *puja*. The sweet, spicy scent was at once familiar and alien. It had been years since he had smelled incense like this, sharing in his Hindu neighbours' many celebrations back home. They had ceremonies for everything, he recalled: betrothals and weddings, of course, but also a ceremony when a baby would have its first taste of rice, and ceremonies for the sacred thread. The smell and the memories invoked a stab of homesickness that Rofikul had forgotten it was possible to have. As he passed through the narrow landing his gaze lingered on the images of deities that hung on the walls: the many-armed goddess, Durga, beloved, revered and feared by all, and Lord Shiva from whose hair flowed the River Ganges.

Rofikul had trespassed on Uncle Deepu's hospitality for several weeks, sleeping on a small foldaway camp-bed in the living room by night, and walking the streets looking for work by day. He was open to anything at that point, putting in applications to manage shops and restaurants, citing his experience of managing a garage, and even contemplating applying for a position to wait tables in one of the curry houses that were mushrooming in the area. In the end it had been Uncle Deepu who had suggested a job for Rofikul. A travel agency had opened up near Uncle Deepu's homeopathic clinic and he had heard that they were looking for new staff. The agency was owned by Mr Patel, an Indian fellow who had been in England for many years and already had branches of his travel agency in Hounslow and Tooting and other parts of the city that Rofikul did not yet know.

Rofikul was offered a job and enjoyed the work, organising flights and travel arrangements for his clients. The travel on offer was mainly to and from India or Pakistan, occasionally to Saudi Arabia for those performing pilgrimages, and some-times – more exotically – to places in East Africa like Uganda and Kenya, where some Indians also lived. Booking travel for other people, day in day out, did little to assuage Rofikul's waves of wanderlust. But for the most part, he was happy in London, with his newly established life, his friends and a different sense of freedom to anything he had experienced before. He felt like the person he had always hoped to be – engaged in things, part of a wide circle of friends.

The years seemed to slip by without much attention; he moved out of Uncle Deepu's flat and into his own bedsit, and Rofikul found himself becoming increasingly embedded in the community of his countrymen that he found here in England. It felt like home when they all banded together in someone's front room: one person would be folding triangles of *paan* stuffed with betel nut and tobacco to pass around, while someone else heated tea sweetened with condensed milk over a primus stove. All around there would be talk of politics and the price of land and the future of Bengal, and the increasing cost of rents here in London.

It was on one spring afternoon that Rofikul finally decided to share with his friends an idea he had been mulling over for months. Heartened by the chirping of the birds in the chimney pots and the contented-looking orb in the pale blue sky, Rofikul made his way down Commercial Road and turned off down one of the little side streets to find the house where he and his friends had agreed to meet that day. They all lived for these snatched moments of real life amid the routine of survival – days when they could gather to discuss politics without worrying about how they would pay the rent. Their weekend salons began to feel like a little bit of *desh* away from *desh*.

Rofikul rounded the corner and strode up to number 62a, the ground-floor flat of a terraced house with an untidy front yard, that was inexplicably nestled between numbers 59 and 63. The blue door stood slightly ajar and Rofikul could already hear voices drifting from inside. Outside, an ice-cream van tinkled a nursery rhyme. It was early in the year for them to be out, but it was already warm. He rapped on the door to announce himself, and pushing it open stepped straight into the front room – there was no hallway. The others were already there, lounging on sofas and sitting backwards on dining chairs, hot cups of tea in hand and plates of fried snacks being passed around. In the corner a cassette player was amplifying *palligeeti* – those well-loved folk songs that constituted compulsory background music for any such gathering.

'*Salam, bhai,*' Rofikul greeted Mr Uddin, the host for today's socialising, and an accountant by background.

'*Salam,* Rofikul.' Mr Uddin, a portly man in his late fifties with a greying beard, patted his guest's arm warmly. '*Kemon achho?*'

'I'm well, thanks.' Rofikul proffered the carrier bag he had brought with him of biscuits and fruit. 'Just a little something for the afternoon.'

'Ah, there was no need.' Mr Uddin took the bag graciously. 'My wife has been frying up treats all morning – do you like *shingara,* Rofikul?'

'Does anyone not?'

'Nobody I would trust.'

Rofikul took the cup of tea that had been thrust into his left hand, and found himself holding a thick, triangular pastry stuffed with potatoes in his right. He took a big bite and closed his eyes. 'Delicious.' He seated himself on the arm of the sofa where some of the other regulars were already ensconced, deep in conversation about the recent political developments back home.

'It's a disaster,' Mr Malik, one of the old guard, said, shaking his head and sighing. 'What makes you think the army are going to be any better than the old government?' Mr Malik was a veteran in England, having been here since before the war. Rumour had it that he had come to England on the ships, a boy *lashkar,* and had lived here ever since, even surviving the demolition of his house during the Blitz, but nobody ever dared to ask him to confirm this outright.

'I don't think they are,' Shafiq, a round-faced, pleasant-seeming lad from Chittagong, replied. 'But it's got to be good news for the Bengalis, doesn't it?'

'What – the fact that President Ayub Khan has just handed over power to the Pakistan Army? Since when has martial law been a good thing for *anyone*, let alone us Bengalis?' Mr Malik took another *shingara* and dunked it heavily in his tea. 'General Yahya Khan has no interest in representation for us in the East.'

'Well, neither did Ayub Khan,' Rofikul interjected. 'But it's a chance for change, isn't it? There's talk that the general is going to introduce direct parliamentary elections.'

Mr Malik sniffed. 'I'll believe that when I see it.'

Rofikul could see the reasons for Mr Malik's scepticism. Things were undoubtedly in a state of political flux back home. The well-established divisions between West Pakistan and East Pakistan – or Bengal as it was known to its people – were as apparent as ever. There had been no direct parliamentary elections since the country's inception over twenty years ago. The electoral college system most certainly favoured the political establishment of the West, and the Easterners were rapidly losing patience. In the end, President Ayub Khan had clung on for as long as he could, but handing power over to the army was a desperate final act.

'It's true that they see Sheikh Mujibur Rahman as a conspirator with India against a unified Pakistan,' Shafiq began earnestly, 'but—'

'But what?' Mr Malik cut in irritably. 'He *is* a conspirator! As he should be! How else will we get any kind of representation for our people? The idea of a unified Pakistan is a sham. The sooner we all recognise that, the better.'

Rofikul couldn't help agreeing. Sheikh Mujib, the leader of the Awami League – the majority party in East Pakistan – was fast becoming the most prominent figurehead for Bengali nationalism. Despite having been tried for sedition the year before, accused of conspiring with India to dissolve the unified state of Pakistan and to bring about the secession of the East, his position was far from ruined. If anything, support for Sheikh Mujib and his party had boomed in the aftermath. Nobody knew where things were headed, but it was apparent to all who were following the situation that they were on the precipice of something unknown but undoubtedly significant.

Rofikul decided that if there was any time to share the idea he had been nurturing for so long, this was it. He cleared his throat self-consciously.

'Brothers' – he looked around the room, pausing as some of the chattering died down – 'we all know that we are living through a time of considerable change . . .' He paused. The other eyes around the room were cast upon him, some amused, some sceptical. Rofikul was known for his fanciful ideas. 'I believe' – he sat up, eyes focused steadily ahead of him – 'that we should start a newspaper. A new one. Written by Bengalis in Britain, for Bengalis in Britain.' He looked around the room triumphantly. He could see some of the others contemplating the idea, mulling over what it would mean for them. They all read the news from home, but it was true that it always reached them a little late; if they wanted current updates, they had to make do with a language that was not their mother-tongue.

'What do we need another newspaper for?' Mr Uddin followed Rofikul's gaze quizzically around the room. 'We have Bangla newspapers already, don't we?' Uddin was a pragmatist, which was a term Rofikul used occasionally as a neutral adjective, but more often than not as a borderline insult. Uddin's inability to see the potential in an idea, the scope for growth of a project, was always limited by his accountant's brain, his need to see the outcomes and forecasts on paper. Still, Mr Uddin, an accountant and one of the community's most successful business investors, was exactly the kind of person Rofikul needed to make this idea happen – to turn it from a vague thought and into a viable, real enterprise. He could make sure the numbers added up, that they were within their budget, that the newspaper – like so many others – would not disappear from circulation after a few print runs because of an exploded budget and no cash-flow planning. Moreover, Rofikul knew from their many discussions at events such as this that Uddin was a patriot, in the best sense of the word. And that was what this paper would be – *patriotic.*

Rofikul nodded sagely. 'Yes, you're right, there are newspapers here, Uddin *shahb*, but they're not the same as what I want *us* to create. Those ones are more like pamphlets – they are volunteer-led, they have no proper budget, no real business plan. They can't keep up with the demands of a regular newspaper – sometimes they have a break for two, four, six weeks because the editor has gone on holiday, or the printing budget has been used up . . .' Rofikul waved his hands emphatically. 'You know how it goes, people get excited with a side project and then drop it when they run out of money.'

'Yes, that's my point exactly. How would this one be any different?'

'It won't *be* a side project. That's how.' Rofikul grinned broadly, proud of his definitive explanation. 'This newspaper will be the main focus of those of us who work on it. The editors, the writers, the business managers – this will be our main project. Even if it doesn't pay at first, it will be our priority. And we will make a point of never having a break. Ever. We won't miss a week. The news won't wait.'

Mr Uddin smiled wryly. 'All right, all right, no need for your hard sell, I understand what you're saying.' In truth, Uddin was moderately sympathetic to the idea, but there

143

were plenty of practicalities to consider. Moreover, he knew better than to show Rofikul that he was almost convinced.

Mr Malik piped up. 'But what about funding? How do you propose to raise money for this project of yours, this "main focus" as you call it?'

'The usual – investors, other people's donations, my savings, your savings – that's if you believe in the cause, of course.' Rofikul paused – he was only half joking. 'And . . . we could take out loans?'

At this point Mr Uddin stood up. 'Rofikul, I like you a lot, and I respect you, but you have no head for money – and if we do this your way, this paper of yours will be in the gutter before it hits the shelves.' The others in the room had their eyes glued to the scene playing out before them. Shafiq crunched a *shingara* audibly. The silence lasted several seemingly endless moments. Mr Uddin sighed. He had a sneaking suspicion that this had been exactly Rofikul's plan all along, to goad him into salvaging a compelling idea that was artfully presented to be on the brink of financial ruin.

Someone called out from the edges of the room. 'So, you'll help him do it then?'

Mr Uddin sighed again and looked around helplessly at the assembled group in the room. He hadn't seen them so animated – and they were not an unexcitable bunch – in a long time. The idea had clearly captivated this audience, at least. He pushed his glasses up on top of his head and rubbed the bridge of his nose. 'Do I have a choice?' He pushed the frames back down his nose and raised his eyebrows at Rofikul.

Rofikul grinned. 'Oh, there's always a choice, Uddin *shahb* – I'm just delighted you made the right one.'

15

As it turned out, Mr Uddin was not the only one who was willing – if at times, despairingly – to help with Rofikul's cause. By the time they were ready to go to press almost a year later, the project was backed by a suite of modest investors. As Uddin discovered through his financial solicitation, few were able to give significant amounts, but it turned out that many were willing to give modest sums: usually small local business owners, or established families who were idealists and who believed that having a Bangla-language mouthpiece in London would somehow advance the nationalist cause. Uddin unconditionally banned any of the newspaper team, including Rofikul, from applying for any personal loans to fund the project, foreseeing destitution for all if they were to go down that particular black hole. Instead they opted to trade heavily in adverts, offering full, half and quarter pages to all the shops and restaurants in the area, both Bengali owned and not. Estate agents, grocery stores, travel agents and clothing wholesalers all bought up inches in the newspaper's advertising pages, determined not to be left behind on this new venture.

The newspaper team itself was formed of five individuals. Rofikul served as editor-in-chief, overseeing the editorials and commissioning content; Mr Uddin was accorded the well-deserved title of chief executive. Mr Pasha, a friend of Uddin, was brought in as news commissioner, responsible for sourcing stories and content from his contacts in Britain and back home. Finally, they hired two wiry staff writers, former reporters for pioneering British-Bangla newspapers that were no longer in print, who were responsible for churning out stories that were handed to them, investigating loose leads, and generally scooping up what needed to be done. Their headquarters were at a small upstairs office donated to them by one of their business-owning benefactors, located just south of Commercial Road.

Despite Rofikul's well-intentioned assertions that the newspaper would be everyone's priority – and in truth, when it came to levels of passion, it was – most of the team had day jobs and conflicting responsibilities, himself included, which required them to be flexible with their hours. Only the reporters were given salaries; the others agreed they would hold equity in the newspaper and forgo payment in the meantime.

The newspaper went to press on 21 February. The name *Ekushey* and the inaugural date were chosen to commemorate 'language martyrs', as they had become known. These were university students who had protested at the exclusion of Bengali as an official national language of Pakistan and who had been massacred by the military police for doing so, eighteen years earlier. Some of them had been among Rofikul's peers.

As he worked on the draft for his inaugural editorial, Rofikul contemplated the events that had led them to this point. The refusal to recognise Bengali as an official language of Pakistan was just one of a series of state aggressions against the Bengali population of the country – his people. East Pakistan had spent the years since the Partition of 1947 being treated as the hinterland of West Pakistan – under-resourced, under-developed, and largely dismissed by the political elites who resided in Karachi, Lahore and Islamabad. The state's capital moved around the critical triumvirate of cities like a movable feast, but never once ventured eastwards to Dhaka.

Most crucially for his purposes, it was important to recognise that diaspora Bengalis, particularly those within Britain, needed to make their opposition to the Pakistani government known. *Ekushey* was to become a mouthpiece for that movement; the new publication would be a platform for Bengalis in Britain to mobilise in support of the political efforts back home, but also to feel connected somehow to what was going on. If he was honest with himself, Rofikul could not deny that that had been one of his motivations in driving this initiative. He had dedicated over ten years to building a life in Britain; he had thrown himself headlong into working, getting used to the culture, having relationships even, here in this country, and yet it never quite seemed to fit. Something had always been missing.

The first editorial was the most important thing he had written to date: it carried a mission, a vision that needed to extend beyond just himself and his colleagues at the newspaper. It needed to rouse and inspire his fellow diaspora at a time when they — their land — needed it the most.

Ekushey News
Editorial | Issue 1 | 21 February 1970

Over one hundred thousand Bengali people live in Britain today. It is no small number and we are growing day by day. The aim of this paper is to connect and to acquaint Bengalis in Britain with the situations prevalent in our countries – both here in Britain and abroad.

It is our belief that it is imperative that one should have the ability to exchange views on political, social and religious matters in one's own mother tongue. This is what we seek to offer our readers and to allow them to keep abreast of issues that matter.

We also wish to identify and resolve the day-to-day questions of the huge number of Bengalis living here in Britain. Living as a minority in a larger nation comes with its own intricate set of issues, complexities and resolutions, and we seek to address this in our newspaper.

As a nation, Bengalis are a distinct entity, with a proud history, a vibrant language, and a unique and colourful culture. We may not have a homeland we can call our own, but we are still a nation and this newspaper proudly promotes our right to self-definition.

16

JUST TEN MONTHS after its inaugural edition, the newspaper had grown to a circulation of ten thousand copies
per week. Each Thursday the printers rolled out the copies,
inked and folded, which were then stacked, packed and
shipped to far-off depots in places like Leicester, Bradford,
Manchester and Birmingham. More and more businesses
were enquiring about advertising spaces for their services
– travel agents, restaurants, wholesale retailers – and not just
in London. The paper was living up to its intention of being
a truly national representation of Bengalis in Britain.

As well as allowing the founders to pay back their cred-
itors, the increasing advertising revenues were comfortable
enough to offer the staff salaries for their work. Those with
full-time jobs resigned from their previous work in order to
turn their full attentions to the paper. The success was liberating for all of them, but especially for Rofikul who had
hoped more than any of the others that they would one day
reach this point. The newsroom had an energy that made
him feel alive and engaged in his work for the first time in
years. There was always somebody there typing, or passing
around a kettle of freshly brewed tea, or tucking into the
boxes of biryani that they ordered in for lunch from
the café across the road.

He was the closest to happy he had been in a long time.

In the years that had passed, Manchester and the life he had lived there faded from the forefront of Rofikul's mind. It was being edged out by the late nights after work when he would stay up with the other writers and, once their articles were filed, play cards, smoke and occasionally dabble in a glass of Scotch. His memorisation of the Manchester tram routes was replaced by the intricate squiggles of the London Underground lines. But sometimes, just before he fell asleep, and as the early morning light was hovering around the edges of the night-time darkness, the image of an auburn-haired woman with soft eyes would float into his mind. He was powerless to banish it.

Keeping abreast of the developments in Pakistan was what captivated Rofikul's thoughts by day. This month had seen the first general election the country had ever held since its inception in 1947 and Rofikul had worked all hours of the day and night on columns analysing the outcome. All commentators had predicted a close tie between the two major parties: Bhutto's Pakistan Peoples Party, and the Awami League, led by Sheikh Mujibur Rahman. Although both were socialist in slant, their dividing line was along regional borders: the PPP enjoyed a majority in the West, while the Awami League dominated the East. The newsroom had tuned in to the radio with bated breath to hear the results being announced. It had been a landslide victory for the Awami League, taking home almost twice the number of votes as their rivals. The room had erupted into cheers of celebration. There would finally be a Bengali-majority party leading the government of Pakistan. The East would be marginalised no more. But the joyous celebrants had reckoned without the political wrangling that would ensue. For weeks afterwards Rofikul's columns scrutinised the unfolding developments:

the incumbent President refusing to give up power; the Awami League being denied taking the seats they had won in the National Assembly.

It was the most exciting political development that anyone had seen in years and it was killing Rofikul that he was so far away from the source of the action, having to report events second-hand from news off the wire. There was no way he could stand by as a spectator from this distance any longer; he had to find a way to get home.

'Yes, I've heard what you said, and yes, I am still going,' Rofikul calmly repeated while Uddin Shahb's face turned an increasingly violent shade of puce.

'You're a madman.' Uddin shook his head disbelievingly. 'Do you have some sort of death-wish? Why do you need to be there covering it "on the ground"? That's exactly why we have connections with reporters *there*, who can cover it *on the ground*.'

'Yes, reporters who may be filing to who knows how many different papers at the same time. How can we guarantee that we will be the first to break the news if we don't have one of our own stationed there?'

'I am not *paying* to send you to an early grave, do you understand me? This newspaper *Will. Not. Let* that happen.' Uddin looked as though he were about to explode. 'Besides,' he continued, 'what's wrong with the newswire? Plenty of respectable news outlets rely on updates from the Associated Press – does it do them any harm?'

Unable to retain his self-control any longer, Rofikul thundered, 'This is *our* story, you understand? It is happening in our country, to our people, and *we* have a responsibility to report back on what is happening FOR OUR PEOPLE. Do you understand this, or should I say it again louder?'

Uddin knew it was useless to continue arguing, but what Rofikul was proposing was utter lunacy: to step down as editor, for Uddin to take over and fly Rofikul out to East Pakistan, and to continue paying him to be a reporter covering news about the election fallout. Uddin had no desire to be an editor; his interest was purely in the business angle of the paper. But it seemed as though Rofikul was pulling rank here.

'Look, it will be hardly any different to how it is now.' Rofikul changed tack, opting to cajole his agitated colleague rather than continue at loggerheads. 'You'll carry on being the business operator here, and I'll be sending you regular updates as much as I can. All you have to do is run with them; there'll hardly be any editorial decision-making because all people will want to hear about will be the war. Just lead with those stories.'

The sudden and unrelenting desire to be at the forefront of whatever political movement he could sense was bubbling up ought not to have been unexpected, but it still took Rofikul by surprise that he had felt so deep a need to find a way of getting there – getting *home* – as soon as he could. It wasn't born out of any latent sense of duty in wanting to see his family, to assure himself of their protection during any potentially dangerous times ahead. It wasn't even particularly born out of a strong sense of ideology; certainly, he'd been an activist during his time at college, but he was hardly one of those earnest enough to dedicate his life to the nationalist cause: he'd left the country as soon as he'd been given a chance. But somehow, the opportunity to be out of England and away from everything that had been his life for the last decade or so – had it really been so long? – tugged at him with such ferocity that he could not ignore it.

'Uddin Shahb, I'm going. If you want me to send my

reports to *Janomot*, I can, but I'm offering you my exclusives first.'

Uddin took off his glasses and rubbed the bridge of his nose with a bony thumb and forefinger.

'Very well,' he sighed, replacing his glasses carefully. 'We'll send you. I want a weekly report wired, Wednesday evening, GMT, five o'clock on the dot. You write them ready for us to put them straight on the Thursday press. You pay for your own travel there, but we'll keep paying you at your current rate. If your head gets blown off, or the Pakistanis arrest you and throw you into prison, that's your problem and we aren't paying out any insurance money. Fair?'

Rofikul grinned. 'Fair.' He pumped Uddin's hand excitedly. 'You won't regret this. This will be the thing that sets *Ekushey* apart from all the other papers. You'll see.'

17

WITH HIS HAIR sharply parted at the side, a neat moustache and heavy square spectacles, Sheikh Mujibur Rahman, the leader of the Awami League Party, cut a distinguished-looking profile. It occurred to Rofikul, standing in the crowds below the podium at the Dhaka racecourse, that Bengal had not seen a leader as charismatic since before the Raj. He was certainly not alone in thinking so: the people had bestowed upon Sheikh Mujib the title of Bongobondhu – the friend of Bengal. Along with his seemingly effortless charm, Mujib's popularity was rooted, somewhat contrarily, in the obstacles to his political success.

Following his conversation with Uddin just a couple of months ago, early in the New Year, Rofikul had stepped off a plane on to the red earth of the country he once called home. He had arrived just on the cusp of seeing it transform into this living, pulsating entity of hope and change. And now here he was, witnessing a moment he knew would be historic. The leader stood before two million people on the grounds of the racecourse in Dhaka. They were citizens whose votes had up to now been ignored by those in power, whose voices had been silenced. No longer.

As he waited for the speech to begin, Rofikul found himself reflecting on the undulating pattern of the nation's history that had led them all to this day. It had been building for years, ever since the British withdrawal in 1947 and the creation of the two new states. The retreating imperialists had decreed that religion would be the dividing line along which the independent nation states would exist. India for the Hindus. Pakistan for the Muslims. No state was allocated to the Sikhs of Punjab; nor to the Christians of Kerala, or the Parsees in Sindh and Gujarat, or the handful of Jews who remained in Calcutta. Partition meant exodus. Sikhs, Hindus and Muslims moved their homes and families across the new borders, fearful that they were no longer safe now that their ancestral villages lay within the redrawn boundaries of these new countries.

And just like that, overnight, the people were expected to feel love and affiliation for these infant nations – *Pakistan Zindabad! Jai Hind!* Standing in rallies, waving flags that had never existed before. The pale crescent moon on the background of green – motifs that had been carefully borrowed from Muslim nations in the Middle East. The orange and green flanking the strip of white with Buddha's wheel in the middle. Anthems were composed, constitutions ratified, elections held. What astonished Rofikul the most was the fierceness of the nationalism that had taken root in barely one generation.

Now it was 1971. Twenty-four years since Partition, during which Bengal had been carved up into East and West, each falling into the boundaries of a different, newly invented country. West Bengal went to India; its capital, Calcutta, a fading memory of the Raj. The rest of Bengal, renamed East Pakistan, lay in its watery Bay separated by several thousand miles from the rest of the country.

The spring air felt fresh. Rofikul turned round and looked out behind him. As far as he could see, the crowds stretched like an ocean of dark hair and waving fists. They erupted into a roar as Sheikh Mujibur Rahman was called to the podium. Clad in a black, Nehru-collared waistcoat over a white *kurta*, Sheikh Mujib issued the rallying cry that was to be heard and responded to across Bengal, in a voice that trembled with emotion. Rofikul noted it down in his book, never once taking his eyes off the man standing before him on the stage.

'*The struggle this time is the struggle for our emancipation. The struggle this time is the struggle for independence.*'

Rofikul felt almost physically lifted by the power of the words. His heart was beating with the momentousness of the event. It was a declaration that would change the future of this nation for ever. And here he was, able to witness it and to share it with the world. He was witnessing history, and he needed to chronicle it. This was why he had returned.

The boarding house that Rofikul was staying in was a relic from a bygone age. Dark wooden shutters flanked every window of the rickety bungalow, the walls washed with white lime. It had been extended to accommodate more rooms, with corridors winding around the back of the original building, each with several doors leading off to individual spartan rooms. Each room had a bed with a mosquito net, a small dresser and a desk and wooden chair. The bathrooms were communal, with no running water; every morning the servant boys went to collect water from the pump outside, heat it on the fire in the kitchens, and then lug the pails to the rooms so the guests could wash. Meals were taken in the communal dining room; simple fare but well cooked and always hot and fresh, and ladled out in generous portions. A wireless set took pride of place on the sideboard of the room, and it was often on during and after meals when the residents would take their tea and smoke and listen to the latest news updates. The guests were a strange assortment of travellers, students, businessmen who were transiting through the city, and journalists. As well as Rofikul there were a couple of other correspondents, one from India and another from an East Pakistani broadsheet. They were friendly enough and keen to discuss the unfolding events as they happened.

In the two weeks since Sheikh Mujib's legendary speech at the racecourse, developments were happening day by day. Negotiations had been taking place between the incumbent President and Sheikh Mujib, but few had been hopeful that they would be peaceably resolved. The sceptics had been proven correct: the recent days had seen a heavy-handed military crackdown in Dhaka resulting in mass arrests and violence. Rofikul and his fellow reporters had taken care to remain discreet when investigating what was being carried out under Operation Searchlight: the military targets included journalists, as well as students, academics and anyone who might have been considered traitors to the idea of a unified Pakistan.

It was in the early hours of 26 March 1971 that war was finally declared. Rofikul had been awake, working late into the night on his latest article. He preferred to work in the dining room for his nocturnal sessions – his own room seemed claustrophobic at that hour, and he liked to keep the wireless on, the sound turned low, for background comfort. Shortly after midnight, the programme he had been listening to was interrupted. He did not notice at first, fully absorbed in the rhythmic clattering of typewriter keys, but there was a pause and the fuzzy crackling stopped, and then the confident, familiar voice began to speak. '*This may be my last message; from today Bangladesh is independent.*'

Rofikul leaped across to turn up the radio. For Sheikh

Mujib to be broadcasting at this hour, it had to mean something serious. He listened, hardly daring to let out the breath he had drawn.

'*I call upon the people of Bangladesh, wherever you might be and with whatever you have, to resist the army of occupation to the last. Your fight must go on until the last soldier of the Pakistan occupation army is expelled from the soil of Bangladesh and final victory is achieved. I have given you independence. Now go and preserve it.*'

The broadcast ended, leaving just the crackle of white noise. Rofikul had sat unmoving. War had been declared.

The next day, news began to spread that Bongobondhu had been arrested and taken from his home shortly after the broadcast had been issued. His whereabouts were unknown: some suspected he had been taken to West Pakistan and imprisoned there; others feared his assassination. Rofikul and his fellow reporters had scoured the streets and government buildings for news, updates and rumours, to try to piece together what was taking place around them. It felt as though the whole nation was waiting to see what would happen, uncertain, roused with the spirit of resistance. The people did not have to wait for long. In the days following Sheikh Mujib's arrest, the original broadcast was repeated, amplified and bolstered by other political leaders reiterating the same proclamation of self-determination and the calls for resistance, until every citizen of the newly declared, 'independent' state of Bangladesh had been made fully aware that they were now at war.

18

SEVERAL MONTHS LATER, Rofikul sat hunched over a table in a roadside tea stall trying to meet his deadline. His column was due, and he needed to start telegraphing it to his editor in London. Radio Peking – one of the few stations for which they managed to receive an uninterrupted signal – was playing on a crackly wireless.

He was working on a piece about the newly formed alliance between the Indian Army and the Mukhti Bahini. He had been to interview them at their makeshift, temporary training camps in the jungle. Nobody could fault the guerrilla fighters for their passion; that much was indisputable. They were a ragtag assortment – students, doctors, farmers, traders – but what they lacked in stature, both physically and militarily, they definitely made up for in zeal. The Mukhti Bahini were not particularly well equipped, wielding cast-off Russian weapons from a different age, but most could be suitably put to use to keep the Pakistanis busy – booby traps, decoys and, occasionally, the odd shooting. The Indian Army had been tasked with training the freedom fighters ever since India had joined in the war on the side of the liberation movement. After all, a weaker Pakistan – or whatever the fragments ended up calling themselves – could only be a boon to India. And it would be far more strategic to have an indebted ally in a newly independent Bangladesh.

Rofikul had expected zeal but he was taken aback by the red-eyed hunger for revenge in the freedom fighters. They regaled him with stories of women bleeding to death, torn inside after whole battalions of Pakistanis had forced themselves on to them; of men who had ended their own lives after watching their families being raped, unable to bear the shame. The freedom fighters were avenging this pain, this shame. Rofikul struggled to find the words to set down on paper. He rubbed his eyes and took another sip of tea, finding himself listening in to the conversation the tea stall owner was having with another customer.

'They do that? And they call themselves *mussalman*?' The tea stall owner spat derisively in the road.

The customer shook his head slowly and sighed. '*Pak*. Pure. There's nothing pure about what those monsters are doing.'

Rofikul's ears pricked up. He had heard about every atrocity the Pakistanis were committing: the rapes, the mutilations, the night-time executions of doctors and lawyers. 'What have they done now?' he called over to the two men, laying down his pen momentarily.

The customer shook his head again. 'The usual. Brutes. Can't control themselves, not enough goats here to keep them busy. Except now, they're sick of the women.' He paused and recomposed himself. 'They stopped a boy in my village yesterday, claimed that he "seemed Hindu". When he insisted he was Muslim, they made him say the *kalimah*. When he could do that, they made him recite *Fatiha*.' The man's voice shook with rage. 'And when he could do that, they made him . . . they ordered him to lift up his *lungi*, to see if he was circumcised. Said that a dirty Hindu boy wouldn't be.'

Rofikul felt sick, though he knew this wasn't the end. 'Then what?'

'Then, when the boy passed that test, that bastard Pakistani officer . . . he said that if this lad was really a good Muslim boy, then he wouldn't enjoy what he was about to do to him. And then the officer . . . well, he . . . interfered with him. And now the lad won't talk. Can't talk. We only know that's what happened because one of his friends was there too, but for whatever reason, they left him alone. They probably ran out of time . . .'

Rage surged through Rofikul's body. The hypocrisy of the army sickened him. They pretended it was a war to maintain unity, to preserve a shared religious identity — and yet there was nothing more ungodly than the actions of the 'Pak' army. He wondered how the war was being portrayed to the citizens in Pakistan, whether they had any idea of what was going on in the name of their country. The truth was, most West Pakistanis probably wouldn't lose any sleep over it, even if they did know what was happening. Bengal — the East — was seen by most as a hinterland. A kitchen garden, at best — like the breadbasket the Ukraine was to the Soviet Union, he mused.

'What happened to them? The soldiers?'

'What do you think happened? They got in their jeep and drove off. Nothing ever happens to them. They think they're untouchable because they are.' The tea stall owner returned to wiping down the counter with a greasy rag.

Rofikul sat silently for a moment, turning the conversation over and over in his head. He was glad that he was present to witness events, to describe them and make sure that everyone knew what was happening. People back in England needed to be aware of what was going on here. This war could not afford to go on for too long. He drew a long breath and turned back to the pad of paper in front of him, trying to focus on his deadline. Elsewhere the war raged on.

19

WHEN HASHIM READ the newspapers these days, all he felt was an ache right in the middle of his ribcage. He wasn't usually one for reading, but once war had been declared back home, everything changed. He would pore over the papers, both English and Bangla – *The Times*, the *Telegraph, Ekushey, Janomot* – at the kitchen table, at the shop counter, on the bus, wherever and whenever he could. It was an obsession, but a bleak one that had no root in pleasure, only in a pervading sense of something disconcertingly close to guilt. He read accounts of the atrocities committed: the Hindu villagers fleeing their homes to avoid incineration at the hands of the Pakistani armed forces; the horrors inflicted on the pro-Pakistani Biharis who were opposed to Bangladeshi independence; the women's breasts ripped off with curved knives by those claiming 'patriotism'. Every day there was a new story, warnings from British MPs of impending famine; eyewitness accounts about bodies of murdered civilians piled up at the side of roads.

He wrote to his family, wiring as much money as he could to help them buy the most basic provisions. But the infrastructure was being obliterated day by day, the institutions that remained being passed over to West Pakistani government control. '*Business as usual*' was the Pakistani motto; the intention was to minimise institutional disruption as little as possible, to deny the existence of a Bengali uprising, and to press on with daily matters. To this end, Hashim learned, national school and college exams were scheduled to continue as usual. Educational facilities remained open, but with dual occupants: students and soldiers. Schools were classrooms by day and torture chambers by night. Hashim read a horrifying article in which a high school principal spoke of having to wipe down blood in the classrooms in the mornings before his students arrived, to erase the presence of the Pakistani Army's executions from the previous night. This was not the land he had left; he wondered what remained of what he had called home.

Hashim placed a collection bucket on the counter of the shop to raise funds to send to Bangladesh in support of the war effort. Munira had written a sign for him, explaining what the collection was for. People gave generously, to his relief – the Bengalis and even the English customers always emptying their change into the plastic container. The Pakistanis pretended not to notice it, politely paying for their purchases in exact change. It heartened him that the British seemed largely in support of freedom; he kept the radio in the shop tuned in to the news, listening carefully for any mention of Bangladesh. Some of his English customers spoke to him about the situation, offering condolences and enquiring as to the safety of Hashim's family. Each night Hashim prayed for his family far away in Bangladesh as well as those with him in England, offering thanks for God's continued protection, as well as gratitude that his destiny had led him and Munira to the safety of this land that had now become the closest thing they had to a home.

He had learned about Rofikul's whereabouts from the paper. *Ekushey*. It had landed on his shop counter like a thunderbolt. A whole stack of them, dispatched from the depot where he got the other foreign-language newspapers. He'd heard about it from other Bengalis – this new Bangla-language national weekly. His regular customers had seemed so excited by the prospect and the papers sold out in his shop every week. It wasn't until he was flicking through the pages that he saw his cousin's name in the editorial section and the tiny black and white picture that accompanied it. Blurry but unmistakably Rofikul. It had caught him off guard, this snapshot into Rofikul's life. So that's where he had gone when he left them all. Left Hashim and Munira to help Helen raise the son Rofikul had never even bothered to meet. In a rare explosion of anger Hashim had flung the newspaper across the shop. Unfortunately, he had timed his outburst for the very moment Munira had walked in. She had demanded to know what was going on, of course, and Hashim had had to show her. Her body bristled beside his, and he laid his arm heavily on her shoulders and pulled her close. *Shall we tell Helen?* Munira had asked before answering her own question. *We have to.*

And so Munira had told Helen, very matter-of-fact, that the father of her child was living in London and running a newspaper. Helen had sat so still that Munira wondered if she had heard her. Eventually she had asked in a clear, low voice, *Which newspaper?* Munira had told her the name. Helen had got up from her chair and marched down the stairs to the shop. She picked up a stack of the newspapers tarnished by Rofikul's name and walked over to the door. She yanked it open, sending the little bell above it jangling, and while Hashim and Munira stared at her, she launched the pile of newspapers into the street. *Don't ever bring that newspaper into this shop again. I swear to God.* Hashim felt part of him wither under Helen's stony gaze. Munira took her arm and led her back up the stairs. The other customers in the shop shuffled around

164

uncomfortably, one or two of them furtively slipping out into the street to pick up one of the abandoned copies.

Hashim had given in to Helen's demand and the offending newspaper never made its way back into the shop. But he would read it whenever he could: sometimes in the library, or in one of the other Bengali grocery shops, or even on the bus on the rare occasion when someone had abandoned their copy. He pored over the articles and the features, and studied the photograph of his cousin, drinking in his words. It was like Rofikul was right there beside him, narrating the unfolding conflict in a way that Hashim could fully absorb. And then, some time the following spring, Hashim had noticed an addition to the byline: *Rofikul Ahmed, reporting from Dhaka.* He was in the library at the time, just a week after independence had been declared. So Rofikul was living in a war zone now. He had *chosen* to go there.

Hashim wondered whether he ought to tell Helen and Munira about this latest revelation, but how would he be able to share it without revealing his secret one-sided relationship with his cousin – conducted through the words one wrote and the other read? There was a part of Hashim that resented Rofikul, even hated him at times, for what he had put them all through. And not just with Adam and Helen. Hashim had been forced – or at least co-opted against his will – into guarding secrets embedded deep in Rofikul's past. It was true that Rofikul had never asked him not to reveal those secrets, but it was implicit somehow – a mutual understanding that Hashim told himself he was powerless to refuse. Hashim feared that if he told Helen and Munira about Rofikul's whereabouts now, it would spiral into an obligation to reveal the full extent of what he knew of his cousin, and his apparent return to their homeland. No; it was far better to remain quiet, not to admit to any knowledge of Rofikul, past or present. It seemed as though the only way to maintain harmony in his life would be to cut his cousin out of it, at least in the sight of others.

And so Hashim never mentioned his cousin's name to Munira or to Helen. Sometimes when he held Adam he wanted to whisper in his tiny ear. *Your baba would love you. If only he knew you. He would.* But he never did. Instead, once a week he caught the bus down to the library and stayed for about an hour, reading *Ekushey* from start to finish and imagining he had company, with Rofikul narrating the editorial to him as though Hashim were the only person present. Rofikul banging the table emphatically to emphasise a point. Just him and Rofikul. The tone was so familiar, Hashim felt transported back to the way things were before. Before things got difficult, before all this pain, before war. At night, he prayed for Rofikul, that he would continue to be safe, would be cloaked in Allah's protection, and then perhaps – maybe, one day – Rofikul would find his way back to those who were waiting for him.

20

THE GIRL IS no more than five; six at the most. All she can hear is the sound of her rubber sandals slapping against the ground and her own panting breath as she runs through the thick forest, clutching her mother's hand. She knows she has to be quiet – one loud sound and they could all be discovered.

There are about twenty or thirty of them, women and children, fleeing as quickly and soundlessly as they can. The village lookout had raised the alarm only minutes before – that the Pakistani Army was rolling in on their jeeps, the soldiers already hungry for Bengali flesh. The men and older boys have hidden in the *dhan*, among the tall rice stalks in the paddy fields. It is safer for the women to flee: stories of mass rapes by the army have spread like wildfire across the country. The soldiers are told that they are raping for their country, to spread their pure – *pak* – seed, to reform the uncivilised Bengalis through fertilising them with the correct genes. They violate women with no regard for age or health; pre-pubescent girls and grandmothers alike are considered fair game.

The women will seek refuge in the neighbouring village, higher up in the hills, where the Pakistani Army – unfamiliar with the terrain – will not bother to search. But to get there, they must run for miles with no light. The women chide and coax their children to move quickly and quietly, fearful of what they may be forced to witness if the army catches up with them. The girl hears a shout behind her, a hushed reprimand, and the sound of her sister crying: she has lost her sandal and is sobbing because her aunt, who has grabbed her by the arm, says she cannot go back to retrieve it.

After a journey of what feels like days, but has only been a couple of hours, the exhausted women reach the village. They are welcomed into homes, offered mats to sleep on, rice to feed their children. It escapes no one that things could have ended very differently had the lookout not been on duty that day. The men of the host village are sombre, knowing that against the army they would have no means to protect their own women, let alone shelter any others. A few of the men carry a *da* – a curved knife – but firearms are available only to the Mukhti Bahini. Some of their sons have joined the Mukhti Bahini, a proud fact among the villagers. But with an absence of young men in the villages, there are fewer means of protection for the more vulnerable against the terror of the Pakistani Army. They have to fend for themselves.

Only one woman stayed behind. Bibi was the oldest woman in the *gram*. Nobody knew her exact age, but she was somewhere between seventy-five and eighty. Her legs had all but failed her years ago, but her mind was still sharp, and, as many of the young village miscreants knew, her tongue was sharper still. When the lookout had arrived in the village square and breathlessly warned the residents of the approaching threat, Bibi simply nodded slowly and creaked her way back to her house, leaning heavily on her stick. When some of the village women tried to persuade her to come with them, she shook her head impatiently.

'Do you think I'm stupid? Are *you* stupid? If I come with you, we'll all get caught – and shot – and worse. Leave me; I can take care of myself.'

Although they were reluctant to leave her behind, the women knew Bibi was right. Who could carry her? There was no way she'd keep up with her stick. Some of the men came along to persuade Bibi to hide with them in the paddy fields. Again, she was insistent.

'What makes you think I could crouch out there for that long? You're all insane. Leave me; I can take care of myself.'

The villagers held up their hands in defeat. They had done what they could. It lay in Allah's hands now – His, and, apparently, Bibi's. As the women and children made their way on foot towards the hills, and the men hid themselves in the *dhan*, Bibi hobbled around the outdoor courtyard carrying a clay pot full of rice. She washed it, and drained it, and set it on the stove to boil. Then she waited.

Sure enough, the roar of the army jeeps grew closer. They screeched into the village *meydan* and doors slammed as soldiers hopped out, berets set back on their heads, rifles in hand. They fanned out like rats, darting into houses, ransacking the rooms when they realised that the houses were empty. They had been denied their promise of Bengali bodies to use and maim. Furiously, beds were overturned, cupboards smashed, gardens trodden on. Livestock was gunned down; cows and goats lay bleeding in the compounds amid the rifle smoke.

'Hey!' A soldier shouts at his partner, motioning him to come over. 'Look over there!'

Clad only in a dirty white sari, the old hag crouches in the corner of the empty compound. Her hunched back is towards the soldiers and she rocks slowly on her heels, leaning heavily on a stick for support. The soldiers look uncertainly at one another. The woman has given no indication that she knows they are there – perhaps she is deaf, or maybe insane. Either way, she is certainly ancient. But there are no other women around, and orders are orders. One of the soldiers slaps the other on the shoulder.

'Come on,' he says grimly. 'Let's do our job.'

They walk towards the old woman, who is now muttering to herself and stirring the pot before her. The second soldier feels sickened but follows his comrade. They are now only a few feet behind her. The first soldier is already unbuttoning his trousers. He's an expert at this. The second soldier feels as though he might faint. The old witch creaks up, leaning on her stick. In her right hand is the handle of the pot she was stirring. It is bubbling. She turns around to face the soldiers, and at the same moment they realise what is happening. With every last fibre of strength, the woman hurls the contents of the pot at the soldiers' faces. Their howls fill the *uthan* and they sink to their knees, covering their faces with their arms. The woman looks down at them and sniffs, creaking her way back into the house.

It is not long before the soldiers are found by their comrades. Shouts and expletives are followed by angry hissing and the sound of boots marching towards the house. The soldiers find Bibi crouching in the corner of one of the inner rooms. One of them hits her face with the butt of his gun, knocking her backwards. As she lies on the ground, a heavy boot flies into her stomach, and another to her back. As the beatings rain down on her, the sky closes in and Bibi drifts out of consciousness.

The villagers find her huddled in a heap on the floor of her house. Her white sari is torn, covered in red and brown smears. Her eyes are swollen, her arms both broken. The few teeth she had left are now strewn across the floor of the *uthan*. A crowd of women huddle around, keening and wailing, as a villager wipes the blood from Bibi's broken body. A fresh sari is brought to her and she is carefully wrapped in it, before being placed in a bed in a village elder's house. For two weeks, Bibi does not move. Only her eyes are alive, streaming with silent tears. After the two weeks, even her eyes deaden. For the rest of her days, Bibi lies in the bed, unable to speak or respond. When her death finally comes, after six cruel months, the villagers offer grateful thanks to Allah that Bibi is finally at peace. They also pray for divine retribution, for justice for her – their – suffering.

But punishment for the oppressors does not come.

It was late afternoon when the soldiers arrived in their convoy of jeeps – the quiet time when people took their naps indoors, or simply rested in the shade for a couple of hours. Mala and her sisters-in-law were sitting in the shaded part of the *uthan* seeking refuge from the slow, languid heat, when they heard the screech of tyres braking on the dirt road outside the compound. Then the thud of boots and car doors slamming.

It all happened with no regard for any normal flow of time. It felt like years and seconds in the same instant. The rough hands grabbing Mala's sari, the knees in her stomach, the blows to her ribcage as her thighs were prised apart. She knew what was coming next. She forced herself out of her own body and floated above herself, looking down on what was happening. She saw the sweating khaki body heaving on top of her, the women who had run fast enough, who were hiding behind the outhouse building, shaking, praying they wouldn't be discovered. A searing tear between her legs and she came hurtling back down to the dry, rough earth.

Around her she could hear screams and grunts, the sound of flesh beating against flesh. It felt like she was underwater, with sounds muffled and slurring. The heavy blow of a gun handle across her face brought her sharply back to the surface. The sounds were piercing now, wails like sirens filled the *uthan*, and Mala lost consciousness. She remained in the black safety of her empty mind as eventually the soldiers retreated, buttoning up their trousers and fastening their belts as they strolled back to their cars. One or two of them adjusted their cloth berets. Ready to report again for duty. The car doors slammed once more, the screech of tyres: and they were gone.

At first nobody spoke of it. Then, a few weeks later, they found the body of Najma floating in the river behind the old schoolhouse. She was the daughter of a poor family from the next village who worked for Mala's in-laws on the farm and had been helping thresh rice on the day the Pakistani Army came to visit. A prayer was said for her and a swift burial was arranged. It occurred to Mala how thoughtful Najma had been, even in her own suicide, by opting to drown herself in the free-flowing river rather than the stagnant *pukur*, the watering hole for most of the village. But still nobody spoke of what happened: of what had driven Najma to weigh her sari down with rocks and sink herself into the depths of the water. Of what had happened to so many of the women and girls of the village. Silently, they all prayed that the rapes would be the end of it all and that there would be no lasting legacy of the horror. But then Mala had started vomiting daily.

Her in-laws afforded her the dignity of not speaking of the matter. It was the same for so many households, who silently absorbed the children of these unholy and unconsenting unions into the family, for the sake of their mothers if nothing else. And so, protected by the silence of all who knew the truth, the baby in Mala's belly grew under the folds of her sari.

21

EVEN THOUGH THE symptoms were familiar from her first time, Mala was astounded anew by how much the life growing inside her was already dominating her daily existence. It made no pretence of masking its presence, instead making itself known in the most tangible of ways. Through the frequent visits to the small shack at the edge of the *uthan* to relieve herself, or by how tautly the fabric of her blouse now stretched against her engorged breasts, so that she had to unpick and re-stitch the hooks at night to allow a little extra give. Or through the smell of frying onions, that made Mala's head and stomach swim with nausea. One afternoon Shapla found her mother leaning heavily outside the cowshed, a pool of vomit lying on the dusty ground beneath her feet. Mala had not fully explained it to her, but, at thirteen years old, Shapla knew enough to work out that she was soon to have a brother or sister, and that, for some reason, this was a fact not to be freely discussed. Had this happened a few years earlier, Shapla would doubtless have been unable to contain her joy. While her school friends knowingly chattered about their expanding brood of siblings, swapping anecdotes of first steps and protruding teeth, one of Shapla's great sorrows was that she was forced to sit out these discussions, having nothing by way of personal experience to offer. Sure enough, she had many cousins, but as for a sibling of her very own, the possibilities seemed slim. No one had ever made a secret of the fact that her father had gone *bidesh* – quite the opposite, in fact; she held it as a badge of honour that her father was supporting them all from a faraway land that was governed by a Queen who had once, they said, ruled most of the globe. But somewhere along the line, Shapla realised that the absence of any siblings was a direct consequence of her father living abroad. She was puzzled as to how this fact of life had somehow been overruled, without the return of the charming, charismatic father she had heard about, but never met.

Shapla decided to broach the question a few days later with Choto Fufu, who was the closest thing she had to a best friend, and was, by all accounts, the favourite of her father's sisters. She was squatting on a low wooden *khat* while Fufu poured warm mustard oil over Shapla's temples, rubbing it in gently. The smell of *shorisha* always made Shapla relax, the tension in her brain unfurling like little fronds before her aunt's soothing touch even grazed her scalp.

'Fufu?'

'Mmm?' The nimble fingers worked quickly down Shapla's scalp, parting the hair to reveal tracks like tiny silver rivers.

'Where is my Abba?'

'Silly girl, you know where he is.'

The truth was, Shapla didn't. *Lon-don*, she was told. *Eng-land*. Gone to be *ranir mehman*. Guest of the Queen.

'Then how is Amma . . . how are we having a baby?'

Fufu's hands stopped momentarily. 'You know about the baby?' And then she sighed. 'You're a good girl, Shapla. You'll be a help to your ma when she needs it. Allah knows best.'

The conversation was over, Shapla knew, but the platitude was disappointing. She expected more from Fufu. Fufu who was energetic and bold, and who never tried to fob her off – at least not until now – like the others did. Fufu who had refused to let the war interrupt her education, and who was still going to classes at the ladies' college, even though it had been partially occupied as an army base. Wars ended, she said, and when this one did, she would need her HSC certificate as much as anyone. And besides, what else was she going to do – sit around the *uthan* peeling rotten skins off jackfruit seeds with her surfeit of sisters-in-law? Dada feared for his youngest daughter's safety travelling to and from the college every day, having to field checkpoints and bored soldiers. But, he conceded, the sense of restlessness was consuming her. It was good for her to have some kind of outlet, to concentrate on her studies.

In the classroom across the courtyard, Fufu was seething after seeing one of the soldiers spitting into the flowerbeds. The soldier caught Fufu's eye before she turned away in disgust. She carried on walking towards her classroom, clutching her books to her chest almost for protection. *How dare he.* These soldiers were told that they were being deployed to a heathen land of idolaters. A place full of *junglee* women who went bare-breasted under their saris, and effete men who favoured checked loincloths over the civilised *pajama*. If there was any question as to which side was 'civilised', Fufu was confident in the position of her people.

The flowerbeds had been untended since Sonu the gardener had fled with his family across the border in the dead of night. He had left without so much as a farewell to his neighbours, whose grandparents had been neighbours with his own. He had locked up the ancestral home, burying keys to locked trunks in the *uthan*, and taking whatever they could carry with them. The family, along with so many others, had gathered together their belongings in the middle

176

of the night, throwing together practical necessities and family heirlooms in one muddled sweep of belongings. Puja *thalis*, photograph albums, school certificates and clean petticoats tied up together and slung over weary shoulders as they made their way across the border on foot. India had opened up the borders to them, declaring that refugees would not need passports or visas: Hindustan, a welcome refuge. A place where they could feel safe until the madness of war died down, and order was restored.

The intention had always been to come back – no doubt Sonu had believed that his neighbours would guard his property faithfully in his absence. But war brings out an ugliness in everyone. Only a few days later, Fufu had watched with her family across the fields as she saw Sonu's old house being set ablaze, shouts of looters drifting across the distance. Hot tears streamed down her face. She wondered if Sonu's daughter had been able to take her *alonkar* with her – nothing grand, only two gold armbands and a pair of gold hoops – or if they were part of the loot this mob was taking off with. Fufu's father turned his face away as he saw the mob making their way back, laden with spoils. He did not want to recognise those who had pillaged an innocent man's property in his absence, did not want to see their faces in the market place or the masjid the next day and pretend not to know what they had done. This war had turned good people into savages.

Then there was the indignity of being stopped and inter-rogated everywhere you went. The random stops and interrogations had become a feature of everyday life in the area, a sort of daily dose of humiliation, just to remind everyone that this was a war. The nearest large town, Srimangal, had been taken over as a Pakistani military base and all roads in and out were blocked by checkpoints and young, khaki-clad men with rifles slung carelessly against their bodies. From Chittagong in the south-east, to Rajshahi in the north-west, the air was rank with boredom. It emanated from the soldiers who had been promised the glamour of war and were instead landed with the thankless task of administering an occupation.

Going anywhere beyond the town alone was out of the question, but even when Fufu travelled with a brother or her father, they were met with a tirade of questions – always in Urdu – that her father always pretended to find incomprehensible. He would simply turn his eyes, translucent with age, upwards to the heavens, lift his hands helplessly and shake his head, with a plaintive *meh Bangali hoon. I am Bengali.* A statement at once rebellious and starkly truthful. She was always struck by the entitlement of these soldiers, that they could occupy a land and not even bother learning how to communicate with the people. That they even arrived on these shores, expecting that Urdu would be widely understood, let alone spoken, was indication enough of their sheer arrogance. Still, as with any occupying force, they found ways of making themselves understood: detentions without explanation; slow, tedious lines to get through checkpoints; the imposition of curfews; limiting movement in any way. Orders barked, demands for identification cards. *DANDY CARD! NOW!*

The obsessive checking of documentation was a particularly tiresome habit of the soldiers, no doubt born out of their own frustration. There was little else to do, other than standing around in heavy uniforms, day in, day out, in villages and towns that offered nothing by way of entertainment. So the sport was to intercept as many passers-by as possible: *moulanas* on their way to masjid, students returning from college, shopkeepers, elderly women accompanied by their daughters-in-law. What the soldiers did not realise was that this passive-aggressive obsession with 'dandy card' checking provided the Bengalis with an especially delicious act of resistance. People would take dares among themselves to see what they could get away with presenting as a 'dandy card', knowing full well that none of the soldiers were able to read the Bangla script – they could be shown their own death warrant and not have a clue. Library cards, doctors' prescriptions, school report cards, even bus tickets, were earnestly presented to soldiers, all amusement being reserved until they had passed the checkpoint. The 'identity cards' would be scrutinised, squinted over, and then roughly handed back. Childish in any other context perhaps, the charade provided some small amusement for a people whose every other freedom was being eroded, and the vital sense that they had not yet given up the resistance.

22

THE NEWS OF disappearances had been spreading through the shadowy streets of Dhaka in the days leading up to 16 December. There was talk of raids; professors and journalists being pulled from their beds and executed in front of their families. Others being bundled into unmarked vans and driven off into the dead of night. Rounds of gunfire were heard in Rayer Bazar and there were reports of freshly dug mass graves in the brick fields. As the rumours spread, prominent academics went into hiding. Journalists vacated their newspaper offices. Dhaka was eerily still.

Rofikul knew that, like so many others, his life was at risk. In the pitch black of the early morning hours, he had got into a car with two other journalists and driven fifteen miles out of the city. They had pitched up on the outskirts of a small village and slept in a barn for four nights. A local farmer had brought them food and water every day and had asked no questions. He squatted with them as they ate hungrily, listening to the crackling wireless radio they had brought with them. They had all been together when the first news of a ceasefire emerged. Victory has been won, the radio announced. *The war is over.*

They returned to Dhaka the next day. Rofikul spent the following days walking the worn city streets, going from house to house to ask the whereabouts of his colleagues, his former classmates, his professors, anyone he could think of who might have been a target. As he spoke to the grief-stricken families, taking down eyewitness accounts of what they had seen, the full picture began to emerge. It had been increasingly clear that the Indian Army's heavy military backing of the Mukhti Bahini had led to the likely defeat of Pakistan. Pakistan's final act of aggression would be to leave this nascent state on its knees: a whole generation of academics, poets, lawyers, engineers, all taken out in the course of a few bloody nights. In total almost one thousand public figures were reported missing or found dead in the days leading to *Bijoy Dibosh*. Victory Day. It was an intellectual blow from which the newly independent state of Bangladesh could never recover; a parting kiss from Pakistan.

Rofikul felt numb as he collected interviews, carefully noting every last detail. A female journalist was taken from the home she shared with her seven-year-old son. Her mutilated body was later found, with a bayonet through her eye, one through her stomach and two bullets for good measure. A renowned playwright had his fingers severed one by one before being taken away. His body had not been recovered. As Rofikul typed up his articles each night, the numbness that had carried him through each day of walking, interviewing and taking notes gave way to an indescribable ache in his chest. He continued to type, the rhythmic clattering of the keys providing some comfort in the lonely dark that enveloped him.

The blood orb rises above the paddy fields, baptising our new land in a wash of crimson. Rivers course through this fertile country like veins, carrying new life and new hope. After the nine months it took to bring her into existence,

Bangladesh took her first breath on the sixteenth day of December 1971.

Cries ring out, Joy Bangla! Flags are raised across the country. The red disc denotes a new sun stained with the blood of martyrs, and the green background symbolises the land. The golden silhouette of the country sits proudly within the circle completing the first official emblem of this new nation. The new flag will hang in every classroom, in every office, in every public space. Every student will start the day with the words of the national anthem. Amar shonar Bangla, ami tomai bhalobashi. *Bangladesh and her children are risen.*

23

Rofikul had tried to delay the inevitable for as long as possible. He had dutifully informed his family that he was in Bangladesh when he had arrived the year before and had made vague promises to visit once his business in Dhaka was complete. But then war broke out, and Dhaka was the epicentre of all the news stories – there was no way he could leave. The work was never-ending, the stories thrilling, and, besides, it was a relief to have a reason to postpone his visit – and his return to domestic responsibility – a little longer. He assuaged his guilt by wiring money and even sending occasional telegrams.

SALAM. ALL WELL IN DHAKA. NEWS BUSY, LOTS OF WORK. HOPE TO VISIT SOON. R.

Mala saw the telegram unfolded on the bed in her father-in-law's room as she swept the floor that morning. Only one person ever sent telegrams. She read the words, almost exactly the same as the last two messages had been. It was surreal to imagine them being said out loud by the person who was at once so familiar and yet a stranger to her. Her husband. *Rofikul.* A name that had never spilled from her lips, not even when they were alone, lying still under the *moshari* on the *palong.* A woman had no right to call her husband by his first name – who was she, his mother? And yet seeing even his initials in print was enough to bring the colour to her cheeks. This was how he had signed his letters to her, back when there had been letters.

They had petered out slowly – the weekly letters becoming fortnightly, and then ever more sporadic until gradually the slim white envelopes with the red and blue edging stopped arriving altogether. Mala used to keep the stamps, cutting them from the front of the envelopes and keeping them in a small wooden box. She always intended to get a book and paste the stamps into them, but she never got round to it. Instead, she kept them individual and separate, like jewels in their own case. All of the stamps had the Queen's profile on them – a slim, elegant-looking face, with the crown settled atop the low swoop of hair. Occasionally the stamps had emblems for different occasions: a red cross for the national day, a looping dragon, landmarks like the bridge that split in two, each side lifted up like the arm of a machine, flanked by two ancient towers. For a while Mala re-read the letters each week, buoying herself with the belief that more would come when her husband was less busy. Work was going well for him, and there was probably a great deal to do. She overheard this much from conversations between her father-in-law and his friends when they visited. And besides, he was always very regular in sending money to them and ensuring they were all cared for. If that wasn't a sign of his commitment, what was?

And yet, she could not forgive her husband for the complete lack of interest he had showed in their daughter over the years. Yes, he provided for her, with the clear stipulation that a portion of the monthly packet sent over was to be used towards Shapla's schooling. But he had let twelve long years slide by without even setting eyes on his only daughter. She had been born in the weeks after his departure. Mala had been a *notun bou* – a new bride – unable to articulate what she so desperately wanted: for her husband to stay, to delay his departure to England. To be there in the hours after she had given birth, to whisper the *azan* into the delicate shell of her baby's ear. To chew a date softly in his mouth and gently brush a little of the sacred fruit on to the baby's lips with his little finger. To help her choose a name, to wonder together at the life they had just made. But Rofikul was not interested in the same things she was. Mala could already sense his restlessness, his excited impatience at having to wait longer than they had anticipated for his passage to England to be confirmed.

His sponsor voucher – government-issued from the British – had arrived one afternoon in the early months of Mala's pregnancy. She had wept when he arrived home with it, silent tears brushed roughly away with the corner of her sari, but Rofikul had barely noticed. Another opportunity like this would not come by so easily, he told her. She knew that he was right, that this move *bilath* was the best thing for all of them. And so he had left, in a flurry of well-wishes and a pressed new suit, white collars that she had starched herself, handkerchiefs that she had embroidered with his initials in beautiful copperplate. He would write, he told her. Send me photos of our baby. I won't be gone long. Mala smiled through the tears, nodded dutifully, and hung back as her mother-in-law howled at the feet of her departing son. It would be all right, she told herself, lying on the *palong* at night, her hair loose around her, her hand resting on the softness of her belly. But still, over the weeks, the hollowness in the pit of her chest grew more cavernous as her body swelled with life. Eventually that life had been pushed out of her, screaming and red and impossibly perfect, and she had poured all the love she had left into her fatherless baby.

As Mala's eyes raked over the word in the telegram, the pinpricks of a vaguely familiar emotion began to needle her body. She lingered on the letter of his initial. The confident print, unaware of the pain he had caused, so arrogant in black ink against the white paper. It was rage, she realised slowly. A hot, surging rage that came up from the very soles of her feet, and burned like searing irons against her legs, into the pit of her groin, up her chest and looped around her throat like a snake. Tendrils of anger crept up the back of her neck, delving into the mass of black curls she had swept up into a bun, and tightening around her head. Her eyes grew hot. She wanted to scream. Her fists clenched the telegram, crunching one corner of the paper, and then gradually screwed the whole sheet into the ball of her hand.

Let him. Let him come back. Let him see what happened to me.

Any hopes Rofikul had of making a discreet arrival in the village were completely dashed. There was a gaggle of enthusiastic locals crowding the platform when his train pulled in. They jostled against each other, eager to see this returner – one of the earliest conquistadors who had travelled abroad. He saw them from the train carriage, waving eagerly, jostling against the khaki-uniformed soldiers who patrolled the station. Rofikul stiffened at the sight of them; he had grown used to seeing them in Dhaka or in the other towns and cities he had visited over the last several months, but to see them here – on his own home ground – made him sick. So the war had come even as far as here. He was surprised, stupidly so, at the realisation. In some way he had compartmentalised his idea of the war – he knew it was going on in the cities, in other towns, in other villages. He just never really thought that it was happening *here.*

As the rickshaw approached the *bari*, weaving through the fields on a raised, winding road, he could see the newly built boundary wall that surrounded the *uthan.* Good for security, especially in these times. *A few months' wages*, he thought to himself wryly. He did not begrudge his responsibility to support the family – and it did give him a twinge of pride to see how well kept the place looked – but even so, it had come at a cost to his own comfort. Having to house-share with other adult men at his age was an indignity that too many like him had to face back in England. Yet the family here in Bangladesh would have no comprehension of the sacrifices he, and many prodigals like him, made. As the rickshaw-wallah pedalled round the corner, Rofikul could see that the main gates of the *bari* were open, and a crowd had gathered in the courtyard. The rickshaw drew to a halt; Rofikul swung his legs round and leaped from the seat.

His mother stood a little ahead of the others. A few stray grey hairs had escaped the shawl that was draped over her head, but her eyes were as keen as ever, and the hands that clasped Rofikul's face were strong.

Ma!

Rofikul knelt before her, touched her feet, and lifted both his hands to his chest. He repeated this three times and then stood up. *Live a long life,* she whispered. Rofikul turned to his father, and performed the same act of graceful submission, the trio of movements symbolising respect. This had been his final act when he had left them over ten years ago for England, the last time he had seen them. Rofikul rose, Baba's warm hand on his head. Rofikul felt tears in his eyes. He was not expecting this. He looked towards where the rest were standing – his younger brothers, so much taller,

187

but no broader than before. His younger sister – a college girl now, he knew, and wearing a simple green sari, rather than the short colourful dresses he had last seen her in. The women he did not recognise were his sisters-in-law, he presumed. He must have three or four of them by now – he lost count. They were flanked by open-mouthed children with cropped hair, some propping babies on their hips; the infants all had a large black dot drawn on the side of their heads to ward off the evil eye. Rofikul welcomed his brothers' *salams* warmly and nodded politely towards the group of women, who inclined their heads in acknowledgement. There was to be no physicality in their greeting. He ruffled the children's hair at random, not pretending to know their names or to whom they belonged.

Shapla watched the whole scene from the steps of the *pukur*. This strange man in a strange suit the colour of stone was doing all the right things: touching her grandparents' feet, hugging her uncles, patting her cousins' heads. But there was an air of awkwardness to it all, as though these were motions that had somehow been forgotten and were now being performed unrehearsed. Although she knew that this was her father, it was a fact that remained as abstract to her as knowing the height of Mount Everest. *Eight thousand, eight hundred and forty-eight metres.* A fact she learned in school. *This man was her father.* Shapla knew what it was to have a grandfather, or uncles and aunts who ranged on a scale from indulgent to harsh, but while she knew what a father was, she simply could not imagine what having a father would possibly mean to her.

She saw her mother hovering at the edge of the crowd. Mala's sari was draped loosely across one shoulder and brought back over to cover her hair. She clutched the edge of the sky-blue fabric tightly, drawing it around in an attempt to disguise her protruding stomach. Her mouth looked so small, her eyes so big. Shapla wanted to look away – this was not her pain to witness – and yet she found it impossible to tear her eyes from the blue form, making its way to the front of the crowd, ushered along by relatives, countless hands gently pushing from behind. There was a look of confusion and then slow realisation that spread across her father's face as the blue form bowed before him, hands emerging to touch his feet, and then stood up, slowly letting the edge of the sari fall to the dusty earth.

Rofikul felt a vague familiarity in Mala's presence as she approached and knelt before him. His stomach knotted and he closed his eyes as her hands gently pressed the tops of his feet with three rhythmic touches – the first between them in over ten years – and he laid his palms on the top of her head. *Live long. May Allah bless you.* She rose and fixed him with an unashamed gaze. Her expression was hard, unapologetic. *I am here. Where were you?* It startled him. In his memory, Mala was so young, he considered her to be almost vacant; her head stuffed only with old wives' tales, and housework, and a paltry excuse for a primary-level education. It was true that he had dismissed her for the brief duration of their cohabitation as being too naïve, too dull to regard as an equal. And then he had left, and had hardly given her a thought for years. Rofikul's eyes lingered on her face. He wondered why the crowd around them had fallen silent as she stood before him, so still. As the edge of her sari fell to the ground, he realised the terrible thing that he had allowed to happen, simply by being absent.

From her hiding place near the *shupari* trees that flanked the *pukur*, Shapla saw her father raise a hand. Her heart lurched and for a moment she thought he was going to strike her mother, but then the palm came down softly and cupped her mother's cheek. Mala lowered her eyes, and the crowd around them dissolved into hushed mumbles of relief. The public display of tenderness made Shapla feel warm and uncomfortable and inexplicably sad all at once.

As the weeks passed, Rofikul settled back into being in his old home. The domestic familiarity jarred with him at first – the scent of onions and garlic frying in aged iron skillets, and the sound of stone pounding against stone, turning pods of turmeric and whole chillies into piles of yellow and red pastes, all seemed too much – an assault on his senses that had been dulled by England, by Dhaka, by war and sadness. But the slow rhythm of village life kept time as it always had, beating along to barefoot steps in the dusty earth, punctuated by the *azan* that sounded five times a day from the whitewashed masjid. He woke every morning to the sound of water lapping the steps of the *pukur*, and noted the onset of dusk by the earthy, wholesome smell of cows as they returned to their shed from a day of grazing in the sparse fields. Slowly, somehow, Rofikul felt himself returning, as though part of his own being were being poured back into his tired, worn body.

The warmth of Mala's body was part of this restoration. He had not expected, on his first night back in the *bari*, that she would come to him. He had been lying on the *palong*, in the dimly lit room that had once been his, when he saw Mala's figure hover tentatively at the door. As he rose, she had crossed the threshold, and softly closed the door behind her. She had lain still as he moved over her, and although she felt like a stranger, Rofikul could not bring himself to stop. When he had finished she had turned over, drawing the covers to her chest, and slept. He did not expect her to return the next evening, having already performed her duties the night before, but Mala arrived at the threshold once again, still hesitant and tired and beautiful. Afterwards, he had reached around her from behind and placed his hands on her swollen belly, and her shoulders trembled, and he held her as his own silent tears fell on to her hair. Each night she returned, and with each wordless rediscovery they became a little less like strangers.

Rofikul was pleased when he realised that the growing ease between them was not just reserved for the evenings but was entering their everyday interactions. It warmed him when he caught Mala's gaze as she served him rice at meal-times, under the watchful eye of his mother or his sisters-in-law. Even watching her from across the *uthan* while she performed her daily chores – sorting out grit from lentils, or swirling rice in water and pouring away the milky waste – made him yearn to go over to her and touch her softness, lay his head on her chest and be held. He wondered how Mala felt, whether she found as much solace in his company as he did in hers. And for the first time since he had married her, he found himself caring about what she thought.

Shapla watched her parents with a detached interest. After the initial awkward *salam* when she had eventually been seized from her hiding place by one of her uncles, presented in front of the strange man and instructed to touch his feet, she had refused to go near her father despite the coaxes and threats of her aunts and grandmother. When Mala tried to persuade her by giving her cups of tea to deliver to him, Shapla would take the cup and saucer without argument, and pass the task on to whichever younger cousin happened to be walking by at the time. She felt uncomfortable in his presence: he was always staring at her, searching her face for something that she felt she could not give him, and it made her feel somehow inadequate. And it needled her that this man who had been nothing to them all these years was suddenly able to stride right back into their lives and command their attention, make demands on them, disrupt the routine that had evolved in the years he had been away. It seemed to Shapla, who had always enjoyed an unchallenged monopoly over her mother's attention, that she was increasingly being edged out. It was *his* room that her mother slept in. It was *his* favourite foods that her mother spent hours preparing. The choicest fruits were prepared and sent up to him, rather than being shared among the children of the *bari*. Usually her father would call and invite all the other children to join him, passing around the mustard oil to smear on their faces before diving in, so that the sticky sweet juice from the *katal* would not stick to their skin. But this generosity did not absolve him in Shapla's eyes. Her cousins loved him, revelled in the attentions of this exciting new uncle who had travelled abroad, even *lived* there. But they did not know what she knew: what a fraud, what a liar, her father was.

It had happened one Friday afternoon. Her mother had instructed her to put away a pile of her father's clean, folded clothes, and Shapla had acquiesced only because she knew her father was at Friday prayer with all the other men and would not be back for at least an hour or two. She stepped into the bedroom, feeling his unfamiliar presence in the objects he had left strewn around the room. The bed was in the middle of the room, the white *moshari* looped up over the top of the four posts. Pressed against one wall was a heavy wooden desk and a chair pulled up against it, her father's jacket that he had brought with him from England draped over the back. Against the other wall were a wooden dresser and a tall steel *almari* with a stern-looking lock. Shapla deftly put away the folded clothes, the chequered *lungis* in the dresser, and the white cotton vests next to them. She pushed the handle down on the *almari* door, which swung open, and she hung up the pressed formal shirt that was reserved for special outings.

Her task completed, Shapla moved towards the desk and chair, and pulled off the soft woollen blazer. She slipped her thin arms into the sleeves, and fastened the smooth, round buttons. It hung down to somewhere between her knees and the tops of her legs. She was drowned in it. Her hands slid into the cool, silk-lined pockets. They were empty save for a packet of cigarettes. Shapla sat in the chair and leaned back. She imagined what it was to be her father, writing important articles on sheets of thin white paper that were stacked in one corner of the desk next to the ink blotter. Idly, she tugged on the knob that dangled under the desk, and to her surprise the drawer gave way quite easily. In it was a black leather-bound diary, with the year '1963' embossed in gold on the front cover. Without hesitation, Shapla opened it. The pages felt thicker than the paper she was used to, and the dates were all printed in English. Her father's slanted handwriting crossed the page, also in English. She could make out the odd word, mainly places she had already heard of: on this page she spotted 'London'; on the next 'Manchester'. She flipped through the pages carelessly, not reading but wanting to feel the paper against her hands. As she got to the end, she noticed a small black and white photograph wedged in the back cover flap. She gently pulled it out, placed it on the desk, and surveyed it carefully. It was of a woman standing outside somewhere – it looked like a house. She was pale, so pale – with light-coloured eyes and hair that was swept back in a messy kind of bun, a few stray tendrils framing her face. Her body was facing away from the camera, but her face was turned back, and she was smiling over her shoulder at the camera. It was not a posed photograph – it seemed as though the photographer had caught the woman off guard – and yet she was smiling at whoever that person was with an expression that seemed vaguely familiar.

The photograph had clearly been carefully preserved – the edges were still smooth and unfrayed. She thought of the one black and white studio photograph that her grandmother had of her father. The paper had worn to an almost cloth-like softness from the constant wearing and showing to visitors, guests, anybody who paid any interest, and, often, those who did not. This photograph had not been shown to anyone. It was for one person only.

Shapla stood up and carefully placed the photograph in the waistband of her salwar. She returned the diary to the drawer, slipped the blazer from her shoulders, and draped it over the back of the chair. The corners of the hidden photograph grazed her skin, a sort of delicious secret. As she pulled the door closed behind her, Shapla remembered where else she had seen the same expression as the woman in the photograph – that tentative wonderment, mixed with happiness and a fear that that joy might dissipate at any moment. It was the same way her mother looked at her father.

Mala knelt on the rug that she rolled out every morning, before there was enough light to tell a white thread and a dark thread apart, as the religion instructed. It was in this brief window of time before sunrise that Mala was able to exist without any attachments, before her duties as daughter-in-law, and mother, and wife of the house began, to be alone with her thoughts. Her morning devotions had taken on a stronger, more urgent character of late. The weeks had drifted seamlessly into months, and with the seasons her body had also changed. She could feel motions inside her, tiny kicks that demanded to be recognised as the life that she had brought into being. She alone. She did not allow herself to remember the pain and humiliation and wishes for her own death that had surrounded the conception. Instead, she told herself she was like Maryam, the virgin mother of the Prophet Isa, who bore a child only through the grace of God. Mala's unborn child would have needed no father, because she would be his everything, and together they would have the mercy and protection of Allah.

By the morning hours, and by the night when it is still; your Lord has not forsaken you, nor is He displeased.
And surely what comes after is better for you than that which has gone before.
And surely your Lord will give you that which will make you well pleased.

Her prayers did not go unheard. The protection she asked for, day after day, was granted in a way she had never imagined. Her husband had returned to her. He had embraced her and her body, knowing what grew within it, and had promised that he would never leave her again. For the first time in months, Mala felt safe. And for the first time in years, Mala felt happy. She turned her palms flat and raised them up, as if to receive heaven's blessing directly.

Ya Allah, You did not forsake me. You did not forsake my children. You led him back to us. You gave us that which has made us pleased. All praise is to you.

Ameen. Ameen. Ameen.

24

WHEN SHAPLA STOLE the photograph, she had had no plan. All she knew was that she did not want her father to have this token of a life that had taken him away from her, from her mother, for all these years. She hid the photograph in a small tin box that she had been given as a gift years ago. It had a painted geometric pattern that was scuffed with age and enthusiastic wear, and contained her most precious items: some beads, an old lipstick that she had rescued from Fufu's cast-offs, a cut-out picture of Meena Kumari looking doleful and seductive, and a fountain pen that had once been her grandfather's. The tin box lived underneath her pillow. For weeks, she watched her father carefully, waiting for him to notice the absence of the photograph. But no such discovery appeared to have been made – there was no outburst, no accusation, no interrogation as to who had been in his room or touching his belongings. In fact, he seemed increasingly at home as the weeks passed into months.

He took a constitutional every morning through the paddy fields and along the banks of the river. Often, he would pass Shapla and ask her to join him, and she would always respond with a shake of her lowered head and a mumbled excuse of some chore she had to perform or a demand from some family member she had to attend to. Her father would then nod understandingly, sigh and stride off, and each time something in Shapla's chest would lurch as she saw his retreating back. When he returned in the early afternoon, he would sit at the very same desk day after day and write, typing letters and reports and articles that he wired to far-off places, to be printed in foreign newspapers, read in distant offices by distant people. He would drink the tea that Mala brought him, and occasionally persuade her to lie down with him for an afternoon nap, to which she would acquiesce if her work was done and nobody else was around. The list of chores and duties and other people to care for – Shapla included – would disappear as Mala stepped into the room, pulling the door shut behind her. And the diary of 1963 lay untouched in the bottom drawer, the photograph unmissed.

It could so easily have been an innocent mistake. In the months that followed, and beyond, Shapla repeated the half-truth to herself over and over, willing it to become whole. She could have forgotten that she had the photograph hidden in the small tin box when she had asked her mother to guard it for her one evening. Rabia's big sister was getting married and, as Shapla's best friend, Rabia had invited Shapla to stay over on the night before the celebration. Together they would stay up late, devouring *mishti*, and wondering secretly what their husbands would be like when their time came. It was a rite of passage, witnessing an older sister's wedding, and as Shapla had none of her own, she was more than delighted to be invited to take part in the colourful rituals.

'Do you think no one has anything better to do than to guard your little treasure chest?' Mala had feigned exasperation but extended her arm to receive the little box that Shapla was holding. 'I'm joking, darling. I promise to guard it with my life,' she added solemnly, seeing her daughter's crestfallen face. Shapla had handed over the box carefully. She had given no instructions not to pry inside it – partly because it would almost certainly have been an invitation to her mother to do just that but also, as she told herself several times over, because she had no idea it could have such dreadful consequences.

The evening had been everything she had hoped it would be: they had gorged on sweets and pastries, talked, told jokes and stayed up late swapping stories about weddings – romantic and horrific alike. Along with the other girls, Shapla shuddered in gruesome delight as she heard the retelling of the story of a girl married off to a man in a distant village who had a glass eye that he took out at night and tucked underneath his pillow. She had swooned at the great romantic tale of a cousin of Rabia's who had been fixed up with a man she did not want to marry and was saved only because a distant cousin, who also happened to be the love of her life, interrupted the ceremony to declare his affections for her, much to the scandal of both sets of parents, and to the delight of all the wedding guests. By the time the sun was edging its way into the sky, the girls had finally dropped off, lying horizontally across Rabia's grandmother's ancient *palong*, covered with thin blankets.

Shapla arrived home next day brimming with stories to tell anyone who would listen. It was late afternoon and the *bari* was quiet; everyone had gone to lie down to escape the heat and, save for a few of her cousins playing in the *uthan* outside, Shapla could see nobody around. She made her way to her mother's room, eager to regale her with amusing tales of how nervous the groom seemed, how Rabia's deaf grand-mother had audibly bellowed that 'he wasn't a looker but he'd do' and to sigh over how beautiful the bride had looked all decked in *kumkum* and gold. She found Mala lying in the bed, the *moshari* looped up over it.

'Ma . . .?'

Mala lay still, almost too still to be asleep. Shapla crept closer and sat down gently on the edge of the bed.

'Ma? Are you awake?'

Mala spoke without stirring. 'I'm here, darling. I'm just resting.'

Shapla sat for a moment or two waiting to see if her mother would say anything else, but Mala returned to her silence. Shapla stood quietly and made her way to the door. On the dresser by the door she saw her small tin box and her heart began to race. She picked it up quietly and made her way out to the *uthan*. Hesitantly she opened her box. She counted through her possessions: here were her beads, the old lipstick, the picture cut-outs of actresses, the inkless fountain pen. Frantically, Shapla tipped the box and all its contents straight on to the dusty earth – she rummaged through the beads and the picture clippings, but it was not there. The photograph she had taken from her father's diary – the woman with the light skin – was gone.

In the days that followed, Shapla felt as though she were continuously holding her breath, waiting for something – she did not know exactly what – to come crashing down. But life continued as usual: her father seemed unchanged, still chatty and vivacious when he was not wrapped up in his writing. Her mother seemed a little subdued but it was hard to detect much of a difference. Even before the night of the wedding sleepover, Mala had been growing more tired and less talkative as she grew closer to giving birth. Her aunts and grandmother whispered that it could be any day now, and Shapla had no idea whether her current quietness had anything to do with the photograph or because her mother was simply weary at the end of her pregnancy.

It happened in the early hours of the Friday morning about a week later. Shapla, who had taken to sleeping with Fufu while her mother grew larger and less comfortable over the last few days, woke to cries coming from her mother's room. The low keening reminded Shapla of the sounds the cows made as they came in from the fields at night. At first she thought the moans came from her mother, but as she listened more carefully she realised that the sounds were from more than one person. Shapla got up and walked out of the bedroom. Fufu was standing outside, red-eyed. Her father was sitting beside Fufu, his head buried in his trembling hands. Inside the room Shapla could make out the moans of her grandmother and other aunts. Frantically Shapla gripped Fufu's hand.

'Is it all right? The baby, is the baby—'

Fufu nodded, tears streaming down her face. 'It's not the baby. It's your ma, Shapla. *Ya Allah.* She's gone.'

For weeks afterwards, Shapla would not let anyone come near her baby brother. Neighbours began to repeat the story: of how Mala's daughter Shapla – not yet even thirteen – had walked into the bedroom, picked up the crying baby from the crib beside where her dead mother lay, and taken him away with her. So the story went, the girl did not shed a single tear. The mother had lost too much blood; had barely had a chance to hold her newborn son before she slipped away. They had asked her what to name him, but she was too weak to answer. The father – was it right to call him that? Well, anyway, the father was beside himself, they said. Tears, actual tears, and rage, and he had refused all food for days after.

If Shapla heard any of these anecdotes, she ignored them. Her time was taken up with bathing, changing and soothing her baby brother. If she could have nursed him, she swore she would have done that too, but that task had to be left to a woman who came to work in the *bari* and had children of her own. At night Shapla stayed up, keeping vigil over her brother as he slept beside her in their mother's bed. She ran her hand lightly over the soft fuzz of his hair, and prayed that the evil eye, the curse unleashed by the photograph of that light-skinned woman, would not take away her brother as it had her mother. It had all been her fault: she did not know how, and it did not make sense, but somehow, Shapla believed that this – the loss, the pain – could all be traced back to the woman in the photograph and her father.

Shapla was ever more protective of her brother on realising that she was all he had in this world. He had no other blood relative to speak of. His very existence in Shapla's ancestral home was a favour granted by her grandparents and her father. Her brother had no claim over this family, this land, this home; only on her. Shapla belonged to him, and he to Shapla. They were all the family they needed.

Part III

1974–1980

25

FOR THE MOST part Helen did not think about the past. She had no reason to – memories were only ever painful, whether they were about her father, or her sisters, or the father of her son. She had learned long ago, well before Rofikul entered and then subsequently left her life, not to look back. She knew that when she packed her bags to leave the Merseyside docks for the sprawling promise of Manchester. She had known that when Aileen had traded in Helen's deepest confidences in the futile effort to win approval from their mother. And she had known it when Rofikul failed to appear at the hospital as she lay waiting in the bed, exhausted and in pain, their tiny son in the cot beside her. Helen was good at not looking back. She knew it didn't amount to anything of worth.

Adam was all that mattered. At almost ten years old he was growing up so fast that Helen barely recognised him from the baby she had cuddled and soothed all night in that empty flat, her heart nowhere closer to healing. His perfect chubby knees and arms, the ones she used to cover with kisses, were bony now and scarred from playing outside and falling over. She had cried the first time she saw him dressed in his little school uniform, with a grey jumper and striped navy blue tie. Hashim had taken a photograph of them both standing by the front door, hand in hand, Adam's face almost all grin, and Helen's eyes both steely and soft. Munira had framed the photograph and given it to Helen for her living room mantelpiece. She and Hashim had kept a copy, too, which stood proudly on their bookshelf. It was sandwiched between a photograph of Adam as a baby, and one of Munira holding a two-year-old Adam outside the shop. It had been taken in summer, just after England had beaten the Germans to bring home the World Cup. In it, the sign *Hashim & Family* was decked out in patriotic bunting, and Munira was squinting at the camera with Adam in her arms, her gold nose-stud catching the light. Helen knew that Munira had been pregnant when the photograph was taken, but the baby, like so many others, had been lost only a few weeks after Hashim had taken the photograph. In the picture, the ghost baby nestles comfortably in Munira's belly, its kicks possibly causing the faint smile on her lips.

Helen had been managing perfectly well looking forward and never backward, until one morning, four years ago, when a stack of newspapers had landed on the shop counter. Some of the regular Bengali customers had been asking Hashim to stock this new paper – a Bengali-language newspaper that was printed and edited in London. Helen had known nothing of it, until Munira had gently informed her that this successful new newspaper was Rofikul's endeavour. That *this* was what, apparently, he had left her and Adam to go off and pursue. Helen remembered how she had gathered up the bundles and thrown the pile of newsprint out into the street, declaring to the onlookers and to Hashim as he stood behind the counter that it was never to be brought into the shop as long as she was there. And Munira and Hashim had respected her wishes. *Ekushey* never crossed the threshold of their shop, despite their customers' requests. Instead, the Pakistani-owned corner shop two streets away profited from stocking the newspaper, and Hashim's customers found themselves seeking updates about the war back home to the financial benefit of old man Zia and sons, not recognising the irony of the whole situation.

Since that day, despite her vehemence at the time, Helen sometimes went alone to the local library to find the newspaper. She recognised it by the English lettering underneath the Bengali script. The date and edition were also printed in English. Everything else was in that familiar-unfamiliar script; beautiful and swirly and unintelligible. She always flipped to the pages where Rofikul's updates were, his blurry black and white photograph just next to his byline. She had no idea what the columns said: she could not read the words but sometimes photographs accompanied the article from which she could guess the topic; occasionally they were of the Prime Minister, before he went into exile, but usually they were horrifying yet generic-seeming scenes of war. Men with sinewy bodies and loincloths brandishing guns. Twisted corpses, all bones and loose skin, lying by the side of the road. Skeletons of houses that had been looted and razed to the ground. It made her sick that Rofikul was living there among all that. Despite everything, she wanted him to be safe.

Today was Adam's tenth birthday: 10 June 1974. Ten years of life for her healthy, loving boy who was kind to everyone he met and had a gentleness that he seemed to have inherited from his Uncle Hashim. Maybe it was true that nurture counted for more than nature. When Adam was younger he had shown little interest in the absent figure of his father; Helen remembered overhearing him in the playground after school telling a friend that he did have a dad and his name was Uncle Hashim. After that, Helen had made a concerted effort to integrate Rofikul more into Adam's life, by mention at least, if not in great amounts of detail. Thankfully, Adam had not seemed particularly concerned and had listened more out of politeness than interest when Hashim, having been given the go-ahead by Helen, regaled Adam with tales about Rofikul, their childhood summers spent playing together outside and their early arrival in Britain. It could be, Munira suggested to Helen, that Adam had not yet understood the biological definition of what a father was, and if he was unbothered by it then that was reason enough to leave him be. *He'll ask more when he wants to know more*, Munira assured her. And so Rofikul was dropped from the curriculum of Adam's life for several years until recently, when he had started to ask Helen more questions about his father: who he was, where he lived, what he was like. Helen always tried to answer her son's questions as fairly and as matter-of-factly as possible, but more often than not she found herself deferring to Hashim to answer certain questions. His memory of Rofikul was fresher somehow, less tarnished by the betrayal of abandonment. Hashim seemed to remember details of specific conversations they had had, Rofikul's likes and dislikes, how he had been when they were children. It occurred to Helen sometimes when she overheard these anecdotes that really she had hardly known Rofikul at all.

For his birthday, Adam had asked for his favourite dinner: Aunty Munira's *aloo*-chicken curry and a chocolate cake from Martin's Bakery. When Uncle Hashim had asked him what he would like for a gift, Helen had been taken aback by Adam's shyly delivered answer: a typewriter, because he wanted to be a writer like his baba. *How do you know your baba writes?* Helen had asked. Adam looked back at her in wide, unblinking certainty. *Uncle Hashim told me*, he replied. *He writes for a newspaper. But I can't read his stories because I can't read Bangla.* Helen had nodded. *You and me both,* she thought. Anyway, of course it made sense for Hashim to share these details about the boy's father with him. Later, Hashim had asked Helen whether she was comfortable with Munira and him giving Adam a typewriter. Helen had been overly dismissive. *Of course not, why would I mind?* Although she urged Hashim not to splash out on anything fancy; a second- or third-hand machine would more than suffice for a ten-year-old's attempts at the Pulitzer Prize.

Hashim had therefore come home a few days earlier with a 1969 Hermes Rocket tucked under his arm. Munira had wrapped it up in bright coloured paper and now it stood on the kitchen table, next to a stack of Hardy Boys mystery books, a gift from Helen, ready for Adam when he tumbled in through the front door after school. With his birthday being in June Adam was always one of the youngest in his class. Helen wondered sometimes if it would have helped his confidence had he been a little bit older in the school year. But these things weren't worth fretting about.

A quick rap at the door interrupted Helen's musings. Munira pushed the door open before waiting for an answer, and backed into the flat pulling a buggy behind her.

'Oh my God, it's roasting out there.' Munira swung the pushchair around, manoeuvred it into a corner of the little flat, and clicked the red pedal brake on with her foot. She leaned into the buggy, clicked the straps off and lifted out the sleeping toddler. Helen went over, arms outstretched, to take her niece.

'There's some water out.' Helen nodded to the jug on the table, gently rocking the baby at the same time. 'And how is my little Joy?'

'Being a pain.' Munira rolled her eyes and poured a tall glass of water. 'Can't sleep, won't sleep, running around; in the end I just had to strap her into the pushchair to get her over here, even though she wanted to walk, and only then did she deign to drop off.'

Munira gazed down at her sleeping baby, the mop of dark hair escaping the headband she had carefully put on, and felt herself soften. She could never stay irritated with her Joy, her miracle baby. They thought it was never going to happen, them being married all this time and nothing to show for it. Hashim had been upset when she had said that to him. *Munira. How can you say we have nothing to show for it? We have so much.* Munira had nodded but she knew, and he knew, that she wanted – needed – more. She had all but given up trying; she was sick of marking calendars, taking vitamins, doing exercises that all seemed pointless – and then, by some gift, they had conceived Joy, and Joy had tenaciously clung on until it was time to bring her into the world.

'It's probably the heat.' Helen kissed her niece's head, the tiny fronds of hair stuck to her forehead. 'Makes everyone go a bit funny, doesn't it?'

'Can't wait for it to turn a civilised temperature,' Munira huffed.

Helen suppressed a smile. Munira had become more British than the British in the time that they had known each other. It was always too hot, or too wet, or too cold, or too sunny – if adopting a national cliché was a part of naturalisation, then Munira had surely taken Gold Medal for Britishness. Helen went into the bedroom to put Joy down, covering her with only a light sheet. When she returned to the living room, Munira had poured herself a second glass of water and was fanning herself with a folded-up *Woman's Own*.

'They shouldn't be too much longer.' Helen glanced at the clock. 'Hashim said he'd collect Adam straight after work.'

'It's all right – gives us a chance to catch up.' Munira was eyeing the bowl of chopped watermelon that stood on the table. 'Thanks,' Munira said, taking the fork Helen handed her. 'Honestly, it feels like I never have any time these days. If it's not the shop, it's the baby, if it's not the baby, it's Hashim.'

'Oh, come on now, you're being unfair.' Helen smiled. 'Hashim is hardly a complainer.'

Munira shrugged reluctantly. 'I'm not saying he complains, I'm saying he's just one more thing I have to think of when I can't even hear myself think.' She stabbed a piece of melon dejectedly. 'Anyway, I just miss you, that's all. I feel like we never talk these days.'

Helen nodded. 'Oh, love. I see you almost every day still, don't I? But it isn't the same, I know. It's hard having someone so tiny demand so much of your time, who can't even talk back or give you much.' She leaned over to squeeze Munira's arm. 'But we're doing all right. We managed to get Adam to a decade between us all, didn't we?'

'He's all right, that one,' Munira agreed. 'Maybe if Joy slept like Adam did, I'd feel a bit more sane.'

'She'll get there, just give her some time.'

A key shifted in the front door lock and the sound of Hashim's heavy tread in the hallway, followed by Adam's patter, alerted Helen and Munira to take their places behind the table. As Adam burst into the room, Helen and Munira yelled, 'SURPRISE!' and pulled the little cotton threads on the plastic cones, showering Adam with bits of coloured paper and wafts of smoke. His face beamed with pleasure as they all broke into a chorus of singing, heralding the happy completion of Adam's first decade.

Later that evening, as Hashim washed the dishes in the kitchen, Munira and Helen sat on the sofa, having put the little ones to bed. The party had been a success. Adam had insisted on cutting his cake first, although he agreed to save eating it until after the *aloo* chicken feast, and Joy had clapped delightedly while Adam tore the shreds of paper off his gifts, revealing his long-coveted typewriter. Hashim had flushed with pride as Adam flung his arms around his uncle's thickening waist, declaring it the best present ever. Helen had shown him how to install the ink ribbon and feed paper into the machine, and how to slide the carriage along when he had finished typing a line. His first, slightly oddly spaced typewritten page had read:

I am Adam Ahmed Doherty To day I am tenyears old.
I h ave the best fam ily inthe uni verse.

*

'Helen?' Munira put down her magazine and turned to face her friend. 'Does it bother you at all? That Adam wants to, you know, write . . . like his father?'

'What?' Helen looked up, her reading glasses perched halfway down her nose. 'Does it bother me that he's a ten-year-old kid who has decided he wants to write stories? Or that writing is something his dad does? Are you asking me if it bothers me that he might turn out to be like his father?'

'Of course that's not what I'm saying – I mean, he's totally different.'

'Not totally. Different in some ways, yes. But I suppose – well, it's natural, isn't it? That they might have some similarities?'

'Well, of course it is. I just mean – well, you seem awfully sensible about it.' Munira's stress on the word 'sensible' betrayed what she was not saying.

'Is that a bad thing?'

'No, not at all, I just . . . Well. If you ever do want to be irrational, or unreasonable, that isn't a bad thing either, you know.'

'I'll bear that in mind – thank you. But you needn't worry.' Helen slipped her glasses back up her nose and continued with her book, leaving Munira no choice but to turn back to her magazine. As her eyes flickered over the words, not taking any of them in, Munira's mind lingered on the conversation they had just had. Helen was always so terrifyingly *calm* about these things. So measured. She didn't seem to allow even a glimmer of rage or hurt or any other kind of plausible emotion to enter conversations about Rofikul, and his hitherto absent role in Adam's life, or Adam's newfound interest in him. Maybe it was a coping mechanism, a ruse that she and Hashim bought far too easily. But whenever either of them broached the subject of Rofikul as anything less than an abstraction, they were met with utter detachment from Helen. It wasn't natural, thought Munira. It surely had to come to a head at some point. She folded the magazine and put it down on the coffee table. She dreaded that moment, whenever it might be.

26

THE STUFFY HEAT and tinkling ice-cream vans of the summer had given way to autumn, with its gold and russet leaves and chilled air, and then came the steady march into the snow-clad, brightly lit festivities of winter. Hashim never tired of the seasons in this land. How much the landscape altered in just a few weeks, the scenery changing colour before his very eyes. And with the seasons came the inevitable changes in activity: summer had been filled with the usual hard work at the shop, ensuring the deep freeze was filled with brightly coloured ice lollies for the school kids on their holidays, and taking Adam to the swimming baths whenever Hashim had enough time off work. Autumn brought with it dying leaves and new beginnings: Adam was in a new class at school and Joy was at nursery one or two mornings a week. Then the boiler had packed up in the flat above the shop, so they had to get that fixed. And before they knew it, they found themselves already in the earliest days of winter, no snow yet on the ground, but a decided nip in the air and frost on the inside of the window panes every morning.

More importantly, it was the season to celebrate the anniversary of another birth. They marked it the way they always had, with a cake and party hats, and cards with lovingly wrapped gifts and food, and their small, but closely knit circle of friends in attendance: Vincent and Marie, of course, as well as Hashim, Munira, Helen and Adam. Hashim remembered the birth as though it was yesterday, and not three years ago to the day.

'Bhaiya!' Helen had waved down the hospital corridor at Hashim. 'There's someone you need to meet.'

Hashim had whirled around, empty Styrofoam coffee cup still in hand, and searched Helen's face for clues. 'A girl? Boy? How's Munira?'

He had been engaged in the proverbial pacing for almost twenty-four hours, treading the length of the maternity ward corridor. Other expectant fathers had come, paced, offered him cigarettes, bought their wives flowers from the hospital gift shop, collected their newborns and gone in that time. Hashim had been going slowly mad with worry; the nurses would tell him nothing, Helen was in the delivery room with Munira, and he had had nobody to distract him from his increasingly dramatic thoughts of what might be going wrong at that very moment with Munira while he was uselessly traversing the hospital waiting room. It was at moments like this that Hashim especially missed his cousin. Rofikul would have been able to provide the requisite combination of light relief, comfort and distraction needed at such times.

'She's fine, and so is the baby – but she's asking for you.' Smiling, Helen gently led Hashim to the small curtained cubicle Munira had now been moved to. It had been a difficult birth – unsurprising given the many complications that Munira had endured so patiently during pregnancy. They were just grateful that this baby had clung on, and not slipped away before its time like the previous unborn children. Munira had been prescribed complete bed rest for her final two months, which had driven her to the brink with restlessness, but Helen and Hashim had been firm in enforcing the edict and had managed to keep the shop running between them. The midwives had been sparing with their details but from the snippets Hashim had been able to catch from their exchanges, Munira had lost a lot of blood and had to have transfusions: the word alone terrified Hashim. If anything had happened to Munira he would not have been able to carry on living. Tentatively Hashim drew back the curtain, and his eyes fell on his wife – pale, tired-looking, but smiling. How tiny she looked – his strong, vivacious Munira – lying among the pillows. She smiled up at him and pointed to the small plastic tray on wheels beside her.

'Look who wants to meet her abbu.'

'Her?' Hashim looked into the tray on wheels and saw a bundle of wool topped with a cotton hat. Amid the folds of white, he discerned a tiny face that he promptly fell in deep and unending love with.

'*Alhamdulillah.*' Hashim's eyes grew hot and full, and he let the tears fall down his face as he picked up his daughter and cradled her close. He buried his nose in the soft blanket, drinking in the smell for fear it might end.

'I was thinking we could call her Joy.' Munira spoke softly as though her words might blow away the scene before her.

'Joy is perfect. She is perfect.'

In that moment the whole of Hashim's life seemed suddenly to make sense. It was true, then, that God had a plan. There was a reason he had married Munira, only to have to leave her after a few months, and move to England alone. There was a reason he had endured years of monotonous, relentless factory work, a reason why Allah had blessed him with the means to own his own business. And, as much as the thought was painful – and he could never share this with Munira – maybe there was a reason why they had been burdened with so many losses before the safe delivery of their daughter. It had all been in preparation for this – the raw appreciation of what it meant to be blessed. It *was* all for a reason: Hashim had always trusted in this idea, but it never rang true until that December day in the maternity ward of St Mary's Hospital when he found himself holding the whole of his and Munira's future in his arms. He knew then that this was where home would always be.

'We were going to go back after five years, do you remember?' He smiled at Munira.

'Plans change,' she replied, kissing the top of Joy's head.

Her name was as apt as any could be. Joy. In Bangla, it meant Victory. She had been born on the same day as Bangladesh. The sixteenth day of the last month of the year, 1971. After over seventeen hours of labour, she had emerged victorious from Munira's womb, purple-faced and irate, and loved more than any other child who had ever been born. Her very existence was a victory for Munira and Hashim, a balm upon the decade of lost babies and lost hopes. Munira said her name would work in both languages, with both meanings, and it was true, thought Hashim as he cradled his daughter, feeding her with one of the bottles that Munira boiled and sterilised several times a day. He felt such joy when he looked into that tiny face and saw her big, dark eyes staring back in that slightly unfocused newborn way. He found joy in each tiny breath that swelled her rounded stomach as she lay sleeping. He found joy in how her fingers curled around his, each nail perfectly formed and surprisingly scratchy.

This was not the first time Hashim had fallen in love with a child, but it was different this time. With Adam there had been the sense of responsibility, of having to compensate for Rofikul's absence, of stepping into the breach. His enjoyment of helping to raise Adam was always tinged with the recognition that he was performing someone else's role, and while he loved Adam beyond measure, Hashim was, at the end of the day, the boy's uncle – not his father. With Joy, there was no sense of having to make up for anyone else's absence. His whole purpose was to love and tend to her, and he did, so diligently and carefully that even Munira was astonished at the new side to her husband.

'He's just smitten,' she had remarked to Helen one afternoon while Hashim was napping upstairs with the baby. 'He's always been wonderful with kids, you know, you see how he is with Adam, but this is—'

'It's daddies and their daughters, Munira.' Helen smiled. 'Or so they tell me. Maybe when your daddy isn't an alcoholic, he might actually be an all right person to have around. I never knew myself . . .' She threw a faux solemn glance at Munira and then laughed.

Munira smiled back, but Helen's comment made her a little uncomfortable. They had spoken about their childhoods before; Helen had been remarkably matter-of-fact when describing the situation in which she had grown up, and how she had left home as a teenager and had not seen her family again until her father's funeral. It was about as far removed as Munira could imagine from her own loving, protective family, where she was treasured as the sheltered only daughter; spoiled even. It disturbed Munira that Helen had grown up amid so much routine violence. Privately, she wondered if this was how Helen had been able to cope with Rofikul's abandonment. Helen had, after all, endured situations that were far more traumatic in some ways, although probably not as painful – at least not in the same way. Munira wanted to ask Helen whether growing up with such a father had somehow influenced how she was raising

Adam with such gentleness. But although the questions sat heavily on her tongue, she could not quite find the right way to ask them.

Once again, as they had with Adam, Hashim, Munira and Helen watched over Joy with such care and amusement at all her actions, it was as though she were the only baby ever to have been born. Except, this time, a fourth devotee was added to their number: Adam himself, the former most-worshipped baby. He spent hours holding Joy when she was too small to do anything else, and when she began to smile and laugh, Joy always reserved her biggest and loudest laughs for Adam. When she started crawling, it was Adam who laid blankets out on the floor, ensuring the corners of tables and bookcases were padded so that she wouldn't hurt herself, and sat with her dutifully fetching and carrying whatever toys or books she wanted to play with.

Watching the two of them, Hashim was reminded of his own cousin, and the bond they had shared since boyhood. It hurt to accept that the two had had no contact since even before Rofikul had returned to their home country. It still puzzled Hashim as to why his cousin had chosen to do that; Rofikul had seemed so at home in *this* country, so at ease with the way things were, ever confident in his meanderings through what still seemed to Hashim an opaque and hostile society. When Joy was a few weeks old, Hashim had drafted a letter to Rofikul, intending to send it to the address of the newspaper in London where his cousin worked. But Hashim had never sent it; Munira had found it months later in the top drawer of the heavy wooden dresser in their bedroom, and had wondered whether to ask about it, but decided against it. She guessed her husband had wanted to finally reach out to his cousin, to share his news of fatherhood, but something – perhaps the fear of not receiving a response – had stopped him from inviting the congratulations and happiness that he deserved.

All that had been three long years ago. Now things were good, thanks to God, better than ever. It was tiring work, naturally. Hashim was spending back-to-back shifts at the shop while Munira looked after Joy. In the years since he and Munira had bought the place, they had set about slowly expanding the services they offered: there was now a small butcher's counter in the corner of the shop, for which Hashim hired an older Pakistani chap by the name of Mirza. Mirza could fillet the meat of a leg of mutton in about three and a half minutes flat, skin a chicken in two minutes, and wielded his de-boning knife with such ferocity that Hashim made a point of standing well back during their conversations about what orders to place from the wholesalers. There was also the small 'newsagents' corner, which had been Munira's idea: they had built in a stand for greetings cards and stamps and envelopes and wrapping paper; even though they weren't quite a post office, it was proving to be a successful initiative. Now that Joy was a bit bigger, babbling and able to charm customers with her ready smile, they brought her down in her carrycot and placed her on the counter while Munira and Hashim busied themselves with serving customers and doing stock-takes. Helen helped out where she could but had decided some months earlier to return to her office job in the legal firm where she had worked before Adam was born. She'd stayed on good terms with the office manager there – Esther Holden could be a bit of a dragon, but she'd always been fair to Helen. When Helen saw an advert in the paper for secretarial staff, she had nervously sent in a letter. Miss Holden had rung her the next day. *Come in on*

Tuesday for an interview, she had barked. *We could do with a girl like you here again. They don't make them like they used to.*

'It makes more sense,' she had told Munira. 'I need to support the two of us, and I can do that better on a secretary's wage than I can in the shop. You understand.'

Munira did understand, and even though she had offered Helen an increase in wages, she recognised her friend's pride in wanting to work independently.

'It's not that I'm not grateful,' Helen had said. 'But I don't want to have to feel grateful any more.'

Both Munira and Hashim missed working alongside Helen, not least because it meant Hashim was doing more of the day-to-day shifts. But despite this, Munira welcomed Helen's return to her old career, secretly hoping that by getting out of the shop and meeting new people, Helen might even meet someone who could make her happy again. Whenever anyone brought up the issue – Marie had a steady stream of potential suitors who she would periodically suggest to Helen, only for Helen to politely, and then not so politely, decline to meet – the conversation was stonewalled. Munira could understand the hesitation, especially when Adam was young, and Helen was working hard enough just to get by in one piece, but it had been ten years now.

Munira had no idea where, or with whom, Rofikul was living back in *desh*. But whatever he was doing, it hardly seemed plausible that he was as weighed down by the consequences of his actions as Helen – and even Munira and Hashim – had been. He was unburdened, Munira presumed. Living a happier life, somewhere new, with someone new, no doubt. It wasn't that she wished Rofikul ill, but the injustice of the discrepancies of these two lives – Helen's of hard work and sacrifice, and Rofikul's, envisioned by Munira as a life of pure hedonism – plagued her. Not that she expected ever to bear witness to whatever present or future Rofikul might have, but the thought that he might be feeling pain proportionate to what he had inflicted made it bearable, somehow. *May Helen's load be lightened*, Munira would pray at night. *And may it be that Rofikul bears the weight that is fair to him.*

Although neither of them knew it, Hashim's prayers differed from those of his wife. In his supplications, he called on Allah for a softening of his cousin's heart, a change in Rofikul's priorities and the divinely inspired realisation of his duties to his family. Hashim knew, perhaps more than he wanted to, and certainly more than Helen or Munira, of his cousin's conflicted responsibilities – but there was no justification for outright abandonment. He resented the burden he had been forced to take on, preserving Rofikul's secrets for no benefit to anyone other than Rofikul himself. In the early days, Hashim had asked Allah what he should do each time he prayed, but the resounding silence that came back to him from the cosmos left him despairing. With no other option but to preserve the status quo, Hashim continued to serve his family, and his cousin, with his silence and his actions, paying the price with the guilt that sat heavy in his stomach.

As well as Joy's birthday, the season also heralded another milestone for the family, although one that Hashim had never formally observed. That New Year's Eve would mark the fourteenth year since Hashim had arrived on these shores, clad in his cheap new suit and no overcoat, with shoes that would fall apart at the faintest hint of snow. To Hashim, New Year's Eve usually meant a steady stream of business from those wanting to buy a bottle before midnight, and the inevitable slurring drunkards in the small hours who banged on the shopfront meant he needed to be sure to deadlock the door. But beyond that, the date didn't hold much significance. Once or twice Munira had remarked upon it, teasingly wishing him a 'Happy Englandiversary', but for Hashim, marking the onset of years was alarming somehow. He had been happy so far, managing to live a good life, but the time had slipped by, well beyond his intended five-year stay in this country. As the days ticked into years, and the years took him into his second decade as an immigrant, Hashim began to wonder whether returning 'home' would ever be a dream he could realise.

27

A T THE RIPE old age of ten, and almost at secondary school, Adam Ahmed Doherty could see no logical reason why he ought not to be allowed to walk to and from school by himself. Children younger than him made the twice-daily trip across the Balfour Estate to St Stephen's Junior School: a point he had put before his mother countless times with a consistent lack of success. His mother would proffer inadequate excuses as to why she should accompany him: 'I like the exercise,' she would say. Or, 'It gives me a chance to pop to the shops on the way.' Humiliated at still being treated like one of the babies, Adam persisted in his negotiations with his mother, using pleas and threats alternately, until eventually one November morning Helen relented.

She stood in the doorway, her housecoat wrapped firmly around her waist, her nose reddened from the flu that had incapacitated her for the last few days. It was for this reason alone that Helen had finally acquiesced in Adam's pleas for independence.

'Got your lunch, love?'

'Yes, Mam.' Adam rustled the paper bag at his mother as a demonstration. At break-time he would swap his satsuma for a chew bar from Tony whose dad owned the Italian corner shop up the road – but his mother didn't need to know about this.

'Be careful now, mind. Don't slip on any ice.'

'There's no ice, Mam.' Adam started trudging across the estate. 'It in't cold enough yet!' Halfway across the concrete paved play area, he turned back and waved at his mother, who was still watching anxiously from the front step, her hands pulling the housecoat closer around her neck.

'Arrite, Adam!' Tony, the corner shop heir, yelled out as he did a wheelie on his push-bike.

'Arrite, Tone.' Adam wasn't *jealous* of Tony, but he couldn't help feeling pangs of envy whenever Tony showed up at school with a new toy or the latest football magazine, or, in this case, a Raleigh Chopper bicycle.

'Where's yer mam then?' Tony stood upright balanced on the pedals, letting the bike roll forward alongside Adam without moving his feet. 'Let yer act yer age finally, did she?'

'She's poorly. Anyway, she always lets me walk by meself if I want to.'

Tony had the grace to let this evident lie slide. They were good mates, him and Adam, not least because they lived so close by. As they arrived at the wrought-iron gates of St Stephen's Junior School, Tony wheeled his bike over to the sheds and chained it up carefully. His father had made it very clear to him what the consequences would be if anything were to happen to that bike. Adam waited impatiently on the steps of the main entrance for his friend.

'Hurry up, we're already late! Yer know what Miss Moorgate's gonna say.'

They slipped into class unnoticed just after the bell had rung. Luckily there were still a few students who were hanging up coats and changing into their indoor shoes, and Adam and Tony managed to stow their jackets safely and change their shoes without being noticed by the pedantic and sour-faced Miss Moorgate, who was a known hater of little boys and, by all accounts, a suspected witch. The day dragged on slowly: prayers, arithmetic, break, prayers, lunch, history, prayers, and then, at the end of the day, English.

'How do you wander like a pissin' *cloud*?' whispered Tony to Adam, who dutifully sniggered as such wit warranted.

'Is something particularly amusing, Aaaah-med?' Miss Moorgate loomed over the desk, so close by that the boys could smell the mustiness of stale sweat. If Miss Moorgate hated little boys, she loathed this one in particular: the proverbial black fly in her lovely white ointment. She insisted on addressing him by his middle name, painstakingly drawing out the 'A', as if to highlight its foreignness.

'No, miss.' Adam shuffled in his seat. He hated it when she did this, which was almost on a daily basis. Picking him out in the class and asking him a series of questions he had no idea how to answer. The fact that she always addressed him by his surname – and the other children by their first – was something he barely noticed any more. It was the consistent public humiliation that bothered him. Last week it was about his times tables – he had failed to answer a question involving his fourteen times table: something that none of the class had covered.

'Wordsworth was not known to be a comic poet, was he, Aaahmed?'

'Er – no, miss.'

'What sort of poet was Wordsworth, Aaahmed?'

'Sorry, miss?'

Miss Moorgate smiled, the way a cat might smile at a cornered mouse right before pouncing on it, thought Tony who was frozen in his seat beside Adam.

'What. Sort. Of. Poet.' She repeated it loudly and slowly, as though he were deaf.

Adam squirmed and looked around the class for help.

226

The students all looked back at him equally baffled. What did she mean, what sort of poet was Wordsworth? A rubbish one, if Adam was honest. Tony was right, how did you wander like a cloud? And what was so great about daffodils anyway? They either looked forced – the deliberately planted yellow bunches in the concrete tubs on the corner of the estate – or scruffy, like when they grew in the dirt on the edges of the rec, where dogs would piss all over them or they'd get trampled on by kids chasing a stray football.

Adam hazarded a guess. 'Erm. An English poet, miss?'

The sneering look on Miss Moorgate's face was replaced by one of contempt. Susan Moorgate had had enough of these coloured kids, with their insolence, their total lack of respect, and no manners. This half-caste one was even worse than usual – his mother was clearly a woman of loose morals to fraternise with, let alone allow herself to be impregnated by, a coloured man. Susan Moorgate had taught only a handful of non-white children – rowdy blacks, dirty Asians, a couple of mute Chinese – but each experience had served only to support her existing belief: that they were far less able than their white classmates. She also conveniently ignored evidence that countered her thesis: that Jenkins boy from a few years ago was a cheat, she had decided, who copied from Stuart Brown in the class tests. The fact that Jenkins always scored higher than Stuart – higher than anyone else in the class and two classes above him, in fact – was of no consequence. He was a cheat. He was black. And this one – this Ahmed – was even worse. He was a mongrel.

'An . . . English . . . poet?' Miss Moorgate hissed the words back. Adam did not move. The rest of the class looked on nervously. 'Yes. Actually. He *was* an English poet. I was looking for the term *Romantic*. He was a Romantic poet. But you've brought up a very interesting discussion topic for the class.'

227

Miss Moorgate smiled disconcertingly at Adam. He knew something was not right. 'Are you English, Ahmed?'

'Me, miss?'

'Is there anyone else here named Ahmed?' Miss Moorgate gestured around the classroom with her hand.

'No, miss. I mean. No there isn't, miss. And yes I am, miss.'

Susan Moorgate raised an eyebrow. 'You think you are English, do you?'

Adam was desperate. He had no idea what the right answer was. It seemed that he'd offended Miss Moorgate, but he didn't know what else he was supposed to say. He lived in England, didn't he? He was born here, wasn't he? But even as the thoughts went through his mind, he knew that wasn't what Miss Moorgate meant. Adam looked different. His skin had a permanent tan that grew even darker during the summer months when he was off school and played football all day.

'Isn't your mother Irish, Ahmed?'

'Yes, miss. Well, she grew up in Liverpool, but—'

'So your mother isn't English. And . . . well, I would imagine your father isn't either, wouldn't you agree?'

Adam's face grew hot. He couldn't understand why Miss Moorgate was asking him all these questions.

'He's from East Pakistan, miss.'

Miss Moorgate smiled smugly, a slight incline of her head signifying that her point had been made. 'So – not English, then. Now, let's see. If your mother isn't English. And your father – whoever he may be – certainly isn't English . . . then tell me, does it make sense that you would call yourself English?'

Adam had nothing else to say. He shook his head miserably, his eyes fixed on the blackboard ahead of him, ignoring the slightly scared expressions of his classmates, trying not to catch Tony's eye in the corner.

'No, I don't think it does either.' Miss Moorgate walked back over to her desk and sat down triumphantly.

Adam silently burned with shame for the rest of the class until the shrill ringing of the bell at three o'clock signalled release. He grabbed his coat from the pegs and fled before he even had a chance to put it on, running towards the safety of home. Adam didn't want to see anyone from school on the way – he didn't have a word for how he felt but he knew he wanted to be alone. If Adam were to walk the normal way home Tony would soon catch him up on his bike, so he decided to take the more roundabout way, up by the rec and across the Downing Estate. Mam never let him go up there by himself usually, but today Adam couldn't care less what Mam or anyone else thought or said.

He set off towards the rec. There wasn't much there – a dog park and a kids' playground with a sad-looking broken seesaw and a couple of swings that had lighter marks on the rubber seats where kids had tried to burn them. He stopped to put his coat on – it was getting chilly now that he had walked off some of the hot embarrassment from before – and then slumped on to one of the swings. He pushed himself back using the balls of his feet and then let himself sail forward, craning his head towards a sky that was already turning a shadowy grey. The links of the swing chains made rusty lines that looked like they stretched right up to heaven when he tilted himself back on the swing. He pushed back and forth, emptying his mind of what had happened at school.

Lost in his own thoughts, Adam didn't hear the footsteps approaching from the other side of the rec, the stifled sniggers, the clink of glass bottles. There was the sound of a heavy thud and Adam found himself suddenly face down on the ground, his mouth full of tarmac and dog piss and the iron taste of blood. He pushed himself up on his hands and knees, but before he could get up, he felt a heavy boot to the small of his back and he collapsed again on to the ground.

'Stay down, yer piece of shit.'

Adam didn't recognise the voice. He felt the sting of his cut lip but stayed with his face to the ground.

'Who's he?'

Another voice, slightly higher pitched and nasal. Neither of the voices sounded familiar: older boys, maybe fifteen or sixteen – but already hardened.

'Dunno, Paki who wandered a bit too far?'

Adam felt another kick to the side of his body and cried out.

'Nosey Paki, in't he?' Another kick. 'Where yer from, Paki?'

Adam didn't know if he was supposed to answer or not, but when he opened his mouth to try, no sound came out. A rough hand grabbed the back of his coat and heaved him up, before dropping him on his back again so he was now looking up at the iron-grey sky and the looming heads of his assailants.

'No need to cry, Paki, we're just talking. Can't yer speak English?' A different hand grabbed his face, squeezing his cheeks hard together until they pressed against the sides of his teeth, before roughly pushing his head away.

Adam could no longer see. His vision was blurred by the hot tears that swam around his eyes, but still he didn't make a sound. He could hear a low hum, like a helicopter over-head, and he wondered if it was a search party coming to look for him. Mam would definitely be worried by now, it was almost dark. The hum got louder and somehow hotter and he realised that it was no helicopter, but the low growling of a dog just inches away from his face. The heat of its breath was on his cheek. In that moment, Adam gave up.

'Oi! What you two doin'?' It was the voice of a girl by the sounds of it, maybe the same age as the others. The dog stopped growling and started barking instead, running over to where the new voice was coming from. 'What you doin'?' The voice was angry.

'We just found him here.'

'Well, leave him alone, poor bastard, he's just a kid.' The voice started addressing Adam, 'Oi, kid, you alri—' It broke off. 'Oh my God,' it said in disgust. 'Kid's pissed hisself.'

Adam lay on the ground in a growing warm pool of shame, betrayed by his own body. Liquid leaked silently from his eyes too.

One of the original voices rose. 'Fuckin' baby, we din't even do nothing – could've given the dirty Paki something ter—'

'Oh shut up,' the girl's voice said. 'I got better things to do. Am off home, you coming or what?' The voices retreated across the rec, the sound of the dog's barking accompanying them.

Adam lay on the ground and closed his eyes, the dark sky closing in overhead.

''Ere, 'ere, Mrs Doherty, I found 'im!'

Adam woke to the sound of Tony's voice shouting, and the sound of heels clattering over the tarmac, and then a cry, and then there was Mam. Worn, pale-looking Mam, who scooped him up, not noticing the stench of his trousers, as he curled into her arms weeping.

'What happened? What happened to you, my love?' But Helen already knew the answer. She had been dreading the day when this would happen – the inevitability of her son's suffering as a result of choices she had made.

'Not now, Helen.' Chacha's gentle voice saved Adam the

burden of having to answer. 'Let me carry him to the car.' Adam felt himself being passed into the stronger arms of Chacha, and he pressed his face against the lapel of his uncle's jacket, inhaling the faint scent of sandalwood and mints, and wept into Chacha's chest.

Mam sat in the back of the car with Adam, her arms wrapped tightly around him, while Chacha drove them home, dropping Tony off on the way. 'Thanks for your help tonight, Tony,' Chacha had said, 'you're a good boy.'

Tony had nodded and scrambled out of the car, his usually jolly face drawn tight. He'd heard of Pakis being bashed, he just didn't think it'd ever happen round *these* ends. 'Specially not to Adam. The proximity of the brutality scared Tony, but he knew that if he told his mam, she'd only fret and warn him 'not ter hang around wi' lads like *'im'* – whatever that meant. Tony waved at the retreating car, the cold fingers of guilt creeping over him. He'd failed to protect his friend twice in one day: once from Witch-face Moorgate, and now from these amateur Paki-bashers. Tony shuddered at the thought of what might have happened if a real gang had got hold of Adam. Tony's older brother had told him stories of blokes who walked around with knuckle-dusters and chains, beating up blacks and Asians for laughs. It was disgusting, Marcus said, but nobody would do nothing cos deep down no one really liked the blacks and Asians anyway, and if they did, they were too scared to admit it. Even from Tony's young worldview, this warped logic held some kind of truth. When people came into Tony's dad's shop complaining about the noisiness of the Jamaican family on the corner with their all-night parties and their lads going with white girls, or the grocery prices at the 'Paki shop', Tony's dad just nodded and listened, and doled out change, but he didn't ask them to stop saying stuff.

Back at home, a pan of hot water was heated, and Adam was sponged down in front of the fire in the living room before being dressed in a pair of clean pyjamas and tucked into bed. Helen stayed with him until he fell asleep, and then came back into the living room where Munira and Hashim were sitting waiting.

'How is he? Did he say anything about what happened?' Hashim's concern was graven on his forehead.

Helen shook her head, sinking into the armchair nearest the gas fire. 'I asked him what had happened; he said something about his teacher, and then being upset at something she said, and that's why he went to the park after school.' She held up her hands helplessly before they dropped heavily again into her lap. 'I didn't know what to say to him.' Helen's voice was small and weary. 'There was nothing I could say that would make it right.'

Munira went over and wrapped her arms around Helen's shoulders, holding her close. 'There are some things you shouldn't need to explain.'

'But I do. I have to find a way. It's not going to go away . . .' Helen's voice broke. She had been aware of it all for so long, but until now the vitriol, the danger to her son and her family, had been theoretical. She remembered that speech several years ago, and how the country had been split in its reaction to such an assertion: that people like her son would cause the rivers of the land to run red with blood. It had angered her at the time, the stupidity of such a thing. She and Munira had talked about it, reading the subsequent stories in the newspapers: the spike in attacks against blacks and other immigrants as a result; the resignation of Powell from office; the boorish cries to return Britain back to 'real Britons'. But now here was her son, harmed and in pain, for no reason other than the fact that he was a product of love between a mother and a father who hailed from two different lands.

As she clasped her arms around Helen, Munira's eyes met Hashim's across the room, and she could see the tears forming in them. None of them had the answers for the challenges that they all knew they would be faced with, in different guises, over and over again.

28

AFTER THE INCIDENT in the playground, Helen tried to broach the subject with Adam more than once, but his stubborn refusal to discuss what had happened that day worried her.

'He needs to talk,' she would tell Munira, 'but I can't get him to say anything.'

Munira's suggestion had surprised Helen. 'Maybe he needs to talk to someone other than you, Helen. Maybe Hashim? You know, someone who might understand it in a way he can relate to.'

It had hurt Helen, the insinuation that there could be something she perhaps would not understand about her own son's experiences. She had responded to Munira more brusquely than usual, and Munira, sensing the change in tone, had lightly shrugged and said it was just a suggestion, but not to worry. In the end, though, Helen did ask Hashim to speak to her son.

'I'm losing him, Hashim. He doesn't want to talk to me any more.' Helen knew that this was part of growing up – but to think that it was happening to her Adam, that her once loving, chatty little boy was withdrawing into himself, keeping things from her, was too painful.

'You're not losing him, Helen,' Hashim reassured her. 'He just needs a bit of space to work things out for himself. But of course I'll try to talk to him.' But when Hashim tried to bring up the subject, Adam was just as closed off as he had been with his mother.

By the time Adam started secondary school, he was even less willing to engage in these kinds of discussions. There was nothing to be gained from talking about this stuff, in Adam's view. He was already aware of what he needed to know. It wasn't a slowly unfurling consciousness, or anything like that. It was just something that was always there, hanging dense and heavy in the air around him, the knowledge that the very presence of his family, mixed and mingled as it was, was precarious. That a single false step – or even no step at all – could mark them out as legitimate targets. That incident at the playground only heightened what he had always known. And what everyone else knew, but never admitted. Even though his family never talked about it, he knew it was the reason why the windows in the shop were smashed and replaced so frequently, and why Mam and Chachi went everywhere in pairs once the clocks went back and the dark nights drew in earlier. He knew it was why Chachi would start anxiously glancing at the clock from ten o'clock at night, when the shop lock-up started, and wouldn't go to bed until Chacha had walked safely through the front door. He had pieced enough fragments together from overheard conversations to know that it had happened to other people he knew too; like the time Aunty Marie and Uncle Vincent were set on when they were walking together in town, or when the Farooqs had fireworks posted through the letterbox.

The Farooqs were what the kids on the estate nicknamed 'freshies' – new immigrants who had come over from some- where in East Africa, even though they didn't look African to Adam – and everything about them radiated cluelessness. Fat Faisal Farooq lived in the next block over from Adam and Helen, and had only been on the estate three weeks before he learned his lesson. You had to be alert to get by. It wasn't taught or learned, but was some kind of instinct for survival. There were consequences for not learning fast enough, and the consequences were real. Adam overheard Mam and Chachi whispering in the kitchen once that Fat Faisal's mother had almost fainted when her son had walked through the back door after school, forty-five minutes late and with a crimson shirt collar and two swollen eyes. After that Mrs Farooq banned her son from walking home alone after school, insisting that he wait in the classroom for his uncle to finish work and come to pick him up on the way home.

Faisal's Uncle Ali was only twelve years older than his nephew and, perhaps because of this fact, was an object of admiration for most of the Asian lads on the estate. Ali wore a leather jacket and smoked Camels and had longish hair that he swept back in a kind of mane. He looked like one of those white men on *Top of the Pops* with skinny arms hanging out of loose vests and torn trousers – not at all like Adam's Uncle Hashim or Faisal's own dad. On the rare occasions Ali spoke, it was with a laconic drawl that only added to his enticingly dangerous aura. He'd moved up to live with his sister – Mrs Farooq – shortly after the family arrived on the estate. Rumour had it he had been in jail before then for trying to assassinate a man called Idi Amin, but Fat Faisal never confirmed nor denied this, realising perhaps that too ardent a denial would impede what morsel of popularity he could enjoy as the tubby, permanently frightened nephew of the mysterious and brooding ex-political prisoner.

Adam didn't particularly like wet-eyed, dumpy Faisal, but at the insistence of his mother he sometimes spoke to him in the playground, and on the days when there was no one else to play with after school, he endured his company in the hope that their paths would cross with Ali and he would agree to take them for a ride in his beaten-up Ford with the broken door handles that could not be opened from the inside. It was a delicious kind of thrill to be allowed to ride in the car on dusky evenings after school and go on long drives to the edge of town, knowing that they were at the mercy of Ali as to whether he would eventually let the boys out of the car or not. Sometimes Ali's drives to the edge of town involved picking up a pretty girl on the way. These additional passengers were always received with disdain by Adam and Faisal – it meant that instead of Ali occasionally responding attentively to their questions, the boys would be in for an evening of having to listen to the girl's over-enthusiastic chatter while awkwardly watching Ali's hand snaking up the open expanse of thigh towards the hem of a short skirt.

But for the most part, these drives seemed to have no discernible purpose to Adam and Faisal. Ali would drive to a remote spot where sometimes two or three other cars would also be parked. Sometimes Ali would exchange a few words with the other drivers, swap cigarettes, and occasion-ally small packages of what Adam assumed to be cash to pay for the cigarettes. These transactions also held little interest for Adam and Faisal, who were far more fascinated on those still summer evenings by playing with the car stereo and catching pop songs on the airwaves, than they were by watching the goings-on of the older men who weren't Ali, their silent and sinewy protector.

But despite Faisal now having his own personal bodyguard escorting him to and from school, Adam knew that being in the supposed security of one's own home did not automatically translate to actual safety. Chacha and Chachi were always having things stuffed through their letterboxes – plastic bags filled with dog shit, rubbish, even a used nappy once. These at least were considered to be harmless enough compared to the fireworks that some unfortunate homes were targeted with, around November each year. Adam remembered one weekend morning last year, watching Chacha attaching a metal box around the letterbox on the inside of the front door, like a cage. At the time he thought it was to catch the letters as they dropped through the flap so they didn't just sit on the doormat. But after the Farooqs' firework incident, Adam realised that the cage was more of a safety measure. He wondered whether Mrs Farooq and her family might have stayed on the estate, had Mr Farooq had the same combination of foresight, caution and access to scrap metal as Chacha.

They were just blessed, as a tearful Mrs Farooq sobbed to Mam and Chachi the day after the fire, *so blessed*, that Ali came home late that night and raised the alarm at three o'clock in the morning, shouting and pounding on all the bedroom doors, hauling the kids out of their beds and practically throwing them down the stairs towards the back door. Never again, she vowed, would she ever try to police her younger brother's movements, saviour that he had proven himself to be, because of, not despite, his nocturnal wanderings.

Nobody ever talked about what really started the fire. A man from the council came over the next day and stood in the middle of the charred kitchen, next to another man from the police station, and said it was most likely faulty wiring from the new fridge freezer that Ali had procured from somewhere. These units were not standard in local authority-provided housing, said the man from the council, and had been installed at the tenants' own risk. Really, said the man from the council, *we* should be fining *you*, for bringing unsafe electrical equipment on to the estate. But you've learned your lesson now, we hope, and we will just leave it there, shall we? Because you're all very lucky that you escaped unhurt, and what's more that the fire didn't spread to the neighbours. And with a sniff and a snap of pen on to clipboard, the man from the council left the estate. But the acrid smell of smoke and melted carpet fibres lingered in the air for weeks.

Helen, infuriated by Mrs Farooq's account of the incident, asked whether the Farooqs had mentioned the charred firework wrapper they had found in the hallway, or the marks on the sloping roof over the stairs that had four messy holes bored into the plasterwork from strapped-together rockets, or the hate-filled letters 'N.F.' spraypainted on to their front door the month before.

Mrs Farooq, taut-faced and pale, shook her head slowly. 'They wouldn't listen anyway, Helen, you know that. It's easier for them to blame it on us than to make it a police matter.'

Soon after that, the Farooqs left the estate and moved to a smaller block a few streets away where Mrs Farooq said she felt safer because the letterboxes were outside the front doors and you needed a key to open them. Plus, they were on the fifth floor in a block with no lift, and everyone knew that even the most dedicated of troublemakers would never be bothered to climb that far. It made her legs ache, and some days she wouldn't go out because the climb back up was too much, but Mrs Farooq declared it was a price worth paying to be safe. Helen didn't see Mrs Farooq much after that, unless she made the effort to go round, but Adam still saw Faisal at school and sometimes hung around with him afterwards. Faisal lost a bit of weight climbing those stairs every day, and Ali had started teaching him how to box; he said Faisal should learn how to protect himself, that if people knew he could land a blow, they wouldn't lay the first one on him.

Not wanting to be outdone by Faisal, Adam was desperate to learn too. But his mother was firmly against it.

'You're too young to be hanging around with the older guys in those boxing halls – and besides, what if you get hurt?'

'The point is that I *won't* get hurt, if someone starts on me,' Adam exasperatedly explained. 'As it is, we all get hurt anyway without being able to hurt them back, so why shouldn't we learn how to defend ourselves?'

Helen tried to hide it, but Adam knew that she cried a bit after that in her bedroom, having left the table without clearing away after dinner. He washed and dried the plates and stacked them away, and was just starting on his homework when Helen came back, still red-eyed but not crying.

'You're a good boy.' She kissed him on the head and for once, these days, Adam let her. 'You really want to learn boxing?' she asked doubtfully.

'Yes, I do.'

'And it's – for exercise?'

Adam hesitated, sensing that the expected answer was to agree. 'Yes, Mam. Exercise. Just like football, or something.'

'And this – this Ali, he'll drop you back home afterwards?' Helen's hands were twisting the hem of her cardigan anxiously.

'Yes, Mam, he drops off Faisal too, it isn't far from here.'

Helen nodded. 'All right then. You can try it. Just for a week or two at first, and then we'll see. All right?'

Adam scrambled up from the table and threw his arms around his mother. 'Thanks, Mam! I'll be careful, I promise.'

The first burst of spontaneous affection from her son in months made Helen well up again. 'That's good, love.' She patted his cheek and went back into her bedroom.

The next day, Adam started learning how to box.

29

THE BOXING CLUB was in the basement of a rundown community centre just off Dickenson Road. The centre consisted of an echoey ground-floor room, which was grandly referred to as the community 'hall' and was mostly used for Sunday school classes, coffee mornings and the occasional local fête. Its only contents were several folding tables clustered in the middle, and columns of uncomfortable plastic chairs with holes cut out of the back stacked around the perimeter of the room. Off to the left was a small kitchenette with a kettle and an electric hob and a cupboard containing paper cups, teabags, sugar cubes and long-life milk. Sometimes people hired the hall for special birthdays or christenings or engagement parties, and then it was transformed with paper tablecloths and bunting and home-made cakes, and the thunder of children stampeding on the scuffed floors and the chatter of attendees.

On Adam's first day, he had been instructed by Faisal to meet by the sheds after school. Together they walked the mile to the community centre, kit carefully stowed in their backpacks, and descended the stone steps to the basement. It was the lightness that struck them at first. The exposed stone walls had all been lime-washed, and the concrete floor was painted a bright blue. Overhead were exposed fluorescent strip lights nestled between white ceiling tiles. The overall effect was dazzling. Everything seemed clean and bright and almost clinical. Everything, that was, except for the smell, of leather and sweat and rubber mats and frustration and release. It was a smell they both came to love, along with the feeling of damp warm air that enveloped them each evening as they came in from the cold dusk for training. Adam and Faisal were thrilled by the idea of having 'training'. It felt so adult, so masterful.

To Adam's fascination, the boxing class seemed to draw in men from all backgrounds and hues. They sparred against one another, sweating honestly and swearing colourfully in more languages than Adam had ever heard. Caribbean, African, Irish, Asian, Polish, Russian – the club did not discriminate. If you agreed to subscribe to the rules, could afford the entry fee and brought your own towel, then the club was open to you. A kind of casual camaraderie began to develop between the members: acknowledgement by way of exchanged nods gave way to greetings and then, in time, to conversation. The one person who did not partake in conversation was Adam and Faisal's coach, Ali. A laconic nod was the most either of the boys could expect before their instruction began. Ali was tough, and at times unsympathetic, especially towards Faisal, but he was fair and his coaching was effective, if frustrating.

'I can't believe we're still on bloody skipping,' muttered Faisal breathlessly to Adam, on what felt like their hundredth turn of the rope.

'When you can say that instead of panting it, I might let you wear the pads.' Ali sauntered past, casting a derisive glance at his nephew. 'You might want to ease off some of your mum's fried snacks too.'

Faisal reddened but it was hard for Adam to tell whether it was shame or exertion. Besides, he too was breathless from jumping. Mercifully, Ali instructed them to put their ropes down, and to get some water. Once they had hydrated, it was time for Adam and Faisal to strap in.

'Hand out.'

Adam extended his arm and Ali bound his right then left hand tightly with a broad bandage-like strip of cloth.

'Gloves.'

Ali held the glove still while Adam plunged his hand into the leather hole, four fingers extending into one section, isolating his thumb in another. The glove encased his fingers, and Ali tightened the strap over his wrist so that Adam had to move his whole hand as though it were one inflexible block at the end of his arm. Ali positioned Adam's feet, left foot forward, hips at an angle, leaning forward, leaning back, keep moving. Ready.

'Right. Now see these pads? See where the red target sign is on the middle of where my palm would be? That's where you aim.'

Adam nodded. He could see Faisal out of the corner of his eye, sulky at not being allowed to go first but curious as to how Adam would fare. Adam was determined not to allow Faisal the satisfaction of seeing him struggle. He extended his right arm towards the pad held up by Ali, but his aim fell just too short, only lightly skimming the leather surface with the top of his glove.

'Okay – that's the right place. Now just extend your arm further. From the shoulder.'

Adam tried again, and this time landed a satisfying punch on the pad. He grinned at Faisal.

'Good. Now the left.'

It was trickier than it looked, the boys discovered. It took weeks of practice just for the boys to land their throws on target, to keep their faces guarded at all times, to bounce and dodge. But the sound of leather on leather was almost melodic, and the rhythm of ducking punches and keeping moving on the balls of their feet felt almost meditative. It was an addiction, the sound and smell and physicality of a release. But it was an obsession not everyone understood.

To the amusement of his mother and aunt, Adam began to swagger around the house talking about 'crosses' and 'hooks' and his 'training regimen'.

'You know what else gets trained? Puppies,' Aunt Munira had solemnly declared before descending into peals of laughter. Hashim had chided her for being unkind about the boy's interests, but Munira had waved him off. 'He shouldn't take himself so seriously,' she said, her arm gently wrapped around Hashim's waist. 'He's only a boy after all.'

'That's exactly why he should feel we are taking him seriously,' Hashim had replied.

Adam overheard the whole conversation from the stairs and his heart had swelled with love for his uncle who *understood* things, even the ones that he couldn't quite put into words. After that Adam took great delight in regaling Uncle Hashim with accounts of his boxing training, of the new techniques he had perfected, of how Coach had praised his lightness of foot, but had said Adam needed work on the strength behind his punches. Uncle Hashim offered – only if Adam wanted – to help him train at home, to hold the boxing pads while Adam practised throwing his weight fully behind his punches, and Adam gratefully accepted the offer on the days when the boxing club wasn't running. It struck Adam as somewhat unexpected that Uncle Hashim was so encouraging about his new hobby – it seemed the kind of pursuit that his uncle would usually have avoided, worrying about injuries or his going to and from the boxing club alone. But still, he thought it best just to accept the endorsement and not question too much, lest his uncle change his mind.

Hashim stood outside Greenfields Community Centre, hands thrust deep into his pockets, his scarf obscuring the lower part of his face. He paced past the signboard, up and down the street, before finally turning on his heel and making his way to the arched doorway. A printed piece of paper with a hand-drawn arrow pointed: 'BOXING THIS WAY'. Hashim took the stairs lightly, two at a time, until he reached the bottom. A warm smog of body heat and fluorescent lights greeted him as he entered the club. In the far corner, Adam had his back to Hashim. A long-haired young Asian man – presumably the infamous Ali – was facing him. Instead of pads, Ali had gloves. Without warning, a hand darted towards Adam's jaw. Hashim gasped and stepped forward, but Adam's left hand had sprung up to block the punch. Hashim looked on anxiously, surprised at the warm feeling of pride that had crept into his chest. So Adam was sparring now and, by the looks of it, learning to hold his own.

It was a fear that Hashim was determined his children – Adam and Joy alike – would never inherit: the insecurity he felt as he traversed the streets of Manchester, a target because of his skin, his accent. The idea that his children, who had been born and were being raised in this country, might experience the same thing was unthinkable to Hashim. He, at least, was an 'outsider' in the way that most people conceived of it. It annoyed Munira when he said things like that; she always pointed out that the land of their birth had been under occupation by the British for centuries. And he knew that she was right, of course.

Hashim lingered a little longer, enough to notice the nascent bulges in Adam's smooth upper arms, and the dark hair curled in the pits of his vest. Adam began to spar with a new partner, a younger, heavier-set lad. The energy of the boys was exhilarating somehow; they looked powerful, unapologetic, beautiful even. Hashim turned and made his way back up the stairs out into the dusky chill, overcome with the feeling of being alive.

30

MUNIRA HAD CRIED on Joy's first day of school.
Hashim clicked the button on his camera as they
both posed by the front door, Joy in her little V-neck jumper
and striped tie and socks that came up to her chubby knees,
and red-eyed Munira trying to smile through the tears.

'What are you worried about?' Hashim had asked Munira
gently as he knelt to help Joy buckle up her shoes. 'You
know she'll be fine.'

'I know she will be.' Munira rubbed at her eyes crossly.
The reversal of their usual familiar positions – Hashim full
of concern, Munira reassuring – agitated her even more than
the distress she felt at the thought of waving her little one
off at the iron school gates. Like a prison, she thought,
despairing of this awful necessity of having to send her baby
off to somewhere so cold and sterile.

'Ammu?' Joy had asked. 'Will I see Bhaiya at school?' That
was her name for Adam – 'brother' – in keeping with the
deshi tradition of never calling anyone older by their given
name, but using their relational title instead. In return, Adam
sometimes called Joy 'Bhaiyu' – a diminutive version of the
name she used for him, and an idiosyncratic example of
Bengalis affectionately calling each other by the same relational title. So when Adam called Hashim Chacha, Hashim
would sometimes call Adam Chacha back. Or when Munira

called her father Baba, he would indulgently call her Baba in return.

'No, Ammu,' Munira replied. 'Bhaiya is at big school now, you remember that? But you can see him after school today, all right?'

Joy shrugged, clutching her new red plastic lunchbox, seemingly oblivious to the significance of the day, despite her mother's tears.

Now Joy had been at school for almost two terms and had taken to it more earnestly than Hashim and Munira could have hoped. *She's very diligent*, her teacher had reported at the very first parent–teacher evening, for which Hashim had dressed especially in a suit. *She's very advanced. You must read a lot with her at home?* Hashim had been barely able to contain his pride. *It's from her mother*, he had beamed at the teacher and at Munira. *She always loves to read*. But where Hashim took unabashed pride in his daughter's school career, Munira found herself set adrift in the first weeks and months of their new family routine.

'I just feel as though my hours are so much longer now,' Munira confessed to Helen one afternoon over a coffee in Helen's kitchen. It was a bank holiday and Helen had had the day off, meaning that for once Munira had some company during the working hours. 'The time between everyone leaving the house in the morning to when I go to pick up Joy just seems endless.' It wasn't only the hours stretching ahead, day after day, that bothered Munira: it was the absence of having anything that she wanted to spend her time doing. There were the chores, and perhaps some shopping, and then a little reading or watching their small colour television – an upgrade from their old black and white set – that Hashim had presented to her a few years ago with great pride, but nothing satisfied her. The feeling she had when she first arrived in Britain – rudderless and useless with nothing solid enough to occupy her days until Hashim came home – had returned tenfold since Joy had started school.

'Sounds like you need something to get you out of the house. A bit of structure,' Helen had proffered. 'Something like a part-time job?'

'I have more than a part-time job – what about the shop?' Munira had retorted indignantly. She resented the insinuation that her role in the shop, diminished as it had been since Joy was born and Munira had been taken up caring for her in the flat upstairs, did not count as work.

'But Munira, you haven't worked full time there since Joy came along. And besides, I'm not sure that really serves the purpose I was thinking of.' Helen looked at her friend steadily and continued in a level voice. 'I think you need a job that gets you away from the shop and from home. Something you do that is separate from everything else. Something just for you.'

Munira had mulled over Helen's suggestion. It sounded so selfish, to do something 'just for her' when Hashim worked so hard for all of them. He had never had a holiday or taken any extended amount of time to pursue things on a whim. She felt guilty at the thought of her husband labouring away for them while she pursued these lofty ideals of self-fulfilment to stave off the disease of those with nothing else to complain about: boredom.

'You're being too hard on yourself,' Helen had remarked when Munira shared these doubts a week or two later. 'It isn't selfish to want to do something else. You aren't taking away from your family; if anything, it will make you feel happier, which can't hurt anyone, can it? It might even make you all get along a bit better. You'd have something to talk about when the others get home.'

It was true, thought Munira. When Joy and Hashim came home, they always had anecdotes to share – who they had seen, what Joy had learned that day, which customers had come into the shop – and Munira nodded and smiled along to these conversations, never really feeling that she had much to offer.

'Even if I wanted to – which I'm not saying I do – what could I possibly be qualified for?' Munira rose despairingly to Helen's carefully laid bait.

'Plenty of things. How about working at the library?' Helen pushed a newspaper across the table towards Munira, a big circle marked around one of the adverts. 'They're looking for a part-time assistant. You should apply.'

Munira had volunteered at the local library before – helping out occasionally with the toddler and parent reading group or at coffee mornings – but a proper job? It was absurd to think she could do it.

'It's nothing you won't be able to handle, Munira,' Helen said, seeing the alarm in her friend's face. 'You've managed a shop, you've volunteered – you've got actual business experience – you could do this with your eyes closed.'

'But I never had to apply for those jobs,' Munira replied anxiously. 'I've never had to do an interview, or even write a cover letter—'

'I'll coach you.' Helen was firm. 'And you've proofread dozens of other people's job applications over the years, so if you can't write your own after that, then, who knows, maybe they should give the job to someone else.' Helen knew how to win, and Munira knew that Helen was well aware of what she was doing, but there was no point in protesting.

Suitably chastened, Munira spent the next couple of days preparing a letter and a page summarising her qualifications and work experience, and Helen typed it up for her at the office. Munira added her signature to the bottom of the letter and sent it off to the library.

'Now to await my imminent rejection,' Munira sighed. She had decided not to tell Hashim about applying for the job. He would get so enthusiastic; she could barely cope with not living up to her own hopes, but to dash Hashim's would be more than she could bear. After two agonising weeks of waiting, filled with pacing the flat and wondering why she had ever been foolish enough to think anyone might want to give her a job, Munira received a formal-looking letter inviting her to interview. Her immediate reaction was one of all-consuming panic.

'What am I going to wear?' she asked Helen, stricken. She had never done this before; never had an interview, never really even considered working at a 'proper' job the way Helen and Hashim did, even though, in the early days at least, she had spent as much time as her husband running the shop.

'Wear what you feel comfortable in,' had been Helen's advice. 'If you feel most confident in a sari, then wear a sari.' But Munira was nervous as to how the interviewers would see her at first glance; just another meek Asian lady who could barely speak English. They'd judge her before she'd even opened her mouth. In the end Helen had agreed to help Munira choose an outfit from her own wardrobe. It was a riotous afternoon, with Helen picking out outfits for Munira, twinning various tops and trousers of different fabrics and hues, amid much laughter. Munira's favourite outfit had been a high-collared white blouse with wide-legged tartan trousers and a sleeveless knitted mustard jumper.

'Ammu looks like an English lady,' Joy had remarked, when she saw her mother teetering around on a pair of Helen's platform shoes.

'You can borrow them if you like,' Helen offered and Munira gratefully took the shoes and the outfit, imagining that perhaps if she looked the part she would convince the interviewers that she could do the job – even if she was still unconvinced herself.

Later that night, Munira told Hashim about the job vacancy that had come up at the library and how, with Helen's help, she had submitted an application – and, contrary to any expectations, she had been invited for an interview. Hashim took a moment to understand what his wife was trying to say to him.

'So that's why I'm borrowing Helen's clothes.' She shrugged and waved her hand at the unfamiliar outfit hanging up on the back of their bedroom door, her meandering explanation gradually tailing off.

'Forget about the clothes for a moment,' he said. 'Do you mean you'll be working – as in, full-time – at the library? What about the shop?'

'It's part-time – just three mornings a week.' Munira glanced at her husband guiltily, not wanting him to feel sidelined by her pursuit, and thinking ruefully that she should at least have talked all this through with him first before pressing ahead with an application. 'And I'll still have time to help out in the shop of course,' she added hastily. But to her relief, Hashim did not seem angry or disappointed with her.

'This is something you want to do?' he asked slowly, his hand resting on hers.

'Yes, it is. I need to . . .' She grasped for the words. She wanted to say, *I need to use my brain for something*, or *I need to feel like myself again*, but she worried that expressing it in that way would hurt Hashim, make her seem discontented with what she had – the life he had built with her, *for* her. 'I just need to do something new.' She paused. 'It's so different now, with Joy at school, and suddenly I have all this time and I don't really know how to fill it, until it's time to go and collect her from school. And I know there's the shop but . . .' She hesitated again, not wanting to admit that the work – well, it bored her, frankly. It was serving the same people, stock-taking, stacking shelves. Aside from a bit of chit-chat with the locals, she didn't really get a chance to speak much to anyone beyond Hashim; she wanted colleagues, new people she could talk to. 'Are you angry?' she asked softly, pressing her hand against Hashim's.

'Why would I be angry?' He shook his head. 'How can I be angry with you? You are so bright – you've always had so many ideas – how could I have expected for so long that this would be enough for you?' Munira opened her mouth to protest, but Hashim continued. 'I don't mean that I think you were unhappy. At least I hope you weren't?' Munira shook her head. 'But this isn't why you studied, is it? To help me price magazines and potatoes.' She would have gone on to college, Hashim thought, if she hadn't married him. She had sat on her own ambitions for so many years, for his sake, supporting his business, raising their family and she had never made him feel like that wasn't what she wanted. But of course she wanted more – she was the cleverest person he had ever known, more even than Rofikul. Her intelligence was different: analytical and sharp, where Rofikul was full of big ideas and radical plans. Munira could get things done; see something she wanted and work to make it happen. Owning the shop would not have happened if she had not encouraged Hashim to take the chance and buy it. He owed so much to her; the least he could do was to support her in the steps she wanted to take.

'When is the interview?' Hashim asked, putting his arms around Munira. 'I'd like to drop you off there, if that's all right.'

'It's on Tuesday.' Munira smiled, her heart lightened from the way the conversation had gone. She was lucky, beyond belief, to have Hashim as her husband. 'And of course that's all right. I would love it if you came with me.'

On the morning of the interview, Munira dressed in the outfit she had borrowed from Helen. She felt different in these clothes: more restricted somehow, the fabric around her thighs feeling too tight, the buttons on the blouse closing her in. In the end, she changed, instead choosing a simple apple-green sari with a white border – a birthday gift from Hashim – to wear instead. Better to be comfortable than to fidget with her clothes all day, she thought. Hashim had taken the morning off work, leaving the shop in charge of Mirza, who ran the butchery counter. Munira and Hashim both walked Joy to the school gates to drop her off – a novelty for all of them – and then Hashim took Munira for breakfast at a café around the corner from the library.

'You need to keep your strength up for the interview.' He beamed at her across their plates of white buttered toast, piled high with fried eggs with brown edges and yellow runny yolks, and baked beans. But Munira could hardly manage more than a little toast and some of the milky, sweet tea.

'It's the nerves,' she explained apologetically to Hashim.

'Never mind,' Hashim assured her, 'we'll celebrate properly when you get the job.'

Munira knew he was trying to bolster her confidence, but talking about the job as though it were an inevitability only added more pressure. She decided not to point this out to Hashim, lest his remorse make her feel even worse. 'We'll see.' Munira sipped some more tea and took a bite of toast. 'Anyway, let's talk about something else.' She looked around the café. 'This place is nice; how did you know about it?'

Hashim smiled ruefully. 'Rofikul Bhai and I used to come here, back in the day.' He gestured to a table in the corner with his head. 'That was where we were sitting when he gave me the papers that said you were coming over.' Hashim and Munira did not really talk about Rofikul much; when he was mentioned it was usually because Adam had asked a question. This spontaneous acknowledgement of their shared lives in a previous, simpler time was not something they allowed themselves often. 'I can still smell the smoke of his cigarettes, you know,' Hashim continued, half to himself. 'Used to try to show me how to do it, but I never really took to it.'

'Good.' Munira was studying her husband's face carefully. He seemed melancholy, all of a sudden, this memory of his cousin haunting their breakfast treat. 'It's a disgusting habit.'

Hashim checked his watch. 'Fifteen minutes to go – shall we walk over now?' He slipped some notes under his plate and pushed out his chair. Munira stood up and followed him out of the café. They did not speak much on the walk, each lost in their own musings. When they arrived at the front entrance of the library, they stood on the threshold slightly awkwardly. Hashim and Munira were affectionate towards each other in the privacy of their own home, although not in front of the children, but neither of them was really used to moments like this in public, where some kind of affectionate or encouraging gesture would be the natural thing to do. In the end, Hashim patted Munira's shoulder gently.

'Good luck.'

'Thank you.'

'I'll wait here and meet you afterwards.'

'All right, thank you.'

Hashim watched Munira turn around and walk through the heavy wooden door and across the foyer towards the reception desk. He imagined her clear, low tone saying all the right things, impressing all those interviewers the way she impressed him every day. She deserved this, he thought. He took a newspaper from his jacket pocket, settled on one of the benches outside the library, and began to read.

Much to her bewilderment and Hashim's delight, Munira was offered the job on the spot: three half days at the princely wage of fifteen pounds a week. Hashim, Munira, Helen and the children celebrated that evening with cakes from the bakery near Helen's work – eclairs stuffed with cream, scones sandwiched together with sticky strawberry jam, tarts filled with egg custard and glazed fruit. Even little Joy was excited, sensing the lightness of mood and relishing the opportunity to stay up with the grown-ups as they talked late into the evening, their low voices a soothing background hum. In the end she had fallen asleep bundled up in Abbu's shawl, the one that was always folded on the footstool beside the armchair, and Adam had carried her to bed, gently unfurling Joy's self-made cocoon of her father's scent and presence and tucking it around her.

Munira started work the following week with the same kind of back-to-school enthusiasm she saw in Joy at the start of each new term. She even bought a pair of sports shoes, like the ones Adam wore, to support her feet which tired from standing and traipsing about the stacks for half of the day. When she had first tried them on, it felt as though her entire foot was enveloped in a warm hug.

'Why have I never worn these before?' she asked Helen when she got home that evening, proudly showing off her new white trainers with their pink rubber sole and matching pink laces.

She quickly took to her duties of re-shelving returned books and stamping the little paper slip in the front covers when people wanted to take them out. It was methodical work and Munira found the pace of it all rather soothing; nobody ever spoke above a whisper and she often sought quiet moments of solitude in the stacks, tracing a finger over the spines of books that felt like old friends and sometimes picking one up just to inhale the dusty, rich scent. Working at the library had reminded her of the things she used to take pleasure in and provided her with a stillness that wasn't rooted in boredom. She sometimes wondered whether that library with its winding stairways and open bay windows had somehow saved what was left of her sense of being her own person.

Hashim gradually became used to Munira's diminished presence around the shop, and although he missed her, he never told her so lest he make her feel guilty somehow. He wanted her to enjoy this new pursuit of hers. And the additional wage helped them both too. It was a bad time for small businesses – well, for everyone really. Every day there was front-page news of another strike, another shutdown, another call for elections, another leader toppled. They were the lucky ones: Hashim's trade was steady enough, although inflation affected them all, but he was having to work longer hours to save money on hiring additional staff. He felt tired, drained from his very bones on some days, with the early deliveries to manage and the late-night lock-ups. He used to be fine with grafting such long days, but his body wasn't what it used to be.

On some days after school, Hashim would be joined at the shop by Adam – usually on his way home from the boxing club which was conveniently close by. Adam would perch at the counter while Hashim did his stock-take, noting down numbers and interrupting the list of orders with anecdotes about his day, what they had learned in class that evening, who had been given detention at school, and so on. Hashim relaxed into the sound of Adam's chatter, occasionally responding, but mostly letting it wash over him like warm, soothing waves of comfort.

'And so we have to do this family history project,' Adam was saying, 'and I'm going to type mine up on the typewriter you got me. It's gonna look the best out of everyone's.'

At the mention of family, Hashim looked up. 'Family history? So this is, what, an exam for history, or . . .?'

'No, we have to write our family stories – who's in our family tree, where they came from and that. The teacher said it will be interesting to trace migration paths; I think she meant, like, where people have come from. She said the other day in class that there's no such thing as "real British". What do you think?'

Hashim ignored the question. 'So have you asked your mother about your family history then?'

Adam shrugged. 'Not yet, but I will. I wanted to ask you, though, about my dad and that.'

'Yes?'

'Well, I know some stuff – like where he's from and that he's your cousin. But I don't know his date of birth, do I? Or when he and Mam got married. And I need that for the family tree. And I don't know his parents' names. Things like that.'

'I see.'

'Yeah. So can I ask you then, some of this stuff and you can tell me?'

Hashim saw no reason not to agree – it was natural, of course, and Adam's curiosity had been increasing over the last couple of years anyway. If anything this 'project' seemed just to formalise an already growing curiosity.

'Yes, all right. If I know the answers I'll tell you. But there may be things I don't know.'

'Okay.' Adam unzipped his school bag and took out a notebook and a pencil. 'Where was my dad born?'

The name slipped off Hashim's tongue with ease: 'Sylhet town. His family was from the city, you see, we were in the village. I think they moved back to the village once Rofikul's father – your grandfather – retired.' Hashim paused for a moment, realising for the first time how small his nephew's family world was. No grandparents in his life, on either side. One aunt and one uncle. How different it all was to the sprawling, untamed, topsy-turvy childhood Hashim had enjoyed.

Adam seemed unfazed at the mention of a grandparent. 'So how are you and my dad related? Like, on what side?' Adam held his pencil poised above the page, like a reporter uncovering a breaking news story.

'My father and his mother were brother and sister. So we were cousins. His mother left our village when she married, and they lived in the city after that.'

'Does my dad have any other brothers and sisters?'

Hashim nodded slowly. 'Yes, he does – he was in the middle of five.' He related their names as he remembered them; nicknames they were called by their family, rather than their official school names. 'That's how we knew each other.' Hashim smiled apologetically.

'That's all right.' Adam shrugged. 'How about when Mam and my dad got married? What was the date?'

Hashim thought for a moment. 'I can tell you that, if you like.' He nodded slowly. 'But why don't you ask your mother the questions to do with her? She might like to talk about it with you herself.'

'Do you think?' Adam seemed doubtful. 'She's always so tired after work and that.'

'Try her,' Hashim encouraged, 'and if she still doesn't seem that keen, then don't worry – I'll answer what I can.'

'All right, I will.' Adam hopped down from his perch on the counter. 'I'd better be getting back anyway, but see you tomorrow.'

'Take care walking back.' Hashim patted Adam on the back. 'Just run up first and see your aunty before you go home.'

Adam swung his rucksack on to his shoulder and bounded towards the door leading to the upstairs flat, where Munira was pottering around cooking dinner. Hashim checked his watch: he still had another couple of hours to go before he could close the shop and head upstairs. He sighed heavily, in the way he only allowed himself when nobody else was around, and sat down on the stool behind the counter. He used to be able to handle this, the standing, the lifting and carrying – and he was hardly an old man now – but everything just seemed more strenuous lately; his muscles ached more than they used to, and sometimes he felt his breath catching at the back of his throat as though he were more exhausted than he ought to be.

He sat for a moment or two, and then heaved himself back off the stool and went over to the front door. With a fleeting sense of guilt, he flipped the shop sign to 'CLOSED' and turned the latch. What was the point in being the owner of the shop if he couldn't occasionally knock off a little early? Besides, he thought, Munira would be happy to have an earlier night together than usual. Perhaps they could watch something on television, a soothing wildlife documentary about somewhere far-off in Africa, or maybe a gardening programme, before tucking Joy into bed. Dimming the lights in the shop, Hashim made his way up the steps towards the warmth of his home, and the familiar comfort that lay within.

31

NOBODY HAD WARNED Helen about the guilt that came with motherhood. It had somehow nestled deep within her, quite possibly at the very moment of her child's conception. As the baby had grown within her, losing his gills and growing fingers and toes, in sweet delicious secret, so too had her guilt. It fed off the love and anxiety and desire to do everything correctly. She barely recognised its presence beside her any more, the cold fingers of inadequacy needling her as regularly as her own heartbeat.

But Adam was changing. Her chubby, red-cheeked baby was hardly recognisable in this lanky young man, growing as tall and as fast as a weed before her very eyes. Adolescence had apparently rendered him almost mute, their interactions reduced to monosyllabic grunts of affirmation or disagreement; the interpretation was open, at her own peril. Sometimes Helen wanted to brush away the dark mop of hair from his face, kiss his forehead and plead for a cuddle. At other times, she felt like shaking him, his laconic gait and brooding stare making her want to laugh and weep from exasperation at the same time. Even Munira sometimes received the brunt of Adam's moody silences. The only person with whom he did not seem to be perpetually on the brink of impatience was Hashim.

But there were indications of Adam's own self-discovery which, in her more positive moments, Helen found reassuring.

The boxing club, as reluctant as she had been initially to allow him to take part, seemed to have given Adam a sense of purpose, a routine that involved something beyond just school and home. When she saw him chatting with the other boys he appeared so confident, so much more comfortable than she had seen him before. Sometimes they swapped books at this club, she noticed. Adam came home with titles like *The Autobiography of Malcolm X* and *Why We Can't Wait* and stayed up late into the night reading them, scratching notes into the margin in pencil. Helen picked up the books sometimes, to leaf through the pages and see what her son was drinking in so ardently. She was struck by the zeal that seemed to leap from the pages, the passion and fire for freedom and justice. No wonder Adam seemed unable to put these books down.

Something had awakened a desire in Adam to know more about himself. It had surprised Helen at first, when he had come home one evening after training and asked to know more about where his family came from. *It's for a history project*, he had said. When Helen had begun to explain how she met Rofikul, Adam had placed his hand on hers – *not about him*, Adam had said gently. *About you. Your family.* It had taken her aback, this newfound curiosity, and moved her at the same time. She had always thought that if Adam wanted to know anything, it would be about his father, rather than her.

It was the first of many conversations the two of them shared; about Helen's parents and how they had come to Liverpool from Ireland to work on the docks. It wasn't the only reason they moved, she admitted to her son. Her mother was pregnant at the time, with Helen, and the couple were not only unmarried – scandal enough – but had formed a relationship that breached the constraints that faith and trad- ition laid out for them. In the end they had compromised, her Protestant father and her Catholic mother conducting their marriage ceremony at one of the side altars in a little chapel in Liverpool; the priest refused to let them marry at the main altar but was open-minded enough at least to solemnise the union in the eyes of the Lord. It was harder to tell Adam about what life had been like in the years she could remember, once the thrill of her parents' act of passionate rebellion had waned and been replaced by anxieties about rent, money for groceries and new shoes. She felt ashamed sometimes, wishing that she could tell Adam happier, more wholesome stories – but he just sat beside her and listened while she recounted fragments from her childhood, memories she had not conjured up in decades. Afterwards, Adam would say goodnight and disappear to his room. Helen could hear the rattle of the typewriter keys, the light from the desk lamp shining out from under the door, well into the early hours of the morning.

When his mother or aunt asked Adam what was so appealing about the boxing club, he found it difficult to put into words just what it had come to mean to him. It was more than simply exercise or routine – although both those things did lend it a certain attraction. And it was more than just socialising too; he could easily have spent less gruelling hours hanging out at the rec with his other friends who eschewed the discipline of the club and its strict training regimen. It was a community. For the first time, and like so many of the other boys, Adam felt invested in something that extended beyond the familiar things he knew and took for granted every day: the comfort of home, the presence of his immediate family, the lessons at school, the games at break-times. Boxing was an example of his autonomy, evidence that he had chosen to commit to something, and measurable only by his own hard work.

It was also an environment where topics that Adam didn't hear mentioned elsewhere were openly discussed. The snatched conversations that he overheard in the locker rooms and between training practice, and the longer arguments that were thrashed out between the older lads sometimes, were about real concerns. Not trigonometry or cell division, or any of the pointless stuff he had to learn for school. This was relevant: how to avoid trouble on the street but the best methods for self-defence if someone started on you. About police harassing guys who looked like Ali and the rest. About politics: who was in power, and why that mattered. This was useful, Adam believed. This would help him, unlike memorising the genealogy of English kings or naming every tributary in the British Isles.

Ali believed it mattered, too. In the years since starting the club, Ali had seen the ranks swell. They were mostly kids, who heard about the place from a mate, who had a mate who went there. The majority came once or twice and never bothered returning. But some of them not only stayed, but came more and more regularly as the months passed. These were the ones who seemed to have something buried deep inside them, a need for routine and discipline and to feel that they belonged. Adam was one of those kids. Ali knew why lads like his nephew, Faisal, and his mates wanted to box: self-defence was a phrase on everyone's lips, with the dark, predictable account of a new attack on someone they knew an almost weekly occurrence. But the more time he spent talking to the kids, and listening to them talk among themselves, the more it became clear that they were more than just afraid: they felt helpless. Perpetrators of attacks went unpunished; violence towards them felt like a non-negotiable price of going to school as a black kid or a Paki. It disturbed him, this sense of paralysis in these kids – the belief that

267

systems were set as they were and nothing they or anyone else could do would change that. These kids needed educating.

And so books came into the training curriculum at the boxing club. Ali prescribed reading for the kids – but unsurprisingly most of the schools did not hold the texts Ali suggested. Instead, he paid to have pages photocopied, at the club's expense, and doled them out to the boys to read. Civil rights treatises. Biographies of leaders. Manifestos of political parties and resistance movements. In between sparring and jabbing, Ali would quiz the kids about what they'd read. Some of them were more diligent than others; Adam most of all. Ali would push them, testing how much they had understood, proffering challenges and expecting a swift retort. It was boxing of a different kind. Adam drank from this pool of knowledge as though parched. Not only did he debate and discuss what he had read, but he wrote his own tracts too, bringing them to Ali to read and offer comments. It was Adam who drafted the memo proposing the establishment of a resistance movement – an 'army' he called it, much to Ali's initial amusement – of lads like him, blacks and Asians and others who felt the same way, who would band together to resist – peacefully where possible, but with the use of force if pushed – threats against them. Ali recognised it for what it was: an attempt to assert some power in a world where they felt as though they had none. A reminder, most of all to themselves, that they had autonomy and they could exercise it at any time.

The Black and Asian Resistance Army, as the group voted to name itself, had a manifesto that was heavy on mission and ideology, and light on how exactly to set about achieving that. It was early days, Adam assured himself and the others. It was more important to agree ultimate goals to strive towards: a society free of discrimination and prejudice;

equality for all races; harsh punishments for those who oppressed or harassed people of other races. Adam drafted letters on his typewriter to get the others to sign and send to their councillors, MPs, even to the Home Office. They talked about direct action – marching, protesting in public places with pickets and signs – but as yet had not taken to the streets to demonstrate their beliefs directly.

It was unsurprising, in a way, that it was Adam who seemed to be the most proactive of the lads at the club in wanting to establish a shared common cause. Ali was well aware of the occasional whispering in the locker rooms about 'the half-caste kid' and had witnessed more than a couple of incidents that he suspected were rooted in the issue, and severely reprimanded those involved. Adam's half-white side of his identity acted as water, in the eyes of some of his peers, serving to dilute his identity as an Asian, washing away the brown. In response Adam could only strive all the more – to train harder than the others, to read more widely than the others, to think and write more prolifically than the others – in order to prove his legitimacy in this particular camp. At no point had Adam ever been asked which, if any, camp he would have chosen himself. It did not occur to him that there was ever an element of choice.

32

'SAME SHIT, SAME stink.' Faisal spat on the grey, gum-spotted concrete and pushed his shirt sleeves up towards his elbows. His arms were smooth, the faint lines of his adolescent muscles showing, having emerged victoriously from beneath the layers of his recently shed puppy fat. 'National Front, British Movement, they can call themselves whatever they want – they're all fucking Nazis.'

'Neo-Nazis,' Adam corrected his friend drily and lit a Woodbine. If his mother saw him now, he would be dead. He put the thought firmly out of his mind. 'They're New Age about their racism, y'know.'

'What's "new" about this lot?' Faisal gestured contemptuously with his head towards the crowd that had gathered in the open space outside City Hall, chatting and cracking tins of cheap lager, ready to begin their procession through the streets. 'Fucking fat bald bastards, too lazy to get a job so they blame their shit lives on us lot.'

They did look much worse than their predecessors, thought Adam. If the Nazis were well turned out – groomed, clipped, smooth in their evilness – then this lot were at the other end of the spectrum. A sea of shorn heads and pink tattooed arms held up placards demanding BLACKS GO BACK and KEEP BRITAIN BRITISH. Some of the banners were emblazoned with swastikas. FREE SPEECH FOR WHITE

PATRIOTS screamed another. RIGHTS FOR WHITES. On either side of the road leading up to City Hall square were metal gates barricading in – or out, depending on how you looked at it – the counter-protest groups who had turned up to rally against the march of Britain's most notorious far-right group. The National Front regularly scheduled street rallies and marches, resulting in an unprecedented display of public activism among a population not generally known for its civil participation. Their activism was matched only by the vehemence of its opponents: from national organisations such as the Anti-Nazi League, to the lads from Ardwick's own Black and Asian Resistance Army.

'Well, they don't get any points for originality,' Adam agreed, exhaling a white cloud of smoke the way he had seen Ali do. Adam and Faisal's exchange was interrupted by Ali's raised voice, rallying the group of young men – teenagers mostly – who had turned out to counter-protest with their painted banners and drums and whistles. It evoked scenes they had seen elsewhere in the country on television: the Battle of Lewisham and other large-scale protests where lads who looked like them gathered to demonstrate against those who wanted to expel them from the country they called home.

'The route of this march,' Ali shouted, 'passes through the heart of this city. *Our* city.' He surveyed the faces of each and every one of the assembled supporters – some Asian, some black, a handful of whites – mostly from the boxing club he had founded. 'It's a smack in the face for people like us,' he continued angrily. 'That the council think it's all right to let fucking Nazis march through this city is a fucking outrage.'

'We need to get them where it hurts. Don't re-elect a single one of them bastards,' Faisal shouted out, honing his skills in the art of rallying a crowd.

Cheers and murmurs of agreement rose from the crowd and then were quieted by Ali's raised hand.

'Yes,' he addressed the protesters. 'The ballot box is one way to target this. Like the great Malcolm X said: *A ballot is like a bullet. You don't throw your ballots until you see a target, and if that target is not within your reach, keep your ballot in your pocket.* And when the time comes, we'll know how to make our ballots land like bullets. But today isn't about the council as it stands – however misguided they are in what they let fly as "free speech". This is about facing up to fascism. Looking at its ugly face straight on and spitting in its eye. This is about showing those bastards that this' – he raised a fist and pumped it in the air with each word – 'is – our – country.'

The Black and Asian Resistance Army cheered, blowing their whistles and banging drums. Ali continued passionately, rousing the crowd and getting them ready for whatever the day had in store for them.

'We're not going anywhere. Let those fucking rivers run, let them run with blood like their man Powell said it would. It's not gonna be our blood. We're not going back to nowhere.'

Vincent Aldridge fancied himself an adventurous man, so it was with alarm that he considered this dawning realisation: he supported these lads and what they were doing, that was God's honest truth. It was right that they didn't take this shit lying down. But he was also terrified on their behalf. These kids were so confidently aware of their rights that there was no way this could possibly end well. Vincent came from a generation where keeping your head down and making the best of the situation was as much as anyone could hope for. He and his peers found themselves embroiled in the draining act of tempering themselves in order to appear as little an inconvenience as possible. When he and his friends tried to have parties, their white neighbours would complain about the noise, making threats against Vincent's record player, cursing the music, and taking moral umbrage over the sordid activities that existed only in the white person's fantasies of what a black person's party might look like. And so Vincent and his friends had had to become timid in their socialising, playing their records at an almost apologetic volume.

Going to the pub was an alternative of sorts, but only if you went to the right ones; daring to set foot in the wrong ones could lead to serious consequences, the type you'd wear on your face. Vincent remembered the first time he ventured into a pub when he first arrived in Manchester: how the other punters' heads had swivelled in his direction as he walked through the door and how the murmur of conversation had ground to a halt as he took a seat at the bar and ordered an ale. Feeling the gaze of the regulars bore like drills into his back, he had finished his pint, every sip more searingly uncomfortable than the last, but he was determined not to be fazed. He got up, wrapped his checked scarf around his neck, left the Queen's Head and never returned.

Vincent had decided to come along to this march today because he was tired. Tired of being told where he was and wasn't welcome, and why that related to his skin colour, as though it were some kind of justifiable rationale. He was tired of it spilling over into another generation, and then another. He helped out sometimes at the boxing club; he'd been a bit of a sparring champ in his own right, back in the day, back when they were self-taught and you had to know how to fight mean to stay all right on the streets. It was Marie who had suggested it to him: *Why don't you go down that new boxing club where Adam and his mates go? You could teach them young things a thing or two.* It was Munira

273

who gave what he was doing a name. *You're a mentor to those boys*, she had said, and the word had reverberated around Vincent's mind like a shiny gold star, telling himself that at his age and with forty years as an outsider, he had something of value to offer these lads. It didn't often feel like he did; Vincent felt as though he had spent half his life waiting for something good to happen, and the other half feeling nervous that when something *did* come along, he wouldn't somehow be ready for it; not prepared, or even not deserving.

There had been encounters of course – but nothing loving; nothing that he would call a relationship. He had made his peace with it. Love did not come to people like him, men who desired love, but not with women. Not in these times, in this place. Instead he busied himself with work – the garage had grown over the years. Nothing huge, just a modest outfit with a steady stream of reliable customers. He saw the girls often, especially his Marie. He wondered sometimes if, despite her numerous affairs, she hadn't married all these years or even had kids of her own because of him. He tried not to think about it too often; when he did, he could feel the snaking sense of guilt wind its tendrils around his gut and squeeze. He'd have liked kids of his own, a little angel whose hair he'd tie up with ribbons and parade around town, the proudest daddy in the city. But to do that he would have had to love women.

Vincent stamped his feet against the cold and raised his placard over his shoulder – GO HOME NAZIS – and nodded along to the rallying cries from Ali and the cheers from the lads. They were decent kids. Not spoiling for a fight, just sick of it. Over in the distance, beyond the metal barricades, the fascists were gathering in an angry sea of pink and white. Why they gotta be so goddamn ugly? Vincent wondered. He remembered his mother's warnings: that ugly thoughts gave you an ugly face, *so mind you don't be having no ugly thoughts, boy.* But this lot, it wasn't just their thoughts, surely. He wasn't a fan of this eugenics stuff that Hitler and his pals were all so interested in, but it baffled him that these fellas could think they were the top of the racial hierarchy. *This* lot? Vincent chuckled despite himself.

The roar from the crowds surged like distant waves drawing closer and closer before crashing against Adam's ears. The chanting, the stamping, the calling for blood: it was like a battlefield before the first horn had been blown. It was primal. The two armies had assembled. The fascists had the advantage of space, with the council having granted them right of way to march down the wide streets of the city. The protesters were confined to the sides, flanking the length of the roads through which the fascists marched. The police lined the streets like ravens, clad in their black uniforms, an intended peace-keeping force between the two groups. Further back, other police constables were perched on large chestnut horses, holding the reins tight as though they truly were preparing for battle.

Adam looked at the crowd surrounding him: almost every face was brown or black, and overwhelmingly youthful. Despite the presence of a handful of older men, this was not a fight for their fathers to face. Several allies, white-skinned and bearded, zealous in their progressive outrage, were interspersed in the crowd too. In total, they were almost equal in number to the assembled National Front supporters. In the road, the fascists were chanting and waving their Union flags. They were veterans at this by now, having marched through places from Lewisham to Bradford. The counter-protesters were not as practised in the art; for most of them, this was their first demonstration, feeling the need

275

to defend themselves against these outsiders who had come from all over the country to declare that 'Britain is for Britons'. The shouting sounded like a football chant, strangely melodic in its synchronicity. *Go home, Paki bastards*, they chanted, *keep Britain British*.

'The fuck does that even mean?' Faisal muttered to Adam.

The crowd was marching through the streets now, the red, white and blue flag held aloft in triumph. Sounds of drums and whistles floated along the route of the march. There was something almost carnival-like about the whole thing, thought Adam, with the rhythm of feet pounding and voices chanting in unison and the huge waves of communal movement. Barricaded down the sides of the route, the counter-protesters raised their voices too, waving placards and stamping their feet.

'Fucking outrageous,' Faisal complained with a scowl, 'that we get caged in like animals, but the Nazi bastards get to parade through the streets like gala queens.'

'Funny sort of gala queens,' Adam replied, hoisting the heavy sign higher on his shoulders. ASIANS AND BLACKS WON'T GO BACK it read in block letters. A roaring seemed to erupt a few metres ahead of them. 'What's that?' Adam asked, craning his neck to see beyond the assembled crowds.

They heard a crash, the sound of a metal barrier being overturned on to the road. The crowd surged forward, releasing a collective roar, carrying both Adam and Faisal along with it. It was impossible to move in any direction, except to be swept along with the flow of the crowd, even as it burst into the street and crushed those at the front into the iron railings. Before they could realise what was happening, they found themselves spilling out into the main section where the National Front were marching. Adam looked behind him and saw the sea of bodies flooding into the road over and around the barriers that came crashing down with every wave.

Police whistles rang shrilly as officers lurched into the crowd, batons swinging. Raising his arms above his face to shield himself, the way he had learned in boxing, Adam stumbled his way through the crowd which had stopped marching, instead erupting into full-blown violence as the demonstrators, counter-protesters and police descended into chaos, with placards, batons and fists raining down on one another.

'Adam!'

The cry came from somewhere behind him. Adam turned to see where Faisal was shouting from, but his friend was lost to him in the swirling masses.

'Faisal, where are you?' Adam yelled, but any reply was drowned out in the din.

A police officer barged past, shoving him roughly to the side, and Adam stumbled into what was left of the metal barrier. He clung to it tightly while watching the scenes unfold around him. A white man giving a Nazi salute before getting kicked in the head by a young black man wearing a leather jacket. A couple of Asian kids being beaten by police with batons. Right in the middle of the street a couple of long-haired white students were trampling the Union Jack, dragging it deliberately under their feet. Riot police were lining up with their plastic shields, ready to form a barrier. Adam heard a sound like a rush of wind and the explosion of a bin that had been thrown into the crowd. He had to get out of there. He had no idea where Faisal or Ali or any of the others were.

'Adam!'

He whirled around at the sound of his name and saw Vincent, his blazer torn and missing the hat that he always wore. Vincent pulled Adam close, clapping him on the back tightly.

'We need to get outta here, lad,' Vincent gasped. 'It's getting ugly.'

'I know, but I need to find the others. They might need me.' Adam twisted around desperately to see who he could spot in the crowds, but the smoke was thick and the police had sprayed something that stung his eyes and made him choke.

'You can't be waiting for no one, Adam.' Vincent was firm, his hand gripping Adam's arm tightly. 'You're just a lad, they'll throw you in jail without even thinking. We've got to go.'

Vincent's hold was surprisingly strong and Adam felt himself being dragged along.

'All right, okay, I'm coming.' Adam shrugged off Vincent's hand and the two of them made their way through the crowds, trying to stick to the edges. Sirens were blaring, police horses whinnying as they reared up and kicked at the crowds indiscriminately. Across the street, Adam caught a glimpse of Ali squaring up to a police officer, surrounded by three or four other officers with batons.

'Through here, lad.' Vincent motioned to Adam to follow him down a narrow passage between two of the metal barricades.

Adam slipped through and glanced behind him. All along the street, barriers were overturned, plastic bollards scattered across the road amid torn fronds of police tape. Crushed beer cans and cardboard signs lay abandoned in the gutters while bodies hurled against one another in a soundtrack of carnage.

Vincent rubbed his skinned knuckles and nodded at Adam. 'You all right?'

Adam nodded. 'Yeah, fine. We need to find the others

though – last thing I saw was Ali getting laid into by a couple of coppers, and then I lost him.'

'There's nothing we can do right now, lad.' Vincent's tone was steady. 'Best thing is to get home, and then later we can head down the club, see who made it back.'

Together they walked along the deserted streets away from the centre, sticking to the side roads to avoid any hassle out on the main route of the march. The afternoon sky was still bright on the horizon, the autumn wind nipping at their hands and face as they made their way home, exhausted and uncertain.

Hashim had almost keeled over when Vincent and Adam came into the shop later that afternoon, the front door jangling. Adam had blood crusted down the side of his face, while Vincent's clothes were torn, and both looked exhausted.

'What on earth?' Hashim practically leaped over the counter towards them. 'What happened to you?' He grabbed Adam's shoulder and tilted the boy's face towards him to examine the cut. It was shallower than it looked, thank God.

'We were at the demonstration.' Adam winced as Hashim took a tissue from his pocket and started rubbing the cut. 'It's okay, Chacha, I'll wash it later.' He reached up and touched the tightening brown mark on his cheek, almost surprised at its presence.

'The demonstration?' Hashim threw a glance over to Vincent. 'What, you too?'

Vincent shrugged, refusing Hashim's implication of irresponsibility. 'Yeah, me too.'

'What were you thinking, both of you? You know these things can be dangerous.' Hashim's voice rose; a couple of customers looked over curiously.

'We're fine, Chacha, honestly,' Adam tried to interject.

279

'Yes, you look "fine". I'm sure your mother would agree.' Hashim glared.

'Hashim,' Vincent tried again, more conciliatory this time. 'We are all right. Just a few scratches and bruises, you know what it's like.'

Adam looked over at his uncle. Did he really know what it was like? Hashim was steely-eyed in a way Adam had never seen before.

'I do know what it's like, and that's exactly why you have no business getting yourselves mixed up in something that could be so dangerous.' If Hashim realised he was shouting, he made no effort to modulate it.

'We had no choice, Chacha, we have to resist—' Adam was vehement but his uncle cut him off abruptly.

'Don't tell me about having no choice.' Hashim was enraged. 'Do you think you're the first person who has ever been black or brown in this country? Why do you think I encouraged you in your boxing, lad? Do you think I did it so you could have a hobby?'

Adam at least had the grace to remain silent in the face of his uncle's uncharacteristic tirade.

'You're supposed to be able to defend yourself, not go looking for trouble. Getting involved in marches – who do you think is going to be on your side? You think the police will listen to you over the white people? Do you?' Hashim turned to Vincent. 'And you! You should know better. At your age, you think you're gonna become a revolutionary? Taking up arms, are you?'

Vincent looked Hashim coolly in the eye. 'I'm not going to fight with you, Hashim. I did what I thought was right. These people are marching through this city, *our* city, saying we ain't welcome. Saying *we* gotta go back.'

'What do you care what they *say*, Vincent?' Hashim banged

the counter hard with his fist. 'People will always say things. We just have to get on with our lives, not go chasing trouble.'

'Hashim.' Vincent's voice had an air of finality in it. 'We *can't* get on with our lives if there's people wanting to do us harm. And we can't be relying on the police to protect us. Adam here, he and his mates, they know this. That's why they was there. And you should be praising him, Hashim, for standing up for himself and his kind.'

Both the men turned and looked at Adam, as if remembering the source of their argument. He stood silently between them, listening to the exchange. Hashim cleared his throat. He did not agree with Vincent's point of view, but now was not the time to have this conversation.

'Adam, I'll take you upstairs. You'll wash your face and then we'll ring your mother and she can come and collect you.' Hashim turned to Vincent. 'Get home safely, Vincent. And thank you for bringing Adam home.'

Vincent nodded and raised a hand to touch his hat before realising that he was not wearing it. 'I'll see you around, Hashim. Take it easy, Adam.' He jangled through the front door and stepped into the street. It was getting dark now, and the crowds had probably already dispersed from the march. Vincent pulled his jacket around himself a little tighter, thrust his hands into his pockets and started walking towards home.

He could understand Hashim's fears – Hashim didn't want the boy to get hurt, of course not – but now wasn't the time to sit tight and hope this ugliness would just go away. Vincent and Hashim had been in this country for long enough to know that it didn't work like that. Nobody was going to turn around one day and simply give you your rights, packaged up with a dainty bow on the front. You had to demand them, and if you still didn't get them, well, then you had to stand up and take them – by any means necessary.

Any reprimand that Adam might have faced for his actions was that day overshadowed by the news that reached them later that evening. Helen had come to collect Adam after Hashim telephoned her to tell her about the events of the afternoon and, at Munira's insistence, both Helen and Adam ended up staying for dinner. It was a silent affair, with only Joy and Munira keeping up any effort at conversation. The telephone rang and Hashim excused himself to go and answer it. The others could hear the brusque conversation on Hashim's side floating in from the hallway – *yes . . . no* – and then, *I'll go and fetch her.* Hashim returned to the room, grim-faced.

'It's for you,' he said to Munira. 'Mrs Farooq. Her brother's got himself mixed up in something.'

Adam looked up in alarm. 'What, at the march?'

'What, were you involved too?' Hashim threw his nephew a look. 'She wants to talk to you, Munira.' He shook his head. 'Thinks you'll be able to help somehow.'

Munira got up and went to take the call in the hallway. Adam and Helen strained their ears in an attempt to hear what was being said. Joy and Hashim continued eating silently. After a few moments, Munira returned to the table, with a face to match Hashim's.

'What's going on, Munira?' Helen asked anxiously.

Munira looked at Adam, debating whether or not to speak in front of him.

'You can tell me, Chachi,' Adam pleaded. 'I'll find out anyway from the lads at boxing.'

'Like hell you will,' Hashim interjected. 'You're not going near that place, not now.'

282

Joy blinked at her father's uncharacteristically rough tone, a little taken aback. Adam was mutinous.

Munira glanced from Hashim to Helen and sighed. 'Ali has been arrested.'

'*What?*' Adam slammed the table with his hands. 'Why, for what?'

'That's enough from you.' Helen put her hand on Adam's arm to quieten him. 'But yes – why?'

Munira held up her hands. 'I don't know the specifics. Neither does Mrs Farooq. All she heard was that Ali and a few of the other boys from the boxing club were arrested today at the march and they haven't been released yet. Faisal managed to get away safely and came home and told his mother she needs to hire a lawyer for Ali.' Munira looked over to Helen. 'That's why she rang – she knows you work in a law firm. She wanted to know if you can help.'

'As a *secretary*.' Helen was baffled. 'How on earth could I help?'

'She doesn't know anyone else who can. Is there anyone you can recommend? Someone from work maybe?'

'I don't know; we usually do family law, not criminal cases.' Helen paused to think. 'There was a chap who left soon after I joined, I think to set up his own firm. A bit odd, but awfully nice, he was. I think he did cases to do with the police.' Helen rubbed her temples. 'Stone, I think he's called. Maurice Stone.'

'All right.' Munira nodded. 'Find out his contact details from your work and I'll get in touch with him first thing in the morning.'

They returned to eating their dinner in silence, even Joy giving up her lively patter, trying not to think the worst of what could happen to Ali and the others.

33

MAURICE STONE WAS the kind of man who believed that in a world with such injustice, being righteously angry was a moral obligation. Well, part of it. The other part of that obligation was to stand up and *do* something about it. At first appearances, Mr Stone didn't seem to exude fiery conviction. He was a mild-looking middle-aged man with a slightly receding hairline, glasses that sat partway down his nose, and hands that seemed a little too big for his wrists. But on closer inspection, it was possible to detect a warmth in his eyes and the determined – even belligerent – set of his chin. He was the kind of man who would listen first, and then ask questions, and then carefully come up with a reasoned, detailed and often watertight plan of how to approach an issue. He was the kind of man you wanted on your side. He was also the kind of man who his opponents arrogantly dismissed as being a bleeding-heart activist, led by his gut rather than by reason.

Mr Stone took no offence at being underestimated; it was how he had won numerous cases during his time as a civil rights lawyer, disarming his opposition with carefully constructed arguments delivered with quiet confidence. He took a perverse pride in toppling the Goliaths of the world. The descendant of Jewish refugees who had fled pogroms in the old country, Mr Stone was made of a steelier core

than was apparent at first meeting, and was a passionate
– at times, even fierce – advocate for those he considered
to be the underdog.

It had not taken much to convince him. Glancing through
the highlighted papers that Munira had brought along to
their first meeting at his cramped, third-floor townhouse
office – testimonies she had collected from neighbours, clippings from newspapers, facsimiles of documents she had
pulled from the library archives – Mr Stone had taken off
his glasses and wiped them with the corner of his shirt.

'How long did it take for you to find this information,
Mrs Begum?' he had asked incredulously.

'Two and a half days, but I could have done it faster if I
hadn't had to work at the same time,' Munira had replied
matter-of-factly.

Maurice had shaken his head in disbelief. The woman
must have worked like a machine.

The evidence that Munira had so meticulously gathered
concerned the number of arrests that were made of blacks
and Asians, almost all of them young men, in the local area
over the last twelve months. Most of the arrests had taken
place at public events such as marches and rallies, or counter-
protest demonstrations. Munira had also researched similar
arrests of white men who attended these same public events,
but on the other side of the fence. Her hunch had proven
to be true: less than half as many white men had been
arrested. The police seemingly viewed one group as more
of a threat to public order than the other, and it was not
the self-described fascists.

Maurice's request for Ali either to be charged or released
had been turned down, and Ali and some of the other
boys remained in police custody. Maurice and Munira's

task was now twofold: to secure the release of the detainees; and to prepare their evidence of unfair and disproportionate arrests against black and Asian men. The next stage would be to interview the men who had been arrested, gather their testimony as to how they had been treated in custody, and see how many of them ended up being charged. They also needed to gather testimonies from the families, eyewitness accounts of the beatings the detainees had claimed to have sustained at the hands of the police authorities, often before eventually being released without charge or apology.

Since that first meeting, Munira had spent many hours in the offices of Stone & Associates, going over paperwork for Ali's case. While the others had eventually been released without charge, the accusation brought against Ali was that of *inciting racial hatred*, citing the formation of the Black and Asian Resistance Army at the boxing club as evidence. Ali's defence – that the group was formed as a counter-movement to protest against the rising number and frequency of marches by the National Front and other right-wing groups that snaked through his neighbourhood with alarming ease and with little objection from the law-enforcing authorities – would not stand up in a court of law, Maurice feared. They would have to take a different tack: to say that Ali was wrongfully arrested in the first place, and that the information about the boxing club was simply the police digging around to try to justify their decision to detain Ali for so long. The police were unduly focused on issuing punitive actions against a community they ought to have been protecting at such times.

For the first time in years, Munira felt as though a fire had been stoked somewhere deep within her, and it excited her. Together they worked to overturn the case against Ali, as well as compiling a log of incidents: arrests without charge, abuse during custody, instances of 'random' stop and searches. Every document she read uncovered a new potential lead, another possible incident of misconduct, another interviewee to trace. They were painting a picture, and the faces that appeared on the canvas were familiar: boys who looked like Adam and his friends, trying to get on with their lives in a society that, it seemed, was preoccupied with vilifying them rather than giving them a chance to flourish.

It had taken Hashim longer to get used to Munira working at the library than he cared to admit. The idea that she was not pottering around in the flat above the shop during the day made him feel somehow less rooted as he went about his tasks. Everything seemed more orderly, more as it was supposed to be, when Munira was home; even if Hashim couldn't see her, the idea that she was there was comfort enough. But now she was spending even more hours out of the home working on the case preparation with the lawyer, Mr Stone. Hashim had patiently taken up the mantle, picking up tasks such as packing Joy's lunches and collecting the washing from the launderette. When Munira's meetings with Mr Stone ran late, Hashim waited for her at the bus stop armed with an umbrella and walked her home. On the way, Munira would update Hashim excitedly about the case – the latest findings, information they had uncovered – and Hashim would listen, asking questions at the appropriate times.

Nothing made Hashim happier than seeing Munira happy. But he could not help feeling left out, somehow, from his wife's new field of interest. It sounded ridiculous for a man of his age. He tried to put the thought firmly to the back of his mind, focusing instead on the way Munira's face seemed to glow when she told him of a new aspect of the case she and Mr Stone were exploring. Except she called him Maurice now, rather than Mr Stone. Hashim tried to see this development as a natural result of the increasing familiarity between the two, and nothing more. It was ludicrous for him to think anything else and he hated himself when the irrational fear flickered across his mind. It was wonderful that Munira was enjoying her work so much, and the fact that she wanted to tell Hashim all about it reassured him.

But he was tired, too. The shop was more than a full-time job and ever since Munira stopped working there altogether, Hashim had had to take on longer shifts with fewer opportunities for any serious time off. His bones and his muscles and his chest seemed heavier these days, as though he were carrying around more than he was able to bear. And now he had to come home and take care of Joy and the cooking and the domestic side of things as well. The creeping sense of resentment was something Hashim occasionally noticed and tried to banish immediately, refusing to entertain it even for a short while. But he couldn't deny that it lurked in the corner of his mind at times when he sat at home reading the newspaper and trying not to check the clock too often as he waited for Munira.

It struck Hashim that the two of them had lived their lives to date almost as opposites to how, and who, they really were. Hashim had been forced to leave his village from sheer necessity: his family needed one of the sons to try to make a fortune abroad, and the eldest brother was too precious to spare. Hashim had never intended to leave the place where he had been born, where he knew the scent and colour of the earth in all its seasons. If he closed his eyes now he could still remember the exact layout of the *bari*, could picture where each fruit tree grew, taste the sour tamarind fruit and feel the cool, soft flesh of mango against his face. By contrast, Munira had yearned for the world outside the four walls of her home since the day she was born, almost as if she had been preparing for the moment she would leave behind everything that was familiar to her. She was the one who had devoured books about different countries, learned the language of England, could wield a pen as well as her tongue in this foreign land. Yet, since they arrived on these shores, they had been forced into roles that they would not have chosen. Hashim, engaging with customers and traders all day when he would rather have been tending a garden, enjoying his quiet time at home. And Munira, traipsing about the house performing chores that bored her, when she would rather have been talking to strangers and learning more about this new world that she had been thrown into. Perhaps it was good that now, finally, Munira was able to unfurl her wings a little – to stretch her mind and find her voice within these public spaces with which it had taken her so long to connect, but which undoubtedly, at least in Hashim's mind, needed her and her talent more than ever.

34

IT HAD TAKEN months of meticulous research, gathering evidence and scrutinising case law late into the night, to finally bring about this day. The four of them – Munira, Adam, Mrs Farooq and Faisal – huddled into a tiny room on the second floor of Manchester Magistrates Court. Aside from Mr Stone, Ali, the prosecutor, the judge and a laconic-looking reporter from the local paper, they were the only people present.

Hashim had squeezed Munira's shoulders that morning before he went downstairs to open the shop. *Good luck*, he had said, smiling. *It's going to be a success. I can feel it.* Helen had also offered her encouragement when she came around that morning to drop off Adam before work. *You should be proud, Munira*, she had told her friend. *You've put so much into this.* But the buoyant words had done nothing to unknot Munira's stomach that morning. Ridiculous really, given that she was hardly the one the case rested on: she would not even be speaking in court. But the outcome from today mattered; it mattered so much. This was bigger than Ali, even. This was about holding those in power accountable for their actions; this was about the safety of her children, *all* their children.

On the front bench the journalist lounged with a note-book propped on his knee into which he scribbled without taking his eyes off what was happening in the centre of the courtroom. The Crown Prosecution Service was making its opening statement. The narrative proffered was that Ali was a petty criminal with a history of offences such as handling stolen goods and drug possession: both of these revelations were new to Adam and Faisal, who remembered their drives into the countryside with Ali and the resulting meet-ups with other friends without realising what the trips actually warranted. Still, neither of these things amounted to violence or incitement to it and, as Maurice Stone interjected, were not the charges being brought against Ali in this case. The prosecution went on to outline its accusations against Ali: that he was an instigator of racially based violence and that he had formed a club with premises for the exact purpose of gathering together and indoctrinating local youths, leading them to violent direct action.

Listening from the benches, Adam could barely control his desire to shout out. It was only the warning glance from his aunt that stopped him the few times he opened his mouth to protest. It was so unfair, the way they were making Ali sound: like he was some kind of thug who brainwashed kids into beating people up. It wasn't like that at all. He could feel Faisal bristling beside him and took comfort in the fact that at least they knew the truth. Once the prosecution had finished, Mr Stone began his opening statement with a scathingly measured delivery.

'It is beyond irony – perhaps veering into absurdity – that the case brought against my client is founded upon a provision under the Race Relations Act. An Act *supposedly* intended to promote racial equality but, in this case, serving as an excuse to go after the very demographic it was supposed to protect.' Stone paused to give his listeners time to reflect on the absurdity of the situation. 'The clause regarding *incitement to racial hatred* has wrongfully been wielded here by Her Majesty's Crown Prosecution Service to justify going after my client for forming a club, the aim of which was simply to empower young men to protect themselves against abuse and violent attacks.' He paused before adding gravely, 'Violent attacks that are increasing both in severity and frequency week by week in our community.'

Maurice Stone went on to describe the vicious attacks that had taken place under the guise of 'rallies', regaling the court with eyewitness accounts of how supporters of the fascist organisation, the National Front, had attacked anti-racist counter-protesters while police stood by and watched. The prosecution shifted uneasily in their seats; they had plenty more hearings related to the march to get through in the coming weeks, and the outcome of this one would surely set the tone for the others. At the front of the courtroom, Stone was enjoying delivering his address to the judge. 'In this case, going after a young entrepreneur – a man who has fled persecution in the land of his birth, and who, since arriving on these shores, has founded not only a business but an important meeting-place for his community – is nothing short of a travesty. We should be celebrating those who work towards justice and equality, not trying to pin false accusations on them.'

Opening statements having been made, it was now time for the witnesses and the cross-examination to begin. While Munira whispered updates to Mrs Farooq, translating the heavy English legalese into a language she could understand, Adam and Faisal watched the court proceedings enthralled. The ceremony of it all, the standing and bobbing, sitting and shuffling, was both pompous and impressive to behold. It seemed to Adam and Faisal that the prosecution was trying every trick in the book, including wheeling out a copper as a witness who claimed to have seen Ali leading the attacks against the National Front supporters.

'Funny how none of us who were actually there could barely see a thing, but this guy has 20:20 memory vision,' Faisal muttered to Adam.

None of the video footage or photographic evidence from the protest showed Ali or any of the group he was with engaging in any criminal activity. The film reel from the local news that had been used as evidence by the defence had shown members of Ali's Black and Asian Resistance Army standing on the sidelines with their pickets chanting slogans while the assortment of National Front supporters barged their way down the cordoned-off roads, where helmeted police were stationed on every corner. Then somebody broke rank – it was unclear who – and the crowds descended into chaos.

Eventually, Ali took the stand, speaking slowly and quietly to confirm his name and address. His responses were clear but short, following Mr Stone's advice, Munira noted with relief, to say as little as possible, as politely as possible. Ali maintained his cool even under the cross-examination, which had been formulated deliberately to goad him into displaying some kind of anger. Mrs Farooq watched with a tissue held to her mouth, her eyes anxiously searching her younger brother's face for some kind of reassurance.

Once the closing statements had been made by both sides, the judge banged his gavel wearily. This was just one of the hearings in the aftermath of this march, and there would undoubtedly be plenty more to follow. Clearing his throat, the judge declared that there was insufficient evidence to press charges against Ali specifically, and ordered the immediate release of Ali and the reopening of the club. The whoops and cheers from Adam and Faisal's bench almost drowned out the judge's stern warning to Ali that any future misdemeanours reported at the club would receive the full force of the law. The prosecutors shrugged their shoulders and rearranged their papers; the next hearing would be in a matter of hours.

Mrs Farooq looked to Munira. 'Is that it?' She searched Munira's face anxiously. 'He can go now?'

'He can go.' Munira repeated the words as though not even believing them herself. She hugged Mrs Farooq. 'It's all over.'

The paperwork took another hour or so to finalise before Ali was able to leave the courthouse, flanked by his sister on one side and his lawyer on the other. He looked haggard, thought Munira, his face all angles and bone and dark crescents beneath his eyes. Still, he smiled wanly at Adam and Faisal as they bounded up to hug him tightly.

'You're looking skinny, mate.' Adam clapped Ali on the back.

'I'll be making gains in no time, just wait and see.' Ali grinned. Munira noticed he was missing a tooth. Ali turned to Maurice and shook his hand, clasping it in both of his own. 'I can't thank you enough, Mr Stone,' he said quietly.

Maurice inclined his head graciously. 'It was the only right outcome.' Gathering his briefcase and overcoat, he politely refused Mrs Farooq's invitation for celebratory tea and biscuits at her home. 'I have a lot of work to be getting on with – I'm afraid it doesn't stop here,' and he nodded at them all in turn before striding off to the bus stop, briefcase in hand. Watching his retreating back, Munira found herself feeling suddenly exhausted, and glancing over at Mrs Farooq she could see the same faint lines around her eyes.

'What do you say to a taxi home?' She put her arm around Adam. 'I think we deserve it.'

Adam dutifully flagged down a cab and they all piled in.

As she was getting ready for bed that night, Munira tried to suppress the feeling of hollowness that had been growing inside her all evening. It had been wonderful to share the good news with the others when she got home and to enjoy the celebratory dinner Hashim had pre-emptively prepared. But after all those months spent researching and gathering information and preparing a case, it was all over so quickly. It had only been a few hours from start to finish before the judge gave his verdict. Of course, it had been a solid case – Maurice had done his best to reassure Munira of that beforehand – and the refusal to release Ali on bail all these months had been nothing short of a travesty. But even so, there was something so unnerving about the fact that it was suddenly – well, over. Part of Munira was elated by the result, yet a more surprising part felt bereft that her work was at an end.

'Munira?' Hashim's voice was low, questioning.

She turned from where she was sitting at her dressing table to face him. He was standing in the doorway, clutching a thick envelope.

'Yes?'

'I want to show you something.' Hashim walked over to the bed and sat heavily on the edge of it, the envelope in his hands.

Munira got up from the dressing table and went to sit beside her husband. Hashim pressed the envelope into her hand, almost nervously, and watched as Munira slid her index finger under the white flap to open it.

'What – what's this?' Confused, Munira pulled the shiny paper catalogue from the envelope.

'It's a prospectus – for college.' Hashim took Munira's hand in his, his eyes fixed on hers.

'A college – for Adam? Why do I need to see his college prospectus?'

'It's for you, Munira. For you to find a course you can do. I thought' – he cleared his throat nervously – 'something to do with law. I highlighted some sections for you.' He flipped to the pages he had bookmarked with stickers he had borrowed from Joy's pencil case. 'I thought these ones might interest you.' His finger pointed to the headings of the different pages. *Law. Sociology. English.* 'And your high school certificate from *desh* will count here. I – I asked at the college. So you can start straight away with A-levels,' he said, turning to another page.

'But Hashim.' Munira's head was close to swimming – these pages with courses and the idea of college and her husband suggesting what she could study – it was all too much. 'I don't understand. Why would I do A-levels? What are you talking about?'

'Munira.' Hashim removed the prospectus from her hands gently, and took her hands in his. 'I have watched you over the last few months. How happy you've been, reading so much, learning about new things. And it made me think about the girl I married.' He smiled at this. 'The one who was top of her class in school, the one who could have achieved so much.' He paused. It was difficult to say the next part. He didn't want to put it into words lest it became even more true. *Had she not married him. Had she not followed him to this cold and distant land.* He cleared his throat. 'You gave up a lot for me. Now I want you to have something back.'

'What do you mean?' Munira shook her head, overwhelmed.

'I gave up nothing. I only gained, from marrying you. You know this . . .'

'Look, Munira,' Hashim tried again gently. 'We have enough money saved up for you to study some courses. And we can apply for grants from the local education authority.' He laughed when he saw Munira's face. 'I do know something about institutions in this country, you know.'

'But the time – what about Joy, and the shop?' Munira ran through excuses. 'And the library, how will we find the time?' *But I want this.* Something inside her felt like it was singing. *I could study, pass exams. I could achieve something.* She stopped, catching sight of Hashim's steady, dark eyes. Her voice lowered. 'Do you mean this?'

'I mean this.' He wrapped his arms around her tightly, and she leaned in to him, feeling the solidness of his body against her. Allah had been good to them. Hashim closed his eyes, counting the blessings he had been given, and gave thanks for the grace his wife had always shown him. Because of him, his wife had suffered loneliness in a land that was not her own; endured pregnancies that ended before their time. She had never complained, never made him feel as though he was less than what she wanted. In the end they had been rewarded for their patience, with their gift – their Joy. And now Hashim could give Munira something just for her – something that was not tied to making him, or Joy, happy. He was not a rich man; he could not afford to shower her with heavily embroidered *banarasi* saris, or the intricate gold jewellery that winked and flirted with him from the shop windows of Wilmslow Road. The opportunity and the time to learn was all he could offer his wife, and knowing that this would make her happier than any piece of gold or fine clothing, was yet further proof that Allah had truly blessed him.

35

I T HAPPENS AT around ten o'clock at night, just as Hashim
is locking up the shop. Shifts have been relentless the last
few weeks, following the sudden departure of the lad who
used to do the late nights. Immigration dodge probably, but
a word of warning would have been nice. Mirza had already
scrubbed the butchery counter clean, the sharp smell of
Dettol somehow reassuring: Hashim keeps a close eye on
health and hygiene. By the front door the day's unbought
newspapers are stacked, ready to send back to the depot.
Hashim has already emptied the till, locking away the cash
float in the small back office. He is ready to go upstairs, to
slip into bed beside Munira, the sheets already warmed from
her body, and wrap his arms around her as she sleeps before
dropping off himself.

Bundled up in his coat and scarf, Hashim steps outside to
pull the shutters down over the shopfront. He hates how
they look, so standoffish and industrial – but it is getting
too costly to replace the windows that are being repeatedly
smashed by louts. It seems wrong that anyone should harbour
such malice towards him, such resentment for what he has
built, that they would damage it continually, without knowing
anything about how hard he has worked for his modest
enterprise, the sacrifices endured on the way. He tries not
to blame them; they are restless too, embittered by the closure

of their workplaces, the gradual depletion of their own incomes. Their horizons seem narrower than ever. But still, why should he be blamed for their suffering? *When we've spent three hundred years in their country, like they were in ours, looting, taking what we like, exploiting the land – then maybe they'll have reason to blame us.* Rofikul used to repeat this mantra often. *Until then, we have every right to be here. We've already paid our price.*

Hashim rolls the corrugated iron down and kneels to padlock the shutter. He doesn't notice the footsteps – two, maybe three sets of them – until they stop right behind him. He stays kneeling, padlock in hand, holding his breath. He waits for the steps to resume and move on, but everything is still. Not this again. He's been here before, many years ago, when he first arrived in this country. It's never far off – stories of this abound. Even Adam has encountered it. If anything, Hashim has been lucky that he's had such a long gap between incidents. Hashim stands up and turns around.

They leave him crumpled on the pavement, his body a crescent, his coat fallen open and leaking crimson. He is discovered shortly after by a group of passers-by returning from some late-night revelry at the Florist's Arms down the road. Shouts in the night, an ambulance called, and Hashim is rushed to Manchester Royal Infirmary in a haze of red and blue flashes, sirens wailing.

Amid all the chaos outside, Munira wakes up. She thinks she heard sirens in her sleep. She gets up, careful not to wake Joy who is sleeping beside her, and goes to the window. She lifts up the white net curtain and sees a gathering of people on the pavement outside the shop. They are talking animatedly but their expressions are worried. A woman she does not recognise is crying. A man bangs on the front door of the shop. She notices that Hashim is not among them. Panic swells and rises; she throws on her dressing gown and runs downstairs.

At around eleven o'clock at night, the doors to the A&E department burst open. Two women, pale and frantic, rush to the reception desk. They are ushered to the wards, stumbling blindly along the white corridors, amid trolleys and bright white lights. They arrive at a room humming with machines and wires – and inside lies the patient, unconscious but alive.

They are made to wait outside, peering anxiously through the glass window, while the doctor talks at them. He has suffered a cardiac arrest, they are told. Does he have any history of heart problems in the family? Any pre-existing irregularities? Munira doesn't hear them. What happened to his face? she asks. What happened to him? The doctor explains that the cardiac arrest was brought on by the shock of acute physical violence. But they also suspect an underlying heart condition. Munira has stopped listening and pushes past the doctor into the room. Helen tries to go after her but is stopped by the doctor. Immediate family only, she is told. So one woman stays outside the room, pacing and praying, while the other goes in to keep vigil at the bedside. They stay like sentries in their positions all night, guarding against the shadowy fingers of death, willing the man in the bed to stay alive.

Hashim is surrounded by machines humming, one issuing a low beep at regular intervals. He is reassured by that steady pulse-like sound, and reasons that he must still be alive. He is strangely proud of staving off death for a little while longer. He knows already that this is a temporary victory. Hashim has never fought a day in his life – it's just not in his nature

– and his deathbed seems an odd place to start. He can feel Munira close by. His eyes are closed but he can picture her, her hair now streaked with strands of grey swept up into her customary low bun, her cardigan pulled tightly around her small frame. He wants to touch her, to hold her close. He wants to tell her that she is everything. That he doesn't want to leave her, but it seems as though this was what is written – who are they to argue with what God has decided? But he wants more time. He wants to stay. He reaches out to touch Munira's arm.

Munira jolts upright at the sound of the machines breaking into a high-pitched beeping as Hashim's arm rises off the bed and then drops heavily back down. His eyes are still closed but when she grabs his hand she feels his fingers tighten around hers. He is here, she thinks. He is still with us. Doctors crash into the room and Munira is jostled away from Hashim's bedside as nurses surround him, shouting numbers and readjusting wires while the doctor gives instructions. The beeping turns into a shrill screech and the medical staff heighten their efforts, shouting and pushing Hashim's chest forcefully. *Stop, stop it,* Munira wants to say. *You're hurting him.* She looks around for someone to tell this to, and Helen appears in the doorway at that very moment, face blanched, holding out her arms. Munira crumples into them as the shouts around them begin to quieten and the doctors and nurses gradually step back, their heads down, and all is silent except for the flat, continuous hum of the machine.

36

EVERY MORNING MUNIRA opened her eyes. Lying perfectly still she waited for the inevitable pain in her ribcage, as her heart swelled at the thought of rolling over to kiss her husband good morning, and then shrank as she remembered that he was gone. It had been six months, six whole lunar orbits around the earth, but the mornings were still the hardest. Adam or Helen would get Joy ready for school, giving her breakfast and then dropping her off at the school gates. By the time three o'clock rolled around, Munira was always dressed and ready to greet her daughter by the iron railings in the playground with a kiss and a warm hug. But each breaking morning still seemed impossible to Munira, lying in bed and anticipating a whole new day without Hashim.

They had all had to make room for it, that pervading cloud of grief that sat among them, still and silent. At first it had felt as though the cloud lay heavily on top of them. The months had moved the cloud off them; now it took its place beside them, continuing to emanate low, periodic pulses of sadness.

In the first few weeks, Adam and Helen had stayed over at the flat to keep Munira and Joy company. None of them had wanted to be alone. After the fifth or sixth week, Helen had sat Adam down and asked how he felt about living there permanently. He had unreservedly agreed, and Helen had almost sunk under the weight of relief. In truth, she had always found their own flat so dull and listless after returning from visits to Hashim and Munira's – especially after Joy had been born and her gurgles and toys and cries filled up their cosy flat over the shop. It was different now; the grief hung in the walls, in the air of the flat, and Helen could not leave Munira to face it alone. It was a terrible thought to entertain, so for the most part Helen refrained from it, but sometimes she was struck by a strange kind of envy of Munira's grief; the permission it granted her for a temporary suspension of the need to function. Where Munira was allowed a reprieve in working and parenting, Helen was afforded no such space. If anything, it fell more to Helen to make up that space, to look after the children, to manage the household bills, to ensure Munira attended her doctor's appointments, all the while pushing her own grief to the furthest corners of her day-to-day life. But it was as it should be, Helen always concluded. She had lost a dear friend, but Munira had lost her husband, the only man she had ever loved. And while Helen had also tasted the bitterness of loss, this seemed crueller somehow. Hashim hadn't wanted to leave.

The very next day after her conversation with Adam, Helen packed up a van with the things that they would be taking with them to their new home. All the furniture, save for their beds, would be sold. Even though Helen and Adam were the ones leaving their flat, to Helen the move felt as though they were finally coming home. They set up Adam's single bed in the tiny boxroom, with only a narrow strip of floor space around the bed. The sloping ceiling meant that Adam could only stand upright in certain parts of the room. Helen moved into Joy's unused room – Joy had been sleeping with Munira ever since that unthinkable night, and refused

303

to be prised away from her mother. When Helen and Adam moved in, Munira had slept through the night for the first time in weeks, with Joy on one side of her and Helen, through the wall, on the other.

Below them the shop continued to hum along, subdued without the man who kept it alive. Mirza, who ran the butchery counter, had wordlessly stepped into the role of acting manager, much to Munira's gratitude. The day after the funeral, Mirza reopened the shop, turning the sign that hung in the door to show that *Hashim & Family* was open for business again. He opened and locked up the shop each day, sometimes assisted by Adam who came home directly after school, rather than stopping at the boxing club. And while it was Mirza who oversaw the day-to-day running of the place, taking stock orders, doing the staff rotas, keeping the books in check, it was Helen who took over ensuring the bills and utilities were paid.

One of the most striking things about death, for Munira, was the endless amount of administration that needed handling. Maurice Stone had helped with the legal paperwork, the certification of death, the sorting out of Hashim's will. The mosque committee had mercifully overseen all the elements of the funeral: from setting a date, to acquiring a burial plot, to notifying the community when the *janazah* prayers would take place. It was a co-operative system, one that Munira was barely aware Hashim had even been paying into. Each member of the congregation paid their monthly dues to the co-operative, and in the event of any death, the committee would step in to cover all expenses. Hashim was, Munira realised, as considerate in his passing as he had been in life, ensuring that all the financial obligations had been seen to. For weeks after he died, people from the community sent food; the dishes sent by well-wishers, including Mrs Farooq, Mirza's wife, and so many others, were almost inappropriately decadent. It felt wrong, somehow, to be feasting on tender lamb curries, bhuna chicken and fragrant pilau rice, but this was the nature of condolence food. Nobody would send a simple dal or boiled rice; the grieving had enough to suffer without the addition of poor sustenance.

There was even an announcement in the local newspaper the day before the funeral. Munira had no idea who was behind it, but there had been a touching piece about Hashim and the shop in that week's edition. The next day, flowers sprang up – bunches of them, in pots and in baskets – placed carefully outside the shop with its shuttered windows. Cards too, signed by well-wishers – regulars at the shop, and people who had never visited alike. Reading them, Munira, Joy, Helen and Adam discovered things about Hashim that they never knew before. There were cards from names they did not recognise: a student refugee from Lebanon who wrote of Hashim's generosity; an elderly lady with copperplate hand-writing who fondly remembered long chats with Hashim over the morning papers. It made them realise that while they had their own lives, Adam with his boxing, Helen and Munira with their work, even little Joy with school, none of them had ever really known the details of Hashim's daily life – what he spent his time doing, who he spent time talking to – until he came home to his family at the end of the day.

Now that the weeks had turned into months, and the months had turned into a whole half year, some of the things that Munira had been deliberately avoiding were beginning to loom large again. First there was the question of what she should do with the shop. Selling it could be liberating in many ways: she would no longer be responsible for managing a business and employing staff, and would be free to pursue new avenues, take up things to occupy her time. It pained her to spend too much time down in the shop, and yet it was the place she felt Hashim's presence most strongly. She felt him – could smell him, even – at the corner of every aisle, behind the till. And the name above the shop was theirs: *Hashim & Family.* To sell the shop would be to sell off her husband's life work: the stability he had built and protected for her, for Joy, for all of them. She could not bring herself to do that. In the end, she decided to ask Mirza to take over as the permanent manager of the shop in return for an annual stake of the profits, while the business would remain in her name. Mirza had willingly accepted; he had been working as the acting manager for months in any case, and it was a good place to train up his own boys. He had liked Hashim greatly and helping to keep things running smoothly was the least he could do.

Munira now also needed to decide about her place at college. In the weeks after Hashim suggested that she return to studying, Munira had held on to the idea as though it were something precious in itself, reading the pages on entry requirements and the application procedure from start to finish in bed each night until she knew them off by heart. Encouraged by Hashim, she had submitted her application and had been accepted on to three A-level courses. And then everything had changed that night, and Hashim had been taken from her, and she had no desire to do anything again. Helen had quietly called up the college admissions department and requested a deferral of Munira's place. But one delayed term had turned into two, and now risked becoming a third, and would soon mean that a whole year had passed. It was Adam who broached the subject with her eventually.

'Chachi,' he had said. 'You know how I'm starting college next year?'

Munira had looked at him, startled. Where had the time gone, that this tall young man with the faintest hint of fuzz on his chin was somehow the same baby whose fat knees she had kissed just the other day?

'I suppose I should have known that, yes,' she had answered, 'but it's hard to believe.' She pulled him close to her and kissed his cheek.

'Are you starting college with me?' Adam had asked directly, gazing solemnly at his aunt. 'Because if you are, I need to know so I can get my crew sorted.' Munira had looked at him blankly while Adam continued, 'You know, get some back-up in case anyone starts messing with my Chachi.'

Munira stared for a moment before realising Adam was joking. She swatted him away.

'Idiot boy,' she said, 'I'm not going to any college with you.'

'Why not though, Chachi?' His tone changed. 'You don't have to come to college *with* me; I mean I know I'll ruin your street cred,' he said sorrowfully.

'I have no idea what you're talking about, Adam.' Munira shook her head. 'What – cred?'

Adam grinned. 'What I'm saying, Chachi, is that we can be students together – but in different colleges, obviously. You still have your place, don't you?'

'I'm not going to college, Adam.' Munira was firm. 'I wouldn't know where to even start. It was your uncle's idea . . .'

'You've already got the place,' Helen interjected gently, having listened to the whole exchange under the pretence of reading her book by the fire. 'It's been deferred for you – twice, now. I made the calls for you, remember?' Munira looked at her anxiously. 'Look, all you have to do is say you'll be attending next term. That's the hardest bit done. And then you just turn up.'

'You know what Chacha would say.' Adam squeezed his aunt's shoulders.

It was true, thought Munira. Hashim was not the type of person to lay down the law, but furthering Adam's and Joy's education was one thing he had been adamant about, stemming perhaps from his own all too brief experiences of formal education. *Education is your ticket*, he would say; *once you have it, it's the one thing they can't take from you*. Everything else could be seized in a moment, Hashim had believed. A person's citizenship, the right to remain, or their business, their home, even their family. To Hashim, education was the sole guarantor of freedom, the ticket that could grant their children opportunities. The great social leveller. And he had been so insistent, in that gentle but firm way of his, that she apply to the college. Maybe Helen and Adam had a point.

'I'll think about it,' Munira said slowly.

'Good.' Helen smiled at Adam knowingly. 'Because I've already told them you'll be enrolling next term.'

Just a few weeks later, Munira began her first day of college, waved off outside the red-brick building by Joy, Adam and Helen. Joy had presented her with a backpack for the occasion, one she had eschewed for being too large – but Munira thought it perfectly sized, able to accommodate her carefully labelled A4 ringbinder with colour-coded dividers. Helen had packed her a lunch in a carefully wrapped Tupperware box. Even Adam had provided Munira with the essential accessories for making friends: a packet of chewing gum and a lighter.

'I'm not saying *you* need to smoke, Chachi.' He had laughed when she looked aghast at his offerings. 'Just that if anyone says "Got a light?" you can say yes, and save the day and people will think you're cool.'

'There's nothing cool about smoking, Adam,' Helen chided.

Munira, too flummoxed to protest, shoved the lighter and gum into the side pocket of her backpack obediently.

'I'd better go in,' she said, gesturing to the crowds who were lining up for orientation. 'I'll see you all this afternoon.'

'Love you, Ammu,' Joy threw her arms around her mother and waved her off.

Munira felt the familiar hot sting of tears as she waved back at Joy, Adam and Helen, then turned to join the throng of people flooding up the steps to the main hall; a tiny, determined figure, fighting not to drown.

37

NOBODY HAD WARNED Adam that grief and guilt went hand in hand. For all the pain of losing Hashim, it sometimes felt to Adam that he had no right to miss his uncle the way he did, when he saw Joy's pain so close to his own. After all, Adam had lost an uncle, but Joy had lost her own father. Adam tried to throw himself into the practicalities of dealing with the aftermath, supporting his mother in the role she had taken on of keeping the rest of the family going, and agreeing readily to leave his own home to move in with them. His aunt was barely able to dress herself in the mornings, or cook or do the shopping, let alone take care of Joy – so Adam had taken on this role unquestioningly, helping Joy get ready for school in the mornings, walking her to the gates, making sure she had money to buy snacks. Sometimes he even made dinner if his mother was working late and Joy was hungry after school. That was their role, Helen's and Adam's, to take care of Munira and Joy through their heartbreak, all the while pushing their own pain and grief aside. After all, where Joy had lost her father, Adam had never truly had one to lose.

Hashim was the only person who had ever really talked about Adam's father. *Your baba was excellent at climbing trees*, Hashim would say, and Adam would nod politely, wondering if these reminiscences were for his benefit or for Uncle

Hashim's. When Adam was older, the anecdotes changed. *Your baba was top in his class at college, you know*, Hashim would say. And Adam would answer, *Was he?* – not really knowing why he was supposed to register or pay any real attention to this information. *That's why you should do your best in school; you've inherited his brains*, Uncle Hashim would urge.

It was only when Hashim was no longer with them that Adam began to wonder how much his own upbringing had been constructed in ways to reflect that of the shadowy figure of his own father. Uncle Hashim had always emphasised the importance of studying, but in that sense he was no different from any of the other parents Adam knew: the only salve over the wound of migration was to gain an education. It was a truth everyone knew. But there were other things, like encouraging Adam's interest in writing and buying him the typewriter, that made Adam wonder whether his uncle had somehow been trying to inject the presence of Adam's absent father into his childhood for all those years.

While Uncle Hashim was still alive, Adam never felt the need to connect with his father directly. If he wanted to know anything he could simply ask Chacha, and bask in the readily granted stories of the past. It was safer, somehow, to do it this way: at a polite distance, with no risk from being too close. But now not only had Adam lost his uncle, the man he loved more than any other in the whole world, but that tenuous, precious link to his own father had all but disappeared. It felt as though everything he knew, the way he made sense of his family and the coexisting presences of the two men who shaped him, through their respective presence and absence, had been thrown into complete disarray.

Helen noticed that the light in Adam's room shone under the crack of the door well into the night ever since they had moved in with Munira and Joy. She debated whether or not to ask him about it; she didn't want to seem accusatory, or suggest that he was under some kind of surveillance. But if he was finding it difficult to sleep, it would be helpful to know. Maybe she could talk to him, suggest ways to get some rest. A warm bath before bed. A hot drink. Opening the window to let a cool breeze through the room. It would be easier said than done, she knew that much herself. Helen could barely remember the last time she slept through the night. More than once, Helen stood on the threshold outside Adam's door, her hand raised as if to knock, and then hearing the clatter of the typewriter keys deciding it was best to leave her son to channel whatever it was that he was feeling through his writing. She was just grateful that he had an outlet of some kind.

In truth, Adam seemed to be throwing himself into his studies. He would be starting at college soon. On the occasions when he wasn't at school, or picking up Joy, or helping down in the shop, or tidying up around the house, Adam seemed to be in the library. *It's easier for me to study there, Mam*, he would say. It was true, thought Helen – there was hardly enough room in the flat for the four of them, and the tiny desk in Adam's room barely had space for the typewriter, let alone his books and papers. To her surprise, Helen found herself yearning for the days when Adam would spend time at the boxing club with his friends; he brushed it off when she mentioned it now. *No time*, he would say. *I've got school work to do.* But it worried her; Adam seemed to be drifting apart from his old friends – even Faisal came around less often these days. Perhaps it was partly the awkwardness that so often came after a loss of some kind; people not knowing what to say to someone who had lost a loved one. It irritated her, this self-conscious embarrassment of well-meaning friends that the bereaved had to navigate on top of everything else. But somehow the days after Hashim's death had turned into weeks, and then months, and now it felt almost too late to prise open the lid of that box that had already welded itself shut. They were coping. They were getting on, in the only way they knew how. But coping was not enough. Helen knew that she needed to talk to her son.

It was a Saturday afternoon when Helen knocked lightly on Adam's bedroom door. Munira had taken Joy to the park after lunch, and the quietness seemed to be a good time for Helen to try to have her conversation with Adam. But there was no answer from Adam's room. Odd, thought Helen. She had not noticed Adam go out. She pushed the door open gently and peered around. The room was empty. The narrow bed had been neatly made with Adam's clothes lying strewn across it. Hashim's gift to Adam, the faithful old typewriter, was perched on the desk by the window. Beside it lay a stack of textbooks and a small pile of what looked like printed letters. Helen was surprised; she thought that Adam was composing teenage poetry or righteous political manifestos in his room into the small hours. Who would her son be writing to? Helen tentatively took a step towards the desk and picked up the first from the pile of letters, both apprehensive and curious about her son's correspondence, and began to unfold it.

'Mam!'

The bedroom door slammed and she looked up to see Adam's face, stricken and white. Still holding the letter in her hands, she heard her own sharp breath as she read the first line.

Dear Baba, it read. *This is your son, Adam.*

*

Tracking him down had not been difficult. All Adam had done was look up the newspaper that he knew his father had last written for – there were copies in the library – and find its contact address. The newspaper was based somewhere in London. Ali talked about it sometimes, from the days when he lived there before moving to Manchester. A shithole, he had called it. Full of racists and high-rise flats and burned-out cars and girls to make your eyes pop.

Adam had typed out different versions of the same letter each night for weeks, testing different salutations and endings, and everything else in between. It was one of those tasks of almost mythical proportions: to draft the letter that would be the first contact with his father, a man he had never known, and yet known his entire life. It had taken Adam weeks to decide on the final version, and although he was far from convinced that it was the letter worth sending his estranged father, he was exhausted from trying. He waited for the typewriter ink to dry, folded the letter into three equal parts, and slipped it into a white envelope addressed to Mr Rofikul Ahmed, care of the editor-in-chief of *Ekushey*.

The lady behind the counter at the post office had looked at Adam strangely as his hand lingered on the envelope, the bright red stamp in the top corner almost mocking him. *You need to pass it under the counter so I can add it to the post bag*, she had coughed impatiently. Adam had lifted his hand and the lady snatched his letter away, tossing it on to the heap of white and brown envelopes behind her. Adam had stayed at the counter, his eyes panicked through the glass, as he saw his letter disappear into the mass of envelopes and parcels. *It will get there tomorrow. First class*, she had coughed again. *Is there anything else I can help you with?* Adam had turned and fled, his heart pounding mercilessly so that he almost tasted the blood in his mouth as he made it on to the cold street outside. Drawing breaths from the depths of his chest, he decided to walk home rather than wait for the bus.

He had known something was not right as soon as he arrived home. It seemed eerily still. The flat had been quieter ever since they had lost Chacha – which made little sense, given that he was the one who had made the least noise out of all of them. It was amazing really, how the absence of one person could change the rhythm of a whole household. Adam remembered that Chachi and Joy had gone to the park and wondered if his mother had joined them. But kicking off his shoes, Adam noticed the door of his bedroom standing ajar. He was sure he had closed it when he left. He heard a noise come from the room. *No*, he thought. *Not like this*. Panicked, he threw open the door.

'*Mam!*'

There she stood by the desk, tall and blanched, one of the many unsent letters, unfolded and smooth, in her hand. Helen's desperate eyes searched Adam's face wordlessly. She dropped the letter to the desk, covered her face with her hands, and wept.

Part IV

1981

38

THE FAMILY BURIAL plot was a place Shapla often visited, usually to claim a moment of longed-for solitude amid the fullness of her days. It was one of the few places where she could actually be alone; going to the *gurustan* was not considered befitting for women, and while her aunts tutted over her visits, the possibility of joining her did not cross their minds. The men usually paid their respects after the Friday prayers, so at all other times the small fenced-off patch of land belonged to no one except for Shapla and those who lay there at peace.

To an outsider, there was nothing obviously marking this plot as a place of rest – the graves were all unmarked, and vegetation grew thick and lush, untamed by any gardener. It was only through memory that Shapla knew where her great-grandparents, and all the others who had died before she had met them, were buried. Her mother's grave was the first she had witnessed appearing – one day there had just been unturned earth, and the next she saw the ground being dug out and filled and covered again, leaving a small mound with her mother's white shrouded body now encased within it. Shapla had watched the whole thing from the edge of the cemetery, her newborn brother in her arms. Nobody had been able to dissuade her. For weeks after, she had continued to visit her mother every day, carrying her baby brother in her arms. Shapla would talk to Mala's grave, telling her mother all about the son she had never met. Shapla described the shape of his head, the downy fluff that covered his skin, the sound of his cries. All the while Mala listened patiently, sending messages through the gentle shaking of branches that she approved, and Shapla saw this and felt strengthened by her mother's silent encouragement. Shapla's grandmother was aghast at the baby being taken out of the house before he was forty days old, let alone being taken to the *gurustan*, but Shapla calmly ignored any protest, and continued with her daily ritual, as the weeks passed into months, until her brother grew older and even more demanding of her time. Her visits slipped to twice a week, then weekly, and then more sporadic, but at night sometimes she dreamed of her mother's grave, and the next morning she would pay a visit again, whispering apologies for being neglectful.

Even now, after all these years, she appreciated the stillness of the place whenever she did find time to go. And as well as her mother to visit, there was now *Dada*, her grandfather, who was laid to rest some years ago, and also now required her presence and prayers.

Ya Allah, please bestow your mercy on all those resting here.
Watch over them the way they watched over me. Grant them
a place in your Jannat al firdous.

Shapla lifted up her cupped hands and passed them lightly over her face. *Ameen*. As she turned to leave the cemetery, she whispered her *salam* to all those who lay there, wishing them everlasting peace in their shady, tranquil resting place.

'*Salam*, Baba-ji,' Shapla called out as she passed by her father's study. 'I went to the post office on the way back from the *gurustan.*' She passed him a letter, which Rofikul took from her, fondly squeezing her hand as he did so.

'It's from him again,' she added.

Rofikul nodded and kissed her hand as he laid the letter on his desk. 'Thank you, Baba. Would you like to read this one at least?'

'No – it's all right. You read it and tell me what you want to tell me.' Shapla gently removed her hand from her father's as she made to leave.

'I want you to know everything.' Her father spoke quietly, and she believed him, but Shapla was not yet ready to read the words, so raw, so direct, that came from this stranger so far away.

'I will, Baba, one day. I will.'

The letters had started coming a few months ago. The first one had made her father crumple when he read it. She remembered seeing his legs buckle beneath him, and she had to help steady him on to a chair. His face was chalk white. She took the letter from his shaking hands and skimmed it. It was written in English. Shapla's reading was adequate but it would have taken time to decipher the long typed sentences that marched across the page.

'Baba?' she had questioned, but her father was blank and shaking, so she had brought him a blanket and arranged it around his shoulders and placed a cup of hot sweet tea in his hands and waited quietly beside him.

'He's dead.' Her father's voice had trembled.

'Who, Baba? Who is dead?'

But her father had sat silently, tears running down his face, clutching at her hand, and Shapla had sat beside him, anxious and waiting, for what seemed like hours, until her father began to speak again. He told her things. *Not everything*, he said. *It will take time for that, and I don't know everything myself.*

But you should know who I am, Shapla, you should know what I did and who I left and what I made happen. She had listened silently, allowing her father time to talk, to explain, to plead to nobody in particular. There were names that she had heard before – Hashim and Munira – and others that she did not know, like Helen and Vincent, and while he spoke, Shapla pieced together parts of a story she had wondered about for so long that she had almost forgotten the parts were live and real and that even her father did not know how they all fitted together.

Since that first letter, there had been three or four more. Each one was long, page after page typewritten on thin paper in those rounded English characters. Her father drank them up like water, and then would lock himself away for hours composing equally long replies. Then there would be a pause of several weeks, even a month, and then another letter would arrive, another revelation, another part of the story that her father had missed out on. Sometimes Rofikul would try to tell her things, and she for the most part listened attentively; but at times she stopped him, not wanting to know too much, the existence he painted being too vivid to absorb. She needed time to piece together this life in her own mind; this whole span of time that did not include her, or her younger brother, or her mother. This life when her father was young and had another family, of sorts, other people who he loved, other work, other interests, another identity.

Shapla noticed a renewed vivacity in her father with each letter he received. A shedding of some layer, a hungriness she had never seen in him before. She was both pleased and worried by this. She feared that the very thing that brought him so much excitement would take him away from her again. But this time, she reminded herself, they had a relationship. They had both changed. They had both lost Mala. There was Abdul Rahim to think of now. *He would not leave her the way he had left her before.*

And so she began to encourage these letters, and her father's replies. She collected them from the post office on her way home, she bought stamps for her father, and ensured the blotter in his study was always clean and ready. She asked her father to read her extracts, and she asked questions, and made suggestions of what he could write. She was still too nervous to read the words themselves, those written by a person at once a stranger, and her blood kin. But along with Rofikul, Shapla found herself thinking about, dreaming about, wondering about – and even praying for – this person whose letters had turned her whole world upside down, but whose name she had not even pronounced out loud.

Adam.

39

ABDUL RAHIM WAS almost nine years old now; only a few years younger than Shapla had been when she adopted him as her own. He had grown up under the fierce protection of his sister and the man they both called Abba. For the first few years of his life, Abdul Rahim had been contentedly unaware of any controversy surrounding his existence. He had known since he was old enough to understand that his mother had died trying to bring him into this world, but it was at around the age of seven when this anecdote about his origins began to eat away at his insides. Abdul Rahim was not oblivious to the whisperings of some of the other children, or the fact that he was always the first one to be discounted from a team if there were an odd number of children playing. At first, he wondered if there was something wrong with him. He was tall for his age; perhaps the older boys didn't like the fact that he was already so much bigger than they were. But his height alone didn't make much sense as a reason why he was always being left out. It took several months of worrying, turning over every possibility in his mind, before Abdul Rahim struck upon the reason: in being born, he realised, he had caused the death of his own mother. Not only that, but his existence had also cancelled out the life of the only mother his beloved sister had ever known. Apa was not as lucky as he had been, to have had a surrogate mother take over when her birth mother had died. The other children must eye him with such suspicion because he was unlucky and because he had caused the person he loved more than anyone else in the world – his sister – so much pain.

One night, unable to bear his silent guilt any longer, he had confessed all to his sister. That he knew it all, about his birth and what it meant, and that he was sorry – so sorry, about the grief he had caused. The light faded from his sister's cheeks as he spoke. *Who told you?* she had choked, barely able to get her words out. *What did they say to you?*

Nobody, he had replied. *Nobody told me anything – they didn't have to. I can see how they look at me.*

How do they look at you? she had asked. Her heart screamed silently. *Who dares to look at you in any way other than the way you deserve?* And then came the answer that broke her heart.

As though I am bad.

It was then that Shapla decided to speak about the thing that she had always sworn she would never acknowledge. She had to be careful how to present it but she wanted him to hear about himself from someone who loved him, who would tell him the truth without hurting him further, if there was such a way. *You came at a time when we were all in a lot of pain,* she had said. *Things were bad for all of us. The war had hurt us all, especially our mother.* Shapla paused, having to hold back the heat behind her eyes. *But out of that hurt, she discovered that she would be having you. And you brought her so much joy. She was happy to be having you. And even though she did not live long enough to see you, I know she loved you, just as I do. And just as Abba does.*

Abdul Rahim was listening, waiting for Shapla to explain what this had to do with how the other children acted around him. *Sometimes people don't know how to act when*

325

something good comes out of something horrible. Like how you could come out of something so unhappy like a war. But that isn't something you should worry about. Abdul Rahim had seemed to accept this explanation readily enough at the time. Over the next few weeks his spirits seemed to have lifted and Shapla was relieved that it had settled the question for now. But that was two years ago and Shapla wondered whether he would reopen the issue or if he had already pieced together the parts that she had not told him.

Time was running out for Shapla to get married. Edging ever closer to twenty-five, soon the only men available to her would be widowers, for the most part with children who needed a mother, or men whose existing wives had long lost their appeal and wanted a second bride to stave off the onset of their looming mortality. Whenever anyone raised the matter, predicting with customary foreboding Shapla's future regret at not having children, Shapla would quietly reply, 'But I have a child.'

It had happened almost by accident; she had been so distracted raising her brother that she had not paid any attention to settling down in the traditional sense. But the responsibility to find a partner did not lie with her; this was a duty for her father, uncles and grandmother, but they too had seemed somehow late to the whole matter and by the time it had been pointed out to them that they had a young woman of marriageable age in their midst, they had been too bemused by this revelation to do anything useful about it: just a few half-hearted introductions to walking paunches with bald heads, old enough to be her father, or gap-toothed young men who eyed her with a hunger that made her feel sick. When Shapla did not express interest in any of her suitors she was admonished for being 'too choosy'. *It's hardly as though you have masses of options now*, reminded her aunts.

Whose fault is that? Shapla wanted to reply. *This was your responsibility.*

Shapla had not wished for it to be this way. As she witnessed a series of younger cousins cross the threshold from girlhood into marriage, and then even into motherhood, it felt as though another small piece of her insides came loose and fell away. She felt it most strongly at night, an ache in her chest and a heat between her thighs, and inexplicable tears. She did not regret devoting so much of her time to raising her brother – he was the person who seemed to give her life any meaning, after all – but she resented the fact that it had rendered her invisible to everyone else. Their lives had continued to tick along while Shapla had taken on the responsibility of keeping Abdul Rahim alive, and nobody had really given the unorthodox situation a second thought until it was too late.

The seeming indifference to finding Shapla a suitable husband was heightened, undoubtedly, by the departure of Shapla's beloved aunt. Having gained a suitable level of qualifications, dutifully stopping before she was educated beyond eligibility, Fufu was married off when Abdul Rahim was only five or six years old. Her husband was an earnest-seeming man with a dimpled moon-like face over which hung two comically shaggy eyebrows. Shapla could barely disguise her disdain when she saw him for the first time sitting on the low *palong* in her grandmother's house, his groom's turban pulled slightly too tight, tiny drops of sweat pearling at his temples. This was the man to whom she was losing her aunt, her closest – only – friend. He was educated, she knew. In some kind of science, chemistry perhaps, or biology. He had studied abroad, in a *laboratory*, apparently.

Do you even know what a laboratory is? Shapla wanted to ask her aunts who uttered the word in breathy awe, every time they repeated this now-established fact. But despite her own misgivings – and they were not insignificant in number – Shapla found it impossible to begrudge the happiness of her favourite aunt. Fufu seemed to glow in the attention she received as a new bride, the recognition far exceeding any congratulation she may have gained for completing her high school certificate, or even her Bachelor's degree. Her studies were valued only in that they made her more eligible for this man, who wanted, it was said with a mixture of great pride and great confusion among the aunts, an *educated* woman.

'Because a woman with a degree will understand the science behind the correct temperature at which to fry an egg,' Shapla had said to Fufu, but Fufu had looked a little hurt at this barb, and Shapla had hated herself. She resolved to be kinder and more supportive of this union.

True to her word, in the years that followed Shapla had come to feel something close to fondness for her mild-mannered uncle who at least had had the decency to allow his wife two annual visits to her parental home as a respite from her new domestic responsibilities, and did not complain when they were extended by a day, and then two, and then a few more. The visits were the highlight of everyone's calendars. Fufu would come and stay for a week, even two, and would be forbidden from lifting a finger.

'You're *nayori*,' her mother would say. 'You're a guest here, save the working for your in-laws' house.'

On these visits home, Fufu would get Shapla to stay with her, sharing a bed like they had in the old days. *What's going on with you?* Fufu would ask. *No plans to marry?* And Shapla would shrug and say that her father and grandmother were the ones to speak to about that, and Fufu would sigh and nod and resolve to take up the issue with her brother the next day, although she already knew the reaction she would be met with. *She's just a child*, Rofikul would say, faking amusement at the ridiculousness of such a proposal. *There's no need to think of that now. Besides*, he once said in an unguarded moment of self-interest, *what would we do without her?*

It's not about you, Fufu had told her brother, but he abruptly announced he was late for a meeting in town and left the room. Any other attempts by Fufu to raise the question of her niece's future were met with similarly awkward avoidance. Then Fufu gave birth to her own child, and then another, and there was nobody left to advocate for Shapla's right to her own future.

40

THE FIRST LETTER had hurtled its way into Rofikul's carefully composed life with all the destructive force of a grenade. He could almost taste the potency of the words when he first read them. His son was a masterful writer, there was no denying it. Within the folds of those pages, Adam – for that was the boy's name – had created a world so vivid to Rofikul that it felt as though he could dive between those sentences and discover this life that had carried on without him for all these years. The names of the characters were soft and familiar, and pricked his heart. Hashim. Munira. Helen. Adam wove the story as though it were a fairy tale, carefully fashioning these protagonists like a craftsman, ducking and diving between their threads as they entwined and fanned out like billowing smoke.

If it was strange to be proud of a child he had never met, let alone taught or inspired or otherwise coached, then Rofikul was oblivious to the fact. It did not matter to Rofikul that his contribution to the existence of this young man had ended before the child had even been born. There was something almost visceral in his pride; the boy had courage, to write to a father he had never met before. *Blood of my blood*, Rofikul thought. *My son.*

The first letter had given no indication that it would be followed by a second. It ended abruptly with the revelation that Hashim had died. Rofikul had been left feeling as though he had been pulled into some kind of parallel world where nothing and everything had changed in the few minutes it had taken him to devour the letter. The Hashim of his memory had suddenly been fleshed out and made whole again, living and breathing, only to be extinguished once more. There was no return address on the envelope. Rofikul had been forced to wait in an agony of anticipation for weeks before another letter arrived unannounced. In it, Adam shared more anecdotes, histories that Rofikul had been excluded from – by choice and circumstance – and Rofikul thirsted for more. This time the envelope had a return address on the back. Taking it as an invitation to correspond freely, Rofikul had penned the first of many letters to his first-born, blood-tied, son.

It was almost impossible to put into words all that had passed in the intervening years since Rofikul had left one home for another, and then yet another – his original home – now here in the newly birthed land of Bangladesh. He had no idea how much Adam wished to know; whether his son sought an explanation or an apology or even acknowledgement. In the end, Rofikul opted to narrate his more recent past. It flowed more freely than the older stories that stuck in his throat and his pen: of abandonment, of war, of pain. Instead, Rofikul regaled Adam with descriptions of his life as it now stood – settled back in the village he had left once before. His job as a newspaper columnist sometimes required his presence in Dhaka, the capital, for on-the-ground reporting, but for the most part – especially now – Rofikul kept such tasks to a minimum. His columns were more think-pieces, ruminations, rather than the journalism of his earlier years. He had, in fact, spent more of his days of late penning his memoirs than filing stories for publication. Rofikul had felt a strange mix of apprehension and nervous excitement in revealing this to Adam; it was a secret he had only shared with Shapla until now. There was something presumptuous in thinking that anyone else would be interested in his life story, but Shapla had encouraged him, fanning his hopes that his memoirs would perhaps be considered worthy enough to read. Rofikul tried to suppress the hope that Adam would one day express an interest in reading them too.

Despite their ongoing correspondence, knowing how much to disclose, on both their parts, had proved a careful exercise in testing the waters. Adam wrote of his mother only in the context of the past; he offered Rofikul no insight into Helen's present-day reality, almost by way of protection. A purdah of ignorance, Rofikul supposed, sequestering the mother from the watchful gaze of the father. Rofikul had mentioned Shapla and Abdul Rahim as his children in his letters to Adam, almost as perfunctory details of his daily life. He made sure not to devote too much time to describing them further, assuming that this was not something Adam would particularly want to hear about, at least not straight away.

Adam had not given any indication to Rofikul that he wished to meet him in person, and Rofikul was nervous of disrupting whatever delicate balance the two of them had arrived at by suggesting it. But Rofikul had found himself thinking about England again for the first time in years. He had left the country in such haste, so eager to return to the land of his birth and help it on its path to self-determination. England had been a place where Rofikul had been the happiest he had ever known, yet experienced isolation to depths he had never before imagined or felt since. The northern chapter of his English years – the time he had lived and worked and loved in Manchester — was a fragile part of his memory, one that he did not care to take down from the shelves and dust off too often. He worried about the ghosts it would awaken. It was easier to remember his time in London: single and eager, driven to work hard and start new things, pursue different ideals. If Manchester had been his confinement, then London was freedom. Both were chapters of his life that he had closed firmly with no intention of reopening until now.

In the time between poring over letters from Adam and writing long missives in reply, Rofikul returned to his memoirs, intending to finally confront the English chapters. Noticing the renewed vigour in her father's work, Shapla stopped by his study one afternoon, a cup of tea and some fried snacks on a tray.

'Baba?'

'Hmm?' Rofikul's fingers clattered noisily on the keys, his glasses pushed partway down his nose. Beside the typewriter a tall sheaf of papers seemed to grow day by day.

'Your writing seems to be going well.' Shapla paused.

'Hmm.' Rofikul continued to thump on the typewriter. The inflection in her father's voice made it clear to Shapla that he was in no mood for a protracted conversation.

'I just wanted to say . . .' Shapla hesitated, feeling her cheeks flushing. 'If you want, I can read your new chapters.'

'Thank you, but that won't be necessary.' Rofikul's hands were flying so fast on the typewriter that Shapla could barely see them. The treacherous tears that had seemed to form from nowhere did not help with the blur. Indignantly she blinked them away.

'Very well.' She willed her voice to remain steady. 'If you change your mind.'

Rofikul did not look up from his typing. 'I'm going to send these pages to Adam. Perhaps once I've revised them, you can have a look, see what you think.'

'As you wish.' Shapla unloaded the teacup and plate on to the desk and carried the tray back to the kitchen. On her relief at finding it empty, Shapla leaned her forehead against the cool mud wall and allowed the hot tears to run down her cheeks and seep into the cracks in the clay.

4I

SHAPLA HAD TRIED many times over the years to forgive
her father for abandoning her and her mother. But
forgiveness sounded grandiose somehow, a spectacle of
contrition and absolution, and that was not what either of
them wanted. Instead they had settled into a kind of unspoken
acceptance in the years since his return, and her mother's
passing. Although sometimes she craved contrition, clearly
articulated words of apology and the promise never to hurt
her again, Rofikul's renewed gentleness towards his daughter
over the years was the only apology she received. For the
most part this was contentment enough for Shapla; the pain
had dulled into a faint background hum that made itself felt
rarely. Instead, she and her father moved to the rhythm of
this quiet acceptance, recognising that their trajectories had
brought them to this stage in their lives.

Since her father's contact with his son in England, Shapla
had struggled to retain this equilibrium. It angered her that
Rofikul did not seem to stop and question how this new
presence, however distant for the time being, might affect
her or Abdul Rahim. Not once had her father bothered to
reassure her, or even ask her how she felt about this development in their lives. Instead he acted as if this was a discovery,
sweet and precious, and to be enjoyed only by himself. But
as Shapla was well aware, if the relationship were to sour, it

would sour for them all. Her father was foolish, old and desperate for the recognition of a foreign son, and it sickened her so much sometimes that she had to look away.

The openness with which Rofikul had declared the very existence of his son to the rest of the family, and the complete lack of any consequence, was also something that bothered Shapla. Her father had simply announced to his brothers and sisters, and even his mother, that he had a son in England, and he was now thinking of going to visit him. The unquestioning acceptance of this fact – and presumably of the relationship from which this son had been produced – and even the excitement from some of the family members, including her own grandmother, felt like a betrayal to Shapla. *How can you just accept this?* Shapla wanted to shake her grandmother. Shapla wanted to shake Rofikul too. *Your son will never be able to forgive you,* she screamed inside. *You left him. Have you any idea what that means?*

As far as Shapla was aware, Adam had not expressly invited her father to visit him. From scanning the letters as they arrived every few weeks, it was clear to her that none, as she recalled, contained an invitation. But her father was forging ahead with his plans, telephoning travel agents in Dhaka and writing letters enquiring about visas.

'It is good that your father is making preparations. Thanks to Allah he will finally see his son,' her grandmother remarked to Shapla one morning while they were hanging out the washing on the hedges in the *uthan*.

'He already has a son,' Shapla replied, daring Dadi to say something contradictory.

But her grandmother simply pursed her lips. 'You know what I mean.'

'I'm not sure I do.' Shapla gathered the skirts of her sari and looped them up between her legs to stop them from dragging on the ground as she heaved the empty basket on to her hip.

'Abdul Rahim is . . .' Her grandmother stopped when she saw the expression on Shapla's face.

'Don't you dare.' Shapla's voice was tight. Her grandmother shrank back at her tone. 'Abdul Rahim is my brother.'

Dadi nodded and shuffled along behind Shapla as they made their way back to the kitchen.

'Yes, yes, of course he is, there's no question—'

'No. No question.'

Explaining the situation to Abdul Rahim was something that Shapla had been dreading. He must have known by now, with gossip spreading like wildfire across the *bari*, that their father had another son in England, and she knew she should have broached the subject with him earlier. But Shapla needed Abdul Rahim to know that this brother would be no rival for their father's affections; she needed to know it herself. It was a conversation that would probably be better coming from Rofikul, although she had no idea how to suggest it to her father without it seeming like an insult. Shapla laid down the basket in the kitchen and rearranged her sari.

'I'm going to the fields for a bit,' she announced. 'I'll be back before lunch.'

Her grandmother simply nodded in acknowledgement.

Shapla set off through the *uthan* towards the fields, her oiled black hair in its tight braid glinting in the sun. Her feet were bare, and she enjoyed the bristle of the plants against her soles as she strode on. She found Abdul Rahim sitting against a stack of *dhan*, already golden and piled high for threshing.

'Abdul Rahim,' she asked sternly, 'what are you doing out here alone?'

337

Abdul Rahim looked up at her, his pale brown eyes framed by thick lashes, and she felt her heart melt.

'*Apa*, the others went over there to play *kana machi*.' He pointed with his finger into the distance. Shapla could see a group of the village children dancing around a boy who was blindfolded with a scarf and trying to catch the others who ran away from him squealing. 'They said I could only play if I was the *machi*, and I'm tired of always being the one who has to chase the others. So I said no.'

Shapla fought the urge to hug her brother; an unprompted outburst of affection would just confuse what she needed to speak to him about. She sat down beside him and took his hand.

'Abdul Rahim, you must have heard by now – about Baba going to England soon, perhaps?'

Her brother nodded.

'Have any of the children . . . have they said anything?'

Abdul Rahim's eyes searched his sister's face for assurance and, finding it, nodded slowly. 'They said Baba has a son. A proper son.'

Shapla spoke sharply. 'What do they mean, a proper son? You are a proper son.'

Abdul Rahim shrugged. 'I don't know. They just said, *Your dad has a real son in England*. And that – that he might not come back.'

'You know that isn't true.'

'Which part?'

'Listen. Baba does have another son, and he is trying to visit him in England.' Shapla draped her arms around Abdul Rahim's shoulders and drew him close to her. 'But of course Baba is going to come back.'

Abdul Rahim sat quietly for a moment. 'When is he going?'

'I don't know. Soon.'

'Can we go too?'

'I don't think so.'

'I'd like to meet my brother.' Abdul Rahim laid his head on Shapla's shoulder.

She let it rest there, as the sun beat down on them both. Abdul Rahim's slender legs were pale compared to hers, compared to their mother's. Shapla wondered whether she would ever want to meet this brother.

'Perhaps one day,' she reassured Abdul Rahim. 'Come, let's go home and I'll make you some rice.'

Later that afternoon, Shapla knocked lightly before pushing the door open and stepping into Rofikul's room. Her father was sitting at the desk writing some dates into a calendar.

'Baba?'

This time Rofikul looked up from his work and smiled at her. 'Yes, my Shapla?'

'I need to talk to you about Abdul Rahim.' She hurried out the words as she stood, barely over the threshold. 'You need to tell him you're coming home.'

'Coming home? What?' Rofikul took off his glasses and laid them on the desk, rubbing the bridge of his nose with his thumb and forefinger. 'What are you talking about?'

'When you leave. To go to England. You need to tell Abdul Rahim that you'll be coming home.'

'Of course I'll come home.' Rofikul shook his head slightly impatiently. 'I haven't even decided if I'll be going this year or not; there's the visa application still, and – and other things.' He put his glasses back on and fixed his gaze on Shapla. 'Where did this come from?'

'The other kids are talking. He's worried.' Shapla turned

to leave the room. 'He just needs to know,' she said over her shoulder as she closed the door behind her.

Rofikul sat at his desk for a moment. Of *course* he would come back, the very question was ridiculous. He would tell Abdul Rahim so. But – when would his return have to be? He had no set time that he needed to be anywhere. Shapla was so self-sufficient, she barely needed Rofikul – it was the other way around, really. And Abdul Rahim could not be in better hands than if he were in the hands of his own mother. Rofikul sighed and rubbed his temples. *Mala*. He thought of her occasionally, less so now than in the early years. Shapla went to the cemetery often, but Rofikul kept his visits to the annual remembrance of her death. She had faded into the backdrop of his life in the village, the memory of their few months together after they reunited still pleasing to recall but ever dimming in colour. He would try to remember to visit the *gurustan* to pay his respects before he returned to England.

Rofikul had been wholly unaware of the time that had passed by while the life of the village carried on. Every planting and harvesting signified another year gone, another year of his life in this place. And all the while, life had been continuing *there* – with Adam, with Munira and Hashim, with Helen. The urgency seemed to flood him; there was no more time to wait. He knew that he should wait to be invited, for Adam to openly express a desire to meet him in person, but it was impossible to hold back any longer. Hashim was already gone. There was no guarantee of any time, for any of them. Rofikul would write, he decided, to inform Adam of his visit. He should also write to Helen to let her know; it would be unfair to turn up unannounced. Not that he expected her to want to see him, but it felt rude to arrive in the city they once shared without so much as a prior warning. He would send the letter care of Adam, and hope that she would agree to read it at the very least. Seeing her again was something he could not bring himself to imagine; it was all too possible that any encounter would be even more painful than he feared. Instead, Rofikul focused on the possibility of finally meeting Adam and the hope that his son would surely want to meet him.

42

WHEN ROFIKUL FINALLY announced his impending departure, he had hoped for at least a glimmer of enthusiasm from his daughter. His mother, brothers, sisters-in-law – all the others – had barely contained their excitement about what this trip would mean for him. But instead Shapla's questions had all been practical: was his passport in date; had he secured the visa; would he need to take any medication with him; did he need her to order some? The absence of any apparent emotional reaction disappointed him, given the significance of this visit. He had hoped to find in Shapla a confidante, a willing ear to listen to the rambling train of his thoughts and hopes and doubts and anxieties. Someone who would help him prepare for the magnitude of what was about to happen and bear the anticipation with him. It did not occur to him that perhaps this was too much of a burden to place on his first-born child, who had borne so much already.

But when the time came for Rofikul to leave, any residual hesitation he had felt had given way to an optimism that could have been construed as being almost wilfully ignorant. If he so much as entertained the thought that the visit would be difficult, even painful at times, the prospect of the journey would seem impossible. Instead Rofikul reminded himself of the endless possibility he had felt on his first flight to

England, all those years ago. It had been a long time since he had made such a journey, and the very thought of boarding a train and then a plane, to travel five thousand miles, was exhilarating. He had not felt so free in years.

Holding Abdul Rahim's hand, Shapla watched her father's retreating back as he clambered into the second-class carriage on the heaving train to Dhaka. Hope seemed to emanate from the blazer stretched tightly across his shoulders, the dancing suitcase he swung in his hand.

'Did Baba say anything to you before he left?' Shapla asked Abdul Rahim.

'About what?'

'Coming back.'

Abdul Rahim shook his head. The train whistled and began to chug out of the station, carrying their father beyond the realms where Shapla could reach him. He would be gone for some time, he said – enough time to make amends, but not so long that he would outstay his welcome. He said this hopefully, almost pathetically so, as though he really believed that anyone wanted him there. Shapla did not expect to hear from her father once he arrived in that place of his dreams, England.

Part V

1981–1982

43

THE MOST STRIKING thing about English winters, in Munira's opinion, was not the bite of the morning frost on leaving the house to drop the children at school, or the way that gardens and entire cars could disappear under blankets of snow, not to re-emerge for days: it was how early night-time set in. The first hint of darkness would begin to creep in at around three o'clock in the afternoon, while they were all still in their offices and classrooms, the warm yellow overhead lights tricking them into believing it was still day-time, and then within the space of about forty-five minutes it would have settled fully into the evening, well before tea-time. It was for this reason Munira loved the festivities that came with winter in this country: the smell of November bonfires with toffee and burned leaves and displays of fireworks bursting across the open star-lit canvas above them. And then, of course, the stringing-up of fairy lights to herald Christmas; the flurry of snow-scene cards to write and send; the photographs on the cover of *Good Housekeeping* magazine of perfectly roasted birds, all crisp-skinned and juicy beneath, surrounded by a halo of saintly potatoes; the sound of carols that floated out of the windows of nearby schools where children practised earnestly for their end-of-term concerts. Sometimes she walked into town to gaze at the elaborate displays in shop windows of carefully arranged gifts: soft woollen scarves and mittens, brightly coloured toys, and jewellery that caught the light and glinted enticingly. She loved how the festivals fell at the time when everyone seemed to need them most.

Putting up the tree was an annual ceremony that Munira insisted on scheduling early in December to allow for the longest possible enjoyment of the decorations. Usually, she and Helen were helped by Adam and Joy, who loved fishing around the box of decorations for their childhood creations – an asymmetrical golden star fashioned out of wire by Adam in art class, a salt-dough heart fashioned by Joy in nursery. But this year, Adam was late at the library studying for his end-of-term exams, and Joy was at orchestra rehearsal practising for her end-of-term school concert. Munira had wanted to wait until they were all together, but they seemed rather ambivalent about the ritual this year.

'You just do it, Ammu, with Aunty Helen – and we'll see it when we come home,' Joy had suggested to her mother earlier that week. 'It'll be exciting to walk in and see it all done already – sort of like magic.'

Munira had tried to take the pragmatic suggestion in her stride, but in private, she mourned to Helen that her baby was growing up too fast. 'She didn't even want me to wait to put up the stockings,' Munira said sadly.

Helen had taken care not to dismiss her friend's disappointment, even though from experience she knew that the gradual fading of excitement for traditions that had seemed at one time an endless source of joy was a necessary part of their children growing up.

Instead she had offered to join Munira that evening to decorate the tree, a suggestion that was seized upon with almost alarming enthusiasm. The shrubby-looking spruce was gallantly hoisted up the stairs by Vincent, whose noticeable puffing, once he arrived at their front door, was discreetly ignored by Munira and Helen, lest it offend their friend's sense of his own youthful vitality.

'Right, gals,' he announced once he had helped them attach the tree to the small metal stand, wedging it tightly in place. 'I'm off to see Miss Marie now, but we'll be dropping in later to see the finished article, all right?'

'Ta-ra, Vincent.' Helen waved him off and closed the front door against the wind that was trying to blow its way in. She walked back into the living room to see Munira in her element, presiding over boxes of coloured lights and tinsel and various hanging objects with wire hooks.

Looking up at her friend in the doorway, Munira beamed and tossed her a bag of lopsided paper angels that had been cut out with Joy's safety scissors. 'Ready to get started?'

They hung and strung and untangled and draped and arranged such decking as Manchester had surely never seen before. Munira was distinctly of the 'more-is-more' school of thought when it came to festive decor, swaddling the tree in tinsel and lights until the green boughs could scarcely be seen.

'Did the distraction work, then?' Helen asked Munira as they eventually sank into the overstuffed armchairs by the fire, their palms cupped around mugs of hot chocolate, surveying their handiwork.

'I'm allowed a break from revision, all right?' Munira sounded distinctly like Adam in her indignation and Helen had to suppress a smile.

'Of course you are,' Helen agreed consolingly. 'You've studied really hard this term.'

Munira leaned her head back on the chair and sighed. 'Still so much to revise. I don't know how I'll possibly remember it all.'

'You will.' Helen felt guilty for reminding Munira about her looming exams after the holidays. 'If anyone can, it's you.'

'I bloody hope so,' Munira groaned. College had been everything Munira had hoped it would be: stimulating, engaging and something to keep her mind active and away from fretting about the wellbeing of her family for a few hours a day at least. She was enthralled by the archaic quirks of the English legal system, the terminology that made no sense, and the vast timelines she had to learn for history. She enjoyed talking to her teachers after class and asking follow-up questions to the material they had covered. But now that exams were looming, Munira was feeling the pressure of needing to pass them, not just marvel at the reams of knowledge she was sifting her way through.

'It's been a long year, hasn't it?' Helen stretched her legs out and rested them on the edge of the heater.

'Not the easiest.'

'No.'

The space left by Hashim was as cavernous as ever. It was a gap that would never be filled, and Munira did not really want it to be. She felt him in his absence, every pinprick of grief a homage to the time they had had together. She was starting to settle into it, wearing the cocoon of loss as a comfort, in some ways – a mantle of memory that she warmed herself in. It gave her comfort, too, to know that what she was doing now with her life was what Hashim would have wanted. He would have been so proud, fussing over her studies, not allowing her to cook or lift a finger around the house while she revised and prepared for exams. She smiled sadly at the thought of what had never come to happen.

'You're thinking about Hashim?' Helen asked gently.

'Always.'

'I know.'

The two women sat in silence apart from the quiet hum of the gas heater and the wind outside.

'Munira?'

'Yes?'

'I need to tell you something. Adam, he said . . .' Helen trailed off, her hands knotted in her lap.

'What did he say?'

'It's Rofikul. He says he's coming to England.'

Munira remembered the afternoon all those months ago when she had come home from the park with Joy to the sound of raised voices in the flat. She had shushed Joy, taking off her coat and shoes, and sitting her in front of the television in the living room. *Stay here*, Munira had instructed Joy, who seemed happy enough to obediently watch afternoon cartoons. Then she had made her way to Adam's room. The door was open and she could see Adam sitting on his bed, his head in his hands, while Helen was screaming at him from somewhere in the room. *How could you? How dare you?* Munira strode into the room. *Helen, what on earth is going on?* she had said. *Shush now. Shush, stop screaming at him. Stop it.* Adam had looked up at the sound of his aunt's voice, his face wet with tears. Munira was stricken. *Helen, stop shouting, talk to me.* It had taken what felt like an eternity to calm Helen down. *How long?* she kept shouting. *When were you going to tell me?* Adam just sat there, immovable, his eyes red, Munira's arm around him protectively, as though to shield him from the terrible words his mother was screaming at him. *Ungrateful*, Helen had screamed again. *Do I mean nothing to you?*

It had shocked Munira too, to learn that Adam had been communicating with his father, but she had simply held on to him tighter as Helen cried at them. *How could he? Why would he keep that from me?* In the end, Munira had ushered

351

Helen into her own room, leaving Adam ashen-faced, sitting on the edge of his bed, torn-up letters scattered at his feet. *Helen*, Munira had hissed, wanting to shake her friend. *You have to stop this. Pull yourself together.* But it was no use. Munira left Helen sobbing into her pillow and went to speak to Adam.

It's my right, he had said, his voice cracking. *Why shouldn't I know my father?* His eyes were blazing with hurt.

It had taken weeks for Helen and Adam to begin speaking again. The enormity of what Adam had embarked on in contacting his father hung over the whole house. He had every right to seek a relationship with Rofikul, but Munira wondered if he had acknowledged the hurt that his actions might cause. In the end, it had been the arrival of a letter from Bangladesh that broke the silence between them. Munira had picked up the red and blue-edged envelope and noted the sender's name. She had handed the letter to Adam on the condition that he make an effort to speak to his mother that evening.

Helen had tried to control her upset that Adam was now in semi-regular contact with his father. Part of her wanted to know whether Rofikul had asked or said anything about her, and at the same time did not want to hear anything about what was going on in his life. *She makes it hard*, Adam had complained to Munira. *She says she doesn't want to know, so how can I keep her involved?* Munira had offered a platitude by way of a solution. *She just needs time*, she assured Adam. But time had turned into months, and the exchange of several more letters, and now apparently an impending visit from Rofikul.

'What do you mean, he's coming to England?' Munira could hardly contain her shock. 'Did Adam *ask* him?'

'He says he didn't.' Helen shrugged. 'I don't know what to believe. I hope Adam would have mentioned it to me first if he really had invited him.'

'So what, Rofikul just . . . announced it?'

'Seems that way. Invited himself over for a visit.'

'He's not staying—'

'No, God, no! Not here. I don't know what he's got planned. He just wrote to Adam and said he was planning to come in the New Year and would Adam like to meet him. He says he hasn't written back yet.'

'Will you see him?' Munira thought it best to be direct. There was no point evading the question. It had been almost twenty years since either of them had clapped eyes on Rofikul, and the idea of him hurtling back into their lives was a prospect neither of them had had much time to consider.

'I don't know, Munira.' Helen shrugged. 'Him being here doesn't change anything, does it? So he comes to Manchester and sees Adam – then what? They talk, they swap stories, they find out that they both love music and detest yogurt. They're both night owls. They eat in the same way. And?'

'And what?'

'Exactly. And what?'

Did they expect that it would happen so easily? That they would recognise their own eyes in each other's faces, identify a few shared preferences and attribute them to a genealogical link, and that would be that – almost two decades of abandonment accounted for? Even though she knew that it had been Adam who had traced Rofikul all the way to Bangladesh, she couldn't help thinking that it showed a remarkable degree of temerity for Rofikul now to make arrangements to come and visit Adam without even checking with her to see how she felt about it.

'The thing is' – Helen spoke slowly, considering every

word as she uttered it – 'it's been too long.' She paused and looked over at Munira, who peered back over her glasses. 'I don't love him. I don't have to like him. But I don't miss him any more.'

You can't hate him for ever, Adam had said at the end of one of their most recent conversations about Rofikul's impending visit that, like the others, had descended into an argument. *Try me,* thought Helen. *I've been doing a pretty decent job of it the last seventeen years.* And why the hell couldn't she hate him for ever? Surely that was her prerogative, nobody could deny her that, and especially not Adam. *If I've forgiven him, why can't you?* Adam had blinked at her, so youthfully confident in his conceptions about the world and the tangled threads of relationships. *Idiot boy.* She had wanted to shake him. *You don't know anything. What could you possibly know about forgiveness?* But instead she had taken a deep breath and retreated to her bedroom to seek solace in the softness of her bed, mercifully unshared for over a decade.

The feminine imperative to forgive was, in Helen's mind, one of the most significant obstacles to genuine equality between the sexes. This idea of the endless bounty and grace of women meant that they – she – were duty bound to forgive transgressions over and over; to turn a blind eye to the hurtful behaviours of their loved ones. The hearts of women were expected to stretch to accommodate the sensitivities of every person, even those who had wronged them, regardless of whether or not the process tired out those hearts, making the edges of them less elastic, less inclined to hold anyone close again. But the alternative – to continue to feel hurt – was to bear a *grudge*; something petty and unbecoming in a woman. In a man, though, it would be seen as bearing honour, being principled. Helen was exhausted. She had not asked for any of this.

The worst is over, she thought. Adam was free to try to connect with Rofikul, to try to forge whatever kind of relationship he was comfortable with. But it didn't need to come at the expense of the years she had invested in cultivating a bond with her son that no other could rival. Almost two decades without the father of her child had hardly left her lacking; Adam had been raised in a home more loving than any she had known herself. In Munira, she had a family with whom the shared bonds may not have been of blood, but they were stronger, warmer, and more nourishing than any other she had ever had. What they created together had withstood war and heartbreak and thrived on dedication and love. They had navigated a world for which they had been given no instruction manual, forging their paths in their work, in their homes and beyond. They birthed two children, loved them and nurtured them, raising them in the best way they knew how. It may not have been what any of them had imagined twenty years ago, but when she pictured the twenty years that stretched ahead of them, she couldn't imagine anything else. The thought warmed her from within.

'What are you smiling about?' Munira glanced up at Helen, noting the lightness in her friend's expression.

'You,' answered Helen. 'This.' Helen waved a hand, gesturing to their little living room, the decorated tree in the middle, the cheerful roar of the Calor gas heater in the corner, the bookshelves crammed with story books and encyclopedias and Munira's textbooks, and the four chairs tucked around the wooden dining table where several stacks of highlighted papers, covered with neat writing, lay. 'I don't need anything else.'

'I know,' said Munira, smiling gently. 'Nor do I.'

44

A S HE STOOD on the airport arrivals concourse dragging
on the last inch of his cigarette, Rofikul thought about
Hashim. It was New Year's Eve – twenty-one years to the
day since his cousin had arrived in England for the first time.
Rofikul remembered the sight of Hashim shivering outside
Manchester Victoria station, clad in that ridiculous cheap
suit, and smiled despite the welling sadness the memory
brought him. They had not spoken since the day Rofikul
had boarded the bus to London, suitcase in hand. Moving
cities, and then countries, and the deep shame he carried
made it possible for Rofikul to finish what he had set out
to do: to erase himself fully from the past. A past that still
existed, thrived even, in another place, another life, some
kind of loophole in time.

When he allowed himself to think of his past, this was
how he imagined it: with a defiantly beating pulse that lived
on in the very existence of Helen, and their boy, and Munira,
and Hashim, and even Atiq and Marie and Vincent and all
the rest of them. Their lives carried on unchanged in Rofikul's
dream world, where time played on a familiar loop. Here
was 1961 and Hashim in a bad suit with even worse English.
The scene was chased out by Helen running into the café,
her damp hair pushed back behind her ears, breathless and
lovely. Then came Vincent, laughing from underneath a Rover

P4 demanding wrenches and plugs be passed to him. In this loop Rofikul was the viewer, never being present in the scenes himself, and for years he had comforted himself with the belief that the lives of those he had left behind were safe and familiar and unchanged.

And then. Only months ago, his cherished show-reel had come to an abrupt halt with the news that Hashim was dead. When Mala had died, Rofikul had felt it almost bodily in its immediacy. Just hours before he had held her warm body, stroked her hair as the birthing pains intensified, refusing to be banished from the room until the last possible moment. The next morning, he had borne her weight on his shoulders, one of three other men who carried her to the cemetery and lowered her into the dry red hollow that seemed too big for her shrouded body. His grief was heightened by the sheer palpability of Mala's absence. She had been such a staple figure of his daily existence that everywhere he looked it felt as though something or someone were missing. There could be five women sitting in the *uthan*, but all Rofikul noticed was the one who was no longer in her usual spot in the shade against the tamarind tree. Someone would bring him his lunch, but in the arrangement of the rice and fried egg, without Mala's usual scattering of seared onion and chilli, he felt her absence all over again. His clothes were washed differently, the bed made up differently, the shutters opened differently. Rofikul felt the absence of Mala even more potently than he had felt her presence.

With Hashim's death, it was entirely different. Part of the shock Rofikul felt was the realisation that Hashim – evergreen in the show-reel of Rofikul's imagination – had aged at all, let alone grown old enough to develop complications with his heart. This time, Rofikul's grief was marked less by a physical absence and more by the harsh realisation that time had not stood still. And he, Rofikul, had no window into the world that he had left behind, no knowledge of what had changed among those who remained, who they had all become. He grieved for the lost time, the wasted years when they had not spoken, the renewal of a relationship that could never happen.

Rofikul dropped the cigarette butt on to the floor and turned on his heel, exhaling a steady stream of smoke that blew over his shoulder as he strode towards the bus stand.

'*Wait.*'

Rofikul stopped mid-stride. The voice came from behind him. It was familiar in its quietly spoken warmth – it sounded like Hashim: a young, uncertain-sounding Hashim. But it could not be Hashim because Hashim was dead, and the letters had not come from Hashim, but from someone else; someone who had haunted Rofikul's dreams for years but had no face, no voice, no discernible features. Rofikul turned and saw him – a stranger – standing with hands thrust deep in the pockets of his woollen coat, his collar turned up at the neck. The moonlight was behind him, and Rofikul couldn't make out the expression.

'Adam?'

The two men looked at each other, unspoken words reverberating between them. Standing only a few paces from one another, the years stretched out like an ocean, uncharted waters that neither knew how to navigate. The letters they had exchanged bobbed around like tiny, hopeful buoys. The words they had written, read and committed to memory the only evidence of any connection between them. He's tall, thought Rofikul. And he contemplated the fact that his son's height was somehow a revelation, as everything else would be. He would exist in this realm of anticipatory excitement, uncovering each new truth as though it were treasure. He was almost ashamed of his hunger, the desire to know everything there was to know about the young man before him. There was so much to learn.

'I'm sorry I'm late – there was traffic . . .'

Had he not been so struck by the surrealism of it all, Rofikul would have smiled. *Such politeness.* There was Hashim's influence in him. Even after everything Rofikul had done – or not done – here was Adam being the one apologising. Hashim was the one who had known this boy: knew what he liked to eat; how to comfort him when he woke in the night from a bad dream; the sports he liked to watch on television. Hashim had raised him, loved him actively. Hashim had shaped him. As Rofikul stared at his son, he struggled to discern where Hashim stopped and Adam started. *There is so much to say*, thought Rofikul. *I don't know how I can ever find the words.*

Adam shifted from one foot to the other. He had not felt nervous until now. His father was at once so similar to the person he had pieced together from the fragments he had collected – dark with a shock of wiry hair that was now almost entirely grey; bright-eyed and alert, almost as though he were ready to jump at any point – and yet older and smaller, and somehow alarmingly fragile, in reality.

'I hope you haven't been waiting long.'

Rofikul shook his head, unable to trust his voice. *Too long.* He stepped forward, his palms turned upwards as though asking to receive some kind of divine blessing. Tentatively, Adam offered his hand. It was warm, alive, coursing with their shared blood. Rofikul's arm shook as he extended his hand to take Adam's. As he looked at Adam he saw tears gathered in his son's eyes. Neither counted time as they stood, hands clasped, while buses drove on by, their headlights casting beams of warm yellow into the dark night.

45

T HE STREETS OF Manchester were as familiar to Rofikul
as the fields of his home village. He was pleased by the
realisation that he had not forgotten the wide paved roads,
the grand Victorian buildings, the markets and the bus routes.
The people in the city had changed though; there were so
many faces now that must have come from different countries: there were more Chinese, and Vietnamese, and many
more Asians and blacks than he remembered, lending colour
to the patchwork of citizens. He remembered when he first
arrived, even before Hashim, back in the fifties, and how
different it had all been then. White men who surveyed him
suspiciously on the bus to work. Women with carefully set
hair who shut guest-house doors in his face. Now the whites
hardly blinked at the sight of him, or any of the other people
who would once have stood out as being different.

Rofikul had, however, forgotten just how inhospitably cold
it got in this part of the country. His years in London had
dulled the memory of the biting north wind, the dampness
in the air and the early onset of dusk. His old coat was still
reasonably thick, but he was thankful for the scarf that Shapla
had knitted for him in preparation for his great English return.
He wound it around his neck each morning, tucking it into
the front of his woollen coat. It had been two weeks since
his arrival in England but it felt somehow as if he had never

been away. It was reassuring, knowing how to get around on public transport by himself, and knowing where to go during the days when Adam was not free to see him. He spent hours at the museum, browsing the shelves at the central library, and going up and down the escalators of Lewis's department store. Everything seemed more brightly lit here. Even the buses seemed to glow from the outside, the lights on board gleaming attractively to those waiting in the cold.

In the beginning, Rofikul had seen Adam on most days. When he had first arrived, it had been the middle of Adam's school holidays so they had all the time they wanted. It had come as an enormous relief to Rofikul that Adam wanted to see him at all, let alone as often as this. Mostly they saw each other in town at a café near Rofikul's hotel, but once term started again, sometimes Rofikul would come to meet Adam at the library where he was supposed to be revising for his exams after school, or Rofikul would treat him to lunch at the weekends at one of the kebab houses on Wilmslow Road. Their initial meetings had been an exercise in strained politeness; offering to buy each other cups of tea, sticking to conversational niceties, navigating the newness of being in each other's company. There were times when Rofikul had to stop himself from staring at his handsome, strong-jawed son. But after a couple of weeks of this, Adam seemed to tire of the pretence.

'I want us to talk,' he had told Rofikul squarely over a piece of cake and a Coke one afternoon. 'Talk properly.'

'What do you want to talk about?' Rofikul was relieved that Adam had been the one to bring it up. He had not wanted to push Adam before he was ready, or to bring up topics that perhaps Adam did not want to discuss.

'It's obvious, isn't it?'

Rofikul sighed, although he was on some level impressed

by Adam's refusal to let him off the hook: he would have to be the one to put it into words, to breathe life into the situation by offering some explanation.

'You want to know why I went away.'

'Yeah. Why you left us.' Adam cracked open the can in front of him and took a deep sip.

'I didn't mean to.'

Adam looked incredulously at Rofikul from across the table. 'So, what, it was some unfortunate accident?'

'No. I'm not making excuses.'

'Yeah. Don't. There isn't one.'

'No – there isn't. Well . . .' Rofikul closed his eyes for a moment. He knew this moment would come, he was no fool. But fool he must be, because despite knowing that this was surely one of the first questions his son would ask, he had no prepared answer. It had been so many things: the pressure he suddenly felt at being a father again, this time in a different place with a different set of expectations; the guilt of the secret he had carried for so long, with only Hashim its unwilling guardian. But mostly, he knew, it was selfish. He wanted freedom; that was why he had left his homeland in the first place, and the prospect of marriage and a child, again, was too much.

'Adam. There is something I need to tell you.' Rofikul drew a deep breath. 'You know that I wrote to you about . . . about the children I have in Bangladesh?'

Adam nodded silently.

'The thing is, Shapla – my daughter – she is older than you.' Rofikul looked at Adam, hoping that he would piece together the details so that Rofikul would be spared from saying it out loud. But Adam remained silent. 'I was married to her mother before – before I came to England. Before I met your mother.'

362

'But – you and Mam. She said you got married.'

'We did. When we found out she was carrying you.'

Adam looked confused. 'So what, did your other wife – you got divorced or what?'

'She died. But not until many years later. She was alive when I married your mother. And Shapla was a young girl at the time.'

Adam shook his head, the pieces falling into place. 'So you were already married when you married my mum?' Adam's voice was rising. 'You'd already left one family. Did she know?'

Rofikul spoke quietly, not meeting Adam's fierce gaze. 'Not from me. I never knew if Hashim told her.'

'Chacha? He – he *knew*?'

The look on Adam's face made Rofikul realise he had done this all wrong. He tried to reach out, to hold Adam's hand across the table, but his son swatted his hand away.

'Are you saying' – Adam's eyes were flashing – 'that Chacha *knew* you had another family, and that he never told us?'

'I . . . I don't know.' Rofikul's voice was desperate. He had ruined everything. 'No, I am sure your uncle didn't . . . he probably had no idea, he—'

Adam interrupted him angrily. 'He knew, and you left us for your other family? That's it, isn't it? Just admit it.' Other customers were turning around in their seats, witnessing the scene.

Rofikul shook his head miserably. How could he explain it? In some ways, it would have been better if he *had* left one family for the other, but the truth was, he hadn't. He had left each of his families, his wives, his children, in search of his freedom, wanting to pursue a dream, a vision of something bigger than himself. It was fate that had carried him back to his first family, and now back again to this one

363

– as though he were some kind of swinging pendulum, unable to settle into a rhythm in any one place.

'Adam, please. Let me explain.'

Adam stood up from his seat and started pulling on his coat, packing up his rucksack. 'I can't do this right now.'

'But, Adam – when can I see you again?' Rofikul could feel the pressure rising in his throat.

'I don't know.' Adam was already halfway across the café and almost out of the door. The waitresses were barely concealing their stares. 'I need to talk to my mam.'

The door of the café swung shut behind him, the gentle jangling of the bell the only noise in the hushed room. The glass pane in the door was already fogged with the warm breath of the punters inside. Rofikul's eyes were swimming, and he could barely make out the figure of his son striding down the snow-covered pavement. He covered his face with his hands and let the tears run silently down his cheeks, not caring about the gossipy whispers of the waitresses or the other customers who had now awkwardly turned their attentions to one another, or the paper in front of them, or the bottom of their coffee cups.

Rofikul did not hear from Adam for days after that conversation. He wrote short letters every day apologising and posted them to Adam but there was no reply. He even tried to see him after college, but Adam either changed his route or left the building early, because Rofikul never saw him at the gates when four o'clock came around. Rofikul took to pacing the streets unhappily, wrapped in his coat, the chill in the air and his inner coldness numbing him. He had handled all this so badly. His first mistake had been coming here in the first place, uninvited, without even checking to see whether Adam wanted it. Instead, he'd thoughtlessly announced his arrival as a fait accompli and Adam, probably out of politeness, had simply gone along with it. Rofikul had not even checked with Helen, even though he knew it was the least courtesy he could offer.

And to make things worse, now that he was here, it was clear he was just ruining whatever delicate connection he had managed to forge with his son. Adam had looked so hurt, so angry, when Rofikul had tried to explain the situation to him. About Mala, and Shapla, and the life he already had, and had left once before. None of it was Adam's fault. Or Helen's. Or Mala's or Shapla's. It was his, and his alone, but he had no idea where to begin to try to make amends when Adam refused even to meet him. He was sorry too at bringing Hashim into it. That had been so unnecessary, such a careless slip. To be truthful, Rofikul had often hoped that Hashim had told Helen; at least then she would have known, and Rofikul would not have had to be the one to break the news. It would have been the easiest way. He wondered why Hashim had apparently never shared Rofikul's secret with her – and presumably not with Munira either. Loyalty, perhaps, but Rofikul had done nothing to warrant Hashim's faithful guarding of such a secret for so many years after he had exited their lives so callously.

After almost a week of persisting in trying to meet Adam, Rofikul wondered whether it was time to change his approach. The boy needed space, that much was clear, but in the meantime there was another person who deserved an explanation after all these years. Someone who had suffered even more than Adam at Rofikul's hands. It was time, finally, to explain himself. Forgiveness was not something he could even begin to hope for; but the freedom of confessing, shedding his duplicity, would be an act of salvation in itself. With great apprehension Rofikul wrote a note and slipped it into the tall red pillar box that stood on the corner outside his hotel. The letter was addressed to Ms Helen Doherty.

Helen recognised the handwriting immediately. It had leaped out in its familiarity, the same careful print that lined the front of Adam's envelopes from overseas. The print that was still etched into the front cover of some of the books that remained on Munira's shelf. They were part of the collection that Hashim had salvaged from the black bin bags left by Helen outside her flat once she realised that Rofikul had gone and was not coming back. They were all his books: Bengali and English, hard- and soft-backed, prose and poetry, some with illustrations and maps, some with line after line of tightly set print. Helen had not realised that Hashim had rescued some of these books until she moved in with Munira and Joy all those years later. Here was a collection of Yeats's poetry. Here was *Gitanjali* by Tagore. A Bengali–English dictionary. A volume on homeopathy, a Bengali translation of Hahnemann's *Materia Medica*. A collection of Russian short stories. Hashim had never read any of them, but he could not bear for them to be thrown away, these relics of a time and a bond gone by. Helen had mentioned nothing of them to Munira or to Adam, and instead had duly ignored their presence on the shelf in the living room in the flat they now shared. She wondered if Adam had any idea that these were his father's volumes.

She had surprised herself by the way in which she had read the letter immediately. There had been no hesitation, no wrangling. She had calmly torn open the envelope, pulled out the single page, and unfolded it. The note was only a few lines long: an apology for not contacting her sooner, and a request – acknowledged as being more than he deserved – for her to meet him in the coming days while he was in

England. *There is much I owe you*, Rofikul had written, *but the least I can offer is an explanation, should you wish to hear it.* Helen already knew what it was that Rofikul wanted to explain. Adam had come home the other evening in such a state that she had demanded that he tell her what was going on. He had refused, saying that it was not his place to tell her. In the end, she had told him that she would forbid him from seeing his father again if he did not tell her what had gone on. There was no point him seeing Rofikul if it was just upsetting him. Adam had merely shrugged. He did not want to see his father anyway. *What happened?* Helen's tone had softened. Her initial anger about Rofikul and Adam meeting had given way to a quiet hope that it would provide her son with some kind of solace, especially since losing his uncle so recently. But if what she feared most – for her son to get hurt in all this – was happening, then she needed to know.

In the end, Adam had tearfully told her what Rofikul had revealed. Helen had sat on the sofa beside him, his hand in hers, stone-faced. Her heart was beating so hard it almost hurt. Of course she had expected that Rofikul had moved on in the years that had passed. She assumed he had remarried, had children he had stayed with. But to discover that it was not a remarriage but a return to his first union, and that her own marriage, such as it had been, was invalid from the very beginning, was a different kind of heartbreak altogether. She had fought back her tears, holding Adam close instead. *It's not our fault*, she whispered, half to Adam, half to herself.

The most painful part of all had been learning of Hashim's complicity in the whole charade. How could he have known, and never told them? Did that mean Munira had known too? The betrayal, the duplicity, had stung unlike any other pain Helen had ever felt – and she was no stranger to being let down. But seeing the shock on Munira's face that evening when Helen confronted her, it was clear that Munira had been none the wiser. *Are you sure?* she had whispered, her face blanched. *It's impossible – Hashim would not have kept this from us.* Tears had run down her cheeks at the realisation of the secrets and lies her husband had guarded so faithfully, leaving the rest of them in such darkness. How could he have protected his cousin all these years, over and above Helen and Adam?

Helen drank very rarely, and did not keep any alcohol in the house, but after reading that letter, all she could think of was sinking a very large measure of brandy. She went downstairs to the shop and helped herself to a bottle from the counter behind the till. *I'll settle up later*, she had told Mirza, before disappearing back upstairs with the bottle tucked firmly under her arm. The first sip was warming, nudging her gently out of her shock. The second sip roused her, burning her throat. By her second glass, Helen had decided what she needed to do. Turning the piece of paper over, taking one of Joy's fountain pens, Helen wrote a short response on the back of Rofikul's letter.

I will meet you this Wednesday at six o'clock at the Crown. Helen

She stuffed it back into the envelope it came in and crossed out her address. She went back downstairs to the shop, asked Mirza for a stamp, and marched around the corner to post it before she had a chance to change her mind. Her hand lingered on the hungry mouth of the letterbox that sat in the wall. She shivered, the skin on her arms prickling like gooseflesh; she had left the house without even a cardigan. Her fingers gently released the envelope and it fell to the bottom of the letterbox with a faint thump. *It's done.* She returned to the flat, her head swimming. Seeing that nobody else was yet home, Helen retired to her bedroom, taking the rest of the brandy with her to stave off the long, sleepless night.

46

IN THE TIME that had passed, Munira had grown accustomed to the emptiness that crept into her chest whenever she thought about Hashim, but the discovery of Rofikul's secret and Hashim's complicity in guarding it all these years had complicated her grief. The loss she now felt when she thought of her husband was tinged with the pain of betrayal, the hurt at not being trusted enough to confide in. She had believed they shared everything. As confused and hurt as the revelation had left her, Munira reserved her hatred for Rofikul alone. As if he had not caused enough problems by leaving his family – or families – in the first place, Rofikul had tarnished the memory of her beloved husband in making him an accomplice in his duplicity. And he had cast doubt on her loyalty and friendship with Helen. At first Helen had not believed Munira's ignorance about Rofikul's other family. *How could you not know? You're related, aren't you?* Helen had stormed that evening at a bewildered Munira. But on seeing Munira's palpable shock, Helen had relented. It was apparent that they had both been left in the dark.

It was difficult to understand why Hashim had kept the secret for so long. He must have had his reasons; perhaps he believed it was loyalty, to ensure that Rofikul's past was kept well hidden. Or maybe he thought that it ought to be Rofikul's decision when or if to disclose the details of his private life. Munira went back and forth trying to rationalse Hashim's actions, but she always reached an impasse. It saddened her; this barrier between them that she had been unaware of while he was living, now emerging after his death. She despised Rofikul for his selfishness, the wedge his actions had driven between herself and Hashim, even now, and the doubt he had cast on the bond she and Helen shared.

Amid this turmoil of feeling, Munira – although she wished to be supportive of her friend – could not understand why Helen had agreed to meet Rofikul. It was doubtful that he would be able to tell her anything Helen did not already know by now. So what use was there in hearing his excuses, tired and pathetic as they were sure to be? He had caused them all enough pain; they'd be better off without him, as they had been for years until now. It was only out of sheer loyalty that Munira had hugged Helen close and wished her luck before she left for her meeting with Rofikul that evening. *Do you need me to come with you?* Munira had asked, already knowing that Helen would turn down the offer. *I'll be fine. I've already told Adam that he can come if he would like to,* Helen had replied. Adam had not seen Rofikul since their last meeting almost two weeks ago and, like Munira, had been surprised by Helen's agreement to meet the man whose name she could hardly stand to hear just a few weeks ago. He had been non-committal in response to Helen's invitation to the meeting. In Adam's mind there was nothing his father could say that would fix the past, but still, it had taken them so long to arrive at this place – whatever it looked like – that there was a part of him that wasn't ready to be finished with it all just yet.

Helen kept one eye on the time all day. The arms on the office clock face seemed to inch along laboriously, the minutes ticking into some of the slowest passing hours that she had ever endured. Her colleagues invited her to sit with them for lunch as usual, but she was too jittery today to sit through the light-hearted chatter and exchange of weekend plans and complaints about children and errant husbands. Instead, she worked through her lunch hour, finishing her typing in good time to leave the office a little earlier than usual. As the hand crept towards four o'clock, Helen packed up her handbag and slipped out of the office to briskly walk the ten minutes it took to reach the salon where Marie worked. Marie, already briefed for the task, was ready with towels and shampoo and set about lathering and rinsing Helen's hair, before blow drying it into a neat, clean bob. Marie kept up a professional level of light, friendly patter, sensing Helen's nervousness at the enormity of her meeting that evening. Only at the end, when she waved off Helen's attempt to pay her, did Marie betray any indication of knowing what was taking place later on. Leaning in to hug her close, Marie whispered in Helen's ear, 'Don't doubt yourself for a moment, Helen Doherty,' and kissed her firmly on the cheek.

It was a little after six o'clock when Helen pushed through the double doors of the Crown, the dark wood frame holding the etched glass panes in a firm embrace. It was filling up with the after work crowd, cheerful laughter ringing through from the bar, and the haze of smoke and music blaring from the machine in the corner. She wished she had chosen somewhere a little less busy – a café perhaps, or even a park. She cast a quick glance around the room, and as her eyes fell on him she could feel her breath catching. There he was, sitting at a booth reading a book amid all the din, his glasses perched partway down his nose as they always used to be. She took in the greying hair on his bowed head, thinning a little at the crown, and the blazer, slightly tight around the shoulders. As if sensing her, he looked up. The smile that broke across his face and his evident nervousness utterly disarmed her in that moment.

'Helen.' Rofikul stood up and slid out of the booth towards her. He reached out his hands as if to take hers, and then, seemingly not knowing what to do with them, he clasped them together again in front of him.

'Hello.' Her voice was measured and steady and Rofikul found it difficult to sense any emotion she might have been feeling. 'It's been a while.'

'I didn't think you'd come.' Rofikul could hardly believe Helen was here, living and breathing and talking to him as though the last sixteen years had not happened.

'I said I would,' Helen replied coolly.

'Yes, of course, you did,' Rofikul answered hastily. He did not want Helen to think that he had doubted her word. She looked lovely, her auburn hair shorter now than it had been the last time. Her skin was still smooth and clear, a little tired around her grey-green eyes that were ever direct and fixed on his. He had to blink and look away. 'It's noisy here.' He gestured to the room apologetically. 'Would you like to go somewhere else?'

'I told Adam we would be here if he wanted to join us.'

'Oh.' Rofikul was surprised, but pleasantly so. He had hardly believed Helen would come, and now there was the possibility that they would be joined by their son. It was all so surreal. 'Well of course, in that case let's stay here.'

'We could sit in the beer garden if they have any light.'

They made their way out on to the small patio at the rear of the pub where a couple of heaters stood alongside some scattered tables and chairs. Lamps hung around the decking and waxy stubs of candles flickered on the tables.

Rofikul gestured to a table closest to the heaters. 'This one all right?'

Helen pulled her coat tighter around herself and nodded. 'Least we can hear ourselves here.'

Away from the chattering and laughter and music it seemed almost uncomfortably quiet in the garden.

Rofikul cleared his throat nervously. 'You look great.'

Helen did not reply.

'I hope you don't mind me—'

'What the hell, Rofikul!' Helen's voice was so low that Rofikul almost strained to hear it. 'Why now? What happened in the last seventeen fucking years?'

Rofikul was taken aback – he had never known Helen to speak in that way. They sat in silence for a few moments. A bored-looking barmaid came over to take their drinks order. A whisky, and a gin and tonic. She sauntered off, her thumb tucked into her waistband.

'I'm sorry, I can't say it enough.' Rofikul was almost too nervous to get the words out. 'Did Adam—'

'Yes,' Helen interrupted. 'He told me, and he shouldn't have had to.'

'You should have heard it from me.'

'It was cowardly.'

'I know. I'm sorry.'

The barmaid brought over their drinks and, as if noticing them for the first time, looked at them curiously, trying to determine their dynamic. Neither was wearing a wedding ring. And at their age, it was strange to see a mixed couple. Maybe they were later-in-life lovers. Times were changing, after all. She thumped the glasses down on to the table and picked up a tray.

'Anything to eat? Kitchen closes at eight.' Rofikul looked at Helen who shook her head. The barmaid stalked off, her tray under one arm.

'Thank you for agreeing to see me.' It occurred to Rofikul that he should be grateful to Helen for this gesture, whatever it meant.

'Adam was distraught when he came home the other night.' Helen took a sip of her drink. 'I let him see you on the condition that he didn't get hurt. You broke his heart.'

'I'm so sorry. I wanted to explain things to him, but I – I got it so wrong. I should have done it differently.' Rofikul shook his head. 'I wanted him to know that it wasn't because of him. Or . . . or you.' He looked nervously at Helen. 'I had things in my past that I hadn't dealt with.'

'Like a wife. A child.'

'Yes.'

'What happened to them? Did she know?'

Rofikul had wondered the same, all these years. He and Mala had never talked about his life in England. She asked no questions, and he told her no lies. It was simple, and yet, now he came to think of it, it must have been torturous for Mala, who surely wondered what he had done, and who he had loved, all those years they had been apart.

'She died,' he said quietly. 'Soon after I returned to Bangladesh. I was there during the war.'

'I know.'

Rofikul glanced at Helen in surprise. 'Hashim told you?'

'He stocked your newspaper once. Until I asked him to stop.' Rofikul did not need to know about the hours Helen spent at the library, reading his war correspondent columns, her fingers tracing the faint black and white image of his face. 'How did she die?'

'Giving birth. The child, it wasn't mine. It was a war baby.'

Rofikul took a deep breath. 'I've tried to raise him as my own.'

Helen had no idea how to respond. It was as though she were watching a film, with all these characters she knew and half knew living out the nakedness of their lives in her full view. It sounded ridiculous, but in all these years she had never fully pictured Rofikul as, well, *living*. He was a character in her fantasies, someone who lived through wars and wrote about them, always making it through unscathed. That he had suffered – had his own share of heartbreak, loss and love, even – had never occurred to her. Rofikul existed only as an extension of her own memories, not as a real person playing out his own fate.

'It must have been hard,' was all Helen could think to say.

'It was.' Rofikul hesitated. 'I know I put you through hardship too.'

Helen let the statement hang in the air, neither accepting nor denying it.

'You had another child though? From before.'

'Yes, a daughter. Her name is Shapla.' Helen noted the softening in his voice as he said her name, and felt the snap of jealousy in her ribcage. 'She has been a great comfort to me.' Rofikul wondered whether to carry on; it was probably wisest to steer the conversation towards Helen and Adam. They were his focus right now. 'Helen, tell me what I can do. I'll do anything to try to make this right.'

'It's not that simple, Rofikul.' It was the first time she had said his name. It stung somehow, so familiar and yet so loaded with accusation. 'You can't expect the last sixteen years just to be wiped out by a single apology, one poxy visit in the whole of your son's life. I don't even know if you can make it right.'

'I'll do anything, I'll try—'

'Rofikul,' Helen interjected, forcing him to stop and look at her. 'It's too late for me. I don't know how I can forgive you, and I don't really feel as though I need to in order to move on.' She levelled her gaze at Rofikul. 'I have moved on. I have managed, and we coped – me and Adam, we had everything we needed. I don't need anything from you. I want nothing from you.' She looked weary, as if she were only having this conversation out of some kind of duty. 'But for Adam – I don't know.' She cleared her throat and drank from her tumbler of mostly melted ice. 'He wanted to meet you. It must mean something to him. I've seen him these last few weeks, how he was when he came home from seeing you. I – I didn't like it, but I could see how it was helping him. But after the last time, he was so upset, Rofikul. I can't let you hurt my son like that. If you want a chance, you need to make it right with him.'

Tears had welled in Rofikul's eyes.

'I want to. I will try.'

They sat there in silence, the weight of years of unsaid pain and fear sitting between them, the load somehow lightened by the relief of recognising it. There was still so much to unravel, and sort, and make sense of.

'Mam?'

Helen and Rofikul both turned round on hearing the familiar voice. Adam was walking towards them from the back door of the pub. He looked uncertain as he came to the table beside the heaters and sat down between them.

'I'm so glad you came, Adam.' Rofikul patted him on the back. He wanted to draw Adam to him and hug him so fiercely that he would never let go. It would take time for that.

'You all right, love?' Helen put her arm around Adam's

shoulders and rubbed them firmly. 'It's cold out, you should have worn your big coat.'

'What have you been talking about?' Adam looked from Helen to Rofikul, as if trying to determine the conversation from his gaze alone.

'Many things.' Rofikul's voice had a slight catch in it. 'If you want to we can carry on talking, here – now.'

Adam looked at his mother questioningly. She looked from Rofikul to Adam and shrugged her shoulders.

'It's up to you, love,' she said gently. 'We can stay a little, or we can go home.'

'Let's stay.'

It was an evening all three of them would remember as hardly being real. They talked, about the years that had passed between them, and the years they had spent together. Memories that had been laid to rest for years were shaken out and aired, and shared again. There was something different in this dynamic, no offering or expectation of apology – those were meaningless now – but instead a promise, a hope, of something lasting, something more absolving than repentance.

47

THE EARLY SUMMER brought with it warm long days that stretched into balmy summer evenings accompanied by the melody of ice-cream vans and the sound of people out in the streets, smoking in their gardens and enjoying the return of the sunshine once more. It also brought with it the grim reality of exams. Munira had turned the living room into her study, with colour-coded stickers and piles of notes stacked on every surface and posters with timelines and diagrams pinned around the room. Revising for her A-levels was the ultimate priority for Munira, who had taken a temporary leave of absence from all her other duties.

'Ammu, come and play with me,' Joy would try to persuade her mother, and sometimes would successfully win a short walk around the block, or game of Ludo, but then the resident student would return to her books until well into the night.

'You know what she gets like.' Adam had shrugged when Joy complained that they had lost her mother to days and nights of feverish studying. 'Just keep out of her way, it'll all be over in a few weeks.'

True enough, May and June came and went, and Munira's exams with them. And then arrived July; the school holidays lay on the horizon, a sweet paradise promised to Joy and Adam.

'It'll be you next year,' Joy pointed out to Adam as they lay on the grassy banks of the park eating orange ice-lollies that Adam had bought for them both. 'Doing your A-levels and that.'

'Yep.' Adam snapped the wooden stick of his ice-lolly into two and flicked the pieces into the bushes. 'Except if I do my A-levels, I'll be going to uni afterwards, unlike Chachi. So there'll be a point to it all.'

'What point?'

'I told you – uni. Leaving home.'

Joy was aghast by the suggestion. 'What – leaving *us*? But why? Can't you stay in Manchester for university?'

Adam laughed and shook his head impatiently. 'Why would I stay here? I could apply anywhere. London maybe. See what all the fuss is about.' Seeing Joy's obvious distress, Adam tried to soothe her. 'Look, I haven't even done my exams yet! And it'll be at least another couple of years before I go – if I go. I might not even pass.' He looked solemnly at Joy who rolled her eyes and smiled despite herself.

'As if you'd fail.'

'You never can tell.'

They lay there in the sun, Joy fiddling with the buckle of her shoe.

'Bhaiya?' She squinted up at him quizzically.

'Hmm?' Adam was lying back on the grass, eyes shut, his arms folded over his forehead as though he were trying to block out the sunshine.

'How come your dad is still here?'

Adam opened his eyes to see Joy peering over to the benches near the path that bisected the park, where Rofikul was sitting absorbed in reading the newspaper.

'He said he wanted to stay a bit longer than he originally thought.' Adam looked back towards his father, who had not yet seen Adam and Joy. He added, half to himself, 'Though he was only going to come for a few weeks at first.'

'He came in January.' Joy counted on her fingers. 'That's seven months. I don't know how many weeks that must be.'

'Do you want to go over and say hello?' Adam stood up, brushing the grass off his jeans. Rofikul had met Joy on two or three occasions in the time he had been around, the last time being when Munira and Helen had allowed Adam to bring Rofikul to their house for lunch one weekend. *He's my guest*, Adam had pleaded, and Munira had looked doubtfully at Helen who had shrugged her agreement. *It's just one lunch*, was all she said. Munira had mutinously slaved away in the kitchen for the whole day before, preparing an excess of every kind of dish: beef curry and biryani, whole fried fish, salads, chicken bhuna, and *mishti* for dessert. *I don't want him thinking we are wanting for anything*, she had explained to Helen, who asked why Munira was going to such efforts. Hashim had been a good provider. Munira wanted it known. The conversation at lunch had been stilted; only Adam and Rofikul ate together, with Munira and Helen standing by offering more portions and answering Rofikul's questions politely but curtly. It was customary, this gendered separation of eating with guests, but one that Munira had never enforced before.

Joy had eaten earlier and had shyly watched Adam and this stranger – apparently her uncle – from the sofa as they ate and talked at the kitchen table. He had been nice to her, giving her some money – a note bigger than any she had been given before – to buy some sweets. When it was time for him to leave, after being served tea and *mishti*, he had patted her head and announced, to nobody in particular, *She looks like her father.* Afterwards her mother had taken the note from Joy and stuffed it into the charity box on the counter of the shop downstairs. *We don't need his money*, she had said sharply to Joy, who fought back her tears. She hadn't asked for it, after all. When her mother had stomped back up the stairs, Mr Mirza had opened the charity box and given Joy the note back. It had been such a strange day.

'I think I'll stay here, Bhaiya.' Joy picked at the grass. She didn't know what to say to the kindly seeming man who her mother and aunt apparently did not like, and who her cousin seemed to like very much.

'Suit yourself. Won't be long.' Adam sprinted off and Joy watched as he reached the benches. Rofikul looked up and smiled and stood up to hug Adam. She could not hear the conversation but she could see the broad grin that had spread across her cousin's face and the animated chat they were having. Seeing how happy they seemed to be around each other, Joy remembered her own father. His scent, faintly of *paan* and betel nut, and freshly washed laundry, and Vaseline hair tonic, and how it felt to be wrapped up in his shawl while they sat watching television at night, and the gentleness of his voice as he sang nursery rhymes to her in Bangla. She missed him so much. Some nights it was hard to sleep with the ache in her chest. With the back of her hand she brushed her eyes hastily in case anyone saw her tears, and went back to picking the petals off a daisy while she waited for Adam to return.

'I can't open it.' Munira's hand was shaking as she clutched the sealed envelope. Helen, Adam and Joy were huddled around her in the main hall of the college. Throngs of students were gathered there, some in groups, some with their parents, eager to find out the results of their exams earlier that summer.

'I will.' Joy took the envelope from her mother's hand and tore it open. She unfolded the piece of paper and squinted at it confusedly. 'I don't understand all the bits . . .'

'Oh, give it here.' Helen took the piece of paper. 'Munira.' She looked over the top of the paper at her friend. 'You've passed them all! And not just that, Munira, you got three As. Three!'

'What?' Munira was frozen, hardly able to believe what she was hearing. Joy and Adam broke out into wild cheering and whooping. She took the piece of paper that Helen offered her, and there it was, in neatly typed black and white. Three clearly typed As. This was incredible, it was more than she had dared to hope. Well, that wasn't true, she had hoped – but she had not thought it would actually happen. 'This is—'

'Brilliant! Yes it is. How shall we celebrate?' Helen beamed at the children, inwardly thankful that they were still just youthful enough to be made happy with the promise of ice cream.

'No, you don't understand.' They all turned to look at Munira who seemed to have turned pale from the news. She leaned heavily against one of the pillars in the echoey room. 'Last year, I applied . . . for a place at university.' She cleared her throat. 'To study law. Maurice Stone helped me, he suggested a few courses and proofread my personal statement. I needed two A grades and a B to get into the law programme. And I, well . . . I suppose I did.' She could hardly keep the smile off her face.

'You got *more* than that,' Helen exclaimed. 'You're going to university, Munira!' She pulled Munira into a hug.

Adam, noticing Joy's quietness, pressed her hand. 'Hey, what's wrong, Joy?'

'Is Ammu going away to London too?' Her voice was barely above a whisper.

'What? No! Joy, Ammu is staying here, darling.' Munira looked confusedly at Adam. 'Why does she think I'd be going away?'

'Bhaiya said—'

Adam interrupted Joy hastily. 'I think Joy got confused when I was talking about university, a while ago.'

'Darling, of course I'm not leaving. I'll be going to university right here in the city. Part-time, probably,' Munira added, looking towards Helen.

Joy, seemingly reassured, took Adam's hand as they made their way out of the hall towards the promise of ice cream.

'How are you, you know, paying for it?' Helen asked quietly, making sure Adam and Joy were out of earshot, several paces ahead.

'Maurice has offered me a job researching. I'll work for him part-time, and he'll pay me – and I'll apply for a grant.' She had been grateful for all Maurice's support, as she was determined to keep even the question of university from her family; she could not bear the disappointment if she didn't make it. It was easier to keep it a secret, one that would disappear noiselessly if it never came to fruition. Munira had thought about this opportunity for so long, never really believing it could happen. Going to college had been struggle enough, an achievement she had only dared hope for in her wildest dreams, and thanks to the encouragement of Hashim she had done it. Now here she was, ready for the next wave that would sweep her up and carry her further, deeper into the beautiful, unpredictable waters of her future.

Satiated on raspberry ripple and mint choc-chip, Munira and Joy sat cuddled together on the upstairs deck of the bus. Behind them sat Helen and Adam, arm-in-arm, watching the city go by below them, the grey tarmac roads and stretches of blue sky. Adam wondered what the roads were like in Bangladesh – probably not as wide or as paved as these, he guessed. They would be dusty in the dry season, cracked and parched. In the monsoons, they would turn to sludge, the mud entrapping those who dared to walk along. Lately, he found himself imagining Bangladesh often. It was strange that a country that had shaped him so much, in ways unbeknown even to himself, should be a land that remained unfamiliar to him. Over the past months, his conversations with his father had travelled from Britain to Bangladesh, from the past, to the present, and into ideas of the future. And they had awakened something in him – something he now recognised as a desire, a need, to know more. To see things with his own eyes, without relying on someone else's narration.

He did not know how he would break the news to his mother. She would insist that he at least finish his exams the following summer – and that, he supposed, was an agreement that was fair enough. But the desire to visit his father's homeland was a pull he was unable to deny. He had a family there he did not know. A sister he had only heard of. A brother. Aunts and uncles and cousins he had never met. The thought overwhelmed him, and at the same time, filled him with an excitement, an anticipation that he had never felt before. He could not expect his mother to understand this, but he hoped she could encourage him all the same. His father had invited him to visit at any time. *It is as much your home as England*, he had said. *You will always have a place there.* Adam wondered whether the welcome would be extended if he actually took up the offer. He hoped so – it seemed so, anyway. Rofikul was always so delighted to see him when they spent time together. He had, after all, extended

385

his visit just to be with Adam, moving out of the hotel he had stayed in for the first few weeks and into a room in a small guest house. Rofikul had made no mention of how long he intended to remain; it was a question neither had raised, and Adam preferred to take each week they had together as it was, without the expectation of it extending for ever.

Adam looked down at his mother's auburn head on his shoulder, streaked with bits of grey. Her eyes were closed, the lashes gently resting on her cheek. When she was awake, everything about her radiated strength and purpose, but in her sleep she seemed softer. He hoped she would understand. But this was not a conversation for today, or even tomorrow or next week. They had a whole year to get through first: Chachi's first year as a university student; his school exams; hopefully securing himself a place at university to return to after his visit to *desh*. The possibilities that seemed to stretch out ahead of him were exciting and terrifying all at once. He closed his eyes and rested his head on his mother's as the orange sun lowered in the evening dusk and the bus faithfully carried them along the wide grey roads towards home.

Acknowledgements

This book exists because of the faith and encouragement of some truly remarkable people.

Thanks to my brilliant editor, Mark Richards, for taking a chance on an unknown author with a half-finished manuscript, and to the whole team at John Murray, especially Yassine Belkacemi and Emma Petfield. Thanks also to my agent, Lucy Luck, for her excellent counsel and warmth.

I owe my greatest thanks to my parents, Selina and Muhammad Ahsan Ullah: to Ammu for reminding me to 'stop messing about and just write' and her unwavering belief that it would all amount to something, and to Abbu, for his long stories by the fire and for teaching us our history.

I am indebted to my grandmother, Fatima Nahar Begum, for sharing her experiences of migration so frankly and so unflinchingly with me, and to my uncle, Aman Ullah, for being willing to talk about the war, even when it hurt. Their memories are what forms the heart of this book.

Especial thanks to Shabnam Ahsan, for her thoughtful comments as my trusted first reader of this novel, to Sabreen Ahsan for telling me about the pitching event that led to this book being published, and to Amirul, Safiyah and Yusuf Khan for making visits 'home' always so joyful.

I am grateful for the continued support and encouragement from my extended families in Britain and Bangladesh and from my new families I have collected on the way: the Brams, the Thourons.

Thanks also to my friends, each and every one, but especially to Esther Odida, Amelia Odida, and Natalie Holden for being there right from the start; Uzma Ali and Anne Irfan for offering to read early drafts; Rosie Fearon, Leah Hyslop, and Mary Waireri for continued encouragement and a great WhatsApp thread; Katie Traxton for lending her expertise and sound advice; Carly Friedman and Lauren Jacobs for transcending time zones; Osmana Raie for going above and beyond as a mentor; and Ellen Carter for her wisdom and empathy.

And lastly, thanks to Avi Bram for getting to know and love the characters as much as I did, and for allowing me to talk about them as real people. And for more love and understanding than I ever thought it was possible to share. *Alhamdulillah.*

Author's Note

Ekushey is a fictional newspaper. The editorial in *Hashim &
Family* is an edited translation of *Janomot* newspaper's inaug-
ural editorial from 'Bengali journals and journalism in the
United Kingdom (1916–2007)' by Faruque Ahmed.

The epigraph, *Probashi* by Rabindranath Tagore, was
translated from the original Bengali into English by
Muhammad Ahsan Ullah.

From Byron, Austen and Darwin

to some of the most acclaimed and original
contemporary writing, John Murray takes pride in
bringing you powerful, prizewinning, absorbing
and provocative books that will entertain you
today and become the classics of tomorrow.

We put a lot of time and passion into what we
publish and how we publish it, and we'd like to
hear what you think.

Be part of John Murray – share your views with us at:

www.johnmurray.co.uk

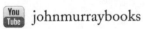 johnmurraybooks

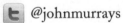 @johnmurrays

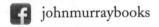 johnmurraybooks